NO MATTER THE WHEN

PAWS ON THE KEYBOARD

NO MATTER THE WHEN

WICK SHORTS
BOOK TWO

Published by Paws On The Keyboard
www.pawsonthekeyboard.com

ISBN 978-1-952763-02-1

Printed in the United States of America

NO MATTER THE WHEN

MAX THOMPSON

with K.A. THOMPSON

NO MATTER THE WHEN

WICK SHORTS BOOK TWO

RED...EMPTION

"There is nothing about missionary work intended to bring converts into the fold," Red Munson said to the talking head. "It's about sending our vulnerable young men into the world to face repeated rejection where they're forced to defend their beliefs day after day after day. Defending the core principles, as well as the history of the church, in the face of crushing rejection cements those beliefs, their creeds, regardless of the validity of those convictions."

The talking head was cut from the same cloth as most Floridian men—very pink, middle-aged, thick, doughy build, short hair with a perfect part on the right side, and known to be incredibly conservative—though he was from a major Midlam news outlet. "To what point?"

Red appeared less conservative to the audience. He was dressed in a suit that Hyrum would deem acceptable Sunday clothing, though his button-down shirt was a soft baby blue, and instead of a dark blue or black tie, he wore a gently striped red and blue one that Hyrum had gifted him for Christmas.

He was seated with his ankles crossed and was quite relaxed as he began to lightly rock the boat.

"By the time they return to the safety of home, where they are surrounded by friends and family who share the beliefs they've grown up with and have been tasked to share with the world, where they are not mocked or belittled for their convictions nor held accountable for church history, they tend to view the rest of the world as 'other,' a place filled with those who are not only wrong but who are also a threat. It's about retaining members, permanently fusing their lives to the church. It's never been about converting others."

The talking head, amused, leaned back in his chair, an eyebrow lifted just so, and asked, "So you're saying your church has been wrong for centuries?"

"I'm saying," Red replied carefully, "that we have suspended and will not resume our missionary program under its current structure. We will no longer use the falsehood of conversion to keep our priesthood holders in line. Instead, we will send our men *and* women into the world to engage in honest service. We want them to learn that the world is not the swamp of evil they've been taught to believe. We want them to see the value in others, the goodness that exists all around us, and where they can, to help."

"Help, how?"

"By building bridges. Literally. Homes for those without. Teach those who cannot read, comfort those who are in pain, feed those who go without. I—we—want our young people to do the Lord's work, and that is not converting the masses. It's leading by example, bringing as much true good into the world as they can."

"You served a mission."

"Not in the traditional sense," Red pointed out. "I was never placed in the position of living in a foreign country, knocking on doors with the hope that maybe *this* time it won't be slammed in my face, or worse. The mission I was assigned was one of education, to learn the written works of the church backward and forward because my father had already decided I would follow in his footsteps. Unlike most men in Florida, I went right from high school into college, and was required to follow that with post-graduate studies."

"You married young."

Red nodded. "As is the norm in Florida. Prior to the division of the United States, missionaries waited until they had returned home to marry. Once Florida became the geographical center of the church, men were encouraged to marry quite young, and leave behind at least one child before serving their mission. Many marry while still in high school, sometimes by parental arrangement. And it was wrong. So very wrong."

"Does this have anything to do with the exceptionally low conversion rates in the last two hundred years?" The talking head tapped at a computer screen, checking his data. "The original church membership numbers through now have declined at a minimum of ninety percent."

"I don't think the membership numbers can be compared. When the United States dissolved, the entire church didn't pull up stakes and relocate to Florida. Florida as a theocracy was originally comprised of a multitude of religions, quickly headed by only one. Most of the foundational church remained outside, in hundreds of smaller sects. Some ended through attrition, some still exist, and those have evolved outside our influence. The Church of Florida does, however, have numbers that exceed those of the beginning of our country."

"Though not from conversion."

"Very little occurred through conversion. It's been through population growth. By encouraging our members to have as many children as possible, often to their detriment."

"And you no longer encourage this?"

Red took his time to answer. "I think it's time to place that decision into the hands and hearts of individuals. No one should feel broken by the family and the number of mouths to feed. The answer should be the result of prayer, consideration for the good of the family, and consideration to the wants of the parents. The church should and will welcome every newborn into its fold but should not dictate how many that should be. That should be wholly between a husband and wife and God."

"Then how do you increase, or even maintain, membership numbers?"

"Knock down the walls," Red said, dead serious. "For too many years we had a literal wall around Florida. The physical wall has been largely demolished, but the other walls, the invisible barriers that turned us into a commune of frightened, holier-than-thou pontificates, must also be eradicated."

"Commune."

"For all intents and purposes, yes. Or if we're delving into honesty, we should name our truth. We've told our members what to think, how to behave, how to vote, who their friends should be, even what the ideal color of their skin should be, what to eat and what to drink. What not to drink. There's only one word for that. Cult. Hundreds of years ago we became a cult. And that ends now."

~

"Red's gonna get in really big trouble." Hyrum made the declaration around a bite of a warm chocolate chip cookie. "He's gonna make all the important church men super mad."

Unlike Aubrey—who was sitting at the dining room table with a giant cookbook and a tablet, creating a grocery list—Jax didn't particularly care if Hyrum had a lapse in manners and spoke while still chewing. He reached for one of the cookies Hyrum had placed on a plate on the coffee table, and took a bite before saying, "I think Red knows what he's doing. And the controlling members who would have been the most upset by this are no longer part of the church."

Many of them were dead, having faded away after Levi Munson was tried and convicted and then murdered in his prison cell. The few who were still alive had either walked away from their positions in the church's quorum or were in jail along with Hyrum's brother, David Munson. The current elders of the Church of Florida had been picked by Red for the most part and would never publicly oppose him.

Hyrum knew this; he had discussed it with Red during long video chats held in the middle of the night when Hy couldn't sleep because he worried about his oldest brother. He understood that Red didn't need to fear a knife in the back from one of the apostles. But he also understood that the church was comprised of more people than those in charge, and he knew from talking to his mother and other brothers that not everyone was happy with the things Red did and the secrets he exposed.

"It's not them," Hyrum told Jax. "Not the apostles. I mean the importanter men, like bishops and high priests. Those are the men who run each, um, I don't know the word. There's the big church, like all of it, but we meet in smaller buildings all over Florida. I forget what it's called."

"Congregation?" Jax offered.

"Maybe." Hyrum scrunched his nose. "It's a different word but that's what it means. Red is making them *really* mad. Mom said she heard that a bishop in Miami said that Red is really the devil or maybe even the anti-Christ."

"He's not, you know."

As far as Hyrum was concerned, God plucked Levi off the face of the earth and gave Red his job so that he could fix everything wrong with Florida. "I just don't want anyone to hurt him because they don't like what he says."

Those people were free to leave Florida, Jax reminded him. And he hoped they did, with appreciation of the irony of their emigrations, because until Red became the President and Prophet of the Church of Florida, they never would have been allowed to leave.

"What if they don't go?" Hyrum asked. "What if they decide to stay and fight him instead?"

"Red has the backing and protection of Pacifica. That's well known."

Hyrum brushed cookie crumbs off his shirt and sat up straighter. "He's not the head of Florida anymore. Just the church. They know that, too. He doesn't get guards the way you do, or even the way the Prime Minister does. What if he tells more secrets, and someone tries to stop him?"

He has guards.

"What, Wick?" Hyrum asked me.

Red has guards. Ask Jax.

When Hyrum asked, Jax nodded. "Red is well protected, I promise. He and Darlene have guards, the same way you do, but it's not something we want the public to know."

"It's a secret?"

"We can't protect the head of every church within Pacifica,"

Jax explained. "And if the public knew, they would be within their rights to demand equal treatment. Red has Pacifican guards because he's the Queen's brother, and, well, she asked it of me."

"Oh. And you don't want to tell her no."

"Would you?" Jax asked with a chuckle.

"No, but that's because I love her and think she's nice. You don't tell her no because you're afraid of her."

"Hey. I love her and think she's nice, too."

"But you're kind of afraid of her."

He wasn't and Hyrum knew it, but it made Jax laugh out loud, and I heard Aubrey snort softly.

Drew's bedroom door creaked open and he stuck his head out, sniffing. When he was sure he smelled what he hoped he did, he limped his way into the living room, one hand on his not-empty-but-wanting tummy. "Chocolate chip or wiener cookies?"

"Chocolate chip," Hyrum said as Drew plucked a cookie from the plate and then dropped onto the sofa next to him.

"Hurting tonight?" Jax asked.

"Little bit. Foot worse than the leg. It's the damned nerve endings, feels like my foot is on fire. But no worries. I will survive."

Mass had warned him following the surgery to replace the leg and foot he'd lost while floating outside Elysium that there would be pain. Drew presumed it would take two to three weeks; Jay reminded him of the pain he'd experienced post-surgery. The worst of it was over in a week, but some lingered for a month.

"Ask Mass nicely, and he'll dispense the fun drugs."

Drew did not want the fun drugs. He wanted to get through it and then remember what he nearly lost.

"Did you see the news tonight?" Hyrum asked. "There was a story about a guy who lost his entire left side on account of it got cut off."

"Wait, for real?"

"Yeah, but he's all right now."

Jax sighed, and Drew soft-elbowed Hyrum in his side. "If I didn't really want this cookie, I'd get up, hobble across the room, and then chuck it at you." He glanced at the screen. "Something happen in Florida?"

"Red is telling everyone about how the church is gonna change," Hyrum explained. "People are gonna be mad."

"He's been spelling out what their conversion missions are actually for," Jax said. "By this time tomorrow, he'll have released church documents supporting his claim that men are not sent out to convert new members."

"Then why are they?"

"To make the young men feel bad about the rest of the world," Hyrum said. "That way when they go home, they feel safe and never want to leave. But now Red wants to send men *and* women on missions to help people learn to read and to feed them, and stuff like that."

Aubrey closed the cookbook and came into the living room, perching on the arm of Jax's comfy chair, and she slid her hand over his shoulder. "Red wants the members of the church to become more Christ-like," she explained, glancing up when Will came in. "He's trying to push everyone to do work that benefits the world, not just the church."

"Will," Jax said, acknowledging the Emperor.

"Security for Red and his family has been increased," Will said.

"Then you saw the interview."

"Indeed." For Hyrum's benefit he added, "It's a precautionary action. There have been no new threats to him."

Aubrey wanted to know about her mother. They still weren't speaking; Aubrey wasn't sure she could forgive Valerie for not stopping Levi's abuse when she could have, though her anger was less about the things he did to her and more about what he'd done to Hyrum. Her anger didn't keep her from wanting her mother protected.

"She has security, as well."

"Does she know that?" Hyrum asked.

"No," Will answered.

"I won't tell her. She wants me to come visit. She keeps asking. Yesterday she cried when I said I didn't want to come on account of she thinks I hate her."

"She'll get over it," Aubrey said.

Will crossed his arms, contemplating the situation. I saw him wage an internal battle for a few seconds before speaking. When he did, he locked eyes with Aubrey. "I think you should go."

"But she'll try to make me stay," Hyrum whined. "Even though I said I'm a Blackshear now. She even has a room upstairs just for me and she made Red and Joe move the window Daddy threw me out of. I don't know why. He can't throw me out it again. And Oz showed me how to kick someone in the nuts if they do something to me. I could do that if I had to."

"I'll go with you," Will offered. "She won't push the issue if I'm there."

Jax sided with Hyrum. "I don't think she's earned the right to see Hyrum *or* Aubrey just yet. If her other kids want to—"

"It's less about earning the right and more that Hyrum should see her soon," Will said.

Aubrey twitched. He was still looking at her, and the reason settled with a sharp sting that made her blink. "Sweetie," she said to Hyrum, "I'll go, too. We'll turn it into a vacation and see all the places we used to play. I'd like to see Miller's pond again."

Hyrum scrunched his nose. "I'm not allowed to go there on account of there are gators."

"There are no alligators in the pond," Aubrey sighed. "Daddy said that to keep you from going there by yourself."

"Mom said so, too."

"I promise, there are none anywhere near the pond. I don't think there are any within five hundred miles of the pond. And if there are, we'll have guards who can take care of them. Wouldn't you like to see our brothers and sisters again? Their kids?"

"Not really."

"Well, I'm going." She got up and kissed the top of Hyrum's head. "I'll call her and arrange a good date. It would be nice if you decided to come."

Drew leaned over and whispered in Hyrum's ear, "Aubrey might feel safer with you there. She trusts you."

Hyrum nodded. "Okay, I'll go. But if she asks me to stay, I'll have lots of words to say about that."

There was no need for Hyrum to unleash however many words he had stored up. Will intended to be there and could have Hyrum home before Valerie blinked more than twice. If she asked him to stay and began piling on the guilt, all Will needed to do was set a hand on Hyrum, tap his jump bracelet, and they would transport to the living room at home, hopefully startling Jax or Drew.

Can I go? To keep an eye on Hyrum? I can hiss if needed.

'No' almost tumbled out of Will's mouth—my presence wasn't necessary—but Hyrum squealed, "Yes! I want Wick to see where we lived. There's lots of squirrels in the back yard and he can play with them."

There was no point in arguing with him. Will sighed, "Just what we need, Wick tormenting unsuspecting yard life."

I won't torment them. I might prefer to observe them from inside. They're kinda like pigeons, you know.

"They don't fly," Will reminded me. "There's nothing for you to worry about. A squirrel is not going to grab you and fly off."

Hey. There are flying squirrels.

I bet they have gangs, too.

I'll stay inside.

Hyrum was certain there were no flying squirrels or little rodent gangs in his mother's backyard or garden. "But I want you to go in the backyard for a few minutes. Lazybones is buried there and I want you to meet him, kinda. And I want to tell him all about you. You woulda liked each other."

I agreed to a short visit in the backyard. Hyrum promised to sit on the ground and keep me in his lap and make sure no squirrels came anywhere near me.

"You're not afraid of squirrels," Will whispered when Hyrum jumped up to tell Aubrey he was going with her. "I've seen you nose to nose with one in the park. More importantly, I once saw you drop a nut at the feet of a small squirrel. You were worried he was hungry."

Yes, but now Hyrum is excited about going. He gets to show me where Lazybones is, and he gets to protect me. He also gets to clean up after me in the bathroom, but you don't need to point that out to him yet.

He'd figure it out.

~

Two days later we jumped from the living room into Red's home office. It would not have been a shock to Valerie if we'd popped up in her kitchen—she was adjusting to the realities of Blackshear life—but Aubrey didn't think her other siblings were aware of Will's ability to transport from one place to another with a tap to his bracelet and she worried that someone might be with Valerie. Red knew all the family secrets and often accommodated Will when he brought Hyrum to visit their mother. No one other than Red, Darlene, or Bree would be in his home office, giving us a safe place to land.

Not unexpected, Bree waited for Hyrum in an old brown comfy chair near Red's desk. Before he had a chance to orient himself to the new location, she rocketed forward to grab him in a giant hug. She had grown a lot since the last time I had seen her and had about an inch on Hyrum. Still, he lifted her a few inches off the ground and spun her around, blurting out how much he missed her and wanted her to visit him at home.

It took a beat for her to register what he meant: Florida was no longer home. Home was San Francisco, in the big gray building on Geary Street, on the fourth floor with the balcony that overlooked Union Square. She recovered quickly and promised him that she would as soon as Daddy let her.

"Maybe this summer," Red told her, ushering her toward the door. "I'm sure I can find business to deal with, and you can tag along."

Bree would not bother him with endless reminders, presuming his "maybe" to be a promise. Hyrum, on the other hand, was going to remind him weekly, calling every Sunday after he had fulfilled his obligation of a minimum half hour video chat with his mother, during which he would swear he had been saying his prayers twice a day, sometimes three if he had questions for Jesus, and he'd been reading his bible stories every night.

It didn't matter that when he had last seen her, their relationship had permanently changed, and not to her benefit. He'd revealed to Aubrey and Will that his mother could have ended Levi's abuse with the touch of her hand to his chest; she had a gift of her own, to cool with a touch, to turn to ice anything she wished, and she could have frozen his heart as he slept. Hyrum believed in the biblical principle of honoring his mother, even if he was mad at her.

When Eli forced Valerie out of the apartment, I thought it spelled the end of Aubrey's relationship with her and presumed they wouldn't speak again. The strain between them was half of why I wanted to be there. If things got heated, I was ready to strike and bite if it looked like Valerie Munson was tempted to use her gifts.

Her house was a sprawling two-story colonial set front and center of a ten-acre lot. As Red's old, sputtering, rusting combustion-engine car pulled into the driveway, I heard Zed's voice in my head, muttering that this was too much for a single family and a waste of space that others could enjoy. The property looked like a park, with trees dotting the sides and rear of the well-manicured lawn, and there was a massive fountain near the arch-point of the curved driveway.

Levi Munson had been rich; there was no doubt about that now.

"This is beautiful," Aubrey breathed as she exited the car. "I don't remember it being so...wonderful."

"Lots of renovation over the last couple of years," Red reminded her. "The house is what, seven hundred years old? It needed work. The things Dad had done were, to be blunt, cheap. Joe and I were honestly surprised that everything inside hadn't collapsed on itself."

Hyrum pointed to a row of windows on the upper left. "That's the girls' bedroom. The boys' is in the back of the house."

"You all shared one room?" Bree asked. "There were a lot of you."

"Spencer, Joe, and I shared a room," Hyrum answered. "It's a big room. Really big."

"And I got stuck in a room with David," Red sighed.

"But you got your own when Daddy let you fix up the attic," Hyrum said.

Red nodded. "True. Which meant David got his own room by default."

"That made Spencer and Joe mad," Hyrum giggled. "Even though the bedrooms are big, they were mad. They wanted their own, too, and said David was spoiled."

"Did you ever get your own room?" Bree asked him.

He grunted. "Yeah, when Spencer and Joe grew up and moved away. I didn't like that very much, though. Daddy was right down the hall and came in—"

Aubrey set her hand under Hyrum's chin and leaned in to kiss his forehead. "Let's not think about him right now, sweetie. I haven't seen this house since I was fourteen years old, and I want to look for happy memories."

"I thought you visited," Bree said as she skipped toward the door.

"I've been back to Florida, but not here."

"You've been here, right, Emperor?"

"I have. And please, call me Will."

"Call him Mr. Blackshear," Red said.

Bree had her back turned to him, but I could hear her eyes rolling.

"Split the difference," Aubrey suggested before Bree opened the door. "Mr. Will. As children in this part of Florida have done for hundreds of years."

"I thought we were all 'Brother' this and 'Brother' that," Bree grunted, pushing the door open.

"Will's not a church person," Hyrum reminded her. "But he's my real brother now, so maybe you can call him uncle."

Bree looked at Red, questioning.

"Whatever Will prefers."

"Will prefers Sweetykins," Hyrum giggled.

Will poked Hyrum's back to get him through the door. "Bree

may address me in whichever manner she chooses. Though perhaps not...that."

She decided he was another uncle; it seemed to matter to Hyrum, so by extension it mattered to her. "It will also annoy Grandma," she whispered to Hyrum. "Let's annoy Grandma. That's always fun."

Grandma—Valerie Munson—was in the kitchen, scrubbing what appeared to be an already spotless counter. She brightened when Hyrum went to her for a hug but swallowed hard when he let go and she had to figure out how to greet her still-outraged daughter.

There was no heartfelt embrace. Aubrey tolerated a quick kiss on her cheek, during which she told Valerie that she looked well. The formalities were awkward—Valerie welcomed Will but said he was unexpected in a way that made it clear he wasn't especially wanted—and Red tried to make small talk until Hyrum couldn't take it anymore.

"Show Aubrey the house! She hasn't seen it in a hundred years!"

Aubrey's left eyebrow ticked upward. "How old do you think I am?"

"A hundred and fourteen, since you haven't seen it since then," he snickered. "But me neither since they moved stuff! Come on!"

Valerie began with the kitchen, gesturing to the new cabinets. The old ones, she reminded Aubrey, had been made from thin painted plywood and had begun to warp when Aubrey was still young. These were stained solid mahogany and ran all the way to the ceiling, more storage than she would ever need. The artificial stone counters were yellow and brown marbled— so much less fragile than real quartz, she said—and the new flooring was polished concrete dyed to resemble swirled copper.

"I wanted something the great-grandkids wouldn't damage. They should play without having to be so careful. And all these cabinets, well, Spencer pointed out that the next people to live here might have a dozen children. The boys considered the next family in everything they did to the house. I enjoy that thought."

She kept one thing from the old kitchen and directed Hyrum to open the pantry. There on the wall, just above the lowest shelf, he had carved *I am Hyrum am 9.* "I couldn't bear to let them cover that. Joe offered to cut it from the wall and frame it, but…"

"She wanted it left where Hy had written it," Red finished for her. "We can move it later, if she wants."

Aubrey knelt and ran her fingers over it. "How did you manage this, Hyrum?"

"I used a knife. Don't tell Daddy. I'm not allowed."

Valerie and Aubrey twitched, but Bree snorted and said, "That old joy-suck is long gone, Uncle Hyrum. Did you know he doesn't even have a grave? Uncle Joe says that sucks because there's nothing to pee on."

We need to spend more time with Joe. I think I really like him.

It took half an hour for Valerie to show them the rest of the house. The room under the stairs was, as promised, gone, replaced by shelves loaded with children's books and a few random stuffed animals. She wanted a quiet place for her youngest grandchildren and great grandchildren. Without saying so, she also wanted to change what that space had once been.

Still, I doubted Hyrum would ever use it. He brushed past it quickly, heading for the room that had one been Levi's office but was now the master bedroom.

"I never realized Dad's office was this big," Aubrey said.

"On account of we were never allowed inside because that was for important people," Hyrum reminded her. "I like that it's a bedroom now. It's pretty, Mom. You got a lot of bright colors and flowery stuff, just like a girl's room. It's way better than the dark stuff Daddy likes."

"Lots of pink," she allowed.

He scrunched his nose. "I like the kind of pink that makes Eli say it feels like his eyes got stabbed."

Neon, dude.

You like neon pink.

"Neon pink," he repeated.

Upstairs, we drifted through the girls' bedroom; there were six twin beds lined 3 against opposite walls, and Valerie reminded Hyrum that Levi wanted extra beds for their friends to sleep over.

"Me and Joe and Spencer didn't get extra beds," Hyrum said. "On account of sleep overs are a girl thing. Don't tell Daddy sometimes I do a sleep over with Drew in my room. He'd be mad. Or maybe not on account of Drew lets me tell him bible stories so he can understand Jesus."

Bree opened her mouth but then closed it when Red set a hand on her shoulder. Hyrum didn't notice, but Bree understood—now is not the time.

The last room, the one Hyrum avoided, was his old bedroom. It was as spacious as the master downstairs, and the first thing he noted was that there was only one bed in it. He'd had a narrow child-sized bed until he left home, smaller than even Joe or Spencer's, and the new one was king-sized with four big pillows and a bright blue comforter.

The walls had been painted a soft blue, but the ceiling was dark and there were hundreds of tiny lights in it. Turned all the way up, the room could be daylight-bright, but dimmed it looked like the night sky. Valerie credited Joe with the idea; when Hyrum visited, he'd said, he could pretend he was camping.

Hyrum was less impressed than she hoped he'd be; the room was nice, but it didn't feel like his room. His room had lots of colors, including bright pink because that was his new favorite color next to red, and no one at home thought it was just for girls. He struck Valerie with a verbal arrow, reminding her of the place he felt most comfortable as he went straight to the window to the left of the bed. It looked out over the back yard, and he stood with his forehead pressed to the glass.

"It's not over the patio now," he murmured.

"We had to replace it anyway," Red said. "There were hundreds of nail holes in the frame, and once we had it out Joe declared it needed to be three feet over, and bigger."

"On account of Daddy." Hyrum was still whispering. "I put the nail holes in it. If he couldn't open it, he couldn't throw me out it. Don't tell him that was me. I don't want a spanking."

Valerie marched past Aubrey and pulled him away from the window. "No one will ever spank you again, Hyrum. I promise."

He shook his head and started for the door. "You didn't stop him before. Why would you stop him now?"

~

While I was not allowed on the table—or even in a chair—while everyone else gathered for dinner, when they were done Valerie picked me off the floor and set me on her brand new shiny breakfast bar, put a finger to her lips with a quiet shush, and she set a plate loaded with Wick-sized bites of fried chicken and a side of mashed potatoes and gravy, minus the potatoes.

Cooking was not one of Valerie's faults. Her fried chicken was as good as Aubrey's and her gravy was—I would never tell the Queen—better.

While I ate, she dropped a kiss onto my head and told me to let her know if I wanted more; there was plenty, and she had cut up an entire breast just for me.

Who are you, and what have you done with Valerie Munson?

Will snickered softly, just loud enough for me to hear over the jabbering coming from Hyrum and Bree in the living room. They'd planted themselves on the floor in the front of the TV, pretending to argue over what show they wanted to see. Hyrum let her win; he didn't care what they watched. He only cared that she was there and was staying until we went home.

"Really, Mom," Aubrey said when she realized I was on the counter.

"I'm taking a page from your book. I own bleach. I'll use it when he's done." She poked her head through the pass way between the dining room and living room to check on Hyrum. "I never let him put Lazybones on the counter. I hope he won't be upset."

Red chuckled. "She never let Hyrum put him there, but I'm willing to bet that she did every now and then."

"I couldn't allow him to see that. Can you imagine? If he'd seen me do it once, eventually he would have slipped up and done it in front of your father. What that man would have done to them both."

No one needed to imagine it. We knew what might happen to Hyrum and could guess what would have happened to Lazybones. No kitty looks good inverted.

With dinner cleared away, Valerie brought a pot of coffee to the table and sat across from Aubrey. "How is Andrew doing?" She poured a cup and placed it in front of her daughter. "Hyrum says he's doing well, but...Hyrum is often optimistic."

"Physically, he's healing. Emotionally?" Aubrey sighed. "He wants us to think everything is fine, but he's quiet now and I know he has nightmares."

Will agreed. "He's shifted his work interests as well. Prior to Elysium, he was focused on development of tools and uniforms to be used during free-float operations outside the space station. He's now back to work on holographic imaging and scaling down the size of nanobots. Worthy endeavors, but neither excites him the way space travel did."

Valerie had watched the news coverage of his space walk and found his wish to keep Oz connected to him admirable and adorable. She'd gotten a private thrill hearing Hyrum's voice on a world-wide broadcast, though was chagrined at his blurting out for Drew to grab onto his nuts. She'd been concerned when the coverage ended abruptly, not knowing what had happened to him, and it took restraint to not call Aubrey at a time when a call would be an interfering distraction.

"Then we heard the news that he had been injured. I could never have guessed how badly until Hyrum filled me in. And don't worry, we've kept that in the family. The only official news I've heard is that he was hit by debris and his injuries were minor."

Red nodded. "Not the entire family, either. Mom and I know. Joe and Spencer know. It doesn't seem prudent to explain to everyone else how Drew's leg and foot burned up in the atmosphere, yet here he is with limbs intact."

Cloned and bio-printed appendages were a reality in Pacifica, but in Florida that level of care was still medical magic.

His new leg could be easily explained with bio-print, but not how quickly he'd achieved it. That would have taken weeks; months if he'd opted to clone it.

Aubrey's voice wavered. "He nearly died out there. He was so far from help, and his air ran out—"

"Then how?" Valerie asked.

"Hyrum," Will said. "If not for his notion of a secondary system to deliver oxygen in an emergency, Andrew would be dead."

Tears filled Aubrey's eyes. "It was such a simple idea, so simple that most of Andrew's team tried to wave it off."

"Simple in theory, yet extremely complex in execution." Will explained Hyrum's worry over Drew getting holes in the tubes that went from his air tanks to his suit, and how he wanted them to come up with something that would carry extra air under his base layer. He had a vision of tubes similar to those used to deliver air into fish tanks, but flatter for comfort, and a filtration system to convert any exhaled breath into useable air. "He admitted he wasn't certain how much air could be stored in those tubes, or how many tubes it would take, but he knew the delivery system needed to be contained within the base layer, separate from the outer suit, and he refused to take no for an answer."

He and Drew worked on it day and night, until Hyrum declared that air could be stored in "man boobs" and an abdominal plate. Drew set about designing a flexible container shaped to his upper torso, with the tubes Hyrum had envisioned carrying just a bit extra and programmed his base layer to activate a nasal canula when in use.

"It gave him an extra hour or so," Aubrey said. "Just enough time for Anthony Myers to bring him another air canister."

"Hyrum did that," Valerie whispered.

"Hyrum is capable of great things when left to his own devices," Will said. "He doesn't always have the vocabulary to articulate his ideas, but he's exceptionally good at getting the point across. And when he knows he's right, he digs in."

"Even when facing the King of England," Aubrey said, laughing. "His Majesty—"

"His Royal Stick Up His Ass," Red interjected.

"—asserted, during an informal state dinner, that children should never be encouraged toward belief in things of fantasy, such as the tooth fairy."

"Oh, no," Valerie muttered.

"Hyrum let him have it. Loudly. He insisted that it didn't matter if the tooth fairy was real or not, but taking magic away from a child is mean, and being mean is never a good thing for a little boy or girl. He was *so* passionate about it, and King Thomas had no idea how to react to King Jackson's brother-in-law confronting him so abruptly. He stood there with his mouth open, until Hyrum asked if he had believed when he was little. And wasn't that fun? Why can't kids have fun?"

"Oh, Hyrum," Valerie whispered, amused.

"He wasn't done. He asked everyone in the room if they'd had fun believing in the tooth fairy, and if they were upset when they learned the truth. Thomas had to concede, because he had believed when he was a child and admitted he wasn't scarred because of it."

Red snorted. "And after that, Hyrum challenged him to prove the tooth fairy wasn't real. After all, he'd gotten money in exchange for his baby teeth. He never saw who put the money under his pillow. And with a finger pointed at the King, he demanded, 'Did you?'"

King Thomas, who had been England's monarch for the better part of four decades, laughed and informed Hyrum that he was much more fun than his father, and kinder to boot. "He told Hyrum he was more like Red, and that was to his benefit."

Hyrum thanked him because he loved Red and Red was a good big brother, but, "I'm a Blackshear now. Eli adopted me. Do you know Eli? He used to be a king, too."

"All that," Red said wistfully, "and he still believes in Santa."

"Good for him," Valerie said. "I hope he never stops. All those years wishing he would suddenly mature..." She wanted to reach across the table for Aubrey's hand, just to touch it, but wasn't sure it would be welcome. "I sent my little boy out to find you. If I had made him come home right after you found him, he would still be a little boy. And he's not, I can see that."

Aubrey wasn't so sure. Her eyebrow twitched up just a tiny bit, so tiny that I might have been the only one to notice.

Valerie wasn't done. "If he'd been here, he never would have gone to work. He never would have explored things the way he does in San Francisco. He never would have felt free. I know he doesn't feel that here." She leaned forward and lowered her voice. "You've noticed, haven't you? He has moments when he acts as if he's forgotten Levi is gone. He keeps looking at my bedroom door as if he expects his father to stomp his way out of the office, angry at a tiny bit of childish laughter."

"'Don't tell Daddy,'" Aubrey sighed.

"He can't stay here," Valerie said, as if she had just realized it. "He doesn't feel safe. I've wanted him to come for so long and had all these things we could do together...he needs to go home soon. Stay tonight, no more."

"He needs to spend some time with his mother," Aubrey countered. "We'll make sure he feels safe. But he needs this time with you."

Valerie stiffened. "Well, we'll see. He might do better if we call each other more often. I'd like to speak to him more than once a week."

They danced around the truth, Aubrey insisting they needed this visit as much as Valerie did, Valerie insisting that Hyrum's safety and mental wellbeing were far more important, leaving Red confused. He finally told Valerie she was looking a bit tired and apologized for keeping her up. She was an early to bed, early to rise sort of person, and he knew she liked to curl up in bed and read before going to sleep.

When she agreed, she confessed that she would not be curling up with the Good Book, but with a *good* book, one that would raise eyebrows all over Florida if people knew. "I love the Lord," she sighed as she got up, "but there's more to life than memorizing those passages, and Hyrum sent me several wonderful love stories."

He'd assured her that there weren't many kissing things in them. Oz read them first to be sure and declared each book to be Suitable for Mom.

When her door closed, Red took a sip of his coffee and then asked Aubrey, "On a scale of one to ten, how angry are you with her, really?"

"The scale *broke*, Red. Do you know what she can do?"

"I have an idea."

He'd begun to suspect on the day Hyrum called to help dig Lazybones' grave. He found his little brother sitting under a tree in the back yard, cradling the dead cat. Though it had been an hour since the call, Lazybones was already cold, too cold for it to simply be the cooling of his post-mortem body. "Hyrum explained that Lazybones had been sick and was howling in pain...but Mom took care of that. She put her hand on his chest to help him stop hurting, so he could go live with Jesus. That's why he was so cold."

He sat with Hyrum and waited, worried that the cat was simply so cold they couldn't feel his heartbeat; he didn't want to risk burying him alive. "While we sat there, I thought back to all the times her hands seemed inexplicably icy, and all the times she sat us down when we were little and served cold fruit despite it having sat on the counter for hours. She soothed little burns so easily. I was in my thirties, Aubrey, and just then clueing into the idea that my brothers weren't the only ones with special abilities. Dad had no idea about any of it, other than Hyrum."

Aubrey sat back. "What? Our brothers?"

"Joe has hearing that's off the charts. Whisper to him from fifty feet away, and he'll hear you as if you'd spoken in his ear. Spencer is..." He exhaled slowly. "What would you call the opposite of an empath? He's not apathetic. But the things you can do, soothing and taking on someone else's pain? He can inflict it. He ignites and inflames feelings and can make a person feel absolutely miserable."

"How awful."

Spencer was not happy with his abilities and felt cheated. No one could whisper secrets that Joe couldn't hear, and Hyrum? Hyrum could burn down the world if he wanted. All he could do was make someone feel sick, and what good was that?

Well, what good was it aside from the few times he'd made Levi hug the porcelain throne while wishing for quick death. Valerie realized when he was very young that he had the potential to be his oldest sister's opposite and protected him against Levi's discovery.

"She tried to keep him from having any idea about you, you know," he said. "He was certain there was something different about you, but I'm not sure he ever really grasped it, not until Hyrum began lighting things on fire. She made sure that Joe and Spencer understood what might happen if he had any idea about them."

"And you?" she pressed. "Surely we aren't the only four in the family."

He glanced in the direction of the living room. Hyrum and Bree were now quiet, absorbed in whatever they were watching. He checked out everything that was on the table, as if choosing between the plate of cookies his mother had placed before them or the coffee, and then told Will to throw his spoon at him after he closed his eyes.

Will whipped it hard, and Red snatched it from the air before it could hit his face.

Wait until he's distracted and then throw a cookie.

"I used to believe I was just quick," he explained. "Right until the moment David threw a knife at me and I felt the world slow down and then plucked it from the air like it was a wayward strand of hair. And yes, Dad was unaware."

David—"he's a dick," Rhys always said when hearing his name, imitating Joe—was the only one of the boys without a discernable ability. He raged with jealousy, though never said anything to Levi, understanding that being a tattletale would invite as harsh a punishment as the little freaks he thought his brothers were.

"And the girls?" Aubrey prompted.

Red didn't know. If they had innate abilities, their mother protected them from discovery.

"She could have protected us all just a bit more," Aubrey said angrily.

"She could have," Red allowed. "But at what cost? He would have killed her if he'd known what she could do."

"That's a risk I would take."

"So would I. If he'd even twitched toward one of my daughters, I would have. But plot it out further. Think like she does. She tries to kill him and fails. He then knows. He suspects about you. Aubrey, he would have turned on *all* his children. He would have been relentless in determining which child was inflicted, and if he so much as suspected any of us?"

"He would have killed his own children," she sighed. "Then why not Hyrum?"

"Because he could control Hyrum. He wasn't in school, had no friends, and only sporadically interacted with people at church. You were gone and there were no indications that the rest of us could do anything. But make no mistake, the only thing that saved Hyrum's life is that he was born male. If he'd been female? There would have been an accident."

Aubrey heard him, but she didn't buy it. "She wouldn't have failed. Red, the woman can freeze a beating heart."

He didn't think she would have failed, either. Yet, he understood how her mind worked; the death of the Prophet, the head of everything in Florida, invited the world in. That he died in his sleep wouldn't matter. There would be investigations, interviews, even with the children. Red thought she knew of Hyrum's abilities long before anyone else.

"Every year she waited was a year more that her kids lived in the only form of stability they knew. Every year was a year more for her to press the boys into secrecy. And every day was another to beg the Lord to protect us *all*, from Levi and from life. That's all she knew how to do, Aubrey. She asked for forgiveness and redemption, begged Him to protect us, and accepted the answers she was given. She lived in terror every moment of every day, knowing there was no way out unless she killed him, all while knowing she couldn't risk it because of the small chance that she would then meet the devil she didn't know."

He swirled the coffee in his cup, now cold. "She did the best she could. She kept herself isolated, played the role of the good wife and mother, and spent every day finding ways to keep her children alive. And that's not hyperbole. Dad was abusive, horrifically abusive, and she did what she could to curb that, but it was also a tradeoff. Because the other option was watching him destroy everything she loved, permanently."

"Tell me you wouldn't have risked death for your children," she countered.

He nodded. "I would die every day for them. What I won't do is risk them dying because I took a leap when I should have taken a step. She was afraid to leap and be wrong. But she was always willing to die."

Aubrey looked to Will.

"And that," Will said, "is why I'm here. She *is* ready to die, Red. Soon. Regardless of your relationships with her, I don't see a point."

"Meaning?" Red asked.

"Meaning that despite her wishes, I intend to prevent that from happening. For no reason other than my Queen needs time to heal, and they both need time to forgive each other, and themselves."

~

Partly because he and Bree intended to stay up late telling stories, Hyrum asked for Red's permission to share the girls' bedroom with her. He reasoned that there were "lots and lots of beds" and he would take one on the far side of the room "on account of that's appropriate." Red chuckled lightly and reminded Hyrum that he was Bree's uncle, and sharing a room was fine. They could even take beds next to each other.

"When Bree was small, he only understood that it was appropriate, because he'd heard Mom say so. Now?" Red sighed. "He understands all too well what we mean. And he's able to articulate that."

Aubrey followed Hyrum and Bree up the stairs. She planned on taking her mother's old room and told Will to take the boys' room.

She never asked Red where he would sleep. I thought she was a little irritated with him, but it also could have been because he was capable of figuring it out on his own.

"He's inquisitive on the matter and is comfortable asking questions," Will said. "Although he directs his curiosities mostly to Andrew now."

"Think he'll ever allow himself a social life? Romance?"

"I'll never discount the possibility."

He won't. He's terrified of hurting someone.

"How so?" Red asked after Will translated.

That's all I can say. I promised. I think.

Will had not promised and knew what I meant. "He isn't convinced that physical relationships don't cause pain to women. He is also unwilling to discuss the matter with an actual woman and believes that Andrew and I have been misled. Somewhere deep down he honestly thinks our wives tolerate physical attention and affection for our sakes and can't possibly enjoy it."

But he believes in the female orgasm. He grasps the anatomy. He giggled about it when Drew explained.

"He won't even talk to Aubrey about it?"

"He has, in a roundabout way. So far he hasn't been able to connect what she tells him to his own experiences."

It's like fractions. He knows the answer, but it won't come out.

Will explained, as briefly as he could, Jo's tests on Hyrum and Rhys. "There are areas of interruption in his brain. He may never be able to override that."

Red didn't think pushing him was necessary. "Look how far he's come, Will. There was a time when Darlene and I prepared to have him live with us for the rest of our lives because we didn't think he would survive on his own after our parents were gone. Every one of us here held him back and no one thought to teach him beyond things a typical first grader would know. Don't be surprised if there comes a day when he allows himself his first real kiss, and then more. I don't know how Aubrey is doing it, but he's thriving, and she might get him there."

"And he will be fine if he doesn't," Will said.

"I know. He's happy now. When my mother returned home so quickly from her last visit? She admitted she tried to force him into coming back with her. I was furious."

"And yet, you understand."

He nodded. "He's her baby and always will be. It's taken until recently for her to accept that she's not the best person to care for him. She's really going to die soon? You know this from your history?"

"The woman in my history died. I will not permit that, Red. She doesn't need to die, no matter how ready she thinks she is."

"How can you stop it?"

He tugged on his sleeve and showed Red his jump bracelet. "I'll get her where she needs to be the same way we arrived. I grab her arm, touch the bracelet, and we jump forward two hundred years. Repairing her heart will take a day, perhaps a day and a half. I've already informed the King's physician and he'll be waiting for us."

And they'll be back in a minute.

"She understands what you can do?"

Will nodded again.

"She'll fight you. You can drag her through time, but once you're there she'll argue until you're not only ready to let her die, but willing to help."

Will had considered that. "That's where you come in. You're going with us. No matter the century, if you order her into the surgical tank, she will obey you. You're the head of her family as well as the head of her church. She wouldn't dare defy you."

"We'll never hear the end of it."

"I can live with that. What I cannot abide is the idea that my Queen, the sister of my heart, will lose her mother before she's able to grant forgiveness. And not only for her lack of action against your father, but for everything. I owe nothing to Valerie Munson, but I will do anything for Aubrey."

"Well," Red said as he got up, "I hope you're willing to take one in the nuts, because she will kick you, and she'll kick you hard."

Aubrey or Valerie?

I didn't get an answer.

~

Hyrum was the first to wake up. Technically. Will hadn't slept, choosing instead to sit in the living room, reading on his tablet, with the lights off. This time his wakefulness wasn't insomnia, but vigilance. He sat where he could hear little noises throughout the house, listening in case Hyrum woke in terror. During the house tour he'd determined he would hear less from Hyrum's old bedroom, and from the living room he would not only hear Hyrum but Aubrey as well.

Sleep still clinging to him, Hyrum sat next to Will on the sofa and leaned against him. "You want coffee? I can make coffee." He yawned and added, "Breakfast, too. Coffee and breakfast are my jobs. Daddy says my coffee is better than Mom's on account of I probably don't spit in it."

Will put his arm around Hyrum and drew him closer. "I'm fine right now and you don't seem like you're awake yet."

"I'm still sleepy but it's time to make coffee. Then eggs and toast. But don't burn the toast. Daddy hates burned up toast."

"Not yet. Sit with me for a bit. We hardly have time to sit together these days. There's always a toddler jumping on one or both of us."

"Okay. Don't tell Daddy the coffee's gonna be late." He closed his eyes and exhaled softly. "Bree wants oatmeal. The kind with honey in it. I can do that."

"I think Bree is old enough to make her own oatmeal."

"I know. She says she gets to cook a lot and she likes it, but I haven't made her oatmeal since she was a little girl. I probably use more honey than Darlene lets her use. Or chocolate syrup. When she was three I made her some with chocolate and I think Darlene was mad but she didn't yell at me."

"Then by all means, when she's up, make oatmeal. But the rest of us can fend for ourselves."

"I know."

Valerie's door cracked open, but Hyrum remained snuggled up to Will. Her mouth opened as if she were going to say something but stopped when Will gave her a look that dared her to complain, and she passed by, shaking her head. A few minutes later the aroma of coffee filled the air and Hyrum's eyes snapped open.

"Oh no!"

"It's fine. Your mother is in the kitchen."

"But—"

"She makes coffee for herself every morning, I'm sure. It's not your job anymore."

He sat up and yawned again. "I make coffee for Jax."

"But it's not your job. He doesn't expect it of you, but he's grateful that you do."

Jax likes spending time with you every morning.

"Indeed," Will said. "That might be the best part of his day."

"Maybe. I bet he likes spending alone time with Aubrey more. Is it light out yet? If it's light outside we can go in the backyard and I can meet you to Lazybones."

Sunrise was half an hour away, but the porch light gave off enough to see by. They bundled up and we went out, with Hyrum leading the way to a spot under the biggest tree in the back yard. There was a long, narrow stone roughly shaped like a bone pressed into the ground. Hyrum kneeled in front of it, brushing away dirt and bits of dead leaves. Scratched into the stone in a childish scrawl was LAZYBONES, the Z and the N backward.

"This is where Red and me buried him," he said quietly. "Red did most of the digging but I wrapped him in a pretty towel that Darlene said we could use on account of she didn't think Daddy would let us use one of his. But I think maybe he woulda because he loved Lazybones even though he was my cat."

Will was honestly surprised that Levi had allowed any of his children to have a pet. Hyrum snorted and sat down, running a finger over the edge of the stone.

"Our neighbor down the street had some kittens and one day Mom and me were taking a walk so I could burn energy up. That's what she said. 'Hyrum, you have bees in your bottom today.' Mrs. Rooter had the kittens in a box and let me play with them and Lazybones crawled all over me and licked me, and I wanted to take him home really bad, but Mom said I had to wait. She had to ask Daddy."

Hyrum suspected the answer would be no; there were few things he wanted that his father consented to, but it wasn't just because he was Hyrum. Levi said no to most things. Valerie warned him that she wouldn't bring it up until after dinner, when Levi tended to be in a reasonable mood. That mood could be thwarted if any of the children misspoke or misbehaved at dinner, and Hyrum knew it.

"I was little, but I knew. I squirmed in my chair during prayer so Red put his hand on my shoulder to keep me still until Daddy said 'amen.' I meant to be good but my tummy was bubbling inside and it kept getting bigger and bigger, and when he said 'amen' I couldn't help myself and I yelled, 'Daddy Mrs. Rooter has kittens and there's a white one and I love him so can I have a kitten?'"

All talk at the table stopped and Red squeezed Hyrum's shoulder, trying to get him to be still again. Valerie didn't know what to do. She braced herself, ready to take the brunt of Levi's anger, ready to take the blame for Hyrum's outburst.

Levi, though, only looked confused for a moment. "You want a kitten? Hm. I don't see why not. Are you willing to care for one? Feeding and cleaning up after it?"

Hyrum nodded enthusiastically.

Levi looked at his wife. "You know who will wind up with most of the work," and when she said she did and didn't mind, he shrugged and turned to Red. "After dinner, call the Rooters and see if they still have the kitten he wants. It'll be good for him."

Red, an adult who was close to leaving home, squared his shoulders as if he'd been given a grave and important assignment and said, "Yes, sir."

"Let's hope that thing is a mouser," Levi said. "I saw a few out back. You take care of the cat, Hyrum. It's one of God's creatures, the same as we are. You treat that cat the way you think Jesus would treat you."

Later, when discussing the conversation with Red, he told Will that was perhaps the most patient and kind he'd ever seen his father. And Hyrum wasn't wrong; Levi loved that cat and when he thought no one was looking, gave him bites from his plate.

"Lazybones was a good mouser," Hyrum told Will. "He didn't eat them but he killed them and then showed me where they were so I could get rid of them. And when Mom was trying to make new grass grow, he chased birds out of the yard so they didn't eat her seeds. But he was also my best friend. He slept with me and listened when I had words to say."

"Except for the birds and mice," Will said, "Wick was much the same for me."

"Wick and Lazybones would have been friends, I think. Like him and Lux are. Maybe they wouldn't see each other a lot but when they did they would be so happy and do things together."

I bet Lazybones and Lux and I would have been amazing friends.

"Can I tell you a secret, Will?"

"Of course."

"I think I understood Lazybones sometimes. Just a few words. But I thought I was making it up, like pretending, so I didn't tell anyone. He called Daddy some bad names, even though Daddy loved him."

Cats, Will told him, can probably sense someone's true self, no matter what face they show to the world.

"I know Daddy's dead, Will," Hyrum said softly. "I don't know why I keep saying things like he isn't."

"You feel him here, I'm sure."

"I keep waiting for him to grab me. But I know he can't. Can I ask you something?"

Will nodded.

"I heard you and Red talking last night. Is my mom gonna die? For real?"

Truthiness is next to godliness. Or handwashing. Something like that.

"I honestly don't know," Will answered. "You understand that when I visit my birth When, I have access to historical records?"

"I guess."

"In my history, the history from when I was a child, yes, her date of death is coming soon. But I'd like to change that by taking her to see Dr. Brian, if she'll allow me."

"She knows?"

"We've discussed it."

"Okay." Hyrum stood, brushing dirt from the seat of his pants. "I should go make oatmeal now. Bree's probably awake."

"Are you all right?" Will asked before he opened the back door.

Hyrum said he was, and I think he believed he was, but he wasn't.

~

Without being asked to, once it was clear breakfast was over, Hyrum began clearing the table and told Bree to turn the faucet on so that he would have hot water to wash the dishes with. Valerie accepted this as a matter of course—Hyrum always washed the breakfast dishes—but Red leaned back in his chair and informed Bree she would help clear the table after she'd turned the faucet on, and then she would help with the dishes.

"Women's work?" Bree snorted. "Aren't we done with that?"

"It's suitable work for an ungrateful child who just had breakfast made for her."

Hyrum froze. "Please don't spank her," he whispered to Red, whose brain had not gone anywhere in that direction.

"He's teasing me," Bree said to Hyrum. "Usually I make fun of *him* for doing women's work when he helps Mom in the kitchen. Mostly because he wears her apron while he washes dishes."

Normally that would make Hyrum giggle, but this time he nodded—I get it, it's a joke—and he began rinsing residual oatmeal from bowls.

Will and Red followed Valerie into the living room, and once she was certain she wasn't needed, Aubrey left, too. I jumped onto the breakfast bar where I could see Hyrum and Bree, with a wary eye on the entryway because Valerie might not be as happy to have me up there as she'd been the night before. Bree chattered on about school and sportsball things while Hyrum half-listened, and he kept glancing over his shoulder, trying to hear what was being said in the other room.

His attention to the fact that there was something going on didn't keep him from startling when Valerie slammed the tip of her cane onto the floor and shouted, "I am *old*! Just let me be!"

"Stay in here," Hyrum told Bree. "I mean it, too."

She shrugged and went on with the dishes. I didn't want to miss it if Valerie whacked Will in the groin with the cane that she didn't really need, so I followed Hyrum and jumped onto the arm of the closest comfy chair.

Valerie's face was flushed with anger and Red looked resigned. Aubrey, on the other hand, seemed sad but willing to let Valerie have her way. Will was the only one who seemed unfazed by her outburst. He stood next to her, close enough to touch, and Red was on her other side, hand on her shoulder.

"Listen to him," Red said as Hyrum came in.

Valerie had no intention of entertaining the things Will proposed. "I've had time enough to think about it, and this is up to the Lord. He'll take me when He thinks it's time. It's out of my hands."

"And maybe the Lord put Will in your path for a reason," Red argued. "My heart says there's still work you need to do, people who will need your help. The Lord very well might have sent Will here to make sure you're around to do that work when the time comes."

She didn't even pretend to believe him, rolling her eyes, sighing loudly.

"Do I need to visit the temple, pray in the Holiest of Holies, and ask Him what He wants? Because I will, Mom. I will humble myself in the most sacred places of our Lord and I will do as He says, no matter *what* He says. And if He tells me you're to live, I will make it a formal declaration."

"You will not bother the Lord in a holy place of revelation," she snapped. "Not on my behalf."

Hyrum took a deep breath, his hands going to his chest the way they did when he was upset, and he clenched his t-shirt between fingers that could not stay still. "Mom, if you go with Will and let Dr. Brian help you, I'll stay in Florida with you when you're better."

Aubrey sucked in a sharp breath but kept from crying out when Will very slightly shook his head.

To Valerie, all but Hyrum faded away. She looked into his eyes, not speaking, and the words she didn't stay hung in the air. Hyrum barely blinked, waiting for her answer, until he let go of his shirt and put his hands behind his back. "I'm not mad at you anymore. And I don't want you to die. Okay? I'll come live here again, and I'll be your little boy."

Valerie reached for Red and Will, and before she could change her mind Will tapped the bracelet and they vanished.

Without saying anything more, Hyrum turned and tumbled into Aubrey's arms. He rested his head on her shoulder; her hand went directly for the soft skin on his neck, trying desperately to soothe him, and she waited until he was ready to speak.

"I didn't mean it," he finally said. "When I said I wasn't mad at her anymore. I am, Aubrey, I'm really mad."

"I know." Aubrey pulled back far enough to look at his face. "I saw your hands behind your back, crossing your fingers."

"I know it was a lie, but I crossed my fingers on account of I think Jesus would be okay with it. Father Dan says that sometimes little lies are importanter than the truth. Like, there's this lady who walks by his church a lot and he always says hi and tells her she looks lovely, but she doesn't, Aubrey. She really doesn't. She looks like I think I looked when Will and Drew found me after I walked to find you."

"Do you know why he says that?"

Hyrum nodded. "Father Dan says that people don't need to hear bad things about themselves, but they need to know that they're cared for and valued. So if someone can't help something and it makes them feel better for someone to say they're lovely, then you say that and Jesus will forgive the little lie."

She kissed him on his forehead. "I am so glad you and Dan have become friends."

"Me, too. I'll miss him."

This time, she wanted to argue. The light in her eyes flared and it was on the tip of her tongue, but Will and Red were back, each holding one of Valerie's hands. They both had a weeks' worth of beard, and Red looked as if he hadn't slept the entire time.

"How long?" Aubrey asked.

"Six days," Will answered. "Three for medical treatment, three for Red to calm down and stop shrieking like a little girl."

"I did not," he protested, which meant he really did.

Hyrum focused on Valerie. "Mom? Did Dr. Brian help you?"

She thought Will could explain it better. Had he not taken her to Brian Massimo, she would have—Mass was certain of it—dropped dead without any hint of trouble ahead. "She would have succumbed to, in his words, a sudden, catastrophic cardiac event. Her entire cardiovascular system has been addressed, and he feels certain she will enjoy the remainder of her life as she would have absent any heart issues."

"But I wouldn't let him make me younger," she insisted. "I *am* old. I've earned that."

"So you're not gonna die?" Hyrum asked.

"She will not," Will answered. "Not anytime soon, barring an accident."

"Okay." Hyrum took a deep breath. "I have to go home for a little bit to get my stuff, but I'll come back like I promised. I'll live here now." His breath hitched as he added, "Can I still wear pink? Even if it's just my underwear?"

Valerie stepped closer to him. I thought she was about to hit him with her cane; she had that look in her eyes. Instead, she leaned a bit closer. "I love you, Hyrum Blackshear, but I will not have you living with me again. You'll go home, where you belong, and you'll do important things with Andrew."

"But I promised," he sputtered.

"I don't want you here." The words slipped out, shaky, sounding like the lie that it was. "If I hold you to that promise, we'll both be miserable. You'll become a little boy again, and I'll treat you like one. And we'll do it with the ghost of that miserable wretch of your father haunting us both."

"I don't know what that means," he murmured.

"It means that this house is no good for you. You feel him everywhere you look, and I won't have that. You'll go home where you feel safe, and when you visit, we'll meet at Red's home if he'll have us. Or Joe's. Or maybe I'll sell this overgrown house and buy a tiny one of my own, someplace your father has never been."

"You can visit me there, too," he said, still sounding unsure.

"We'll see. But you need go home, and I think you should go today. Play with Bree for a while, but after lunch, it will be time to leave."

He twitched in the direction of the kitchen.

"Hyrum," she said, stopping him. "You're a good man. I need you to know that."

She watched him leave and listened for the sound of her son and granddaughter talking in the kitchen. When she was sure his attention had shifted, she turned to Aubrey. "You hate me, and that's fine."

Before Aubrey could protest, Valerie waved her off, and not for the last time.

"You both hate me. You also both love me. And I need you to know that I understand."

"Mom—"

"I also need you to know that I don't know where my footing in this world is. I am angry, all the time. I am hurt, all the time. I will never undo the things Levi did, not to you, not to Hyrum, and not to myself. I don't know how. For the rest of my life, I will question why I did or didn't do something. All I have to offer is that I'm sorry. I was and am still terrified, and I'm sorry."

Aubrey wasn't going to forgive her that easily, but she reached out and gathered her mother into a tight hug. Will and Red brushed past, heading into the kitchen, and as he went by Aubrey Will tapped his finger on her arm, lingering just long enough for her to hear.

She snickered quietly but didn't let go of her mother.

What did you tell her? I asked him once we were back in the kitchen.

"I simply passed along a bit of information, Wick."

Red laughed out loud. "You told her Mass medicated the hell out of Mom, didn't you?"

"Perhaps."

"Grandma's on drugs?" Bree asked, snickering.

Red said they would discuss it later, but without saying anything else, he confirmed it. Mass might have been working on her heart, but he peeked into her head, too, and drugged the hell out of the chemical imbalance that had ruled and ruined her life.

~

Hyrum refused to leave after lunch. There were things he wanted to do, places he wanted to see, and a part of him remained unconvinced that he could leave and then see his mother when the whim suited him. If there was a chance she was going to die soon, he wanted a happy memory to take home with him.

"We're gonna get in the car and go get ice cream and I'm gonna drive because I can."

Bree was invited along; the rest of us were not.

Valerie, Will mused as he sat in a lounge chair in the back yard, was in for a surprise once Hyrum reacquainted himself with her car. It was cold out, but Aubrey wanted to enjoy one of the places where she'd found peace as a girl, and that was under the gazebo near her mother's garden. She made hot chocolate, pointed Red and Will to the back door, and made them suffer the cold with her.

"He's been driving since he was fifteen, I think," Red informed Will. "They'll be fine."

Will had no doubt regarding their safety. The surprise would come in Hyrum's absolute confidence in his ability to maneuver any sort of car. "He drives Andrew and I to work most of the time. He also pushes the speed limits, which are considerably higher than they are here. If he can nudge that car to ninety or higher, he will."

"That car will rattle apart before he gets up to that speed. It's as old as I am. She refuses to replace it because it runs and gets her to church. What more does she need?"

"Forgiveness," Aubrey said, softly. "And I'm not sure I have that to give."

"You'll get there."

Aubrey grimaced, her eyebrows knotting together. "With all due respect, Red, you don't know that. You were witness to the aftermath of Dad's abuse, but you were never the target of it. I imagine you retained much of your innocence until Darlene—"

"I know. And I'm sorry. But if you're going to be angry with her, be angry with me, as well. I didn't know how to stop him, either."

"You didn't sleep next to him every night, knowing you could have ended everyone's misery with a touch."

"No, I didn't." He leaned forward, elbows on his knees, and he gave weight to the words that were about to come out. "But I could have ended it just as easily, Aubrey. I could have killed him. A knife through the heart. Slashed his throat. I thought of it, more than once. I came close, more than once."

Red leaned back and sighed. "Do you know why Dad decided I would follow in his footsteps, and not David? He chose the softer of his oldest sons, and not the one cut in his image."

"I imagine you were far more religious," she said, wondering what his point was.

"Religion never had anything to do with it. Faith was a façade as far as Dad was concerned. He chose me because of all his boys, save Hyrum, I was the least likely to stab him in the back. Literally. And yet over the years, after talking to them all, I'm certain I was the only one who had come close. I had the knife in my hand. I knew what he'd done to you, I had the knife, and all I needed to do was walk across the kitchen and pull it across his throat while he pored over paperwork."

He waited a beat, giving her time to ask why he hadn't. She refused.

"What if I had failed, Aubrey? I knew what would happen if I only wounded him. And I'm not the one he would have gone after. I'm not the one he would have killed."

"Mom," she whispered.

"No." Red shook his head. "Mom's silence was a given. He would have killed *you* as punishment to me for daring to cross him. And he would have done it knowing I would feel destroyed by the guilt every day for the rest of my life. He owned this country. No one would have held him accountable. If your death didn't do it, he would pick off my siblings one by one, until all that was left was fear."

Red drained his hot chocolate and got up.

"Mom wasn't just in fear for her life, Aubrey. She knew if she failed, he would make sure she lived through the worst of her nightmares. He would have destroyed us all, probably youngest to oldest, making her watch, and then he would have accused and blamed her in front of the world. He would have sat at the head of the tribunal ordering her execution. Maybe it was wrong of her to not take that chance, but like it or not, she lived for us. I know you say you'd have taken that chance and died for your kids but be honest. You'd have gone through hell if you knew that your action might mean they would die. Hate her for a while if it helps you heal, but at some point you have to forgive her because if you don't?"

He didn't leave her with an answer to that. He went inside instead.

"That's why you wanted to save her," Aubrey whispered, knowing Will would hear her. "To give me time to get to that point."

"Getting medical attention for her was the right thing to do. I can't save the world, but sometimes I can save one."

There were tears in her eyes when she looked up. "Don't lie to me, William."

"I'm not. But yes, I also wanted you to have time. I somewhat understand what a contentious relationship with one's mother feels like, Aubrey. A very small part of me still harbors resentment toward mine for all the years I lost with Aisha. Yet I also know what that sort of forgiveness feels like, and I think in the last few years I've paid closer attention to mothers in general, and what motivates them."

"But the pain—"

"I know. And if Levi were standing before me, without the restraints imposed by Jax's position and the inflammation of politics, I would kill him before he could blink. Unlike your mother and Red, I have zero doubts about my ability to do just that and would feel neither remorse nor guilt."

I jumped from Will's lap to hers, even though she wasn't as warm as he was. Someone needed to purr for her, and it wasn't going to be him.

You asked Jax not to kill him. Because of reasons.

Her fingers tickled the underside of my chin. "I know, Wick. I didn't want the fallout to harm my family."

"May I ask what might be an out of line question?"

She nodded.

"When you were a child, did you ever harbor thoughts of killing him?"

Her voice cracked. "Every time, Will."

"And do you know why you never attempted to?"

She stopped scratching. "Don't bring logic into my snit, Emperor. Let me have it. I can be a grown up later."

He got up, bending over to kiss her cheek. "You love your mother, Aubrey. Sometimes, that's enough."

~

After dinner—roast beef made with tiny carrots and potatoes, Hyrum's favorite—Valerie insisted it was time for him to go home. She felt the house choking his spirit and didn't want another minute of that for him. Before we left, she stood with him in the living room cradling his face in her hands, whispering to him to not be upset. Still, he cried.

"You have important work to do, Hyrum," she said gently. "I'm sorry I didn't take it seriously before, but I understand now. Andrew needs you to think for him. He needs your ideas."

"Sometimes they're stupid," he said.

"Never. Sometimes ideas are just the seed of something new, and it takes time for that new thing to grow. You always get where you need to be. Even when it's the hardest thing a man can do, when you don't want to take another step, you always finish the job."

He set his forehead against hers. "I found the Queen, Mom," he whispered.

"You found the Queen. And now you're a prince. Will you thank Eli for me? I wasn't gracious or forgiving, but you deserve him."

"I have a daddy who loves me."

"I know. Just don't forget, you have a mother who loves you, too. I'll try harder to be better."

"No, you won't," he said, earnestly. "You mean it now but you'll forget. That's okay. I'll remember that you wanted to."

While they said goodbye, Will reached into his backpack and then handed a jump bracelet to Aubrey.

"I'm staying for a few days," she explained to Red. "I don't think Hyrum is the only one whose spirit gets mangled in this house. I want to help her start the search for a new one."

"With a pool?" Hyrum asked hopefully.

Will jumped before Valerie could answer.

So at least it wasn't "no."

~

For Drew's sake, the drink of the night was cinnamon whiskey, bottle straight from the freezer, and over ice. Eli grimaced at first sip and asked Drew who had broken him so badly that he considered this worthy of passing his royal lips; Drew asked Eli who had coddled him so royally that he thought he had good taste.

Hyrum smiled because he thought the way they teased each other was funny, but he was quiet and didn't join in. His silence reminded me of the overgrown boy who thought taking sips of Drew's whiskey was being very naughty, so he didn't speak to make sure no one paid attention to him and didn't take his drink away. He was fully aware that either Will or Drew or even Jax had always poured the drink and handed it to him, but the part of him that still chewed on pencils and markers thought it was a mistake.

He also thought it was a bit naughty, but only because Aubrey always sighed and rolled her eyes when they took him out drinking. Usually after a drink he was loud and giggled wildly; tonight's silence was notable and noticed, but they waited before pressing him on it.

Part of him wanted to be in Florida, helping Aubrey plan out exactly how they would go about hunting for a new house, but the other part of him was relieved and happy to be out of the house in which he'd survived the first 42 years of his life. He was content to be home, drinking with the brothers and father who had chosen him. Eli reached over every now and then and rubbed his arm, reminding him that it would hurt in the morning if he drank too much.

He was into his second drink when the alcohol kicked down his wall of inhibitions, and he joined the conversation. Jax hoped that Aubrey would be home before Thanksgiving, but especially before her birthday. Surely if they had not found a house by then, Red could handle it.

"She'll be back," Hyrum said. "She wants to have a big birthday and anniversary with you on account of she's gonna be fifty-five and you're gonna be fifty and you're gonna be married for thirty years. That's a lot."

Eli declared that there should be a party. "Reserve that restaurant on the waterfront, the one you were at the night I came home. Invite Andrew's family. Sophia's family. Rent some friends so the world doesn't realize how anti-social you are."

"Bite me."

Aubrey already had a notion of what she wanted for their birthdays and anniversary, but it didn't include a party. She wanted to bolt through a portal to spend a week in Will's birth When, drinking head-sized margaritas while they played tourist. Regardless of how long she spent in Florida they could still do that, but he wanted her home to celebrate in real time, too.

"He just hates sleeping alone," Drew said.

"At least I'm sleeping." Jax leaned forward to see past Will. "You're not. I hear you wandering around at night. Take the damned pain medication."

"I take it," Drew said.

"Not working?"

Before Drew could answer, Hyrum did. "It's not his legs that hurt. It's his dreams. It doesn't hurt as much if you don't dream."

To that Drew nodded. "The dreams are still bad. Less now, and oddly enough talking to Tobias really does help. But yeah. I'd rather not dream."

Talk to Hyrum. He's helped me a lot.

Hyrum shook his head. "Drew needs someone smarter. If Tobias isn't helping enough, maybe Will can help you find a doctor in the place he was born."

"Not a bad idea," Drew admitted. "But Tobias *is* helping. And I know more about him now than Finn does, I think. He's a believer in conversation as therapy. It's starting to feel like visiting a friend, not seeking help."

Has the village forgiven him?

"Some," Drew said. "They tolerate him because they know if he takes a single step toward the dark again, his programming will be deleted. And he's fine with that."

Hyrum turned to Will. "Aubrey always makes my appointments with Dr. Cheshire and I think I need one, but I don't know how. Can you call him for me in the morning? I need to tell him about seeing my mom and that I lied to her."

"It was a white lie," Will reminded him. "It spurred her into getting help."

"Not about that. That wasn't a lie. If she'd said I had to I would have moved there on account of I promised. But I lied when I said I wasn't mad at her anymore and even though Aubrey says that was a white lie, too, it feels like I was being bad."

Eli set his drink down and reached for Hyrum's hand. "You are never bad, son," he said gently. "Out of all the people I know, you just might be the most kind. And being kind is more important than always telling the truth."

"Father Dan says so, too," Hyrum murmured.

"Father Dan has his shit together," Drew said. "Listen to him."

"Is that the only thing bothering you?" Jax asked. "Because even your mother would wave it off."

"Especially now," Will added. "I imagine as her medications take greater effect, she'll be far more...agreeable."

"So, she really was depressed?" Eli asked.

While Valerie refused any medical intervention other than what would save her life, while he had her sedated and in a surgical tank, Mass ran test after test to make sure there would be no surprises in the coming years. He noted that her brain chemistry was less than ideal and could, theoretically, cause massive mood swings. With Red's permission, Mass inserted a packet of slow-releasing medications into her bloodstream; by the time they'd been fully released, her brain chemistry would return to normal and she would be, effectively, cured.

"I just don't want to be mad at her anymore. But even Aubrey's still mad. It makes me feel bad."

"You're allowed to be upset," Drew said. "You don't get over a lifetime of pain just because you better understand what was happening."

"But I *don't* understand. She could have stopped Daddy and she didn't."

Eli started to tell him it was complicated, but he didn't know all the details. Jax knew what Aubrey had told him; Will had heard both sides.

"She considered it," Will told Hyrum. "She wanted to."

"Then why didn't she? I think Jesus would forgive her."

"Perhaps. She had many things to worry about, though. I don't think she was concerned that your father would have killed her if she had failed. Her worry was that if she tried and he lived, he would systematically kill her children, one by one, as revenge. She also worried that if she succeeded, his death would bring scrutiny to your family, and her children had gifts."

"Our things we can do? But nobody knows that."

"Nobody knows that because she was able to teach each of you to hide what you can do. She recognized when Red was very young that he had a gift, and because she had lived with her own, and possibly gifts of her parents or siblings, she understood it was best to keep those things hidden. It would be bad enough if those things were exposed here, in San Francisco, but in Florida it would have turned into a modern-day witch hunt."

"I don't know what that means," Hyrum said, thinly.

"It means your mom was fucked no matter what she did," Drew said.

"Jesus, Drew," Jax sighed.

"Well, I'm not wrong. Hy, maybe she got it wrong, but she was trying to protect you."

"She got it wrong. And when she made me go look for Aubrey, she got it wrong. My daddy hurt me all the time, and walking that far hurt a lot, too."

Eli took Hyrum's glass and set it away from him, on the ground. "She knows that, too, Hyrum. And maybe that's why she's grumpy all the time. She was both right and wrong at the same time, and it hurts her deep inside."

"I know." He blinked, and tears slipped over his eyelashes. "I still wish she had killed Daddy. I'm gonna go to hell because I can't make myself stop thinking that."

"Dude, no," Drew started.

There was nothing any of them could say to make him feel better. Will fished his phone out of his pocket, tapped at it, and then told Hyrum that there was someone waiting for him in the living room.

Unsteady, Hyrum got up, but didn't move until Eli swatted him on his butt and told him to go.

"Red," Will explained when the door closed behind Hyrum. "This goes far too deep for any of us to understand. I don't think even Aubrey would be the right one to help him wade through it."

"But you accept what Red told you?" Jax asked. "Valerie was stuck in a 'damned if I do, damned if I don't' situation?"

"I believe," Will said carefully, "that she weighed her options multiple times per day for decades, and never saw a path that would keep her children from harm. In her eyes, one way or the other, they were doomed. Levi's abuse simply felt like the least destructive option."

Calling it abuse felt too neat, Jax thought. It stripped way the violence and turned it into something spoken about in statistics, one of Those Things that could easily be brushed aside and that history would overlook. In thirty years, or fifty, or a century, history would not know that Levi Munson was a monster; it would only see him as a failed religious prophet, one who elevated himself a few steps too high onto a pedestal he could not grip.

"If it wouldn't hurt Aubrey, I'd expose the bastard for everything he was," Jax said. "The things people heard at his trial were not enough. I just want to—"

"Burn everything down?" Eli finished for him. "You dismantled his government and his legacy. That's not enough?"

"It's not enough," Drew said before Jax could. "What he did to Oz? Hell, yes, I want the world to know how much more than awful he was. I don't just want his legacy destroyed. I want every trace of him to be tainted with what he really was. A rapist. A pedophile. A hebephile. Sodomist. I want history to remember that he fucked little children, he beat his wife, and he did it all in the name of his religion. Because he could."

Jax grunted. "Tell us how you really feel, Andrew."

"How I feel? Valerie is an easy target because she's here. But the more I look at it? This is still all on Levi Munson. Every last bit of it."

It didn't matter.

Jax still couldn't tell the world, not without hurting Aubrey and Hyrum. She might be willing to suck it up, but it was too much to ask of him, and his promise was to protect Hyrum.

There was nothing to resolve.

Nothing to fix.

Nothing they could do.

~

At four in the morning, Red slipped out of Hyrum's bedroom. He'd intended on going into the guest room to get a little bit of sleep before going home and returning the jump bracelet to Aubrey, but Jax and Will were waiting in the living room. They'd sobered up and decided the world's woes could wait until Hyrum wasn't upset with himself.

Red was sure his brother understood that there wouldn't be any celestial blow-back for a simmering wish of revenge upon his father for the years of torture he'd endured. He reminded

Hyrum of the tools he had—prayer, asking for forgiveness, asking for clarity—and to not forget that sometimes the answers he received would come in the form of silence. Jesus might not whisper to him but would place in his path someone who could help—someone like Father Dan or Rabbi Joan. He might see his answers in the words of one of the children, or a baby's unexpected belly laugh.

"I think, at least I hope, he takes my word that his soul is one that will never see the likes of Hell. Though I may have confused the issue by telling him I'm no longer certain there is such a thing. As his ideology now includes concepts such as purgatory and limbo, I imagine we'll have some interesting discussions in the future."

Jax wanted to know how we could help him get over being angry with his mother.

"You don't. This is progress, Jax. Ten years ago, he wouldn't have allowed himself to feel this kind of anger toward her. Let him feel it. He's owed this much."

"Allowing him to wallow in anger seems punitive," Will said.

Red didn't think so. "You can't do it for him. And with this, the only way over it is through it. He'll get there. So will Aubrey. She needs time before she can step back and see the bigger picture. Right now, she's standing in front of a Monet with her nose an inch away from the paint, and the picture is lost in the details of each brush stroke. Give her time. She'll step back and see the whole thing soon enough."

Half an hour after Red came out, Hyrum's door opened and he shuffled down the hall, intent on making coffee for Jax. He was surprised to see Red and Will still up and offered to make breakfast for everyone.

"We haven't even been to bed," Jax said. "Go back, get some more sleep."

"Nuh. I'm hungry. You want grilled cheese? On account of it's not breakfast if you haven't been to bed. I can make soup, too."

Jax opened his mouth to tell him no, cooking for everyone

wasn't necessary, but Will stood up and said he would like a grilled cheese sandwich. He offered to make soup while Hyrum made the sandwiches and told Jax to sit tight until it was ready.

"That sounded like an order," Red mused.

"It was." Jax turned and looked in the direction of the kitchen. "Will is one of maybe three people who can order me around."

"Will, Aubrey, and who else?"

"My dad. And trust me, he does."

"Seriously," Red chuckled, "I know what it's like to be ordered around by a father."

Jax shook his head. "Not like that. The difference is that my dad orders me around. Not my father. And while I thought he was unfair when I was young, I can't even imagine what you went through. What your brothers and sisters went through."

He gave Red the short version of the balcony conversation, the impulse to expose Levi Munson down to the charred, splintered bones of his soul. It felt petty, personal, selfish, and unnecessarily necessary. Aubrey and Valerie had both testified to his character in open court. Oz had testified to the things he'd done to her. Yet it never felt like it was enough, and that justice had fallen a step short when Levi was murdered.

"Yet, we're all glad he's gone," Red mused.

"Except for David, sure."

Red visited David regularly. He kept an open line with his brother; he was the only person Jax had permitted ongoing contact with. If he didn't see David in person, he spoke with him on a video chat at least every other week, often weekly. And he had seen the shift in him.

"David is repentant," Red said. "Granted, he still thinks he should have been heir to the First Minister's seat and current head of the Quorum, but he would agree whole heartedly that our father was a monster and we're better off without him. He enjoys a certain amount of glee over the changes I'm pushing onto the church. Not what he would have done, but he has daughters and is silently cheering them on. He sees the picture I'm trying to project."

That picture was easy to see when there was nothing else to look at. David was in solitary confinement for his own protection. His life was a room, a bed, books, an entertainment monitor, and infrequent contact with the outside world.

"Were Dad still alive," Red said, "David would destroy him."

"He was molded after your father."

"To a point." Red lowered his voice. "He didn't know what Dad was doing to Hyrum. He knew Dad liked to pick on him but had no idea what else was going on. He admits he willfully turned the other way and didn't want to know, but he was grateful he was never taken under the stairs. He thought Dad was beating them, nothing more."

"How could he not know?"

"It's not like we stood up at dinner and announced it, Jax. None of the girls knew it was happening to anyone but themselves. Joe and Spencer only knew because they shared a room with Hyrum and had to comfort him after. If David had known? He wants power, Jax, but never wanted...that. He has no moral issue with obliterating someone in his way. He would be the one to bring down the image of Levi Munson, for no reason other than he refuses to be measured against him now."

"But does Levi need to be exposed now? Or are we projecting our wants as a need that doesn't exist?"

Red didn't know, but he was certain he wanted to pull his church away from the mold Levi and his predecessors had stuffed it into.

~

Less than a week after we watched Red announce the changes to his church's missionary program, he sat down for another interview with another talking head. This time, instead of being speaking with a middle-aged, pinkish, church-acceptable male reporter, he sat with a slightly less middle-aged, world-renowned female reporter who was not pink at all, and she conducted the interview from a studio in San Francisco.

Aubrey mused that heads were exploding all over Florida,

dozens of older white men unhappy that their First Minister was giving this *woman* his time, much less taking her seriously. She'd come home the day after Red arrived, mostly because Red had told her what he was going to do, and Valerie didn't want anyone to see the Queen there if they took umbrage.

Seated next to Red, their chairs turned just a bit so that they sat in a semi-circle with the reporter, was the King of Pacifica. They'd been discussing an upcoming conference with Red, Florida's Prime Minister, Midlam's Prime Minister, and the Governor of Texas. It was to be held in San Francisco, neutral ground, but the decisions made during this conference were not binding.

Red wanted to poke the bear, as it were. He wanted to be seen conferring with Sandra Warren and Shazia Van Hoff. He wanted to appear to be the voice of reason and maturity against the likes of Robert Lopez's flirtatious charm. He and Jax discussed the potential topics—converting to a common currency, sharing of social programs, expansion of the Emperor's shelter system, and creating a uniform tax base—and as the interview wore on, Jax carefully steered the discussion into the conversation he and Red truly wanted to have.

Destroying what was left of Levi Munson's legacy.

"Oh, it's beyond petty," he told Aubrey before he left for the news studio. "It's elevating petty to a new height. For me it's personal, but for Red, stripping away any shred of light Levi still has in Florida is necessary if he's going to drag the church into the twenty fifth century."

Today's talking head opened the door by mentioning the interview Red had given just a week before, and Jax jumped on it. We watched as the reporter gave up control and ceded the conversation to Red and Jax, though she didn't seem at all upset by it. Instead, her eyes glistened under the studio lights, and she was thrilled; she had what no one else had: the King and First Minister engaged in open, public banter, with no publicist hanging in the background, ready to pull the plug.

"Hyrum and I watched that last interview," Jax said to Red. "You stated that missions were the church's way of keeping its members within the fold. So now, what, you admit part of that was an intentional infliction of fear? Not just the fear of the outside world, but of each other?"

"In a way," he replied. Missions pushed men out where they would have to defend their faith to outsiders and gave them a safety net at home. Living among like-minded people was comfortable, and it was easy to feel faithful when life was comfortable.

"It leaves no room for doubt, and silences those who have questions," he explained. "Our children are taught a simplified version of church history, and as they age and those stories change a bit, they're also taught to not question, to accept that they're given information as they're mature enough to process it. But along with that is the unspoken message: if you question, if you doubt, if you give voice to those thoughts, you are in a state of apostacy, and therefore unworthy."

"And worthiness matters?"

"Worthiness is everything to a member of the Church of Florida. It's social currency. If you're deemed unworthy enough that you can't enter a temple? You can't hide that. People notice. And it's deducted from your social currency."

"Doubters are valued less," Jax guessed.

"They are, unfairly, and it's something we need to change. Those with doubt should have their questions addressed. There is always validity in their concerns, something that doesn't add up, and they need it to. Sometimes it's a matter that they've been taught in literal terms when in truth the matters at hand are figurative."

"What, as in possible commandments?" Jax pressed. "I've always taken issue with things such as stoning adulterers. It's right there in the Bible, but you don't see anyone chucking rocks at the neighbor who was literally caught with his pants down."

Red chuckled lightly. "I was thinking more about the foundation of our beliefs. We teach that our founder translated documents written in a dead language by using a seer stone, with his face planted firmly into a hat. This has been perpetuated as fact for centuries, and within our main temple is a display of the supposed stone and hat. Yet were one to carbon date either, they would find both to be relatively contemporary. It would be impossible for those things to have come from the first days of the church."

Jax gave a light shrug. "Seems like a harmless way to pass down the story of how you began. Guy finds some gospel etchings, exaggerates how he came to be able to read the words, and allows people to decide what he means."

"It would be harmless if it were the only mis-truth. It shouldn't be presented as a hard fact. It would be better if it had been told as a story, an allegory, and if members of the church had known it was bits of fabricated hope meant to inspire faith. And frankly, it's one of the things that sparks first doubt in many people. That accounting doesn't add up, so they look for other information. And people are resourceful—even without access to the church's historical documents, some have found ways to research our founder and have discovered glaring inconsistencies with what they've been taught, and the truth."

"Then what *is* the truth? And straight up, I'll admit I've asked Aubrey about this before. She admits she doesn't know. Now I'm guessing she was either too young or never would have been told."

Red wanted to tread carefully. "Understand, the heart of our church is faith in the Lord, and faith in our families. If you strip everything else away, we're left with that, and it's not a bad thing to have. I think those are the most important things to have. But the mythos the church has deliberately created? It's far from the truth. So many things are far from the truth." He considered his next words carefully. "Let's start here. Our founder did not receive personal revelation from our heavenly father that he was to begin taking multiple wives. Simply put, he was caught with women who were not his wife, and he found a way to justify it. He took it further, sending men off on lengthy missions, then in their absence declared their marriages invalid...and then married their wives. They were told and believed that this was what the Lord had declared. He married women who were *barely* women, and there is somewhat debatable proof that he took a young woman by force, prior to having married her."

At home, watching, Aubrey gasped and Hyrum blurted, "No way!"

From the look on Jax's face, I could hear what he wasn't allowing out: *Say what...?*

I could have expounded for him: history is ripe with women forced to marry their rapists. That was nothing new. For someone in Red's position to be so forthright about it, *that* was new.

"The true history of this church is well known to the patriarchy within its hierarchy. The farther up the ladder one goes, so to speak, the more one learns. Every man who has served the Quorum, every man who has called himself an apostle of the Church of Florida, has access to the full and uncensored texts of our history, and has access to every letter written by each president and prophet. We *all* know the truth, and yet all but one of those men are prohibited from speaking the truth because of the detrimental effect it would have on the gospel and the membership."

"Then why talk about it now? Why not protect what you have?"

"Because I'm the First Minister. The Prophet. The one who is not forbidden. It is now well within the scope of my power and my *rights* to release to the membership every text, every document, every letter, and to allow them to make up their own minds. They deserve the truth, every bright moment and every dark, ugly detail."

The talking head looked as uncomfortable as Red looked impish, and she spoke before Jax could. "Your church has always made the claim that its prophet has a direct line to God, and that he speaks for God, as if he *were* God. Are you suggesting that all this time God has told them to perpetuate a lie, but now you have word it's time to tell the truth?"

Red hesitated. "The church has made the claim of divine revelation since its inception. But also understand that as I sit here speaking, I'm not receiving revelation that, were I to repeat it, would stand as the word of God. That only happens in one temple, in its inner sanctum, the holiest of holies. Ostensibly, the prophet and the quorum meet there, pray, listen for celestial answers, and then carry on with God's work as He orders. What really happens is we meet, we bring up issues in need of attention, we argue about everything, men try to persuade me to their side, and then we pray. We open ourselves to receiving revelation. Not one of them is going to tell me that God has given them information different than what I feel I've been given. At least not those who believe that despite the fallacies of our history, the substance of our gospel is true."

Jax snorted. "Don't tell me you don't think you have a thing going with God. I know you do."

"I believe I do," he said lightly. "And I can't speak for prophets long dead, but I can tell you with utter certainty that my father did not. He never believed that he did. He saw his position as one of power and one of control, and he used that position to excuse any number of deplorable and criminal acts. Including—especially—against his family. He tortured my mother so brutally, physically and emotionally tortured, that she feared for the lives of her children and never felt safe enough to speak out against him. Levi Munson molded himself into the worst possible image of our founder, taking his license to do whatever suited him to depths most men cannot imagine. And you may read into that what you will."

Excited, the talking head jumped in again. "What depths are we talking? He beat his wife and kids? Murder? Rape?"

"Yes."

She flinched and looked almost pained as she noted the time left. Red had taken the top off the jar and thousands of tiny bugs were about to crawl out, and she had—by his design—not enough time left to examine them.

"What does this mean overall, Minister Munson? The end of the Church of Florida?"

"Not at all. It means a new beginning, with the truth made available to all who seek it, with doubters being welcome with open arms, and with compassion for those who choose to find another path. Our books, our beliefs, literal and figurative, will be open for the inspection of our members from here on out. I invite the world to study our religion. Our social currency must change, and this is the first step."

"You're going to piss off so many people," Jax said. "Levi still has followers. He still has men in positions of power, and they're not going to sit back quietly while you open the books."

"To quote the Emperor, 'I am aware.'"

At that, Jax laughed, but then quickly sobered. "You're also going to open a lot of wounds. Your brother. My wife. I'm not sure how much the world really knows about what Levi did to them. I'm not sure how much they should know."

"Tell them!" Hyrum shouted at the TV.

Red didn't think the brutal and exacting details of Levi's abuse needed to be highlighted in contrasting colors. But he hoped for transparency, and for the truth—that for longer than Levi was prophet, the position had been used to commit crimes against humanity, and that Levi had, indeed, molested and beaten his own children, and he had mentally and physically tortured his wife—to come to the surface.

"You don't think his abuse remained within your family," Jax mused.

"I would be surprised if it did. I want our members to understand that the legacy of the presidency of the Church of Florida is tainted. It didn't start with my father, but I want to make sure it ends with him."

"To bring the church back to the people."

"I hope that we can reach a place where the least of our members are valued as much as our apostles have been, and that those who feel less than will begin to feel equal."

"Does he mean me?" Hyrum asked.

"You've never been less than anyone," Aubrey told him.

Hyrum grunted. "But Daddy thought I was."

"Freedom of religion needs to spring forth in Florida," Jax said. "That means freedom *from* religion, too. Can your people bear that? Can they hear the truths about your father, and the prophets that came before him?"

"If the right people speak up, I believe so."

Jax tilted his head, thinking, and then asked, "Who else would they listen to?"

"My brothers. One in particular. Help me unleash the ugly truths, all of them, King Jackson. Release David. He's served enough time, and he would speak the truth loud and wide." Red turned in his seat, eyes gleaming, his lips tugged up in a half-smile. "It's time, Your Majesty. Let my brother go."

THE WHEN WHERE YOU BELONG

Thor's tail thumped against the side of the coffee table. He sat still otherwise, his tongue hanging out, little flecks of drool dripping onto the area rug, and the tiniest of whines escaped him. I hovered a foot above where he could get a good look at me, and I let my tail fall over the back side of the hover cart. It flicked once, twice, then a third time to make sure he'd seen it, and when he did it also caught Aubrey's attention.

"Wick," she cautioned, "be nice."

I am being nice.

I leaned as far forward as I could without sending the cart into his head. *You need exercise, right? It'll be a while before Rhys can take you for a walk. Want to run the stairs?*

"Good boy good boy good boy!"

Well, all right then.

I lowered the cart until I was directly in front of him, bopped him on the nose—no claws because why would I do that?—and then took off. I dipped down the staircase and he bolted after me, scrambling on the steps as he chased me from the fourth floor to the first, where we were stopped by the desk guard and his jabbing pointy finger.

"No. You're not allowed out on that thing, Mister Wick."

Fine.

I turned around and headed up, knowing Thor would follow. We raced to the multi-purpose room, shot across it, and then thundered back down the stairs. Every now and then Thor let loose with a tiny *woof*, which meant *I'm gonna catch you* and also *this is fun, keep going.*

He was not going to catch me and knew it.

Catching me wasn't the point.

On the fifth trip down, the guard blocked the door, displaying a complete lack of trust that we understood the rules. "Please, Wick. Just go back upstairs. I know you understand me. Please."

A familiar voice came from the guard's lounge. "Problem?"

"They keep running down here like they're going to barrel out the front door," the guard whined. "If that happens—"

"Auto open was disabled after he got the hover cart." Vicat came out of the lounge, wearing jeans and a t-shirt instead of her usual uniform of jeans and a sweatshirt, which meant she was off duty. "He knows better than to go outside without someone upstairs knowing."

Well, I have in the past. There's a cat door, you know.

"How many laps today, Wick?" she asked. "Remember, he's still a puppy."

Five. But you're right. We'll stop for now.

She reached down and rubbed Thor's head. "You seem fine. Let's go get Isaac and Rhys and maybe we can all go outside."

"Good boy good boy good boy!"

I led the way to the apartment and Thor slapped his paws on the stairs as he walked next to her. He was panting, but in that happy-puppy way; I hadn't overworked him but Vicat was right. He was still a puppy and for all I knew he would collapse in a pile of sleepy golden fur halfway down the stairs, having fallen prey to the spontaneous-nap-monster.

He needed a reserve of energy. He still had a post-work walk to look forward to, when Rhys led him around Union Square or down to Market Street with Will trailing behind, watching and encouraging him in Thor's training, and there was also his nightly roof romp, when Will took him upstairs where he could pee and sniff all the things and then bark at someone in a window across the street. He'd already learned that when Will said "no," he needed to listen or else he would get the wagging pointy finger of disappointment, but when he was outside, he was allowed to bark; at night he rarely let out more than one or two, mostly to hear his own voice.

"He's a toddler," Will explained. "He's learning. It's all right as long as he doesn't continue long enough to become bothersome."

Inside, he'd learned to use a soft bark. He let slip a *woof* instead of an *arf*, and sometimes whined when he was unsure about something. He understood *sit* and *stay*, though often lacked the maturity to remember that he was expected to continue sitting or staying until told otherwise.

He also had no clue what it meant to heel, so instead of staying next to Vicat, when he heard Rhys in Aubrey's dining room, he pushed past her with excited glee and galloped to his boy.

"Good lord," Aubrey sighed. "What did Wick do? Did he tease the poor guard downstairs?"

Of course I did. Dude's got to earn his stripes.

After a short, proper bow to her Queen, unrequired in private quarters but something she would not yield upon, Vicat answered, "He was exercising Thor, as near as I could tell."

Aubrey seemed dubious, but anything else she had to say was lost when Isaac jumped from his seat and squealed "Aunt Vi! Did you see Daddy? Does he miss me? Is he okay?"

The little spot where her temple met her hairline twitched. "I couldn't go today, Isaac. I'll see him this weekend, all right?"

"Can I go?"

The answer to that was no, it was always no, but Aubrey spared Vicat from Isaac's disappointment. "Sweetheart, didn't you already promise to help Jay carry things from his room to his apartment this weekend? And he needs you to pick out things for your room. He wants it to be special for you."

He frowned, but only for a moment.

"I get to help, too!" Rhys reminded him. "If we do a good job Jay's gonna take us for ice cream!"

Vicat bent over to kiss Isaac on the top of his head. "A promise is a promise. And I promised you two that we would go to the playground today."

"Can Thor come for fresh air?" Rhys asked.

Thor was welcome to stay with Aubrey, but Vicat nodded

and told him to get his leash. "And what about you, Wick? Do you want sunshine and fresh air this afternoon? We're stopping at the bakery first. There's bacon in it for you."

I wouldn't mind going outside.

I lowered the hover cart and stepped on the off switch as it settled on the floor. Vicat patted her shoulder, an invitation up, but Thor was learning how to carry me, so I jumped onto his back and settled near his neck. Riding on him was easier than balancing on someone's shoulder. I had more room to make myself comfortable and if he wobbled, I only needed to splay myself across his back. I could flex my claws in his fur and not hurt him—I don't think he even felt it.

As promised, we stopped at the bakery on Union Square for chocolate milk and bacon. I jumped from Thor to the table, lest he steal my bacon—for which I could not blame him, because bacon is bacon and bacon is good—and watched while Rhys tried to get Thor to sit.

He tapped the puppy on his backside with a finger and gave the order to sit, prompting Thor to tilt his head to the left and let slip a tiny noise that sounded a lot like, "Huh?"

"Sit, Thor," Rhys repeated.

Use your whole hand, not just your finger. And use his name first. And then tell him no bacon unless he does.

Rhys splayed his fingers and reluctantly—he didn't want any hint of hitting—used his palm to tap on Thor. "Thor, sit. You want bacon? You gotta sit."

Thor sat.

"Good boy?"

Tell him he's a good boy.

"Good boy, Thor. Now stay. Daddy says you have to stay after you sit, remember?"

Thor did not remember, but Vicat had an entire slice of bacon in her hand and he knew better than to do anything that would place that bacon in front of me instead. He watched, his tongue hanging out, as she crumbled a slice for me. His tail flopped back and forth, and he twitched, but he stayed put.

"Good boy," he woofed when Vicat handed the bacon to Rhys.

"You want bacon?"

"Good boy good boy!"

Rhys broke it into chunks and fed him in bits. He'd learned early on that if he gave Thor the entire slice at once he would try to swallow it whole, and there was a 50-50 chance he would choke on it. Thor was happier when he thought he was getting several bites, anyway, and he vibrated with the sheer joy of getting greasy fried goodness from his boy.

Tasty, right?

"Good boy."

Dude, wait until you taste steak. You're going to 'good boy' yourself into a seizure.

"How come Alex and Charlie aren't going with us?" Isaac shook the milk container and then handed it back to Vicat to open. "They like the playground."

"I know, but you two deserve to play without them sometimes, right?"

Isaac shrugged.

"They needed naps," Rhys declared. "Alex had a tantrum because she can't taste blue, and Charlie threw blocks at Hyrum. They were cranky."

"But it's not fair."

Vicat slipped her arm around his shoulders. "Yes, it is. You boys are older and should be able to do things without them every now and then."

"Like Hyrum plays with us, and then sometimes he goes and plays with Drew," Rhys said. "It's okay when he does."

"Sometimes he plays with Will or Jay," Isaac mused. "Do they go to the playground?"

"They go to Fuzzy's. I think it's a playground for grownups."

"Is that like when Daddy and Odie go to Luke's?" Isaac asked. "Odie says there's a *lot* to play with there."

Vicat bit her bottom lip to keep from laughing and then said, "Something like that."

"How come you call Jay's daddy 'Odie'?" Rhys asked him. "He's James."

Isaac shrugged again. "He's my Odie."

"Other Daddy," Vicat explained. "It's a nickname."

"Oh. That's clever." Rhys set his milk down and jumped out of his chair and shouted, "JayJay!" but he wisely did not run from the table to get to his big brother. "Where you been?"

They both scrambled to him when he was close enough, which made Thor get up and run, too. Jay grabbed his leash before he could zip past and kept him on a short lead back to the table, miraculously not tripping over the kids jumping near his legs.

"We're headed for the playground," Vicat explained. "Just pre-loading the carbs first."

"You wanna go with us?" Isaac asked.

"Please?" Rhys added.

"Sorry little dudes, but I'm here to meet Zed and Sophia and talk about boring things like paint and the thread count on good sheets." He jiggled the leash. "Want me to keep Thor here so you can play without worrying about him? I'll make sure he gets home all right."

Rhys was torn. He wanted to keep Thor with him because Thor loved the playground, but he also wanted to run and play and not have to tell Thor to sit or stop it or keep other kids from climbing on him. His major concern was Will, though.

"Daddy would get mad. I'm supposed to take care of Thor."

"I promise, Daddy won't mind. I'd like to take him for a w—"

"Don't say the word!" Rhys sputtered.

"—alk."

Thor began dancing around Jay's legs, wrapping the leash around his ankles.

"Good boy good boy good boy good boy good boy!"

"You have to *spell* it," Rhys said with a heavy sigh.

I'll stay with Thor. Daddy will be okay with that.

"Lesson learned." Vicat laughed and then scooped up the milk containers. "Come on. Let's go play while there are still kids at the park."

Rhys reached for Thor's leash. "I don't want Daddy to get mad."

"He won't," both Jay and Vicat said at the same time.

"But I promised."

Ask him. He just slipped out of the portal.

Will was halfway across the Square, heading for home.

As loudly as he could, Rhys yelled, "Daddy can Jay take Thor for a w-a-l-k? Isaac and me are going to the playground."

Do not correct his grammar, dude.

"He may," Will said when he was closer. "Go have fun. Thor will be fine with Jay."

When were you?

He'd been in his birth When. His grandparents were there, and he often went to see them, but there was something else pressing him to sit at the table with Jay.

"Dad okay?" Jay tucked Thor's leash under his leg and told him to sit. "Last time I was there, he barely looked at me. He just sat there, staring at George in the tank. Most of what I said to him went in one ear and out the other."

James was fine and would be coming home soon. "Perhaps this should wait until he's here."

"No fucking way. Is it George? Come on, Will. Don't make me sit here and agonize over a maybe."

George Denton—currently Geo Okuda in this When—had been floating in a surgical tank for several weeks. Vicat kept watch over him for the first ten days, until Mass bluntly told her she was more in the way than anything else and her presence would not make a difference in her brother's progress despite her wishes. Jay visited frequently, mostly to see his own father once he'd been removed from his tank.

Physically, James was fine, but he was emotionally distant, his thoughts scattered, and had only asked about Isaac once.

The issue at hand was George. He'd been encased in surgical gel long enough that Mass was concerned about skin degradation. The number of nanobots needed to keep his flesh from deteriorating while others went about rebuilding and repairing his internal organs and spine had reached the maximum amount the tank could safely hold. It was time for him to come out.

"But his back—"

Will gave a short nod of his head. "He'll be paralyzed from

his waist down and will remain hospitalized while he recovers from this part of the surgery. Once Mass is certain that his skin has recovered, he'll go back, and the remainder of the surgery can progress."

"How long?"

Will didn't know. It could be a week or a month. If his skin remained the only issue and there were no sudden infections complicating matters, he would likely return to the tank in under ten days. "There is a more urgent concern, however. The trauma he endured was significant, and there may be repercussions from that."

"He could go into shock, I know."

"Jay."

"He could die. I know that, too. You didn't need to wait for my dad to tell me this." He sucked in a deep breath. "We're not close, Will. I've forgiven him for all the shit he pulled, and I remember when he was really good with me, but after that crap...we just never got close again."

George and Jay were friendly and enjoyed each other's company on occasion, but the odd truth was that Will was closer to George. They'd bonded over the horrible truths of their lives, and then over their sons. For Jay, George was his former stepfather, but for Will his childhood tormentor had become his friend.

"My concerns lie elsewhere."

"Isaac?"

"George didn't simply utter a wish before Rhys froze time. There are legal documents in both Whens naming you as Isaac's guardian. Those documents are quite specific in preventing James from assuming custody."

That gave Jay pause. "Why would he—?"

Will nodded in the direction of the portal. Old Finn had escorted him through, and with a wave to Will, turned around and went back. "Ask, and demand the truth, Jay."

Usually when someone comes out of a surgical tank, they look younger and quite refreshed. James was tired and every year of his life pressed against him. He crossed Union Square slowly, hands shoved into his pockets, and he wanted to be anywhere but there.

Irritation crossed Will's face; confusion covered Jay's.

I was with Jay; James was the good guy, the one we could trust. He never stood in the way of his son, and he'd certainly never tried to kill Will. Yet Will was clearly upset, and barely looked at him when he sat across from Jay.

"Dad?" Jay frowned. "You're back. Why? Is George—?"

"Coming out soon."

"Then why are you here? You should be there when he comes out."

James shifted uncomfortably. "He wouldn't want me there. And I can't bring myself to watch him die. I just can't."

Anger flashed in Jay's eyes. "He's your goddamned husband. You can't let him die alone."

"He's not my husband," James said thinly. "Our marriage ended when he was declared dead."

"Bullshit."

"We intentionally never remarried, Jay. He didn't want to tie a legal noose around our relationship."

"But his name—"

He became Geo Okuda to plaster over the cracks in his old life. He'd been banished as 65-year-old George Denton, declared and presumed dead by the masses, and returned as mid-forties Geo Okuda. Near death when Aisha tackled him through a portal, two weeks in a recovery tank gave him back two decades of life lived away from his birth When; old friends here might pass by and wonder who he resembled, but no one mistook him for his old self.

He'd taken James's last name, but they had never formalized their union.

"He didn't want anything standing in your way when you turn twenty-five. Not him, not us. And he needed to be able to walk away, if living here made him ill."

James was no longer George's anchor; that bond had never returned.

"I don't care what the legal issues are." Jay leaned forward.

"Deep down, he's your husband. You owe it to him to be there, no matter how difficult seeing him die might be."

He squirmed. Under his son's angry glare, James squirmed.

"Just tell him," Will finally said.

Reluctantly, James began. "The day of the explosion. I don't think I've ever been so glad in hindsight for you to be late. We would have been inside. I mean—"

"Get to the point," Will snapped.

"There was a reason we asked you to leave Isaac with Zed, and to have dinner with us. Well, I wanted dinner. George thought it was unnecessary and cowardly of me, but I wanted to tell you in public. I mean...yes, it was cowardly. But I didn't think you'd react badly. I didn't think it would matter much to you at all."

"What?"

"We were there to tell you that we're separating. He was going home, and he wanted to ask you to bring Isaac here every now and then to see Rhys."

"You could have done that with a phone call." He glanced at Will, whose anger was bubbling on the surface. He made no effort to hide it. "Then what else was there? It had to be more."

"That's it. That we were splitting up."

Jay shook his head. "What the fuck did you do? You wanted me in public so I wouldn't make a scene." The realization settled with him. "No, *who* did you do? Holy fucking hell, Dad, the *one* condition Uncle Jax had in letting George come back was that you stopped screwing around. That was it. Just keep your fucking pants on. Who the hell was it?"

James flinched. "Does it matter?"

"I'm sure it mattered to him. So what? Another man? A woman? He used to be pretty good about not caring too much if it was a woman. He understood that. But you gave your word."

"I'm just not monogamous by nature—"

"Bullshit. We're not five years old and left alone with the cookie jar. Anyone can stay faithful if they want to." He stood, knocking the chair to the ground. "If you're not there, if he survives, it really is over. He'll never forgive that. You know that don't you?"

James gave a bare nod.

Jay turned to Will. "Can you get Vicat back here and then send her through? She'll want to be there. And do you mind taking Isaac?"

"I'll take Isaac home," James said.

"Like hell you will." Jay's voice wrapped around an angry hiss. "He stays with me, whether George survives or not."

"He needs a father," James started.

"He needs a stable home." The realization hit Jay. "This is why, isn't it?" he asked Will. "He wanted me to let them see each other, but he wanted to make sure I had custody. To shield him from the inevitable."

"I believe so," Will said.

Jay leaned his hands on the table, facing his father. "Don't you dare try to get him. I will fight you on every front, and I'll win. You know that."

Before James answered, Will told Jay to go. He planned on waiting long enough for Rhys and Isaac to enjoy the playground, and he would then escort Vicat to her brother's side.

"Last chance, Dad," Jay said.

James sadly shook his head.

After the portal had swallowed Jay, James pushed away from the table and stood.

"He'll forgive you eventually," Will said. "But make no mistake, you won't wind up with Isaac."

"Jay's too young to take on the responsibility."

"Perhaps." Will gently yanked on Thor's collar and told him to get up. "But I am not, and Isaac will always have a place in my home, as will Jay. I believe George would be satisfied to have his son living with me, close to Jay."

"He's my son, too," James hissed.

"Jay? Yes, he is. Isaac? While you remain his Odie, his other daddy, you forfeited rights to him when you broke his father's heart. You'll have frequent access, but I will support Jay in this matter. George rewrote his will not long before the explosion. There is a clear line of custody for Isaac, and there are several ahead of you."

"Jay and who else?"

"Jay, Aisha and me, Andrew and Oz, Vicat, then you."

He didn't believe Will. "All of you ahead of his own sister. There's not a chance—"

"He was aware that her career comes first. Vicat would never turn her back on Isaac, but she understands that he'd be happiest surrounded by a large family, and that she would be able to see him whenever she chose. What he did not want for Isaac is exactly what Jay understood. Your history suggests that he would be exposed to a parade of men and women, and while that's fine for you, it is not for him."

He didn't give James a chance to argue. He scooped me up, set me on his shoulder, and we headed off to find Vicat and the boys.

~

The surgical suite was brightly lit and desperately grim. Quiet choked the air, pitted by gentle humming that seeped from the machines surrounding the tank, and the technicians went about their duties without speaking and without glancing at any of the people waiting for George Denton to be eased out of his long surgery.

I'd seen Jay lifted from his tank; the mood had been brighter, and the recovery bed waiting for him was the same type that patients throughout the hospital slept in. The bed waiting for George was a thin pad atop an industrial strength hover pad, one that could speed him into another surgical suite down the hall. Another surgeon waited there, but there was no tank; there was a surgical team armed with scalpels and a breathing machine, and every medication they typically used in an emergency.

Mass told Will privately, while Jay and Vicat were occupied with the sight of George floating in the center of the gel, covered in nanobots, that he did not expect to need the second surgical suite. If George came out of the tank and went into shock, if his organs seized and failed, there was likely no time to get him down the hall.

"I could jump—"

Mass shook his head. "There will be no coming back from this if he goes into shock. The nanobots have kept him alive, but once they disengage, the count is on, and the margin of error is microscopically slim. I have a cardiac stimulator ready to go and if we can keep his heart beating, he'll make it, but we have to get him out of the tank first."

The cardiac stimulator acted as an external artificial heart, forcing the natal heart to pump blood regardless of its condition. Mass answered Will's confusion in a whisper. "If the repairs to his abdominal aorta aren't perfect, it will shred, his heart will seize, and there's nothing to be done at that point."

Now Will stood quietly next to Jay, eyes darting as he checked each monitor in succession, and he repeated that until a tech seated near George's head cracked through the silence. "Nanobots have disengaged and are in the colon."

Still, they moved with precise care. He was not yanked from the tank as if his life depended on the speed with which they acted. They were far more careful with George than they'd been with Jay; his spine was incomplete and could fracture if they hurried. I heard Jay's breath hiccup and felt Will's heartbeat increase, but I sensed nothing from Vicat except stern resolve.

She was not nervous or anxious; she trusted that they would do everything they could for her brother, yet she understood the risks. She accepted the risks. She'd lived over fifty years without him and believed that grief was transient, but her memories of reconciling with him would go on and eventually paint over his loss.

George was gently lifted and then placed on the recovery bed. Instead of cleaning him off or even removing the breathing apparatus, they waited. Mass watched the monitor for signs of failure, paying particular attention to his heart and aortic pathways, and when he was satisfied that George's heart would hold, he began dialing back on the breathing machines, and then instructed one of his technicians to remove it.

The tube slipped from his throat with a horrible sucking sound. It was thick and wet, slurping and bubbly, but what Mass listened for was breath.

There was none.

Jay left slip a tiny sound, a whisper of wanting to see George's chest rise and fall. Mass gestured to another technician who placed a hydrospray against George's neck, and moments after the hiss of the medication hit his skin, his chest heaved, and he drew in a deep, strangled breath. It sounded as if he were choking, but Mass appeared pleased and indicated that they could begin cleaning the gel from his body.

"His skin is like paper," he reminded them. "Leave a residual, and then cover him with wet film."

"Evacuation?" a tech asked.

Mass shook his head. "We'll wait for biology to catch up with him."

"Shit's gonna shine," Jay muttered, which finally elicited response from Vicat. She snickered, but kept her gaze focused on George. She would have stood there until he was awake, but Mass gestured to the door and made it clear we needed to leave the room.

"He's at risk for infection," Mass said once we were in the hallway. "The fewer people in the room as the gel comes off, the better. Once the film adheres to his skin and we've been able to examine him thoroughly, you'll be allowed to see him."

Jay watched the door slide shut after Mass went back in. "What's the film for?"

"It will prevent further degradation of his skin," Will explained. "Once applied, it bonds with flesh and acts as a barrier while facilitating healing."

"It's a body bandage," Vicat said. "Expensive as hell back home and only used for burn victims. Here? Common enough that there are kits in every home."

It was expensive on our home When because it was relatively new, and the patent protection had not yet expired. In under a decade, Ozoo Enterprises would purchase the patent from its creator, file for the dissolving of its protection, and make the formula free for any pharmaceutical company willing to sell the final product at a minimum. Ozoo would continue to purchase protected medical patents, until there was little benefit to them;

medications and life-saving technology should not come at a premium, Prince Consort Andrew Blackshear asserted, stopping just short of a Royal Declaration. The agreements made with competing companies allowed for a profit margin, though it was slim and specifically designed to prevent anyone from getting rich.

Neither Will nor Vicat shared that with Jay.

"How long will it be until we can see him?"

Will thought it would be a day, perhaps two, though the waiting time was irrelevant as far as Vicat was concerned. She intended to remain, even if it meant losing her position as Rhys's personal guard.

"Your position is not in jeopardy from this. Regardless, given as close as you've become with him, we may need to revisit your assignment. He sees you as Isaac's aunt and the person who often plays with them. Not his guard. And he prefers that."

She gave a tight nod. "I'll find a pool of candidates to replace me. There are a few who would do well with his need for social contact without sacrificing the level of protection required."

Oh, look, she can talk like a history teacher, too.

Will also heard the slight edge in her voice. "This is not a demotion, Vicat. If anything, taking the assignment in the first place was a step back."

"It's a promotion," Jay said. "You're going from guard to aunt."

"That would make George his uncle. I presume the Emperor wouldn't chose that direction."

Will gave a slight shrug. "Rhys already views Isaac as a brother. They're close. While I would prefer that he not refer to George as Uncle George, I will not object to a relationship."

"If he survives, he'll take Isaac home," Vicat reminded him. "To here. Now. He won't have much of a choice."

Jay twitched at the idea, but Will let out a soft breath and said simply, "We'll see."

~

Aisha was the one to call James. While Will thought it was important that he know George had survived removal from the tank and that he would be allowed visitors soon, he was still angry enough to not want to speak with James personally and didn't argue when Aisha offered to make the call. Neither did Jay, who hadn't so much as twitched in the direction of his phone.

"Yes, you fucked up," she said after a long silence. "But honestly, I'm impressed it took this long."

"As far as we know," Jay muttered. He was on the sofa, bare feet on the coffee table, scrolling through a list of stories he wanted to read to the kids. "I doubt it."

A loud crashing of wooden blocks popped from the playroom, followed by peals of laughter. Will turned his head to listen, making sure that crying didn't follow the giggles, satisfied when he heard Charlie squeal, "Do it again!"

"Does he want to go back?" Will asked Aisha after she'd hung up.

He did not. "Just keep him apprised. He only wants to know that George is all right, and when he can see Isaac."

"I want to hear from George first," Jay said.

"He was clear," Will said. "No matter what happens to him, he still considers your father to be Odie to Isaac."

"I know."

"They should have time together, even if you have custody."

"And maybe I'm feeling like a punitive little bitch," Jay snapped. "He could be Isaac's Odie for the rest of his life, but he fucking blew it."

Aisha sighed. "If it means anything to you, he swears that he didn't violate Jax's rules. Anything he did, he did there. Never here."

"I'm not sure Jax will see it that way," Will said.

Jay tossed the magazine aside. "And I don't think it matters. He promised he would stop screwing around. There were no timelines attached to that."

George was, arguably, not the same person who had taken a swing at his King. He was not the same man who had pulled a gun on Will, nor the same man who attempted to drag Jay off to who-knows-where. It was more than a change in behavior. He had, by virtue of a rehabilitation tank, had every cell of his body rewritten. The George who had done all of that was in his sixties. The Geo that lived in Pacifica was in his forties. They shared DNA but the resemblance skittered to a stop a step or two beyond that.

"Jax will pay attention to the details. I believe he would consider Isaac's needs most of all."

"George Denton is dead," Aisha reminded Jay. "He might need to return home every now and then to reset, but Isaac seems to need to stay here."

Will nodded. "I could make the argument—and I will if necessary—that prohibiting George from returning to and remaining here is akin to sentencing Isaac to death. I suspect that regardless of where he was born, he is a child of this When."

Jax could order Isaac to stay here and still send George home.

"He wouldn't." Will was certain of that. "He's not heartless."

"It wouldn't be legal, would it?" Aisha wondered.

Jay skipped over that thought. "If he were banished again, George would leave Isaac with me. I'd take him to visit his own father, but he would grow up here, being shuttled between Daddy and Odie, and all under my thumb. He'd hate me, eventually."

There was discussion of carts and horses and the order in which they belonged. I snoozed through much of it, missing when Jay left the apartment to finish cleaning his own, but woke in time to hear Will confess to Aisha that if it came to it, they would raise Isaac.

"Jay could give that little boy everything he wanted, and he would be an excellent guardian."

"But?" Aisha asked.

"But we could give him everything he needs, and seeing him with Rhys? Part of what he needs is family. He's thriving right now, Enzo. Has he been sick once since he began staying with us? "

She didn't think so.

"In the last year he's constantly felt ill. George has been flummoxed by it. Weekly stomach aches and low-grade fever, with nothing being truly wrong. And I've never heard him laugh so much as he has lately."

"He's not our kid," Aisha warned. "I'm attached, too, but he's George's son."

"And if George recovers, this is all moot. But if he doesn't?"

"You want to take custody from Jay."

"No. But I would ask Jay to stay with us. I know he wants to move back to his apartment, but I'm not sure it's the best thing for Isaac."

"He lost Navi, Bilbo. Don't take Isaac, too. I would welcome that little boy to stay forever, but not at the cost of Jay."

~

Jay may have wanted the world to believe he wasn't terribly close to his former stepfather, that the man had blown all reasonable chances for redemption when he pointed an antique handgun at Will, but I wasn't buying it. His soul ached with resentment that occasionally bubbled to the surface, and he still wrestled with anger that had George gotten his way, he would still be fighting against biological hiccups, suffering in the wrong body.

Despite everything, he loved George.

If George died, Jay would mourn him along with all the little bits and pieces of their complicated relationship, and recovery would take a long time.

I left Aisha and Will to ponder what might happen to Isaac and went downstairs to see if Jay needed supervision while he cleaned—which as far as I could tell involved nothing but staring at the video screen while a soft-spoken, color-stained older man described how he achieved a subtle glow in his paintings—and sat on the floor where I was sure to be in his line of sight.

"What, furball?" he asked after a few quiet minutes.

You love George. Admit it. You love Isaac more, but you love George.

"I don't have any food here right now. You could sneak into Zed's and convince Sophia to feed you. Even if Will already did."

She's at work. Zed's home and he's not exactly free with the snacks.

"Well, since I know you understand me, and you're not leaving, I suppose you're here to just stare at me?"

Making you uncomfortable is a highlight of my life.

"Hyrum might want someone to cuddle with."

I'm starting to feel unwanted here.

"You can sit on my lap if that's what you're after. I need better clues, Wick."

He patted his thighs, and while that wasn't what I was after, I jumped up anyway. If I could manage enough cuteness without wanting to hork up a hairball, he might get me something dead and delicious when he was done pretending to clean by way of whatever mindless drivel he'd been watching.

It might have worked, too, if his phone hadn't pinged. He forgot I was there once he'd answered, and the look on his face was a curious mixture of excited and dread.

"Yeah, no, I'm in the apartment." He said it in the same tone people did when they know someone is about to ask them a favor, but they don't want to be guilted into doing something. "Sure. I'll let the guard know you're coming."

I jumped down, because getting up usually followed a promise to make the guard let someone in.

"Yeah, hey, can you grab a slice of bacon or something while you're there? Wick is here and I think he's got a royal case of the munchies."

I knew I liked you for a reason.

"No, that wasn't a pun. Hey, I'm not an actual prince, princess."

Hm. Oz? She's an actual princess. Unless you meant that sarcastically, the way Jax does when he's talking to one of the sticky people.

And technically, you are an actual prince now. Will is Prince William. Your mom is Princess Aisha. Since he named you as his firstborn, you're Prince James. Check your travel visa. It might surprise you.

"You heard me mention bacon, didn't you?"

He didn't wait for an answer. He stepped out long enough to let the desk guard know he was expecting someone, and then darted back, racing to the bathroom to brush his teeth with a stale, weeks-past-last-used toothbrush that I may or may not have licked a few times while exploring the vacant apartment.

"Best behavior, Wick." He cupped his hand over his mouth and exhaled. "Good enough. Not like she's getting that close."

Which she are we talking about? New girlfriend? Some model you're going to paint? Will there be nudity? I'm leaving if there's nudity. Well, unless it's tasteful and then I'm going to critique.

His foot bounced against his knee as he waited, and when she knocked on the door, he jumped like someone had pinched his butt a little too hard and then he lunged for the door.

Yeah, you're not smooth at all.

Navasha Ghai, Navi to anyone who mattered to her and a few who didn't, came bearing gifts of hot chocolate and cookies for Jay, and three slices of hot, crispy-but-not-too-crispy bacon for me. She smiled almost shyly and held the brown bag filled with sugary goodness up a bit, and said, "Snickerdoodles. Not as good as Aubrey's, but still pretty damned tasty."

He stepped out of the way so she could come in, and then took the tray holding their drinks from her and set it on the table. "Hi. Wasn't expecting to hear from you for a while."

Or ever.

That happened with the last timeline. She never came back. Cookies are a good sign, right?

"We're still talking to each other. Right? Besides, I smelled the cookies and thought 'Jay would want one. Or ten.' So I bought a couple dozen."

He had no idea what to say to her. He opened the bag and inhaled, taking in the aroma of freshly baked cookies, pretending that there was nothing awkward about the woman he loved more than anything—who was on a new path that didn't include him—being in his apartment, breaking up bacon into Wick-sized bites. While she plucked a small plate from the cupboard to put the bacon on, he flipped the tops off their hot chocolate and brought them to the living room.

The cups, not the tops.

The tops remained on the kitchen table, where they would most likely accumulate dust while the residual milk products curdled and turned various shades of gross while he contemplated further cleaning of the apartment.

"How's work?" he asked as she sat next to him.

I would have told him he needed to ask better questions, but my mouth was full, and I didn't want to stop chewing.

"I work with a bunch of dicks," she sighed, and then laughed when he wasn't sure if she was serious or joking about the obvious. "Relax, Jay. I'm not here to bite you. Work is fine. Work is kind of why I'm here."

"If Mass wants to handle my junk again, he can wait until my next appointment."

"I think he has his hands full of other peoples' junk. That's not what this is about."

Mass had taken her through the portal for a tour of her potential future workspace. She'd seen the beginning of a surgical reassignment, had been allowed to cross the blue line and handle a dollop of surgical gel, and then before going back, he took her in to see George.

"The biofilm is working well. He'll bring George out of sedation tomorrow."

"Any idea if he's healed up enough?"

"No sign of feeling in his lower extremities. Once his skin has healed over, he'll need to go back in."

"Damn, this is taking a lot longer than I thought it would. I was out in four days. This has been weeks. Months."

"Lots to repair."

"And not why you're really here, is it?"

She took a sip of the hot chocolate and then set it aside. It was less of a delay tactic and more that she was gathering sticks and twigs to brace her nerves for a conversation she wasn't sure would go her way. I heard her breath hiccup and then she swallowed hard, so I finished the bacon quickly and ran to jump onto her lap.

People usually manage to spit the words out when they have a cat to pet.

Now, granted, that didn't always work in my favor. If they were annoyed or angry, my furs wound up being abused. Navi, though, just seemed to want peace, and gentle purring could do that for her.

"I explained myself well enough before, didn't I?" she asked, though it wasn't clear that she really wanted an answer. "When I left, you knew I loved you, right?"

"I know. I still love you, too, if it matters."

"Ever since I started working in Mass's office, I just…I paid attention to everyone around me. Not just in what we were doing, but personally."

He'd heard it before, but he leaned back into the sofa cushions and let her go on. She was the youngest person in Mass's office; it wasn't long before she realized there were no pictures of kids on her co-worker's desks, other than a few scattered here and there in group shots. There was an old photo of Mass with people he'd once worked with, and a boy who seemed familiar but wasn't related to the doctor. No one rushed to get home to care for kids, no one ever whined about canceling plans for sick children, no one laughed over the cute or stupid things their offspring managed.

They worked long hours and socialized mostly with each other. She'd gradually come to the idea that there was no room in their lives for family. Most of them were married, some to each other, but not a single person in Mass's medical practice had children. She noted the long days and how little time there was to accommodate growing kids and reached the conclusion that the job made procreation a bad idea.

"Mass was exhausted when he took me on that tour. And an exhausted Mass is a nosy Mass. He wanted to know what had happened with us."

"So you told him."

"And he promptly told me I was a blithering idiot. Just because I could see something with my own eyes, that didn't equate perception of truth."

He led her to the cafeteria, where she watched kids leaping from the launch pad across the street, jet packs strapped to tiny backs. Mass watched quietly, too, long enough that the silence became uncomfortable.

His voice cracked when he finally spoke. "Those kids should be dead. Every single one of them." He pointed to the cars below. "All those people should be dead. All of them, yet most didn't believe it. They shrugged off the warnings. Surely someone would do *something* to save this planet. They were sure of it. They felt safe, even with the truth of a meteor big enough to end this world hurtling through space, aimed right at them."

He knew better. He'd worked with Jo and Finn long enough to understand the scale of what was happening. He knew they had access to records left protected that spelled out exactly what had happened in a dozen other loops of time, and in none of those had the world survived.

"We *all* knew that," he told Navi. "Everyone who works with me now, except for you, is from here. From now. Some of us have been there for a decade longer than the others, but we all left at roughly the same time, knowing that there was little chance life here would go on. We spent our early adulthood working with Finn and Jo trying to find answers, and only when we were forced out to get the educations that would give us lives *here* did we leave them."

He sounded broken and bitter when he said, "We didn't forgo having children because we didn't want them or because there weren't enough hours in the day. We didn't have them because there were no guarantees we'd be able to leave, and if we had them…we didn't think they would live."

Mass had wanted children; he knew that most of the people in his employ had wanted children. None of them were willing to procreate because the world was going to end, and escape was not certain. The job was not, he told her, an excuse for avoiding something that scared her. And make no mistake, she was reacting from fear.

"After he brought me back through the portal, I wandered through the hospital and looked for people I'd gone to school with. I paid attention to the nurses clustered at the center stations and noticed all the people who I knew had kids. They complained about them *so* often, yet they also bragged about them all the time. And then I realized that every doctor I know, except for Mass and the few in his practice, they *all* have kids.

They figured it out. And I don't know why I thought I couldn't or shouldn't. Unless he was right, and I was just scared."

In the back of his head was the long list she'd given him. At the top of it was the truth of what she wanted for a child of hers: a present mother, and that was something she might not be able to promise. He swallowed it, refusing to remind her.

"What are you saying, Nav?"

"That Mass is right. I'm an idiot. That for someone who's supposed to be just a little bit smarter than average, I don't seem to be able to think straight a little too often."

He waited.

"I miss you, Jay. And I made a huge mistake."

He kept waiting. He wanted her to say it.

"Is there any part of you that would want to start over? Like, right from the beginning. Go out to lunch. Date a bit, get to know the less stupid me."

"I don't want to start over." He spoke in a near whisper. "I don't want to date. We've done that and I think we know each other well enough."

Her fingers gripped me a bit tighter, and I felt her legs stiffen as she prepared to stand up. "All right, then. That's what I needed to know. I'm sorry, I—"

"I just want you to come home."

She stiffened all over.

"I mean, there are new complications," he went on, "and it's only fair to point them out. Like, there's Isaac. He's mine for the duration, and if George dies? He's part of the package. And even if that happens, I'd still want one of my own. But goddamn, Navi, if you're all right with that, holy hell, please come home."

She swallowed hard, and a tear pinged off my ear.

"I'm not in a hurry, either. Kids can wait until you're done with med school. And I'm still pumped by the idea of being the one who stays home or carts the kid off to work with me. And if we stay here—"

"He'll have a huge family, no matter what."

"Other kids to play with, aunts and uncles and cousins. I'd make it work, I swear."

"We," she corrected. "If we have a baby, *we* make it work."

"Please come home," he repeated, softly.

I didn't hear the answer, but given the sudden kissing and groping, I was pretty sure it was yes. I left them to their reconciliation and headed up the stairs, hoping to find someone who wasn't swapping spit or bouncing, or anything else that might offend my senses.

~

Jay's probably spending the night in his apartment. Only telling you so you don't worry.

"It can't possibly require that much cleaning."

He's not alone.

Will lifted an eyebrow.

I think the wedding is back on.

He tapped the side of his leg to get Thor's attention and told Aisha he was taking the dog to the roof for a few minutes. I understood what he wanted: follow. Will typically wasn't a gossip, but he wanted details and I was the only one who could provide them unless he started banging on Jay's door.

Once on the roof he let Thor off the leash and watched as he sniffed his way across the lawn. "All right. Spill it."

Navi brought cookies and hot chocolate over so they could pretend to snack while talking. Mass said a bunch of stuff and showed her kids in jetpacks, and she decided she was kinda stupid and thought that she wanted a baby someday but had been looking at it the wrong way. Then she asked if they could start over, but Jay told her no.

"He told her no."

He asked her to come home. Then the kissing started, so I left.

It was enough information. He seemed both pleased and concerned, but I wasn't sure which he felt more.

It's a happy thing, right?

"It's happy if they reconcile for the right reasons. It's happy if she truly desires to have a child with him and isn't bending to the notion simply because she misses him."

I told him what Mass had said, including the part where he called her an idiot.

He wanted kids. He didn't have them because he didn't want them to die.

"Many people who worked with my parents chose to not have children."

Maybe that's why they were so good with you. You were as close to having sticky people as they were going to get.

"Possibly. But Navi seemed certain that she's on the same page as Jay now?"

She thinks she is. Who knows how she'll feel later? Another Navi in another When left Jimmy and never looked back.

"But this one did."

You always thought she was his Aisha.

He nodded. "I hope she still is. But she now understands, no matter how much we love her, we'll stand behind Jay."

Thor hitched his leg up and peed on the fence that surrounded the grill and then bounded back to Will, his tongue out and drool dripping onto the ground.

"Good boy," Will said as he patted Thor's head.

"Good boy!"

They're going to wake George up tomorrow, if you want to be there. I think Jay does.

"I'll be there. I assume you intend to tag along?"

George might need purr therapy, and his cats aren't there.

"You tried to kill him once, you know."

Only because he was hurting Jay and wanted to shoot you. I'll purr for him now because he's Isaac's dad, and Isaac loves him.

"You're a good man, Wick."

You want to keep Isaac, don't you?

"Not from his father."

George picked Jay for a reason. Just because you might be the better person to raise him doesn't mean you're the right one.

He heard me.

I don't think he agreed.

~

George's new, sensitive skin was shiny-slick and had the tint of too many hours in the sun, his face and shoulders several fiery shades that enhanced every speck of his innate pinkness. Jay grimaced and sucked in a sharp breath, but Will had braced himself and didn't react.

He knew George would appear a bit broken and had tried to warn Jay, but the boiled lobster of a man in bed was not what he expected.

"He's awake," Mass said before we entered the room. "Well, he's no longer sedated. He answered enough basic questions to assure me he's there mentally, but he's groggy and might actually be asleep at this point."

Vicat sat in a chair near the foot of the bed, where she could keep an eye on him. She sat stiffly, ever watchful, guarding her brother with the same attention she afforded Rhys. No one passed the door without her performing a quick mental assessment of their intent, and I had zero doubt that if she hadn't known who was about to enter, she would have blocked the way. Will gestured for her to remain seated, and then asked how she thought he was doing.

"Well enough, all things considered. First thing he asked about was Isaac, then Jay. He knows where he is and when he is, though he didn't ask why he can't feel his legs or why he still feels like complete shit."

George's thick, sleepy voice cut through the air. "I was fucking cut in half. Why would my legs work?"

Jay went to him, leaning over the bed to look into George's eyes. "They will. You just needed a break from the tank, that's all. Like the rest of you, your spine is being a little bitch."

George snorted. "How's my boy?"

"He asks about you every day, but he's good. He plays with Rhys—"

"I meant you," George croaked.

Jay wanted to touch him. His hand twitched and he almost reached for George's arm, but the bright red skin made him think twice. "Really good."

"Talked to your dad?"

"Yeah. And I'm really fucking sorry."

"Hm." He reached for the bed rails, the back of his hand bumping against it, and he hissed with the sting of it. "Sit me up a bit."

"Don't," Will said before Jay touched the controller. "Talk to Mass before moving him at all."

"Still a damned joykill, Emperor." His words rode on his breath, and he sounded beat down. "Do that. Go ask him if I can sit up a few degrees. I don't imagine it matters." When Jay nodded and headed for the door, George added, "Go with him, Vi."

She didn't ask why. She stood and slid the chair over to Will, who pulled it the rest of the way but did not sit in it.

"You have your cat?"

Will stepped closer, where George could see us. "I do."

Slowly, George moved his hand to his chest and tapped at it. "Set him here. It won't hurt."

It would hurt and I knew it, but he wanted me there so Will set me down gently, and I was careful to not move.

Should I purr?

"Please," George sighed.

"Are you aware of the extent of your injuries prior to surgery?" Will asked. "And what else needs to be done?"

He managed a short, tight nod. "Literally cut in half, save a few nerves and tendons. I should be dead. I don't know why I'm not."

"The whims of a little boy." Will set his hands on the bed rail and leaned closer, speaking softly. He told George about Rhys's new gift, how he had frozen time—and George—to give Will a chance to jump him forward and into a critical care surgical tank. The moment he was submerged in the gel, the nanobots scurried over his massive, open wounds and created a film that kept him from bleeding out before the technicians could get an airway working. "We had no idea Rhys was capable of this. He had no idea."

"I am exponentially more grateful now that you were too stubborn to die when we were boys," George murmured. He'd stuffed Will into an airtight bio-bag, taped it shut, and shoved him into the school swimming pool. "Did Isaac see?"

"No. And he hasn't been told of the scope of your injuries. He only knows that you haven't felt well, and needed to spend a lot of time here, at home."

"Home," he grunted. "Don't bring him here, Emperor."

"Not until—"

"No. If I recover, I'll go to him. Here, he feels like shit. He hasn't been sick once while in your care, has he?"

"No. Aisha and I have mused that regardless of his birth When, he's a child of that one."

"I agree. So, if I die—"

Will reminded him he'd survived the worst of everything. The odds were now in his favor. The next surgery would be delicate, but entirely survivable.

"I could die before I get there. Infection, my skin…and if I live, I'm here for a long time no matter what. I need to be sure Isaac is all right."

"He might need to see you to be completely all right."

He didn't want Isaac to see him until he looked healthy; once his skin healed, he was willing to provide a video for his son, but he knew better than to allow him to come forward to visit. "That kid is sensitive as hell, Will. He feels—"

"A gift?"

"No. Just…perceptive. Has he seen James?"

Jay was too angry to allow his father a visit with Isaac. George understood and agreed with it.

"If I die—and don't argue the possibility—make sure Jay gets custody of Isaac. I love James but his life choices are the last thing I want for my son."

"Visitation?"

George managed a bare nod. "How often is up to Jay. But I don't want James taking him. I want better for Isaac. Better than being witness to James's appetites."

"Would you be open to another arrangement?" Will explained his discussions with Aisha, the belief that they could provide the best place for Isaac to live. "We love him. He's not just

Rhys's friend or Jay's little brother. He's welcome and wanted in our home."

"And that would give Jay freedom to explore his own life," George said. "I understand every point you could make on this, Will. I considered it long before this. I have no doubt that you already treat him as your own, and he would have a comfortable and happy life with you. He would feel equal to your own children, the same as Jay does. He'd never question whether he was your son or not."

"But?"

George went quiet as he collected his thoughts, quiet enough that Will wondered if he'd drifted off.

He's thinking, that's all.

"Isaac reminds me of a little boy I once knew," he finally said, his voice growing stronger. "The odd kid out, no friends. He wants them, desperately, but they sense something eerily different about him. We both know how kids treat the odd ones. He never feels well because, frankly, his life sucks and there's no one for him to turn to. He could tell his parents, but why disappoint them? What could they do?"

His fingers went to my back and he stroked my fur, looking for comfort. "You didn't have anyone, Emperor. You never told your parents the worst of what we did to you, did you? But if you'd had an older brother? One invested in your happiness? I think your life would have been much different. We never would have gone after you, not after the first time he loomed over us, threatening without saying a word."

"He would still have that. Jay will always be his big brother."

If Isaac lived with Will and Aisha, he would have a mother and father, yes. Brothers and a sister. But what he would not have were friends. "He needs Jay, and he needs Rhys, but he needs them differently. If you take Isaac, Rhys becomes his brother. You know that would happen. You would treat Isaac as your own, claim him as your own, and your children will claim him. Rhys would think of him as his brother. Jay would be just his brother. He would be absorbed into your family...and I know, that would be a good thing, but not what he ultimately needs. I want Isaac to have the big brother you didn't, one who feels a purpose in that relationship. But I also want him to have the friends you didn't. Because that little boy is so much like you, Will. Isaac is the universe reminding me of what I did, and he's what I can give back. I can't take—"

"I understand," Will said before George could get ramped up any further. "And you're right. I don't want to take away Rhys's best friend, either. If Jay is responsible for him, they'll likely tether to each other."

And when George gets better, it won't suck so much for Isaac to leave. They'll still be best friends and have school together.

"Indeed."

Jay bounced in, declaring it Perfectly Okay to raise the head of George's bed a few degrees. Vicat was in the cafeteria looking for a bottle of grape soda because, apparently, George liked that—Isaac said so—and would be back in a few minutes.

They filled him in on the things Isaac was doing, including skipping preschool in favor of homeschooling with the Queen, which George was wholly in favor of, and his reluctant attachment to Thor, Rhys's puppy.

"Puppy," George said, amused. "Wait, what about the cats?"

"He sees them multiple times a day," Will said. "They are currently residing with King Eli, and you might get them back someday. He is enthralled with the antics of three littermates that alternately adore and loathe each other."

When they'd exhausted the topic of Isaac, the grape soda untouched because it was actually Isaac's favorite and George couldn't stand it, he reached out to touch Jay's arm. "And what about you? You said you were really fine, but the last I heard you and Navi—"

Will gestured to Vicat to leave the room, and he followed.

"We split for a while," Jay said. "But we're working on it and she's moving back home."

George managed a slight smile. "Good. But listen to me. Once you marry her, that's it. You committed. Better or worse and all that. Don't make my mistakes. Whatever the real issues are, you have to deal with it."

"We will. It's still just about kids, but she wants one. That's all I wanted."

"And five years from now if she changes her mind? Or if life has other plans for you that don't include a child? You have to be okay with that. Marry the girl you love, not the potential mother of children that may never be. Life has a way of doing that, forcing you off one path onto another."

"Is that why you never remarried Dad? You knew it would come to cheating all over again?"

"I committed, Jay. I meant it. He just can't, and I knew that."

"I get it."

"He's in love with her," George whispered. "I might have overlooked it otherwise, but he's in love with her. Don't hold that against him."

"When is she?"

"Here. Now. He'll need you to—"

"He blew it and he knows it. I don't know if I can bring him here again. He should have stayed. But he came home."

"Damned idiot," George sighed. "Why didn't he stay? Go talk to him. Be gentle, Jay. He's the only father you have."

Well, he has Will.

"Yeah, cat, I don't know what you just said, but I can feel it. Doesn't matter how great Will is, James is his father." He looked at Jay. "Honor that. If this is the last thing I can ever tell you, honor that. He loves you even if he is stupid as hell."

"He's not stupid, he's just...thoughtless."

George grunted at that.

"I won't help him cheat."

"It's not cheating. We're not married. He made promises to your King, not to me."

"Bullshit. He accepted the terms as a promise to you, to allow you to go home. You took his *name*, George."

"Home," he said softly, "is why I need you to protect Isaac, and keep him there. He doesn't do well here. This isn't home for him."

"No shit. He'll be okay once you're on your feet and home again."

"I was allowed to stay there on the condition of James's fidelity. The terms were clear. I took on a new name, didn't work there, and he had to stop being...him. Even if I survive this, I can't go back, Jay. Isaac won't survive here. The best I can hope for is to live here and have occasional visits with my son."

"George."

"Whatever is best for him, Jay. Promise me. He's the only thing right that I've ever done, and for whatever reason, you haven't jettisoned me from your life. If occasional visits are all I can have, I'll accept that with as much grace as possible. And Navi—"

"She knows he's part of the package."

"I'm asking far too much, and I know it."

"You know what?" Jay leaned over the bedrails, until his face was close to George's. "For the first time in my life I think I really understand you. And dammit, I feel like you're the stepfather I wanted when I was little but didn't quite have. You're not asking too much. We're family."

Will stood in the doorway, quietly, watching them, and I could see the wheels spinning already.

Geo Okuda had to come home, no matter what the King said.

~

Hours later we were on Union Square, heading for home. Vicat stayed behind, supposedly to keep George company, but more likely it was to growl at the student nurse who had tried to peel back a corner of the biofilm to see if it had fully adhered to his skin. It had. He moaned, Vicat growled. That was when Will decided it was time to leave and let him get some rest, with a promise that we would return the next day.

Once on the Square at home, Jay stopped near the lab entry. "Huh. Here. Right here. George had my wrist in a vice grip, a gun pointed at you, and Wick tried to shred his face off."

"And then your mother dragged him through the portal," Will said. "The memory has bubbled in my head recently, as well."

"You're *friends* with him now. How the hell did that happen?"

"Isaac. Multiple apologies on his end. But mostly Isaac and how profoundly attached Rhys is."

Jay's voice cracked when he said, "He thinks of me as his son. Not the daughter he lost. One of his boys."

"Fatherhood can soften the edges. For instance—" he gestured to the other side of the Square, where Rhys and Isaac were running toward them, with Thor lumbering beside his boy, Aisha waving from the door "—the dog. A year ago, I would have denied there was any possibility of this happening. I would have contended that my children would never want a dog, they would want cats. I was prepared for cats, several of them. Then Rhys asked for a puppy and I insisted that he wait until he turned ten. And here we are. I melted at the realization that he needed Thor as much as he wanted him."

"Eh, you've always been a softy," Jay snorted.

Thor reached us first. *"Good boy! Good boy! Good boy!"*

"What's he saying?" Jay asked me.

Just his way of saying hello.

Also, he thinks we need bacon.

"Will, Will, Will!" Isaac squealed, though it sounded more like 'Wilw, Wilw, Wilw,' which was as close to correct pronunciation as he'd ever gotten. "How's daddy?"

Will scooped him up. "Your father," he said, planting a kiss on Isaac's cheek before setting him back down, "is feeling quite a bit better. He wants you to know he loves you and misses you." He bent over to kiss Rhys, too. "And he wants *you* to know how happy he is you've been so good to Isaac."

Rhys scrunched his nose. "Isaac's my friend. I'm not gonna be mean to him."

"Is Daddy coming home soon?" Isaac asked. "I wanna show him how high I can count now. Mrs. B said I was doing really good."

Will turned them toward the bakery. He hadn't intended on donuts and bacon, but he was getting donuts and bacon whether he liked it or not. "It might be a few more weeks," Will said as both boys climbed into the chairs he pointed at. "But he's doing better right now."

Jay offered to get the donuts with two slices of bacon.

"How come it's taking so long?"

"Your daddy was *really* hurt," Rhys said before Will could. "He was kinda squished. They're unsquishing him and it probably takes days and days for that."

Will didn't correct him. Isaac seemed to accept the answer, and it was relatively close to the truth. "I'll see him again tomorrow. Perhaps tonight you could draw a picture, and I'll take it to him."

Isaac turned toward the bakery door and shouted, "Jay, can you help me draw something for daddy? Please?"

I wasn't sure Jay heard him. He was at the door, his hands full, but his attention was diverted to something just past us. He grinned, which made me turn to look, too. Navi was coming our way, dressed in the same professional pajamas Mass always wore. Usually her hair was tied back, but this time it was down, flowing across her shoulders, and she carried an overnight bag.

Both Rhys and Isaac stood on their chairs to get her attention, and Isaac yelled out, "Nabi! Ober here!"

You really need to help him with his speech.

"Hush, Wick," Will whispered.

When it was clear she was intentionally coming to us, Will stood. He greeted her with a hug, and then waited while the no-longer-toddlers collected kisses.

"Did I hear Isaac right?" Navi said as she sat down. "We're drawing pictures tonight?"

"Can I draw one, too?" Rhys asked.

Will was about to tell him no, that Isaac needed to spend time with Jay and Navi, and this might be the night Isaac moved downstairs to his own room, but Navi ruffled his hair and told him it would be extra fun with him. They could sit on the floor and draw while she made popcorn, and while they worked they could tell her what they'd been up to.

Rhys scrunched his nose. "Thirty-seven pounds, I think. Can Thor come? He'll be good."

"Good boy, good boy good boy!"

That evening was the start of family life for Jay and Navi. I tagged along to keep an eye on Thor and lounged on the sofa while a dozen pictures were drawn and colored, and then while Jay shot video of Isaac telling his father he missed him and hoped he came home soon. I listened for voices outside the front door, for Will and Jax to come home from Fuzzy's where I knew the subject of Geo Okuda returning to Now would be raised, his residence permitted despite James's infidelities.

If Navi needed an illustration of life with children and Jay might be, this was it. Shrieking laughter, two temper tantrums, food on the floor and somehow the ceiling, and they faced it without flinching.

And spoilers...she stayed.

~

The Christmas tree on Union Square glowed with bright lights twinkling against the dark of night. Loud, happy voices rose from the skating rink, and music swelled from the far side of the Square. Behind us, in the apartment, baby Eli squealed simply because he could, and the air swirled around popcorn bursts of laughter.

Jax, Aubrey, and Aisha waited on the balcony, taking turns to check on the small children as well as the grown ones watching them. I wore a path between the living room and the balcony, wanting to hear any gossip that might occur outside, but also wanting to hear Will come down the steps.

Santa was coming early. I didn't want to miss it.

He'd promised to text Aisha when he was home, but what if he forgot?

"Finn and Jo," Jax said, looking down on the Square. "Were they here or there? If they were there, Will's probably on his way."

"Will could have left there five hours ago," Aisha reminded him. "But no, Finn was here all day as far as I know."

They wanted to spend Christmas Eve with their grandchildren.

By the time they reached the front door, Aisha's phone pinged. Without even looking at it, she got up and they headed inside, to the living room where the kids sat in a circle, egging baby Eli on, making him crawl back and forth to collect plastic toys that he discarded the moment he realized someone else had another one that surely had to be better.

When Will reached the last step, he bellowed out, "Ho, ho ho!" before entering the living room. Rhys giggled and rolled onto his back, declaring his father silly and telling the others that it wasn't really Santa. Hyrum reminded him that he still had to be good, because the real Santa hadn't come yet, and who knows what could happen before midnight?

"Perhaps I ran into him," Will said. "Perhaps there was one thing he wanted delivered before everyone went to sleep."

Hyrum's eyes went wide. "But we didn't make the cookies yet! He can't come and not get cookies!"

"He'll come back later," Will promised. "But something couldn't wait. Something for Isaac."

"Me?" Isaac got up, and like he'd seen Hyrum and Rhys do so many times, his hands went to his chest. "What is it?"

Will turned and lifted his hand, beckoning. There were soft footsteps on the tile, new shoes squeaking, and when Jay heard them, he jumped up, too.

Twenty pounds lighter, fatigue creased in fine lines around his eyes, George hesitated at the doorway, uncertain what he would find. What there was, what he hoped for, was the sight of his four-year-old son surrounded by the people who loved him. His eyes were already wet, and he barely managed to squeak out, "Hey, buddy" before Isaac asked, hopefully, "Daddy?"

Rhys exploded to his feet. "Your daddy's home, Isaac! Daddy's home!"

George was, thankfully, amused that Rhys was the one Isaac threw his arms around first. When Rhys let him go, Isaac ran to George, slamming a hug around his father's neck that sounded as painful as it did happy. It only took a few seconds before Isaac began to cry, asking between gulps of air if George was home to stay.

It had been six months.

On the day that his world exploded, George left Isaac with Jay because he had a playdate with Marco, and he knew Zed was willing to babysit for a couple of hours while Jay went to have dinner with his dad. He'd left a three-year-old, missed a birthday, missed the start of preschool, missed everything his son had done in those long months. He choked out an apology for all the days he'd missed and battled against tears that threatened to become a wail.

Isaac was taller, though not much heavier; George aged a few years in that time and looked gaunt, but together, it was easier to see that they shared the same DNA. Isaac was literally George's clone, and they'd never looked more alike than they did when he pressed his tiny forehead against his father's.

Rhys went over to Will and tugged on his hand. "Is Isaac's daddy staying?"

Will nodded. "Tonight he'll stay in the guest room with Isaac—"

"Bullshit," Jay interrupted, "they're staying downstairs with us."

"—and after Christmas, they're moving into an apartment across the Square. You'll still get to play every day and have school together."

Will had secured an apartment for Geo and Isaac Okuda just across Union Square, a spacious three-bedroom unit five floors up. Vicat was not far from her brother and nephew, close enough that she could walk over and rescue them from the Queen's math and spelling lessons for an hour in the park.

George Denton kept an apartment in his birth When, a place to go when he needed to reset, a place Isaac would visit once a month, but where he would not live.

In six months, Isaac had not fallen ill. He was not a flea on the hairy back of time, trying to avoid being scratched off. He was either a child of this When, or time had ignored his presence.

It was possible, Will thought, that time could not make sense of Isaac. It made him curious about his own children, whether time would ignore them, as well.

Later that evening, after a loud, joy-filled dinner where George surprised everyone by asking if it was all right if he offered a prayer, he cuddled on the King's sofa with his son. Isaac was clingy and no longer wanted to play, which bothered Rhys less than I might have supposed. They had other days to look forward to; Isaac was still Aubrey's student, and would be until Blackshear Academy opened. He sat on the floor and quietly read to Alex and Charlie, running his finger along the words, encouraging them to read with him. Jay and Navi sat on the floor with them, listening, her hand set casually on his leg. Hyrum had stretched out and his eyes were closed, but he paid attention to the story and laughed at all the right places.

"Thank you." Will spoke quietly, so that only Jax would hear. "If not for Rhys—"

"Liar," Jax chuckled. "You'd have asked even it was just for Isaac. Even if you still hated George."

Jax hadn't hesitated in giving his approval, and he told Will to get the ball rolling as soon as possible to make the transition easier for everyone. By the end of the week George would have a new ID in hand and a new, very impressive resume to use while searching for a job in his field. Where he'd previously been forbidden to work in this When, Jax allowed him the freedom to do whatever he wanted, provided he refrained from crossing old paths.

It was likely he would stumble across people he'd known in his old life, but he resembled his old self as much as a son resembled his father. That was the platform upon which his new identity was built; he was now George Denton, Junior. Isaac's surname would be quietly changed with the aid of a clerk in city hall.

"He feels as if this is home now," Will said. "Isaac does well here, and I believe this separation may have created a tether between them."

I felt that, too. When Isaac hugged him. It was like the anchor dropped.

"Isaac is his anchor."

Why did it take so long?

"Possibly because they moved back and forth so frequently. I'm not certain."

"Eh," Jax grunted. "It doesn't matter. He's back. He's home. If Isaac has anchored him, he won't need to jump forward unless he gets the itch to see someone there."

King Eli is not going to be happy about losing the cats.

Maybe Santa should bring him a litter.

"Are you lonely, Wick?" Will asked. "My promise to get you a kitten of your own still stands."

I'm not lonely. But Eli is.

"I think he's the least lonely he's been in years," Jax said. "Between work, the cats, the great-grandkids, and running off to play with Will's grandparents, he has a fairly full life."

I want more for him.

"As do we all," Will said.

James won't try to take the cats, will he? He's the one who wanted them so badly.

That wasn't a battle Will could fight on behalf of Isaac and George, but he was certain that James wouldn't think of taking them from Isaac. They still had a relationship; Jay made sure of that. He'd moved back into his old apartment, upstairs from where Aisha and Jay had once lived, and he saw Isaac often.

Will that change now that George is home?

"Again, not my fight."

"You would have adopted that kid if the circumstances made room for it," Jax said. "Still would, if I hadn't allowed George to return."

"If George had not been insistent that Jay take him, and Jay had been hesitant, yes. But I understand George's wishes in this and respect them."

"The child of the man who tried to kill you more than once. The child you were taken to court over and would be paying support for if things had gone differently. The irony if you turned around and adopted him..."

That had occurred to Will more than once. There had been several nights when he stood in Rhys's bedroom doorway, watching them sleep, pondering what might have been. He'd wanted a child of his own, but with Aisha, not a random stranger who had stolen his DNA. He didn't want that baby, wanted nothing to do with his mother, and he wanted far less to do with George.

Yet, that was the tipping point, when he became willing to see George as more than his enemy. "He's an asshole, certainly," he'd told Aisha, "but he's working to redeem himself."

They gave George a chance.

He doesn't lie all the time anymore, does he?

"Not as far as I know."

Ask him about karate.

"Wick."

He told James he was a champion and a third degree blackbelt. Ask him. I want to know.

"You're just nosy."

"He's bugging you about me, isn't he?" George asked.

"He tends to find one thing to focus on and does not give up."

"What is it?" he asked me. "Worried I'll eat one of the kids? I promise, I won't."

"Feline curiosity. He recalled that we once trained together in karate and wanted to know how long you'd stuck with it."

"Ah. He knows about the fight I ran from." When he realized he had to spar with Will, he bolted from the room, and as far as Will knew, never returned. But he'd found another dojo, a smaller one closer to home, and trained there until he left for this When. He had, he promised, reach his claimed rank, and had also been the Pacific Rim champion three years running.

"It was a sport-oriented school," George said. "Very little in the way of practical self-defense. I learned how to score points hard and fast, and used my own fear to intimidate my opponents. They had no idea I was terrified in the ring. But my ego kept me there, because it was one thing aside from math that I was good at."

He could teach that, right?

"My skills have faded," George said. "Rhys could kick my ass these days."

Jay snorted. "Rhys can kick *my* ass. And I've been training."

It's in his head. He just needs to work at it to get it back.

"Is your train of thought heading for a specific destination, Wick? Or are you meandering?"

Blackshear Academy will need teachers. He has a skill. And time to work on it before the castle is finished.

He relayed the suggestion to George, who didn't dismiss it out of hand. He had other skills, as well. Before he officially died, he'd been an in-demand engineer and programmer, and much of his work was functioning on Elysium. He was nearly as good at math as Aisha. And he knew about Rhys's gifts. He knew about Will. Those things no longer frightened him; he suspected there were more people like the Blackshears, and no longer felt the need to run from them.

"I'm not certified to teach," he pointed out.

"You have a year until construction is complete. A year and a half before the school opens. Ozoo Enterprises could hire—"

"I can afford a year or two off. That's not a problem. Admission into a university is. My transcripts don't exist yet."

Jax chuckled. "I'm the King of Pacifica," he reminded George. "I have people. We can get your transcripts. Which prestigious university would you like to graduate from?"

"It has to be something kinda far," Jay pointed out. "If he said he graduated from UCSF, people would expect to remember him."

"Where did you go?" Navi asked.

"Northwestern. School of Engineering."

"That's far enough," Will decided. "And quite easy to have someone remember him."

"Richard?" Jax asked. "But they wouldn't have been there at the same time."

It didn't matter. If Richard Van Hoff hadn't attended school at the same time as George, he could easily remember him from social things or even work. They were in the same field, and George was familiar with Richard's work.

I think you have a job. You probably should say that you want it.

He wanted it.

He wanted to start over.

He wanted something for his son.

"I'll do whatever I need in order to make this happen. Even if it means changing who I am and who I was."

Jay raised an eyebrow. "Oh, look. When Mass was doing everything else, he removed George's extra asshole. There may be hope for the world yet."

~

"It would not be Christmas Eve without having a drink on the balcony," Jax mused, swirling the scotch around in his glass. "The kids are asleep. Hyrum will be soon. Eventually Eli will stop crying—"

"The baby, not his father," Jay explained to George, who looked like he needed to be in bed more than any of the kids. "Though he might be downstairs crying, too, now that he knows he has to give up the cats."

Jax growled at him. "The point is...it's Christmas Eve, we have excellent scotch thanks to Finn, and we're damn well going to enjoy it until Hyrum is asleep and Santa can come."

George sniffed at his drink but didn't taste it. "Why does Santa need to wait for Hyrum to be asleep?"

"Because Hyrum still believes," Will said simply.

"Huh."

"We will always foster that belief," Jax added. "No matter how horrible Hyrum's life became—and it was horrific until he left home—Santa was the one person he could count on. The one person who never let him down, never failed to deliver, never forgot him. We'll make damned sure that no matter what, Santa never does."

Promises had already been extracted from Oz, Drew, and Zed; if Jax and Aubrey died first, they would carry on. They would make sure their children carried on. They danced around the obvious: Will would outlive Hyrum. Without a doubt, he would guard Hyrum's beliefs.

Finn will probably be around longer than any of us. He won't let Hyrum down.

"Indeed," Will said. "My father would take joy in being Santa for him. I'm not certain of the sort of gifts Hyrum would wind up with, but he would happily assume the task."

Hyrum is pretty good at making wish lists. He's even stopped worrying about being greedy.

"To a point," Jax said. "He'll ask for things, but never anything big or expensive. Books and toys. Drawing paper and markers. This year he asked for clothes that will make his mother mad."

Jay snorted. "Oh, Zed, Drew, and I made sure of that. We got Mrs. Kovlov to make him three pairs of jeans. Neon pink, neon orange, and neon green. With matching hoodies, t-shirts, and shoes. His mother is going to choke when she sees him."

He's going to wear the pink hoodie with the green jeans and orange shoes. You know that, right?

"I'm counting on it."

With a sigh, George finally took a sip of the scotch, followed by tossing the rest of it back.

"What?" Jay asked him. "You only shotgun booze when something is bothering you."

He nodded. "It's Christmas. In a few hours my son will wake up, as excited as Hyrum probably will be, and I have nothing for him."

Jay snorted again. "Yeah, you do. I mean, we had no idea you'd be coming home tonight, but the bases were covered. There are at least four things under the tree labeled 'from Daddy.'"

"As well as gifts from the rest of us," Will added. "And Santa never forgets."

Before George could tear up or begin rambling his thanks, Jay leaned forward a touch. "I know you and Dad made a big deal out of Christmas for him. But what he talks about are the decorations and music and listening to you sing silly songs. And I'm pretty sure that from here on out, what he'll talk about is the year Santa brought Daddy home. It was all he really wanted."

"What about Odie? How much have they seen each other?"

"A bit. But even when he didn't see Dad for the weeks he was in the tank, it was you he asked for. He knows who his father is. He's content to see his Odie every now and then."

With a sigh, George leaned forward, elbows on his knees, matching Jay's posture. "I need a favor from you. If not you, then...someone."

Jay had "anything" poised on his lips, but George set his glass aside and wrung his hands together, so he decided to wait.

"I need you to take your dad back. Forward."

"What the hell?" Jay sat up straight. "Why should he be rewarded for yet another broken promise? It wasn't too much to ask of him, George. He blew it."

"It's not a reward, I promise. He's going to feel the guilt for a very long time and most of that is over the pain it caused you. But there's a woman in the future that James truly loves, and she might be the one who spurs him into finally getting things right. I've had time to think about it. I don't want to be the reason he's miserable. And he will be. No matter how many people parade through his bedroom, he'll be miserable, and I hate that, Jay."

He didn't want to, but Jay nodded and agreed to take him forward.

"It's not even midnight yet. He's still up, probably wallowing in his feelings since you're here and not there. Call him. It would be the best gift you could possibly give him."

"If I take him and he anchors to her, he'll stay."

George nodded.

"It will mean taking Isaac there to see him, most likely."

"I think as long as Isaac knows he's visiting for a day and not staying, he'll be all right. But I don't expect you to bear the burden—"

"He's my *dad*," Jay said. "If he stays there, I'll be popping back and forth anyway. But are you sure? He doesn't deserve this."

"And I never deserved any hope of redemption for my transgressions, yet here I am. The people who had every right to let me die saved me. They cared for my son when I couldn't. They loved him when I wasn't there. None of us deserve the extra chances we get, Jay, but we're damned grateful for them. It may be the last gift I have for James."

Jay got up and headed inside to call his father. Without

asking, Will poured another drink for George and pressed the glass into his hand.

"From this moment on," he said, refreshing his own and Jax's glasses, "we're square. There is no need to seek redemption for the things done when we were boys, nor for the things you did to Jay and to me."

"I will always owe Jay," George said softly.

Will was willing to give him that. "Jay won't see it that way, but I understand."

"Hey, he took a swing at me," Jax reminded them. "Death penalty offense there."

"Kick him in the groin when he least expects it and you'll be even," Will suggested. "Trust me. Your daughter has managed on a few occasions and the pain does, I believe, make up for any I inflicted upon her in the past."

Hey, you stepped on my tail once. Where's my payback, bitch?

"He just called me a bitch," Will sighed. "No more old movies with Hyrum and Drew, Wick."

I'm pretty sure we've watched all the good ones.

I have plenty more things up my furry little sleeve.

Just wait until your birthday. There'll be a surprise. A blunt one.

"Birthday." George groaned and leaned his head back, eyes closed. "I missed his birthday. I promised him a day filled with fun and was going to surprise him with Disneyland. He'd been begging to go for months because Rhys made it sound damn near magical."

He'd had a terrific birthday. Isaac was greeted with cinnamon rolls for breakfast, then spent the morning at the playground with Rhys and Jay. After lunch, they went to a movie and stuffed themselves with popcorn, and there was cake and ice cream after dinner. Will admitted he flopped back and forth about an appropriate gift, but he'd heard the boys whispering when they were supposed to be sleeping and was certain that more than anything else, Isaac wanted a bicycle.

"I apologize if I overstepped. Aisha and I debated the idea, worried that it was something you wanted to teach him to do, but Jay reasoned you would want him to get something unexpected, something Rhys did not already have—"

"And he did think it was from you," Jax added.

"Jay was right." George let out a soft sigh of relief. "Rhys has always reached milestones first and he's noticed. He knows he's a little older and just wanted to be first at *something*."

Rhys got his bicycle a few weeks later, but Isaac had the head start. By the time Will took them to the multipurpose room to help Rhys get started, Isaac was already riding in wide, wobbly circles, and cheered Rhys on with squeals of "It's easy, Rhys! You can do it!" When Rhys finally got the hang of it and managed a complete circuit of the room, Isaac hopped off his bike and ran to hug his friend, just as excited for Rhys as he had been for himself.

"Hyrum and I go to Disneyland every January," Will told George. "Come with us, bring Isaac and I'll bring Rhys. Provided I get a few hours alone with Hyrum, he won't mind sharing the trip."

"There you go," Jax said. "Give him an IOU ticket to Disney as a gift."

"Or we surprise them," George suggested. "If we tell him—"

He stopped, turning as Aisha came outside. Hyrum was snoring, so they were certain he was asleep enough for Santa to come. Before anyone got up, she went to George, standing behind him with her hands on his shoulders. "The boys are all asleep in Rhys's room and there's no point in moving Isaac now. Unless you'd be uncomfortable, stay in our guest room. He'd be happier waking up with Daddy there, and then we can all come down for breakfast and presents."

When Mass proclaimed him well enough for discharge and Will suggested that he jump home to spend Christmas Eve with the family, George presumed it would be awkward and weird, and if not for his son he would have begged off. His old apartment, absent James, was five miles away, though he imagined it was stale and grim after being locked up for so long. It was not a place he could take Isaac, not on Christmas, and there was a new apartment waiting for them, just across the Square. There were few furnishings, though Vicat had assured him there were beds and she'd made sure Isaac's toys had been collected from their future-when apartment. They had someplace to go, but it was a place where Christmas was absent, something George was not willing to take from his little boy.

He'd worried about the discomfort of it all as he slowly made his way down the stairs, but the moment he stepped into the living room and saw Isaac, all he felt was calm.

"Jay borrowed a jump bracelet," Aisha told Will before George could tell her he was content to remain here. "He and Navi went to get James and they should be back in a few minutes, if they can get James to quit crying. And you know he's going to cry."

She bent over and placed a quick kiss on George's cheek. "You get points for letting him go, you know."

"I should have cut him loose nearly twenty years ago," he said, softly.

She knew what he meant; for a flicker of time, she wanted James to come home to her and to Jay, and he had come close to leaving George. "I'm glad you didn't. Though I hope whoever this poor woman is, she knows what she's getting into with him."

He had no idea and would make no effort to find out. "I don't think I'll remain friends with him, not the way you have, Aisha. I don't know how you managed."

"We had a son. Funny the things you'll tolerate for your kid."

Will stood, scooping me up. "Or your cat. Come on, Wick. I know you have rounds to make while Santa is busy unloading his sleigh. I'm sure he has something for you."

A good night's sleep, I hope.

"Insomnia?"

Lots of dreams. They feel like memories.

"Good or bad?"

Both. But I lose them as soon as I wake up. They'll settle soon enough.

I sat with George on the sofa while Santa's gifts were removed from their hiding places and helped him draw out an IOU for a trip to Disneyland. Will translated without stopping what he was doing, his words riding just behind mine, and by the time we were done George had reached the space where everyone else had when Drew and Will translated, not really hearing them, but hearing me.

You know, your new apartment is right across the Square. If you get Isaac some binoculars, he can see right into Rhys's bedroom window.

"That sounds creepy, Wick."

They're used to being with each other and Rhys helps him get to sleep. Maybe if they can still see each other before bed, it'll be easier. And more fun.

"I'll keep it in mind. But aren't there laws about spying on the royal house?"

It's only illegal if you get caught, George.

"How about I give him video chat access for a few minutes at night instead?" He held the paper he'd been writing his IOU on to show me. He'd drawn a Mickey Mouse head with a dialog bubble that said *Let's go to Disneyland, Isaac!* "Good enough for a four-year-old?"

I'd add 'love, Daddy' so he knows who it's from. Want a box and wrapping paper, too? I'll make Jax go get it for you. The King does my bidding.

Jax muttered, "Bullshit," but with one look from Aubrey, he sighed and went into her office to get the things George needed to wrap his gift.

"Do you ever mistranslate Wick to screw with people?" George asked Will.

"Unnecessary," he answered. "Wick is sarcastic enough on his own. If anything, I sometimes have to tone it down."

Hey. I'm a forking gentleman.

I did not say forking.

But, I was a gentleman for the rest of the night and well into the next day. I watched Christmas happen from the box that Hyrum had given me four years earlier, batted at balls of wrapping paper thrown across the room for me, and batted at Thor's tail when he plopped down beside me.

George was quiet and tired, obviously sore and not ready to move much, but he managed to not flinch when Isaac climbed on him. He melted in gratitude when Jay hugged him far longer than usual, and he spent a long time in quiet conversation with Navi while Hyrum kept the little ones occupied. I could have eavesdropped and listened in; they spoke in near whispers, serious but not tense, but I didn't need the words to understand.

It wasn't awkward or weird.

They'd both found their peace. They'd both found their family.

And like Hyrum, Drew before him, and Will long ago, they'd both come home.

THE WEIGHT OF WHEN

The thing is, no one really, truly understands how the portals work. Or even time travel, for that matter. Will had his theories, Finn had his theories, old Drew—future Drew—had theories practically blowing out his backside, but they didn't really *know*. Finn figured out how to make his original time ship work, utilizing null space, but even that was a concept he was a bit fuzzy on. "It just works," is often how he explained things, though he did have ideas that were clustered around practical applications he had designed and tested and with which he found considerable success.

Finn *knew* how it all worked; he just wasn't sure where all the bits and pieces were hiding in his brain, nor how to access all that data on command.

Will had his own notions and was able to add a space parameter to Finn's work—acknowledging that his father did, after all, know how to transport through space but yet didn't quite grasp that, nor why his efforts often inverted objects—and condensed it all into a bracelet that allowed him to move through both time and space, taking along passengers if they had a hand on him. Or any body part, really. Jam your foot in his mouth, and he can take you anywhere, anywhen.

Their work was built upon research and theories and equipment that old Drew had created and passed along to his grandson—Finn. But the ideas, the first taste of the possibilities of time travel came from knowing his adult grandson when he was only a teenager himself, a paradox that no one wanted to examine too closely.

There was a lot no one wanted to examine too closely.

Will thought it was something that had built upon itself; the first Finn had escaped the end of the world and landed on Drew's doorstep, so to speak. That gave Drew the initial inklings of what was to come, and through loops of time, the number of which they'd lost count, the warning of the meteor hurtling toward earth came earlier and earlier, until our own When, the loop where Finn got it right...because teenaged Drew had an idea.

Everything, all the data on all the loops of time, every effort made to save the world, was time locked in the Old Mint on the edge of the South of Market neighborhood, which meant that—theoretically, of course, because who knows what might really happen—Finn would not need to keep jumping around in time, planting ideas and things and setting up life for his own son two hundred years in his past. Will hoped that would continue in each When because he loved his life, loved that his own great, great grandfather was his best friend and brother, and he especially loved the family he'd created when he hadn't, as expected—as had every known Emperor to precede him—died at age 42.

Will had played around enough in time to know that if he changed something in the past, it didn't necessarily affect the future. He should have died within months of his parents jumping through the portal to avoid the end of everything, but because of Drew's ideas involving the placement and direction of gates built to hold the meteor in place, he didn't...yet when he jumped forward thirty five years, he did not exist. The Emperor of that When had died and remained dead to all the people who loved him.

When Oz was six, she fell from a pier and drowned; he immediately hopped through a portal and prevented it from happening. That one stuck. He jumped back into his own life and watched as she grew up, married Drew, and started a family of her own.

He thought it stuck in his timeline because he'd made the change close to the event, but he wasn't sure.

Now, Lux knew all of this, but listened patiently as I reminded him of everything, the people in each When, where we'd both come from, and where we might wind up. He had an inevitability: he was a domestic housecat with a life expectancy of 20 years or thereabouts. He didn't mind that, mostly because he'd come close to dying when he was very young and was grateful for the reprieve. He understood that Will could find a way to extend his life, and when the end came close he might make that request, but he took comfort in knowing that he wasn't stuck in this life.

I had no such reassurance. I was already centuries old and there was no end in sight, not unless I asked someone to help me move on. But the things that bothered me most were the gaps in my memory, decades I could barely remember. I had thought I would be grateful if those memories returned.

Then the dreams began, and my gratitude was significantly less than I had supposed.

~

"There are three certainties, Wick. Everyone is born. Everyone exists. Everyone dies. Not everyone lives, though, and it seems to me that you've excelled at living. Peace can be found there."

Lux stared out at the ocean as he spoke, watching waves lap onto the sand, watching the children dig in it while the adults lounged in chairs and enjoyed the breeze, and as they played games with each other. There were guards, of course. One for each child stood near the water's edge, ready to stop their assigned little ones from darting into the ocean and being swept away by the strong undertow, and there were others nearby. Today the guards were visible, uniform-clad reminders to passersby that the beach was closed this afternoon, and no one uninvited would be allowed to leave the road that ran alongside the parking lot.

There were detour warnings along the Great Highway, but it couldn't be completely closed off because people did live along the far side, just past the breakaway.

Lux and I sat on the break wall. We'd been on the beach, lounging under chairs when it suited us and jumping on sandcastles as the children built them. We'd played when asked to, but my heart wasn't in it and he sensed that. He sensed why; he knew me well enough. With the excuse that we needed to find a spot to use as a litter box, we made our way to the wall, to soak up some quiet while we watched the family enjoy the beach for the first time in years.

I was happy to be there because they were happy; when had we last reserved this stretch of Ocean Beach? It was once a year when Oz and Zed were small, but I didn't think the family had done this since the summer before Drew came to stay. It was cold and overcast, January being an odd choice for a beach picnic, but I'd looked forward to it. Small children playing on the beach was always fun and funny, and someone—probably Drew—would surely wind up with a bucketful of sand down his shorts.

Somewhere in the days leading up to it, my mood shifted. I couldn't even articulate why, exactly, until the dreams became incessant.

Then there was no denying it.

Lux meant well, but I wasn't sure he was right. I'd been born. I existed. I lived as well as I could, and that was usually enough.

What if I never die, Lux? Isn't that one of the points about living? That one day it will end, so we enjoy it now, while we can?

I should have died before 1925. I should not have survived until the mid-1960's when Finn plucked me from certain starvation and brought me home to be Will's companion and playmate. More accurately, I shouldn't have been sitting on that wall at all; I wouldn't be born for fourteen more years, and my life should be over in roughly thirty-five.

If one counted the years I was stuck in null space—and I did, because I felt them all—I was nearly 500 years old. An exam that would take place in a bit under 200 years had proclaimed me to be a healthy, five-month-old feline.

I've aged one month for ever century I've lived. Do the math. If my intended life span was twenty years...how many more centuries is that?

Lux could do the math; he chose not to.

"What is it you're most afraid of in living that long?"

That I'll forget them.

He didn't tell me I wouldn't. Lux understood that I had already forgotten huge gaps of my life, and he understood that it was likely that I would forget more of it as I aged. Lux did what a good friend does: he listened and when asked, tried to help me root out the reason I suddenly felt sad.

Forgetting you, as well, I added. *A hundred years from now, will I remember this? Will I remember meeting you in Jo's study thirty years in the future? Will I remember how often I slipped through the closet portal in the dead of night to visit you and enjoy some quiet away from toddlers? Will I forget that we convinced old Hyrum to sincerely tell his sister that chocolate milk comes from brown cows, so that means it's healthy and that's all he wanted for forever? Or that we ate so much fish the night JoJo and PopPop took us out for dinner that you threw up on her on the way home. Or—?*

"Or that on the day we met, you saved my life?" he mused. *"Perhaps not. But when I near the end of my days, I'll remember the wonderful tiny cat who grasped that I was in pain and was able to relay that to her. I'd be long gone already, if not for you. I'll carry that gratitude to the end, Wick."*

I didn't want him to end. I didn't want any of them to end.

"You have an agreement with the Emperor regarding the end of your life, do you not?"

Will had agreed that when I told him, sincerely, that I was done with this life he would help me end it. I meant it; I wanted that option. But I was less certain that I would reach that decision during his life, lengthy as it promised to be. There was also the likelihood that Rhys would live longer, and Finn surely would—Liam Finnegan, an older version of Finn, was somewhere between 1,500 and 3,000 years old, possibly more. The number changed with his mood, but Will was certain that he was well over 2,000 years and given the likely reason—time stuck in null space—I would live just as long.

I would not be alone.

But I might forget.

Worse, I might remember.

Lux knew about my dreams, in which I stealthily hopped on sputtering, slow-moving cars in the 1920s to explore San Francisco. He'd listened to tales of the Great Depression and the generosity of those who had little for themselves yet shared their meagerness with me. In my dreams I watched men in uniforms stream onto boats that carried them away, some forever.

He knew as well as I that those dreams were memories beginning to surface.

He grasped the pain of having lived through those years, eons where there was no generosity to be found, years upon years of near-starvation and thirst, abuse heaped upon a tiny, fragile body by people so angry about their own lives that they didn't recognize the pain they inflicted. Lux knew I'd seen history when it was still the present, and that I would trade those years for almost anything.

And yet, when I had the chance, I chose to remain in my own life.

I chose it for another me.

I had no right, I told him.

"You did it so there would be days like this." He jutted his chin toward where the children had scooped up handfuls of sand and were now sneaking up on Drew to throw it at him. *"You did that to Seven so that one day he would be here, with them, where he belongs."*

I made Will give him cheese. Do you know how many years it was before he tasted it again? Fifty, if not more. I hate myself for that, Lux. I hate it, and I can't undo it.

~

Naps were taken in a tent that butted up against the support pole of the heavy canvas canopy that had been set up to offer shade, despite how overcast the day was. Rhys and Marco laid quietly even though they were awake, and the toddlers had gone out like sweaty little lights five minutes after being told to rest for a while.

The adults sat in a semi-circle in plastic beach chairs, gazing out at the ocean, speaking softly so that they didn't disturb their finally quiet offspring. There were bottles of beer, about which Oz and Sophia grumbled because neither could partake, and there were bottles of root beer because that's what Hyrum wanted. Somewhere in the periphery there were, undoubtedly, photographers invading the privacy of the royal family, and the evening gossip rags would be littered with pictures of the King and Queen drinking beer near small children, and how dare they indulge in things that everyone else in the free world did?

The same websites alternately praised and reviled the royal family, depending on the level of outrage they could manufacture, or how sickly sweet they could make an image appear. Occasionally photos taken of Jax and Aubrey while they sat together on the balcony popped up, the running narrative making it appear that they spent an absurd amount of their time with lips locked. Pictures of Hyrum holding hands with whomever he walked had, in the beginning, garnered attention but now were merely cute homages to his innocence yet still appeared weekly. Sophia bristled at the intrusions and had once slapped a camera out of the hands of a younger photographer while growling, "You can fuck right off, sunshine," without realizing that someone else was recording video.

"We're kind of boring," Zed told a reporter visiting Alcatraz for a fact-finding tour. "I'm not sure why there's any interest in pictures of us doing ordinary things."

There was nothing special about this picnic, but someone was out there snapping picture after picture, and they would make something out of it.

"I think I prefer the anonymity of my When," Lux said when Will reminded Hyrum that his waist-high sandcastle would surely appear online later because it was creative and detailed. *"Your family is still known, but not pursued so blatantly."*

Next time around they will be. Jax isn't giving up the throne to Oz for a long time, so when yours rolls around again, they'll still be the royal family.

"Not my When, per se. Jo and I relocated from another, though I am uncertain about the difference in the number of years."

Hyrum got out of his chair to contemplate his castle, head tilted. "Should I knock it down? It got bigger than I meant. If it fell over on one of the babies, it would hurt."

Despite assurances that they were keeping close watch on all the kids, he decided he didn't want to risk it and after Drew had taken several photos, he trudged over to begin the task of pairing it down to an acceptable size.

Lux and I followed.

Kick it over. I mean, when else can you kick a castle until it's just chunks?

"Wick," he snorted. "What if I got all the sand on you and Lux?"

We'll stand back. Kick it and when it's about knee high, we'll help you by jumping on it.

Giggling, Hyrum adopted the stance Oz had taught him, and then wailed at the castle with an awkward but effective round kick. The sand exploded, spraying in all directions, including covering Lux in a fine layer of wet sand.

It didn't matter. When the sand settled and it was no taller than Hyrum's knees, Lux and I both launched, leaping onto it, compressing what was left into random lumps and piles.

"Did that make you feel better?" Lux asked me as I shook sand from my paws.

Little bit. That was fun. Hyrum, you need to build it again so the older kids can knock it over.

He sat down and began scooping sand into little piles. "Were you feeling bad, Wick?"

Just tired.

"You're having dreams again, aren't you?"

Hyrum was my sounding board, the person I turned to when the enormity of Drew's accident in space had become too much for me to bear. He knew about my dreams, and he knew the direction my brain had been taking me.

Dreams and other things.

"He worries about another version of himself," Lux said, though Hyrum rarely understood him. He caught words here and there, which gave Lux hope, but for now he relied on me to tell Hyrum the things he said.

"You mean like how Will goes to the future and sees the other me?" Hyrum asked. "The one Lux knows?"

Like that. But a younger me.

"Will says that guy is me but not really. So I wouldn't worry about him more than anyone else."

"*You have deep concern for others regardless of who they are,*" Lux said.

"We have to think about others on account of that's what Jesus would do," Hyrum reasoned. "You think about others. So does Wick."

But if you could change something that happened to you, would you? Think about it. If someone had plucked you out of your life when you were young, don't you think you would be happier?

Hyrum's nose scrunched as he considered it. There was a lifetime of abuse he could have been saved from, had the right people known and been given iron clad legal reasons to rescue him. If he'd been taken from his parents at birth, Hyrum's existence would have been one of peace and not terror.

"Maybe if it coulda happened after Spencer and Joe and Ruth and Elle and Sarah were born. I wouldn't want to not know them. And I was happy a lot of the time except when I was being punished. Or hit and stuff."

He also had never forgotten Aubrey after she left and missed her horribly. "Maybe if it coulda happened before I had to go walk for so long to find her. That was the hardest thing I ever did."

You grew up a lot on that walk.

"Yeah. Maybe. And if I never went I would have missed that winter in the cabin with you even though you said your name was Major. And I met Will and Drew then even though I didn't know it and thought they were angels." He grabbed another handful of sand and patted it onto what would be a wall of the new castle. "Maybe they really were angels. Sometimes I think angels are people who do the work Jesus needs them to do and they don't even know they're angels. Not like the ones who live in heaven all the time and have wings and halos on account of Daddy said those weren't real, but even Daddy thought that there were people who were mostly here to do work Jesus needs them to do. So I'm pretty sure Will and Drew were angels, and that's something I wouldn't want to miss."

Even though you had so much in life that hurt?

"I don't hurt now. I like my life now."

"Perhaps the pain is why you appreciate what you have now," Lux ventured.

"That's what Dr. Cheshire says. He says everyone has bad things in their lives that weren't their fault, and since you can't do anything about it, you gotta find a way to make the best of things." He sat back on his heels. "Does this stuff have to do with your dreams, Wick?"

In a way.

"Well, if your dreams really are your memory getting better, maybe when it all comes back, you'll feel better on account of it won't seem as bad."

He had one wall up, a thick, three-inch-thick slice of sand that stood six inches high. He reached for more sand to start a second wall, but Lux crouched down, his butt wiggling, and pounced, reducing it to a flattened slab.

"Sorry. I don't often get to play."

Instead of being upset, Hyrum giggled as he picked Lux off the remnants of his castle, threatening him with little balls of Ocean Beach if he did it again. And because I did not want to dwell any further on my dreams or anything else that reminded me of everything I could not remember, when the wall was rebuilt, I looked Lux in the eyes, and we both pounced.

~

I flicked bites of cheese off my hover cart and onto the floor, where Thor waited with his mighty, drool-soaked tongue. He'd already had his treat, and Will squinted over the edge of his tablet, trying to decide if the cheese launching had been intentional or an accident.

It won't kill him to get a bite of cheese, Will.

Lux swallowed his. *"It will if you give it to him too often."*

I'm not hungry. His heart isn't going to explode over a half an ounce of sharp cheddar.

"You're not hungry," Will repeated. "Since when are you not hungry? Are you feeling all right?"

I lowered the cart to the floor to let Thor lick any residual cheesy goodness from the top and stepped off. Lux dove for the far side, still not trusting that giant tongue, though he was no longer afraid that Thor would bite him.

I ate a lot at the picnic. Between the bites of burgers and hot dogs, I'm still stuffed.

So was Lux, but he wasn't about to share any of his cheese. *"Truthfully, I was not hungry, but cheese was my reward for not defecating all over Hyrum when he insisted upon bathing us."*

Neither of us had been allowed to set a paw on the floor when we returned home from the beach. The kids were headed for a bath, and he was determined that whether we liked it or not, we were getting into his tub, where the remnants of the day's picnic would be lathered from our furs and allowed to slide down the drain.

Lux protested throughout the indignity of being bathed, mostly because he went first, and I sat on the edge of the tub mocking him. As Hyrum rinsed the shampoo from his fur, Lux growled, *"I will eat your soul,"* which only made Hyrum giggle again.

Lux froze for a moment. *"He heard me."*

I think he hears when he's not trying so hard.

There was no point in fighting it. He'd made sure the water was warm and had rinsed the tub after Lux, so I jumped in and tried not to complain about it.

"Sometimes I hear things," Hyrum said. "Just like I used to hear things from you, and then one day I just heard you all the time."

"Well, hear this. I am cold and would like to curl up by the fire now."

"As soon as Wick is done."

I would never admit it to Hyrum or anyone else, but the warm water felt good as he poured it carefully over my back, and he was gentle as he worked the shampoo into a lather and then rinsed it off.

He took us upstairs to Will's fireplace, reasoning that it was bigger and had a better blower on it, which meant we would dry quicker. Giggles and laughter rolled down the hall—all the kids were in one tub, probably splashing most of the water onto the floor—and there was one wet dog already lounging in the floor in front of the fireplace.

Our patience, combined with the lack of bloodshed and other bodily fluids, earned us each bites of cheese. I didn't lie when I said I was full, but when the smell hit my nose all I could think about was Seven and his sheer joy in tasting it for the first time. His body had vibrated with happiness, and he spent decades hoping for more.

I didn't want it after that, but Thor had no idea about Seven, and would have eaten a roach if I'd flicked it from the cart to the floor.

We need to find a roach.

Will set his tablet aside. "Do I want to know?"

About roaches? I'm sure if you get online there's a ton of information about them.

"Why do you need a roach?"

To see if Thor would like a crunchy treat, Will. Why else?

With a sigh, he headed down the hall to check on the kids and possibly rescue Aisha from an inordinately long bath time. "Do not feed bugs to the dog, Wick," he called out.

I turned to Lux. *It's on you to give it to Thor, then.*

Thor's tail thumped against the coffee table, happy to hear his name. *"Good boy?"*

"For a dog," Lux allowed.

Thor laid down and let out an exasperated huff. *"Good boy."*

He's just not used to dogs, I explained. *Try to imagine how you look to a cat. You're big and hairy, even your soft voice is loud, and if you wanted to you could hurt us.*

"Good boy."

I know you wouldn't hurt us. But Lux doesn't see you every day and you're kind of scary to him.

Lux peered at Thor from a safe distance behind me. *"When I say you're a good boy for a dog, it's meant as a compliment, Thor. From my perspective, you're the best boy of dogs."*

"Good boy good boy good boy."

If we had more cheese, I'd give it to you. Maybe if you go help keep an eye on the kids, someone will get you more to eat.

"Good boy?"

Well, yeah, it's half the reason I'm so helpful. People give you things when you're helpful.

Thor was happy to help even without an offering of food on the horizon. He bounded down the hall toward the large guest bathroom where three small children were drenching their parents with bubble bath soap and water and likely a significant amount of sand. Lux and I were dry and now warm, and tired enough to sleep without, I hoped, too many dreams.

~

Lux had uncurled from his tight ball of sleep on the window seat of Will and Aisha's bedroom and was stretched out on his back. One paw was smashed against the glass, his tongue was sticking out of his mouth in a tiny blep, and if not for the gentle rise and fall of his stomach, one could have mistaken him as being very, very dead.

Aisha was in bed, pillow over her head, one leg jutting out from under the covers. Will had begun the night with her, but as he often did, once she was deeply asleep he crept out of the room and stretched out on the sofa to read. While his sleep issues were far less intrusive than they'd been before she came back into his life, Will still had nights when it eluded him, though I hadn't heard him begging the sleep fairies for a very long time.

If he was out there and awake, that meant he had thumbs I could borrow. I jumped to the floor carefully, trying to not wake Aisha, but the movement was enough to rouse Lux and he reluctantly followed me to the living room, where I made an impassioned plea for food before I keeled over from starvation.

My stomach growled.

Will looked over the top of his tablet. "So?"

So. When my stomach growls it's your responsibility to fill it.

"There's dry food in the kitchen, Wick."

We've had this conversation before, Will. Dry food is for peasants.

"What about you?" he asked Lux. "Are you hungry?"

"I could eat, thank you."

"He's polite." Will set the table aside and sat up. "In fact, I'm sure Lux would have asked nicely instead of indulging in passive aggressive tactics to guilt me into food."

My way works. Make with the thumbs, food dude.

Now, truthfully, had Lux not been there Will would have suggested things I could do to myself and my hunger would have gone unrelieved until Hyrum was up at 4:30. But I wanted Will to feed us and then go to bed, so that we could start with our day while everyone else was sound asleep and would not notice that we had quietly disappeared into Oz's closet.

"Are we sharing a can?" Will asked. "Or would you each prefer your own?"

Lux was poised to tell him sharing was fine because Lux did not want to seem greedy. I had no such issue and told Will a full can meant me not bugging him in fifteen minutes because I was not quite satisfied, and if he gave us each our own, he could go to bed where he belonged.

Don't you have a meeting in the morning? I heard Oz say the board was finalizing the paperwork on the Wastelands sale.

"I do, and I'm fully capable of being there on little sleep."

Maybe you think you are, but you'll be grumpy and they're all too polite to tell you when you're being a giant, gaping as—

"I get your point," he sighed as he set out plates on the floor. "Was Aisha asleep deeply when you left the room?"

You won't wake her. Charlie could body slam himself onto the bed and not wake her.

"Has he done that?" Lux asked as Will disappeared into the bedroom.

Charlie had launched himself onto the bed while yelling "Mommy!" at top volume more than once, though he hadn't done it since she returned the favor during the tail end of a nap a few weeks before Christmas. To her credit, she didn't fully slam herself onto his mattress; she only sat down hard while gleefully calling out his name, though the mental image of his little body flying into the air if she had truly launched at it made her snicker.

Lux ate half his food and was prepared to walk away when I suggested this was a good time to eat a little more than usual. He needed calories on board because I didn't know when we would eat again and there was no way to carry it with us.

"Why?" he asked, squinting at me. *"Where are we going?"*

To paraphrase Hyrum...we're going on an adventure. But it's less where and more when. So eat up, because if I recall correctly, food won't be easy to get.

~

It was cold and dark on Union Square, and quiet cracked all around us. There were soft footsteps in the distance, a single pair, one man crossing the street at the corner closest to us. Lux sat down, turning his head to look in all directions, confused by the familiar yet wholly different city surrounding us.

"Wick. When are we?"

Nineteen hundred six. April sixteenth. In two days, this entire city will be shaken so hard that anyone survived is a gift.

"We came to observe an earthquake. Wonderful."

We came to help me help myself. And to do that, we're going to follow the Emperor and me from here to Ghirardelli Square. So we need to get to it, before he's too far ahead.

Gentleman that he was, Lux refrained from pointing out my short legs nor how long it had likely been since either of us had run the four miles it would take to get from here to there, and the likelihood of that was never. He ambled along behind me, taking cues when it was clear I was hiding from Will, ducking into store entryways every time he paused.

"What," Lux asked when Will stopped for more than a moment, *"is he doing?"*

Talking to me.

I'd had a question and he was pondering the answer. Having been in another When, where we met Tad, the boy who cared for me through much of the late 1950s and 1960s, I was curious about my memory of that time in my life. I shouldn't have remembered meeting Will—the Happy Birthday Man—because our visits then, spaced out as an annual event, had happened after Will and I had died in the When before us. Merlin, which was the name Tad anointed me with, should never have known Will, yet I remembered him clearly.

Another thing we chose to not examine too closely.

"Perhaps Whens overlap," Lux mused as Will resumed walking. *"Drew has theories regarding the composition and compression of time."*

Time is spaghetti.

"You've spoken to Hyrum, then. Drew envisions time as lines upon lines that form a global pattern, and those lines touch in places. When displayed as a flattened image, it looks to me to be more like—" he paused to consider the notion *"—snowflakes etched into shattered glass. Where the lines touch, there are tiny clusters that have the same tender filaments as the tips on a snowflake."*

The image formed in my mind, frosted glass in winter, the pane having fractured through eons, though not completely broken.

"He suspects there are echoes. Perhaps that is what has allowed you to remember him."

I'm remembering the next timeline then. What's to come, not what happened before.

"Or you remember a previous time when you both survived."

Neither of us could explain how that was possible but it seemed as reasonable an explanation as anything else. Lux chalked it up to ancestral memory, something time had hardwired into my DNA through repetition. I thought it was something more, but being unable to articulate it beyond a *meh, maybe* grunt, I chose to consider his idea.

"I mean," he went on as we turned a corner, *"it's not likely an event I or even Jo or Will could experience. But your years in null*

space, perhaps that's freed some sort of memory cascade? Small windows into the minds of your other selves. You were, essentially, in null space at the same time together, possibly occupying the exact same space. Many of you, while being only one of you."

With that notion, Finn might have memories he was unable to explain. He might not be able to separate them from his discussions with himself, believing them to be things PopPop or Liam Finnegan had told him; it was an explanation for why he understood yet didn't fully grasp time travel. I would have made a mental note to remind myself to ask Will to ask him, but he'd turned another corner and was moving so fast that we had no hope of keeping up.

Another block and we'll lose him.

"You know the way, though, don't you?"

I had a vague notion of how to get to Ghirardelli Square. I'd never walked there on my own; I was always on someone's shoulder or I rode in the front pouch of their sweatshirt. While I paid attention, I hadn't *paid attention*, so the directions inside my head were more abstract than literal. Still, I was certain I could get us there, but not how long it would take.

Once there, we had to make our way back, and I didn't want to do that while it was light out. Sunlight meant people, and people meant dodging feet or meeting the bristly end of a broom shaken by an irate shopkeeper trying to get dirt out of the doorway. It meant avoiding small kids with sticky hands.

And dogs.

We'd inadvertently walked past the street Will turned on and headed for the next corner; halfway down the block stood a mouth-breathing, ear-twitching brute of a dog that was twice Lux's size, and it had noticed us.

"What do we do?" Lux wondered out loud.

We held very, very still, waiting to see if the mouth breather was intent on harm, or simply noting our existence. He was considerably smaller than Thor but that jaw was likely as strong, if not stronger, than that gentle giant's. If he managed to grab one of us, we would become an early morning snack because there was no coming back from that.

Stay behind me.

Lux did as I said and scooted back. He could still see over my head, and I felt his breath ruffle the fur on my ears; his breath came in short, shallow bursts, and if not for my presence—he would never abandon me—he would have run.

Running would be a mistake. If we ran, the dog would give chase, and I didn't think either of us was fast enough to escape.

Behind us, there was little but a dirt encrusted road and darkness. There were several doorways, but none set deeply enough into the building's façade to provide a place to hide. Around the corner there was a short staircase with a railing surrounding it on two sides. It was made from heavy pipe, smooth and round, with little surface to perch on, but it would have to do.

Very slowly, go to those steps. If he moves, run up and get as high as you can.

"And you?"

I'll follow. He'll head for movement, so don't dawdle.

"Wonderful. He'll eat me first, then. Thank you for that."

Better to get it over with, don't you think?

"I think," he grumbled as he inched over, "that avoiding him would be the wisest course. He doesn't seem like the sociable type."

I had no intention of avoiding him, but I wanted Lux out of the way. He didn't argue, but moved as slowly as he could, until Brutus the Mouth Breather decided it was play time, and he began galloping toward us.

"Wick, get up here," Lux hissed.

Get up high. Just do it.

He jumped to the railing, a tiny whine escaping as he adjusted to the narrow rail. If the dog ran up the stairs, Lux was just high enough to stay out of his grasp; I didn't think the dog's short legs allowed him much in the way of a vertical leap, but if he tried, Lux had the option of jumping off onto the sidewalk on the far side, and then running. He had as much time as it would take Brutus to scramble down the stairs to get away, and I counted on it being enough.

"Wick, please."

Brutus is looking at you, not me. Trust me.

"Oh, dear."

The dog was at the curb, and as he lunged toward the steps, I leaped.

Oh, Bast, he's going to taste worse than George.

I landed on his head and sunk my teeth into his ear, pulling as hard as I could while digging my claws into the flesh around his eyes. His yelp echoed down the street and he began thrashing his head back and forth, trying to loosen my grip, but I dug deeper and yanked on his ear until it ripped.

Brutus screamed in agony, head jerking violently, but I couldn't let go, not yet.

Now, the truth is that I didn't want to hurt him. I only wanted him to leave and let us be. But this dog wasn't any saner than George had been when he tried to grab Jay and run; he was focused, determined, and pain was the only thing that would get through to him.

I pushed hard with my rear left paw and felt his skin tear under my claws. He screamed again, bucking hard. I moved my right back claws to his eye and let go with my teeth, warning *Let me off and leave, or else I really will cut your eye out.*

The yelping dulled to a whine, and then one tiny *yip* that I was confident meant, "I give."

I jumped off him, standing in front of the steps that led to Lux. He turned to look at me, blood running down his snout. I'd expected him to bolt, so when he didn't, I pulled my lips back, bared my teeth, and hissed.

I've taken on bigger dogs than you, sunshine. Go now while you can still see.

There was an outraged huff, but Brutus turned and walked away, his tail down but not tucked between his legs. I didn't move until he was back at his position by the door where we'd first spotted him.

Be careful about it, but you can get down now.

We tucked behind the staircase, making sure Brutus wasn't going to charge again. Lux sniffed every inch of me that he could, looking for injuries, and he refused to let me move until he was positive that I was all right.

"That was impressive," he allowed once he was sure. *"Does Thor know you're capable of that? Is it why he defers to you?"*

Thor is gentle and sweet by nature. I don't think it would cross his mind at all.

"Still. I imagine he would behave impeccably if he knew how badly you could injure him."

It would never occur to Thor that I would. It would never occur to him to put me in a position where I felt I had to defend myself, not intentionally.

It's not that dog's fault. He's just out here trying to survive.

"But he would have eaten us, I'm sure of it."

I was sure of it, too, but not because he was a dog. I was sure of it because I had cornered rats and mice and the occasional slow bird and done to them what Brutus felt compelled to do to us.

Dog's gotta eat. It's not personal.

Lux glanced over his shoulder to make sure we weren't being followed. *"It certainly felt personal."*

I reminded him of the life he'd had before moving to a new When with Jo and Finn. There was a courtyard filled with cats who had begun their lives on the streets and had no one to care for them. They survived by eating other animals. The fact that he'd escaped that misfortune because he was born in Jo's house didn't change what he knew about their lives. We hunt, we kill, we eat.

Brutus just wanted to survive, and I didn't blame him one bit.

"My awareness doesn't mean the notion of becoming a meal is palatable, Wick."

It should never be palatable. But it's acceptable. Just promise me something.

He waited.

If you ever find yourself stuck outside, needing to survive, and you kill something for food, eat it all. Don't waste it. And if something gets me while we're out here, if they eat part of me and leave the rest—

"I will not consume your remains."

Leaving my remains would be a dishonor, Lux. It would be a waste. At least eat the meaty bits and then drag the guts where the birds and rats can find me. I kind of owe them.

He huffed but didn't refuse.

"I believe when this is over, I'll be the one fighting horrible dreams."

You'll be fine.

Lux glanced over his shoulder again, at a dog we could no longer see. *"Brutus. That's what we've decided to name him, correct? What did Brutus taste like?"*

Chicken.

~

The horse was Lux's idea.

We'd fallen so far behind Will that there was little hope we'd catch up or even find his scent. At the rate we were walking, the sun would have been out for an hour or more by the time we reached Ghirardelli, and we risked Will seeing us on his walk back to the portal. Anyone else would have glanced, thought, "hey, that kitty looks like Wick," and kept going. But Will? He would know. And then be stuck with two of me. And a bonus kitty. He would not be amused.

Well, he'd be stuck until we got back to a portal, upon which I would receive a lecture typically reserved for wayward teenagers. After that Lux and I would be free to return home and Will would return to his own When, but my reason for being in 1906 would be left unresolved.

Someone had to teach Seven how to be a cat. How to hunt, to quickly kill prey without torturing. How to be cute around people with food, and how to zig zag away from people who not only wouldn't share but would throw things at him. He needed guidance. Direction. Paws-on training in rat-catching and consumption. What not to eat. The best time of day to snag a bird before it could take flight. There were a thousand things I needed him to know without having to learn through trial and error, because I'd had to and it was hard.

He needed a teacher.

I wanted it to be me.

When we reached the halfway point, as we turned onto what I thought was Hayes Street, there was a horse standing to the side of the road, his tether wrapped loosely around a vertical post. His rider—owner, perhaps, I couldn't swear to it but presumed—patted him on the nose and told him he would only be a minute, and then went inside.

"If we ask nicely enough, perhaps he'll give us a ride," Lux mused.

You want to steal a horse.

"It's not theft so much as it is borrowing. We won't keep him, after all."

He's kinda tied up.

Lux marched up to the post, tilting his head as he examined the tether. It was wrapped simply and with one swipe of his paw, it uncurled and dropped to the ground.

Dude. Hey. Big guy. Look down.

He bent his neck and looked at me, head cocked to get a better view.

Any chance we could talk you into giving us a ride down the street? Not far. Maybe a mile or so. It's kind of important.

Warm air popped from his nostrils and he let go a soft whinny.

You can be back before he misses you. I don't want to get you in trouble, but we really need to get as far down the street as we can.

He bent his knees and twitched his head, an invitation to jump up. There was a glimmer in his eye; this excited him, and he didn't care if he got into trouble for it. For the next few minutes, he had freedom, and he was taking every glorious moment of it.

Hold on, Lux. But don't break his skin with your claws.

It felt like flying.

Actually, it felt like zooming down the street on Zed's air bike, but with all the bumps and jiggles I felt while riding in the basket on Hyrum's bicycle, and then some. Lux and I held on as the horse trotted away from his post, and then dug in when he began to gallop.

*Big dude, I totally know a dragon you'd get along with. He'd
have given us a ride, too.*

There was a voice booming from behind us, but he didn't
break stride. Air popped from his nostrils, air that sounded a lot
like laughter.

He ignored his owner's shouted protest to get the fuck back.
We did not get the fuck back; he sped up, somehow prancing
as he ran, and it occurred to me that we had probably enlisted
an equestrian toddler in our quest to get closer to Ghirardelli
Square. This was Charlie, racing down the hallway without his
pants, giggling as Hyrum chased after him with a stern, "No one
wants to see your wiener, Charlie!"

Well, they might not want to, but they're gonna.

We were half a block from Will—I spotted him turning
toward the Square—when a deep, commanding voice shouted,
"Fred, stop!" and the horse skittered to a halt.

Fred?

And that's when the shoe hit me.

~

"*Well, that was quite rude,*" Lux said as he jumped from
Fred's back. "*Are you all right?*"

I was on the ground, on my side after having rolled several
times, and I snorted dirt out of my nose. I thought I was all right,
but I didn't want to move until I was sure nothing was broken, so
I told Lux to give me a minute and to keep an eye on the person
running toward Fred.

He only had one shoe on, so I didn't think he would get
there fast.

Where'd he come from?

"*I didn't see. But he apparently knows our horse and stopped
him long enough for his human to catch up.*"

Before the people could get there, I forced myself up, and
we stepped onto the closest walkway. Fred's rider had caught
up and stood in the street, hands on hips, lecturing his wayward
steed about staying put when he's told to stay put, laughing
when told about the cats that had been riding him.

"You ran because you're afraid of a cat?"

Fred grunted. Of course, he wasn't afraid of a cat. He was helping, dammit.

As his owner grabbed the reins, Fred snorted at me.

You're welcome. I'm glad it was fun. Thank you.

"I don't think the shoe was meant for either of us, per se," Lux said as we made our way in the same direction we'd seen Will. *"I think it was intended to shock the horse into obeying."*

I've had worse things thrown at me.

"What can be worse than being knocked off a horse by someone's filthy footwear?"

Rocks. Boots.

"Boots are footwear."

Literal dog shit.

He thought I was kidding. But, it had happened. I was fairly sure it was sometime in during the early 1930s. The mood throughout the city was one of constant tension and hunger, and there were more people fighting for scraps than there had been just five years before. I spotted a chance to grab someone's lunch while they cleaned up after their now-sleeping dog, and I took it.

When the shit hit, literally, I kept running. I was not about to let that food fall from my grasp, and I didn't stop running until I was up a tree and tucked into the cradle of a large branch. It was just a slice of beef, not even enough to make a sandwich from, but it was more than I'd eaten in days so there was no guilt about it.

If the poop slinger could afford to feed his dog, he could afford to lose what for him was just a few bites of food.

Besides, he shouldn't have left it in the open.

Given the desperation of the times, I suppose he was just as bad off as I was, but I didn't even consider that then. I was hungry, painfully hungry, and that feeling was the only thing I could focus on.

Lux paused. *"Is your early nutrition why you're so small? I can't imagine being that hungry."*

Lack of food might be part of it. It might be because of the years in null space. I was just a baby then, but we'll never really know.

He decided it was a combination of events. He'd never known anyone who could eat as much as I did and still remain as small. Perhaps my hunger was owed to how hard it was to find food in my earliest years, while my stature had been stunted by whatever I'd been exposed to in null space.

Have you met Hyrum?

The sarcasm was intended.

"All right. That's fair. He does indeed require a considerable amount of food compared to the other men I know."

And he's still tiny by comparison.

Hyrum had hit 120 pounds and was thrilled by it. He was still hovering just above five feet tall, but 120 felt so much bigger than 118, especially when Drew suggested it was all muscle.

His legs are like steel. I don't think he's met a hill in San Francisco he hasn't delighted in biking up.

"My Hyrum is softer, but he's also much older. I worry about him sometimes. Every now and then he calls me 'Lazybones' as if he thinks it's my name."

When he was a little boy, he had a white cat named Lazybones. The first time he saw you, he was crushed that it wasn't also your name.

He'd forgotten. *"Oh. Yes. He carried me like an infant. The indignity."*

Worse than what Drew did to you?

There might never be a larger indignity in Lux's life. When Eli was just a few months old, still not sleeping through the night, and his parents were several levels of exhausted, Lux slipped out of the closet in their room. He'd come to visit me but detoured to the baby's crib to get a good look at him and to say hello.

Drew, mostly asleep but recognizing that Lux was there to see me, picked him up, slung him on his hip, carrying Lux with his hand placed where no one's hand had any business being.

Lux tolerated it long enough for Drew to open the bedroom door and then shrieked—loud enough to get every person in the apartment to their feet— *"Unhand my genitals, human!"*

Drew's sleep bubble popped, but he didn't put Lux down.

"I swear, I will file a complaint with management. Put me down!"

Aubrey could not understand a word Lux said, but she was fairly certain about his intent, and she carefully took Lux from Drew. "Let the kitty go, sweetie," she said, snickering. "He's not happy."

Neither was Eli, who began crying.

Drew blinked a few times. "Do you even have genitals?" he asked Lux. "I'm pretty sure you've been neutered."

That wasn't really his fault. I don't think he'd gotten a full night's sleep since before the baby was born.

It was still undignified, Lux insisted, though he agreed that neither that nor being carried like a baby was half as bad as being hit with a wad of fresh dog droppings.

"I suppose you don't blame him any more than you do Brutus."

All he saw was some random cat stealing his lunch and he reacted. No, I don't blame him. I blame the circumstances.

He didn't think I should soften the truths of my life by applying logic after the fact. *"Horrible things happened to you, Wick. That you survived and understand the behaviors of people around you doesn't change the degrees of awfulness you endured."*

It wasn't all awful. I met some nice people along the way.

Tad, for one.

"Wick. You can count the number of decent people you encountered in this When on one paw. The few who helped don't erase those who didn't."

We'd reached Ghirardelli. Will and other-me were seated on the ground, patiently waiting as Seven peeked around a tree, trying to decide if he could trust the giant man. I nodded toward a larger tree at the edge of the stand and we ducked behind it, sticking our heads out just far enough to keep an eye on things as they unfolded.

Seven trembled in fear, yet he took incremental steps toward the other me, and by extension, Will. Lux wisely remained silent as we watched; I wanted to remind him that we didn't want to draw attention to ourselves. I didn't want Will to notice us, and while I thought I would understand what was happening if I had seen us as I sat by Will's feet, I might not keep as quiet about it as I should.

I had no memory of the feeling of being observed.

Seven discovered the stash of cheese in Will's front pocket and began dancing, quivering with excitement. I felt the happiness on his tongue as he tasted cheese for the first time, the overwhelming feeling of Everything Is All Right, even though an older version of himself was sitting there and had decided that no, everything would not be all right, not after the cheese was gone.

I looked into my own eyes, and I saw despair.

Seven showed Will the pieces of the ship he'd crashed in. I hadn't realized how pale Will had gone when he understood how Seven came to be and hadn't noticed how red his eyes went. He fought tears even as he dug slivers of the ship from the ground, and when he sat down again, his face was painted in agony.

There was more cheese and some ham, and I sat there explaining to Seven how the world was going to shake apart, how terrifying it might be, but he had to stay there, stay by that wall, and if he did that he would be safe.

I didn't tell him he would only be safe for a short while. Once the earthquake was over and life began to unfold itself again, he wouldn't feel safe for another 60 years.

"He really is just a baby," Lux finally said, as soft as he could.

Will was nearly broken, but he got to his feet, and gave Seven the last of the cheese just before walking away.

Weeks old, not counting null space.

When he finished the last bite of cheese and ham, he licked the foil clean, then sat back and looked up.

He'd expected to still see Will and me there.

I'd told him we would leave, but he was so focused on the cheese that he hadn't grasped what I meant.

Certain we were close by, Seven picked up the foil with his teeth and trotted to the end of the wall and peeked around it, and when he didn't see us, he headed deeper into the trees.

He looked up; maybe we had climbed up where the birds usually were. When he didn't see us there, he began circling trees, a tiny whine slipping with each failed discovery. I felt his fear build in my own chest, that sinking feeling of being alone again, balancing on the precipice of understanding, and I knew how hard the fall would be.

Another few seconds, and he would begin to cry.

I couldn't take it anymore and stepped out where he could see me.

Seven squealed and then came up to me, dropping the foil at my feet. *'Cheese?'*

I'm out of cheese right now, little dude.

'Big man? Cheese?'

Lux bent over and sniffed Seven's nose.

'Big kitty?'

"*I'm sorry. I don't have any, either. Wick, he smells exactly like you.*"

There's a reason for that.

"*No need for sarcasm. Have you stumbled upon whatever decision you needed to make?*"

I had not.

I'd thought that we could teach Seven how to be a cat, how to better survive through the years he would be alone. I hadn't had that and was left to figure it out on my own. Surely Lux and I could take a few days and show him how to hunt and then hide the evidence.

But then I remembered Lux had no clue about hunting and his food had always come to him from a can and was served with love.

I wanted to stay here for a while, to keep him company until he learned how to take care of himself.

"*You needed a decision for that?*"

No. I was lying to myself.

'Loud. World break. Fire. People yell. Take food. No trash.' Seven boasted. *'Find cheese?'*

If I leave him here, I told Lux, *he won't taste cheese again until Tad gives it to him. That's fifty years from now.*

'Long time?' Seven asked. *'Days?'*

Too long.

I made my way over to the wall, counting on them to follow. When I turned, Lux was right there, and Seven was a few steps behind him with the foil hanging from his mouth.

He'll carry that foil for weeks. I did.

I can't do that to him.

"What's the plan, Wick?"

There was no plan. There was a portal on the other side of the wall, if we could just get to it. If we waited two days, there was a good chance we'd have access, and we wouldn't have to risk walking all the way to Market Street to get to the next closest one.

If only there was a way in.

Seven dropped the foil. 'In? I show.'

There's a way in? You've already explored?

'Warm in. Come.'

He picked up the foil and headed for the far side of the wall and we scrambled to line up behind him. Just around the corner, where in the future would lie a steep staircase, was a cat-sized hole that had little tufts of fur stuck to the edges. Seven wiggled in and I followed, and we waited for Lux, who took considerably longer to squeeze through.

'In,' Seven announced.

Good job.

We stood where there would later be a breezeway, and ten feet ahead of us was the most glorious, loudest, pink-shrouded portal I had ever seen.

"We're taking him with us, aren't we?" Lux asked. "How will we get him through with no transponder? It's not as if we can hold his hand."

You get to be momma kitty. I'm not strong enough, I don't think.

Lux knew exactly what I meant. "You are, but your size rather limits your ability to carry him."

Seven, do you remember how your mom used to carry you around?

'Neck.' He still had the foil in his mouth. 'Ow.'

I need you to let the big kitty pick you up just like she did.

'No. Ow.'

Do you want cheese? Because that's the only way you get cheese.

His little eyes went wide. *'Yes.'*

Foil firmly wedged between his lips, Seven let Lux grab him by the scruff, and we stepped through the portal to home. He was already wiggling to get loose by the time Lux was all the way through, and I was poised to explain the cheese would come when we made it back to the apartment, but the sudden onslaught of light and noise scared him.

He ducked between Lux's legs, quivering.

It's all right. It's just a little louder here. And we have more street lighting. That will make it easier to see our way home.

We managed to coax him down the stairs and as far as the aquatic park. Once on the bleachers, he balked and tucked between them, refusing to so much as look over one. We were still there when the city began to wake and were there when Zed pulled up nearby on his air bike, and I watched as he unlocked a skiff to ride to Alcatraz. If we stayed, there was a chance Hyrum would be by on his bicycle, heading for the island, and I played with the idea of shouting to him to come rescue us.

As the thought came to me, so did the realization that he might think Seven belonged to someone else, and no matter what I said, he might leave him behind.

"Hyrum would not do that," Lux insisted.

Not intentionally. But if he was too excited to listen to us? Who knows?

Half an hour later, he still was not there.

All right, so he probably doesn't work at the island today. We're gonna have to walk if we can pry Seven away.

Little dude, do you remember the giant man?

Seven sniffed and his ear twitched, but he didn't answer.

We still have to walk all the way to him. He has the cheese.

Lux stared off in the distance, calculating how far we were and how long it would take. *"We might be home for lunch."*

He was staring over Ghirardelli. I had other ideas.

We'll go down the Embarcadero to Market Street. Distance is the same but it's flatter and there's more shade. We might even be able to find water.

'Water? Want.'

I can't get you anything to drink if we keep hiding here, Seven. You need to trust me. This is where I live. We'll be okay.

His eyes narrowed and he didn't completely trust me, but his thirst was greater than his fear, and it was all trumped by his want of cheese. He followed me down the bleachers to the sidewalk in front of the beach and we headed for Jefferson Street, which was the closest way I knew to get onto the Embarcadero.

We were near Hyde when I spotted the hotel where Hyrum and I had spent a night. Across the street from that was Piazza's, an Italian restaurant owned by Sean McAllister's grandfather. I'd been there often enough now that nearly employee knew who I was, and there were tables outside we could jump onto in order to draw attention to ourselves. Lux balked at the idea—that was inviting trouble—but I was certain I'd be able to get someone to understand we needed water, and quite possibly, some help getting home.

"They're closed," Lux groaned as he jumped onto the table. *"It's morning, Wick. They won't open until lunch."*

Someone has to come in and get things started. Pizza doesn't make itself, Lux.

'Cheese?'

Yeah, sure, you can get that on a pizza. You can get lots of things. Like meat.

'Meat?'

Remember the ham you just had? That's a meat. There are lots of meats and you're going to learn about a lot of them, I promise.

'Hm.'

"He's never letting go of that foil, is he?" Lux asked.

When presented with more cheese, he would have to let go of it. I wanted to let him keep it for now. It seemed like a comfort item, the same as Hyrum's nighttime stuffed rabbit, and that was not a thing I ever wanted to mess with. We sat on the table with Seven huddled between us, watching air bikes slip past and people walk by, waiting for the first person to come open the restaurant.

Seven stayed low, between us, and I felt him tremble with every loud noise that assaulted his senses.

When Sean came around the corner of the hotel, I felt relief pour from the tips of my furs. He spotted us from across the street and frowned, but I wasn't worried that he was angry. He was concerned. The first thing out of his mouth was "Wick, what the hell? Lux?" and then he spotted Seven.

"It's a baby Wick," he squealed, but in a manly way, of course. "Oh, I know he's not yours. What woman would put up with you?"

"Oh, I like him."

"But damn, he looks exactly—" Sean pulled the chair out from the table and sat down. "Son of a bitch, Wick, *is* he you?"

I stretched and head butted his nose.

"How?" Lux asked.

He knows about the portals and stuff. That's why he's safe to ask for help.

"How can we ask, exactly?"

I opened my mouth and stuck my tongue out, careful to not exaggerate, lest we repeat the freaking out of Hyrum and his certainty that I was dying from thirst. I gave a tiny pant and then waited as Sean considered it, and then repeated it.

"Ah, water. Wait here."

Two minutes later we each had a glass of water, though he had to pour Seven's into his hand because the kitten couldn't get his face into the glass. When we'd had enough, he sat back, and began musing about why we were there.

"You're never out alone," he said to me. "Without a person, I mean. I don't think you'd run away, not without a good reason. Do I need to call someone? I can call Drew. Or just take you home."

Either is acceptable.

He had his phone in hand and was about to dial when Denny of the bike taxi skittered to a stop in front of the restaurant. He was not as friendly as I presumed he would be, and he scowled as he barked, "Hey, what the fuck? What do you think you're doing? That's Hyrum's cat—"

Sean held his hand up, signaling for him to stop. "I know. I was about to call Drew to tell him Wick is wandering around town."

Denny's irritation abated quickly. "So you know him? The Prince?"

Sean nodded. "We're friends."

"Like, first name basis, or just, you know…you've met."

Sean held up the phone. "Well, I have his phone number. Oz's and Hyrum's, as well. I know them well enough to not worry about fallout from texting or calling them."

"All right, fine, I didn't mean to be rude or anything. But Hyrum is my friend—"

"I get it. But I need to get these guys home. I doubt they're supposed to be playing tourist today."

Denny tilted his head toward the back of his bike. "Hop in. I'll give you a ride."

I wasn't sure if Sean wanted to go or not, but I'd been in Denny's taxi enough times that I was comfortable riding with him, and Lux and Seven followed me because where the hell else were they going to go?

"How'd you meet Hyrum?" Sean asked as he got into the taxi.

"He and Prince Andrew hailed my cab once, right after Hyrum moved here. Neither of them had ever been on a bike before. And now look at him. He's all over the place and that bike has more miles than mine, I think."

"Well, Hyrum, yeah," Sean said, laughing. "Drew's not quite that brave."

Oh, you two are gonna get along.

Without me asking, Sean held onto Seven, keeping him firmly in place on his lap. Denny turned around and rocketed down the Embarcadero, not slowing as he made the turn onto Market, and that little piece of foil flapped in breeze. Sean reached for it once, trying to take it, but Seven whined and Sean let it go.

In order to pull up right in front of the royal house, Denny waited to turn until he reached Powell. The sharp rise of the street didn't bother him any more than it did Hyrum, and he lost no speed making the climb. He didn't slow at all until he turned onto Geary, and then stopped abruptly right in front of the door.

The guard at the door stepped forward sharply and had a hand up, a warning for Sean to stay put. He picked me up to show the guard—hey, look, it's Wick, surely someone misses him—when the door opened again and Vicat stepped out.

"Stand down," she ordered the guard, who did not get down at all but who stepped back to his spot by the door. "Sean. Long time no see. Where'd you find the troublemakers?"

"All the way at Jefferson and Hyde." He scooped us all up and climbed out of the taxi.

Satisfied that Sean truly was familiar with the royal family, Denny told him he was heading back to the Embarcadero and if he wanted a ride back to work, just head that way and he'd keep an eye out. No charge.

"And who," Vicat asked as she reached for Seven, "are you?"

"My gut says it's Wick," Sean answered for him. "I'm not sure how, but. Well, you know."

Vicat gestured toward the door, and invitation to enter, but Sean begged off. "I'm late getting the restaurant opened. Any later and I'll get the how-irresponsible-are-you lecture from my grandfather. And his lectures can be brutal."

She held her fist up, making a small circle as she whistled. "Wait just a sec."

A minute later, one of the official cars pulled up and the passenger window rolled down.

"Mr. McAllister just rescued Wick and Lux. That deserves a ride back to work in one of the King's cars, don't you think?"

"Yes, sir," the guard said, grinning. "Hop on in."

"I don't know what you boys were up to," Vicat said as she carried us inside, "but I'm not getting in the middle of it. Go upstairs and confess your sins to the Emperor. And remember, I'll find out if you don't tell him you were out running around."

'Cheese?' Seven asked as she set him down.

"The Emperor is at home," the desk guard informed Vicat. "He hasn't called down about missing Wick. Should I call up?"

Dude doesn't know what you know.

"They're fine," she told the guard, but the look she gave me was clear: confess, or I'll rat you out.

I didn't have much choice.

There was an extra cat, after all.

~

Now, the one thing I forgot to consider came lumbering at us with his tongue flopped out and dripping all over the place, and he was six kinds of excited and happy and *oh my god kitties* as he raced across the floor. We made a beeline for the fireplace and jumped onto the hearth, where Lux and I stood firmly in front of Seven, not letting Thor anywhere near him.

I could feel him trembling behind me, but knew he wasn't going to run, not with That Thing standing there, exhaling dog food breath onto us.

Thor saw him and could still smell him. He didn't want to cause any harm to Seven, but he damn well wanted a good look, and a chance to sniff him from the tips of his ears to the end of his tail. The whining turned to woofing and became a full-on bark when I told him to back off because we weren't moving.

Where's Rhys? Go find your boy.

"Good boy."

Rhys was where Rhys was supposed to be, downstairs in the old staff kitchen with Isaac, Charlie and Alex, and Marco. It was school time; they were probably in the middle of math or history lessons, and Thor was not allowed to attend on days when they studied important things. So he was not going to go find his boy, he was going to stand there and bark his fool head off until Will stomped down the hall to find out what the problem was.

As soon as he spotted Will, Thor shut up.

I need you to sit on the sofa, Will.

"Wick, I don't have time for this."

Make time. This is important. Please, sit down.

His eyebrows knotted, but he sat and folded his arms across his stomach. Aisha followed from their back-room office, curious what the issue was, but instead of being irritated when he told her I'd ordered him to sit, she laughed and dropped onto the sofa next to him.

Call Thor off. It's important.

Will patted his leg and then pointed to the fluffy rug near the coffee table. Thor knew better than to argue and went to it, plopping down with an exaggerated grunt.

"Well?"

Lux and I each took a step to the side, revealing Seven, who sat there with foil hanging from his lips, still trembling.

I heard Will's sharp intake of breath and Aisha began to gush about the tiny kitten, but Seven zoned in on Will and the foil fluttered to the floor as he dashed off the hearth, scrambled up Will's leg and launched at his face.

'Cheese?'

Will cupped Seven between his hands, and Aisha touched a finger to his soft, tender belly.

'Cheese?'

Will, he wants—

Will knew what he wanted, but everything flooded into his brain, the agony and guilt over leaving Seven behind, and without warning, his eyes became brutally red.

Lux turned sharply. *"Wick, what have we done?"*

He's fine. Give him a moment.

It lasted only a few seconds. Seven's tiny paws had found their way to his face, and with it came his tiny claws. Will pulled him away and held him out so that he could get a better look, sniffing, still not sure who he was looking at.

I had to go get him, Will. The dreams—

"He's adorable," Aisha said.

"He's Wick," Will breathed. "Seven. This is the kitten we left behind, in—"

"I figured that out, sweetheart. That was so long ago, though. Wick, why now?"

I needed time to consider things. And what I decided was that just because I lived my life, that doesn't mean he has to. I saw him again and realized that I would never leave anyone else to face the life I had. Why do that to a baby? Especially a baby.

"I agreed with your decision then, Wick," Will said.

And now?

"I agree with this one, as well."

'Cheese? Cheese? Cheese?'

Well, agree or not, you need to get up off your asterisk and get him some cheese. It's all he's been asking for, just more cheese.

"I did promise I would spend the rest of my life stuffing him with it."

Just start with a few more bites. It's been years for us, but to him you gave him the cheese about four hours ago. Let's not make the little guy puke before he has a grasp on the idea that he never has to go back to the scary place.

~

Aisha held the tiny piece of foil, turning it over, amused that Seven had felt it important enough to hold onto. He was on the breakfast bar with a plate of beef cat food, his quest for more cheese satisfied for the time being. Once he'd swallowed the last bite, he asked for more, but Will promised him something he would like almost as much, something that would help his tummy feel fuller.

I carried that foil around for a long time. When I finally lost it, I was crushed. No foil meant no cheese, ever again.

"How could you remember that?" Will asked. "The loop of time before that—"

I remembered the Happy Birthday Man when I shouldn't have, either.

He let it go.

"Bringing him here changes everything, Wick. Have you considered Tad? He became a veterinarian and caring for Merlin might have been the spur for that choice."

Tad loved animals. With or without Merlin, he'll find his way.

"Have you considered the future me, as well? He'll need you."

I know.

Seven licked up the last bite of beef and sat back, looking truly happy for the first time. *'Good.'*

"Well, I suppose you can rename him 'Bob.' You finally have your own cat."

We can't keep him, Will.

He twitched back a step. "What? You're not sending him back."

No, I'm not. But he can't stay here. He shouldn't.

"We have room enough for another cat. Thor will get used to him. The kids—"

We can't keep him because he's me. It's that simple, and that complicated.

Will moved me from the breakfast bar to the table and sat down, listening. It wasn't that I didn't want to share my life with a miniature version of myself. Seven couldn't stay because it wasn't fair to him. If he stayed, he would be living my life all over again, and wouldn't have a fair shot at living his own.

He's small now, but in a few months, he'll be my size. He'll look exactly like me. People will see him from the corner of their eye and think it's me.

"And we'll adjust. Different collars, for starters."

But there are all the expectations that go along with looking exactly like me. Think about how it was when you were four and as tall as most seven and eight-year-old kids. People expected you to behave and know things as if you were older than you were. Then when you showed this huge vocabulary, they were either afraid of you or expected even more.

It went beyond that. If we kept Seven, he would spend his life in my shadow, no matter how badly everyone wanted to treat him kindly. He would be burdened with the expectations they had for me, and that wasn't fair.

If he stayed, he would never become me.

"So then what do you want to do?" Will asked. "Take him to three-year-old me now?"

No. To Hyrum.

"Hyrum."

Not our Hyrum. Lux's Hyrum. He'll understand Seven but he doesn't have this huge history with me. And being with him will give Seven the years I'm taking from him otherwise. He lived for sixty years before Finn found him. He needs those years to grow into the cat you'll need when you're a little boy.

"He could be that cat now."

I couldn't have been the companion you needed if I hadn't had so many years to grow into myself, Will. You needed me to explain things to you, and I couldn't have when my brain was focused on finding cheese.

'Cheese?'

"Later," Will promised.

There's no one better to act as Seven's caregiver than Hyrum. He'll protect him, he'll love him, and he'll teach Seven compassion.

"Wick, that Hyrum is eighty years old," Aisha pointed out.

And he has a lot of years left. And then add onto that the years he'll get if Will takes him to Mass and the rejuvenation tanks.

"And there are Oz and Drew's future children," Will said. "Sam will take over his care when the time comes. She would do anything for her uncle. Including getting Seven to Finn. It might not be the sixty years you spent waiting, Wick, but it would be long enough."

Then you understand?

He understood. He agreed. That didn't mean he wanted to let Seven go, but he grasped that he needed to get things in motion before Aubrey released the children from school. Once they saw him, letting Seven go would be even more difficult.

"What about it, little man?" Will asked Seven. "Would you like to live with someone who will take the very best care of you?"

And you'd never have to sleep outside again.

'You?'

"No, Seven, I'm sorry."

His name is Hyrum. And he has cheese.

'Cheese?' He nipped the foil from Aisha's fingers. *'Okay.'*

Will held him a little closer than necessary and took longer to walk up the stairs to the portal in the multipurpose room. His excuse for not jumping directly there was an unwillingness to surprise anyone; if he went through the portal he could then call and let them know he was there. I didn't buy it at all, because he had jumped before, and no one had died from a heart attack. He always jumped to the landing by the stairs in front of the royal family apartment and then knocked.

We can visit, you know, I said to Will before he stepped into the portal.

"And I'll be there," Lux added. *"If he needs you, I know how to find you."*

"Are you sure?" he asked me one more time. "I don't mind keeping him."

I'm sure. I want him to have years when he's not me. I want him to have Hyrum.

With one more tiny squeeze, Seven's purring making his hands vibrate, Will nodded and stepped into the portal, and when he did, I felt the weight of forever slide off my bones.

~

"It was like Christmas," Will told Aisha later that night, lying together in bed. "I asked him to care for Seven and it was like the year he found Lazybones' whiskers in his stocking. When he could speak without crying, he sat down with Seven and quietly promised him he would be the best cat daddy ever, and he would always love him and take care of him."

Seven nuzzled Hyrum's face, dropped the foil into his lap, and solemnly asked, *'Cheese?'*

Will warned him to not give him cheese every time he asked, given that it was his favorite word, but Hyrum sighed as he got up. "We've had cats before, Will. I know how to take care of them and feed them."

Because Sam was heading off to college—living on campus, something Drew was not happy about—Hyrum had moved back upstairs. He didn't want Oz and Drew to feel alone so much, and with all their kids gone, they needed someone. He took Oz's old bedroom because it had the best view, and squealed with delight when Will informed him that in our When, the wall between that room and the one next to him had been knocked down to create a little apartment.

"I would be happy to come help with doing that again," he offered, without consulting Oz or Drew first.

While Hyrum was in the kitchen, Seven picked the foil off the floor and took it to Oz. *'Cheese.'*

That small square of foil had become currency, one he would continue to trade for cheese.

"Seven was incredibly happy when I left," Will told Aisha. "He latched onto Hyrum as if they were meant to be. It pains me to admit it, but Wick is right. Seven deserves that."

Told you.

His arm came out from under the sheet and he pointed at me. "Don't think we're not discussing your little adventure later."

You never knew we were gone.

"That's not the point. So much could have gone wrong."

I stood and stretched, then jumped off the bed and headed for the door.

Remind me to tell you about Brutus. You'll ground my furry little asterisk for the next ten years.

Spoilers, I was not grounded.

But I did give him ideas.

Big, messy, stuff-he-shouldn't-do ideas.

THE ONE WHERE NOTHING REALLY HAPPENS...

On any other day, I would have launched myself at Goober's face, claws and teeth bared, a loud growl rolling from deep down, and I would have felt exactly zero guilt about drawing a little blood and making him scream like a little girl whose ponytail is caught in a blender. Instead, I sat on the arm of Will's office sofa—the extra one that took up space on a wall near the giant window that looked out over the bay—and waited.

In the span of about 45 seconds, Hyrum removed and threw his shoes, knocked over the coffee table, and unintentionally destroyed several things on a nearby display shelf. A framed photo of Will's kids was on the floor, the glass cracked. An etched copper vase had rolled across the floor and settled at the base of the window. Papers placed on one end of the shelf scattered across the floor.

Hyrum stood in the center of the room, his fingers tied up in his t-shirt, and he wailed. Snot dripped from his nose which made him sniff, but he cried as hard as I had ever heard him cry. Part of his anguish was seeing the destruction he had wrought, but most of it was because Goober—I didn't bother to ask his name; I only knew that he was a chemical engineer who hadn't been employed at Ozoo very long—had grabbed Hyrum's sketch pad and crayons, holding them out of his reach as he taunted him over his choice of break time activity.

He dropped the s-word.

As Hyrum flailed and threw his shoes, he growled—it came from his soul—*I'm not stupid. I'm not!* Though to be fair, Goober had called the use of crayons in conjunction with the activity stupid and had not said that of Hyrum.

On long days, Will's office was Hyrum's sanctuary. He'd learned that when he felt anxious, he needed to step back and get away from whatever project he was working on. This week his tasks included inputting data gathered from research into a more conductive gel, and when he realized he had couldn't make sense of the information and thought it was written down incorrectly, something that it would take several hours to fix, he realized he needed time away from the computer, and time to decompress.

Goober, on the other hand, wanted the finished file twenty minutes ago, and left the lab to find Hyrum. And he did, quite easily. Hyrum was sprawled out on Will's floor, right where his private portal could be activated, and he was drawing a picture of the things he saw out the window. To one side of the paper stood the Golden Gate Bridge, with choppy water underneath and several surfers riding waves.

He was getting good, even with crayons. He paid attention when Jay described how to blend colors, how to highlight, and what to put onto paper first. The people he drew were no longer simple stick-figures but fully fleshed with facial features and the correct number of fingers on each hand. The act of drawing soothed him, so Will kept paper, pencils, and crayons on hand, and Hyrum was allowed to use his office any time he needed it.

Now, I could have ended things before they blew up. The moment Goober stomped into the office and began berating Hyrum for leaving before the job was finished, I could have growled and distracted him. When he bent over and snatched the paper off the floor, I could have used my claws to climb his leg—taking no care to be gentle—and made him drop the pad. When he swiped the crayon out of Hyrum's mouth I could have bitten him. But I did none of those things, choosing instead to let Hyrum deal with the sanctimonious blowhard himself.

I could always inflict damage later, if Hyrum was unable to handle it.

Goober didn't stop there, however. Once Hyrum had gotten to his feet, picking bits of blue crayon from his lips, Goober decided to launch into a lecture on work ethics and keeping one's ass in the chair until the work was completed. Even then, as Hyrum's eyes reddened, I thought I should stay out of it. He needed a chance to explain.

When the words, "You're worthless if you're not going to work," rolled off his tongue, I stood and felt the furs on my tail fluff. This was something worthy of treating a part of Goober's body to a toothy death. "You're not fucking five years old, Hyrum. What the hell makes you think running off to *color* is all right? This—" he waved the paper "—is *stupid.*"

I was ready to launch, but then so was Hyrum. He kicked at the coffee table and turned it onto its side, and when Goober laughed, things on the shelf went flying. "I'm not stupid! Give me back my stuff!"

"Not a fucking chance." Goober held the paper just out of Hyrum's reach. "Come on, Nancy, you're gonna cry?"

That's exactly what Hyrum did. He latched onto his pink t-shirt and cried.

Goober twitched—*oh, I should not have done that, I* really *should not have done that*—and I sat down.

Cat ears, you know.

He knew he shouldn't have done that, yet on he went.

"You want this back? You can have it after you do your damned job. Go finish inputting that data or I fucking swear I'll—"

Will's voice boomed through the open door before he had even reached it. "Or what?"

Hyrum began spinning, his eyes on the damage he'd inflicted upon Will's things, and apologies poured from him before Goober had a chance to register the enormity of the stupidities he had just committed.

"Will, I didn't mean to, I'm sorry, I promise I'll clean it up," Hyrum sputtered.

Will barely glanced at the papers now scattered across the floor and instead focused on Goober. "Explain."

"We'll be a day behind on the gel project now, thanks to him. He just got up and left, the information isn't compiled correctly, and he needs to get his ass back—"

Hyrum bounced on his toes, knees bending the way they did when he was close to breaking down. "Stuff didn't look right and it's gonna take all day and I just needed—"

"You need to get back and finish," Goober said. He still had Hyrum's paper in hand, though he was no longer holding it where Hyrum couldn't reach it.

He called Hyrum 'worthless,' and 'Nancy,' and said his coloring was stupid. Hyrum thought he was being called stupid. That's when he kicked the coffee table over.

Will took the pad of paper from Goober and handed it back to Hyrum. "Are you all right?"

He couldn't make himself look up. "I just needed a break for a little while. I was gonna go back."

"We're getting behind," Goober seethed.

Instead of acknowledging Goober's irritation, Will took a step closer to Hyrum and gestured to the picture. "You're getting quite good, Hyrum. I can almost hear the waves crashing against the rocks. Did you see any surfers wipe out today?"

Sniffing, he nodded. "They're trying really hard."

Will pointed to a smudge near the bridge. "What's this?"

"It was gonna be a boat but then he took my paper away and then he took my blue crayon but I promise I didn't mean to eat it." He clenched his front teeth together. "Do I got any on my teeth?"

There were flecks on his bottom lip but none on his teeth, and it was while Will used a napkin to wipe Hyrum's lip clean that the lightbulb went off over Goober's head and he realized that he had stepped into a giant steaming pile of Blackshear shit.

"What was the problem with work today?" Will asked Hyrum, gently.

The numbers were off, Hyrum explained. He didn't know how but he knew they weren't right and had maybe been written down in the wrong order, but he wasn't sure what order they needed to be in. He knew everything had to be exactly right and he felt fuzzy, so he decided he needed to color for a bit and let his brain think about it while he wasn't paying attention, and then maybe he could make sense of it.

"Who gave you the data?"

Hyrum glanced at Goober but didn't answer.

"There's nothing wrong with the data he was given," Goober said. "A ten-year-old could manage the data entry."

I'm thirty seconds away from biting him.

Just so you know. Fair warning and all that.

"We'll see about that." Will set Hyrum's pad of paper on the sofa and then gestured to the door, an invitation to get the hell out of his office. I scrambled up his leg to get to his shoulder—there was no way I was missing this—and reminded him to tell Hyrum he didn't need to stay behind to clean up. It would be there later, and he was needed in the lab to show Will the written notes Goober had given him.

The lab's main office was most definitely not my favorite place to be. There was a peculiar odor hanging in the air, the collective aroma of unwashed gym socks and cherry-scented candles overlaid with bubblegum. I wasn't sure if it was because of the people working in the lab or because there were misguided attempts to mask the odor of the gels being worked on, but I found it unpleasant and would rather breathe in Drew's armpit sweat.

Hyrum's desk was tucked into a corner near the entry to the room where Drew did most of his experiments on the gel. He had his own computer, placed so that he could see everyone else in the lab and what they were doing; not far from where he worked most days was room seven, the spot where, in fourteen years, a tiny cat who mistook the room designation to be his name would take the first steps into becoming me.

Hyrum, however, didn't know that. He did know his own computer and how it was set up, and he knew in an instant someone had been moving things around on it.

Goober shrugged. "I was looking for the notes."

"Well, I don't leave them out on account of they might get lost," Hyrum said, stopping just short of snapping. He slipped behind the desk and sat, then unlocked the lower drawer and pulled out a stack of papers that he handed to Will. "This is them. I remember what the numbers looked like on the last time Drew played with the gel, and it's not the same."

Goober let out an exasperated huff. "It's a different analysis run. Of *course* the numbers are different."

"And yet," Will mused as he shifted through the pages, "the differences should be minute."

"Page three," Hyrum said, standing to peer over Will's shoulder. "The vis-something-or-other didn't seem right. And when I got to page five it was like someone added numbers wrong. Like when I tried to do times with thirteen and nine but Rhys burped and made me giggle, so I got the answer wrong."

Goober's face pinched.

"Viscosity," Will murmured. "It expresses the magnitude of internal friction—"

"Stickiness. I know what it is, Will, I just couldn't think of the word."

"Apologies. However, you are correct." He flipped the pages back and thrust them toward Goober. "Your math is wrong, and your table is skewed. Start over."

"You're taking the word of a—"

"Tread very carefully," Will warned. "Hyrum has sufficient seniority over you that if he chose to, he could end your employment on the spot."

"He could fire me."

That caused a tiny gasp to escape Hyrum. "No! I don't want him to get fired. He just needs to say sorry."

"A reprieve, then," Will said. "Make no mistake, I will not tolerate any additional abuse of your coworkers. If Hyrum chooses to take his break time in my office, he is welcome to. If he deems the time necessary, accept it and wait for your data, or complete the entries yourself."

"That's his *job*..."

"No. His job is to assist Andrew and to a lesser degree, me. That he undertakes the compilation of notes and turns them into data files is doing you and every other engineer here a favor. He is not your minion. He is also not replaceable, whereas you are."

In a blink, Goober understood: his extremely lucrative paycheck was on the line.

To drive the point home, I growled at him.

Just a little bit.

Hyrum reached up and took me off Will's shoulder. "Wick, you gotta be nice. People make mistakes when they're new."

Yeah, well, he still called you things he shouldn't have.

I've decided his name is Goober.

"No, his name is Nancy. I heard it in Will's office."

Goober's face clenched again. "What?"

"All right, then, Nancy," Will said as he reached for me. "Hyrum has deemed an apology to be sufficient. However, there's a mess in my office to be cleaned, and you have approximately fifteen minutes before my wife and children will be here. So."

Nancy Goober scuttled off, both relieved and about as pissed off as I'd ever seen someone.

"His name isn't really Nancy," Hyrum snickered.

It's not Goober, either, but it fits.

We can call him that, right?

"We will not," Will said. "And if he doesn't apologize soon, Hyrum, I want to know."

"Okay. I'll fix this before I go home."

He would not stay to fix it; Will thought it was something that could wait until morning, and if Goober wanted it sooner, he could do it himself. "Aisha and I are taking the kids to the playground and then out for dinner, if you would like to join us."

Hyrum had other plans. He might have been chewing on crayons earlier, but he was meeting Drew and Sean McAllister for pizza and maybe a drink, but first they were riding their bikes up and down the Embarcadero.

Got your basket on your bike?

He nodded. "I brought my lunch today so I needed it."

Mind if I tag along then? I want to see Drew throw up when you out-bike him.

"Maybe I'll let him win."

"Never," Will said as he headed for the lobby, "let Andrew win. His victories should be well earned."

Hyrum skipped a few steps, trying to catch up. "But he lets me win sometimes. I know he does even though he says he doesn't."

"He truly does not let you win as often as you might suppose."

His brain is too full of things. When he's playing a game he's not focused just on that.

"Indeed. But also consider that Andrew doesn't ride nearly as often as you do, and he'll know if you let him win. His ego might not accept that."

"I don't know what that means."

His feelings might be hurt.

"Oh. Oh! I don't want to do that."

Goober stepped out of the office as we approached, looking none too happy to see us again. He'd straightened out the mess, set the papers on the coffee table, and the broken picture frame was on Will's desk. His consideration in that earned him a point; he'd placed it there because Will had said his children would be here soon, and he didn't want them to get their hands on it.

"A moment, Mr. Gifford," Will said, gesturing toward the lobby. He and Hyrum dutifully followed to the display case against the wall between the elevators, something Will wanted Goober Gifford to see.

"Air gear," Goober said. "I see this every day."

"Specifically, this is the HCB AFMB chest plate. It is, without a doubt, an engineering feat. This containment system is responsible for saving Prince Andrew's life while stranded outside Elysium. It was a last-minute addition to his suit, and there isn't a single member of the royal family who isn't grateful— eternally grateful—for its design and implementation."

"I understand its importance—"

"Do you understand its designation? For whom the HCB stands?"

He'd never given it any thought. Until that moment, he hadn't given it much more than a cursory glance, though he had tucked into the back of his mind the notion that he would inquire about it once he was more settled in his position with Ozoo.

"HCB. Hyrum Charles Blackshear. This is his concept, his design. Even when Drew's team refuted the possibility that it could be done, Hyrum insisted. He knew what he wanted it to do, had a notion of how it could function, and refused to give up until they understood what he wanted them to create."

Goober turned his head to see Hyrum. "You did this?"

"Kinda. I had lotsa help."

"Others took his idea and extrapolated his intentions into a final product. So understand, Mr. Gifford, when Hyrum decides to take a break, he is fully entitled to every minute he chooses. For that matter, anyone employed in this facility is encouraged to step away from their tasks if they need to. We would prefer a delay over mistakes created by fatigue. So if your data isn't compiled by the end of the day, tomorrow is sufficient. Or the day after. Simply keep your supervisor in the loop."

"So noted." He was more interested in Hyrum than Will. "What gave you the idea? And how did you figure out how to store enough oxygen in this to last as long as it did? It looks like it would store ten, maybe fifteen minutes."

Hyrum's eyes lit up. "Oh! I thought maybe we could use tubes like the stuff for fish tanks but make them flatter and closer together. And then I thought, okay, if he started breathing it the air might leak out, so I thought he could have a switch or something, and the nanobots could be the one to work the switch on account of Drew had other things to do."

"That accounts for operation. But storage?"

"Well, the nanobots could only let a tiny bit of air out at a time if they had to. So I thought maybe Drew could have a thingy in his helmet that held onto the air he breathes out, and it could go through a filter that took the bad things out, so that when the nanobots added real air, it would be okay. And that would make it last for a while. There's a tiny computer that lets the nanobots work, and it had all the stuff that said, 'time to do this' and 'time to do that' so that instead of just a few minutes of air, he had lots."

"You did this," Goober marveled.

"Well, like I said, I had lots of help. I didn't know all the right words to tell Drew what I wanted, but they all figured it out." He had more to say, but Aisha opened the door and held it for the kids. Hyrum's distracted squeal meant the conversation was over, and he skipped to them, leaving Will and me with Goober.

"Treat him like an adult," Will warned. "He has a deep need to play and often lacks the vocabulary necessary to express himself, but he is not a child. Grant him the respect you do your other colleagues, and you'll do well here."

I had a gut feeling that Goober treated everyone the way he had Hyrum, but that could sort itself out. He left, and Will turned his attention to his family.

Alex, dressed in a frosted blue gown with a disturbing number of pleats and half the lace in existence, ran to him. "Daddy, I'm a princess!"

He lifted her up for a kiss, spinning her around once. "I can see that."

Apparently, so is Charlie.

Will set his daughter down and crouched so that he was at their height. "And what are you?"

Charlie wore one of Alex's leotards, a bright red set, with a blue satin skirt. "I'm pretty."

"Indeed. Are you a ballerina today?"

"Nuh-uh. Just pretty."

He looked at Rhys, who was in jeans and a dark blue sweatshirt. "You didn't dress up for me?"

With an air of seriousness, he replied, "Well, Alex wanted me to wear her Cinderella costume, but it didn't fit. So I told her that no one should be prettier than the princess, but if she wanted I could be her bodyguard. My guards wear sweatshirts, so..." He tugged on his shirt. "This is it."

Hyrum bounced on his toes. "We should get you a prince costume!"

With a heavy sigh, Rhys nodded. "Sure."

"Oh! Oh! Oh! We can get it at Disneyland! We should go again!"

All four turned to Will, which made Aisha laugh.

"Oh, hon, you won't be able to find a reason to say no. Let's check the calendar when we get home and we can schedule something."

"We were *just* there," Will reminded her. "Two weeks ago. That's reason enough."

Charlie opened his mouth to say something; he probably had several reasons to go regardless of how long it had been, but Rhys tapped his arm, a clear message: Let Mommy handle this. She's on our side.

"It's a one hour shuttle ride away. We can limit them to two days. And consider it, Will. Wear them out, then have drinks by the pool. Hell, *in* the pool. Swim right up to the bar, do shots. We'll take Jay and make him watch the kids."

"Daddy, please?" Alex asked.

Dude, I said to Hyrum, *we're going to Disneyland.*

~

Spoiler.

I did not go to Disneyland.

Instead, after a couple weeks of listening to Will and Aisha ponder how to handle their three kids, plus Marco, plus Isaac—because what's the fun for Rhys if his best friend isn't there, and it would be cruel to go without Marco—while assuring that Thor wasn't stuck in a hotel room, even if it was only for one night, I decided to stay home and dog sit.

Being in the park isn't a lot of fun for me, anyway. I'll stay home and make sure Thor gets fed on time and walked and I'll play with him.

"How you gonna open his food cans?" Rhys was suddenly anxious and concerned enough to not want to go. "He'll pee on the balcony if he has to, but you can't open cans. And someone needs to feed you, too."

I'll ask Drew to help. In fact, Thor and I will sleep in Oz and Drew's room, and we'll go to work with Drew. Thor will enjoy seeing Ozoo.

"Uncle Jax and Aunt Aubrey will help, too," Aisha reminded him. "They watched him the last time we went."

Rhys bounced on his toes. "But what if—"

"The alternative is bringing Thor with us but leaving him alone in the hotel room for hours at a time. Which choice is fairer to Thor?"

With me, he gets to play, little dude. And when we go to Ozoo, we can park in front of the window in your dad's office and watch people play on the beach. I bet we can even talk Drew into taking Thor for a walk on the beach.

"But he's my 'sponsibily.'"

Sometimes being a responsible carer means leaving them at home where they're safe and not bored. It's not like you're leaving him alone. He has me, Jax, Aubrey, Drew, Oz, Zed, and Sophia.

"They'll take good care of him," Will promised. "Would you like me to call Drew?"

Rhys considered it. "I should ask him. Thor is my dog. But if he says no, then I can't go because I promised I would always take care of him."

Ask Aubrey if Drew says no. Then ask Jax.

"Okay, but then I have to stay home. Okay?"

Without Mom and Dad?

"Wick," he sighed, as if I weren't thinking clearly, "if I stay home Aunt Aubrey will watch me. I can sleep in Hyrum's room."

Second spoiler.

Drew did not say no. He came upstairs to let Rhys show him where Thor's food was, where his leash hung, and he took notes regarding his walk and play schedule, and Rhys reminded him that Thor would sleep better if he was allowed on the bed. It was only after that, along with Drew's promise that he would call if there was even a moment where he thought Thor was upset, that Rhys decided it was all right for him to go.

They left in a rented high-speed air van at seven in the morning, and at seven-thirty Drew realized—with a fair amount of horror—that Hyrum's trip to the House of Mouse meant that he had to drive himself to work. He couldn't jog to Ozoo because he'd promised to take Thor, and Thor was not ready to run that many miles. He picked at his breakfast, trying to think of reasons to work from home, muttering to himself about it until Oz finally huffed, "Oh, for fork's sake, I'll drive you. You can't stay home. You have three people expecting to meet with you today."

She did not say fork.

He reasoned that they could do it over a video call, so unless she needed to be at her office, too, he could work from home.

"Feed the dog, feed the cat, get your shit together, and let's go, Drew."

Being somewhat intelligent, he fed Thor, fed me, got his shit together, and went.

After we entered the building—and the security guards had been asked to make sure no one let us out—Drew reminded me to stay out of peoples' ways, absolutely do not enter any room with a red door, let him know if Thor needed out or needed anything in general, and most importantly, do not walk across anyone's keyboard.

"Don't walk across them, don't plop your furry little ass down on one."

But they're warm.

"Wick."

Fine. Where can we run? Thor will need to run.

Drew pointed to an entryway just past the display of Hyrum's air-filled man boobs. "Just watch out, all right? It's a long hall and you can get some decent speed in it, but people might pop out of doors. Don't knock anyone over."

"Good boy."

Thor padded his way to Will's office. The number one item on his list of things-to-do-today was to sit at the giant window and watch the world go by. Unlike the first workshop Will and Drew had, we weren't close enough to the street for people to see us, so no one stopped to wave or tell us how beautiful we were. I felt a bit bad for Thor because of that; he loved people, especially people who gushed, "What a good boy! What a pretty boy!" and he didn't mind at all if someone called him a good girl.

"Good boy."

That's right. It doesn't matter. Unless you want a girlfriend, and it might matter to her.

"Good boy?"

Preferences are preferences, dude. But I imagine if you found another dog you felt that strongly about and the affection was returned, neither of you would care.

"Good boy?"

Just like who you like, that's all. You'd have to actually meet another dog, though.

"Good boy, good boy!"

No, Lux is like a brother. He's like Jax is to Will.

"Good boy!"

Fine, all right, I'm like your brother, too. Your much wiser older brother.

"Good boy."

Yeah, sure, fine, you're prettier.

"Good boy? Good boy, good boy."

He wanted to see things he hadn't seen before. Thor occasionally visited Will at work, but he was typically taken in a straight line from the door to the office, and his view of Ozoo was just this and Drew's office. And the views from the windows in each office were the same.

There was a short hallway connecting their offices to the lobby, and as we made our way out a security guard near the door twitched in our direction and pointed. We were not getting outside, not while he was watching. I stopped and sat, staring at him, my only intention to make him a tiny bit nervous about my plans.

Thor's tail thumped against the floor, a dull thud made louder by the height of the lobby and how easily things echoed. He wiggled a bit, not wanting to sit as still as I was, having no idea what I was doing. I let the guard stare a moment longer and then turned around, leading Thor into the giant workspace and over to Hyrum's desk.

There were red doors here, rooms in which we were not allowed. I reminded Thor of that and he grunted, but I wasn't sure he could see red to begin with.

Just don't go into a room without me. I can see colors I'm not supposed to be able to see.

I jumped onto Hyrum's desk, and Thor stood on his hind legs, front paws resting on the edge.

"Good boy?"

Hyrum works here sometimes. It was super sweet when Drew and Will gave him his own desk. He squealed and hugged everyone and then had to run off because he was so happy, he had to pee.

"Good boy."

Yep, it smells like him.

There were a dozen other desks scattered across the room. Each engineer had their own space to work, and the red door rooms were where they experimented and built things. Near Hyrum's desk was the room where tinkering went on; they built things and tested them, and on special occasions—Reserved for Testing Days, there was a big yellow sign and everything—lasers were fired.

Across the room there was another red door with a giant window. That was the clean room; no one entered in their regular clothes. They had to put coveralls on, booties over their shoes, and giant tented helmets over their heads. Once inside, there was an air blower and sanitizer, and just beyond that a special curtain to keep the cooties at bay.

This was the place Drew worked on nanogel and other nano-projects. From my spot on Hyrum's desk I could see the first tank in which the gel was experimented upon. It was bright red without any shiny things in it, because there were no nanobots in that tank. Someone was standing in front of it, looking at the gauges on the end of a long tube that ran over the top and into the gel, and he was taking notes, scribbling onto a tablet with a data pen.

"Good boy?"

No, It's not Jell-O. You don't want to eat that. I mean, you can, but you wouldn't like it.

Admittedly, Hyrum's desk was about as far as I'd ventured into this room, but as I looked around I noted the numbers above each door. The laser room was 2. Gel room was 1. That meant that two doors down from the place our eyeballs could be fried if we entered at the wrong time was the room where I would eventually be born, and from which young Eli would take me.

I jumped down and Thor followed, curious to see where I was going.

The door was not red, but it was closed. I had no idea what lay behind it, but I felt deeply pressed to go inside, so I stretched on my back legs and pounded my paw against it.

Let me in.

Come on. Open the door. I know you're in there.

"Good boy!"

Sucks, I don't think there's anyone in there. But I really wanted to—

Thor took a few steps back just as I heard footsteps coming toward us. It was Goober, bearing a computer tablet and coffee mug. He stopped short, trying to decide if we belonged there or not.

"Wick, right? You want in there?" He shifted the mug to his other hand and turned the doorknob. "I was going in there anyway. Plenty of room for all of us."

Sharing a room with Goober was not on my day's to-do list, but he was willingly opening the door for us, so I decided to shove aside my distrust for no reason other than I really wanted to see inside.

I remembered what I'd seen on the security recordings at Jo's house, but I didn't actually remember being there and hoped that seeing it for myself would jar something loose. I didn't expect to find the cat tree or litter box that Eli had cleaned out; I hoped the window was there and the shades open so I could see what was on the other side.

But I wanted to remember being there, what those first weeks of my life felt like.

I wanted to see my mother there, to fix into my mind what she looked like. I had no idea.

Goober let us in and braced the door open so that we could leave when we wanted, and he dropped into an armchair near the window. As expected, there was no tree that I would one day climb on. There was a sofa on the wall opposite the chair, and a small desk against the wall just beyond that. Instead of a coffee table there was a small oval rug that Thor plopped down on, his tail thumping against the sofa.

Risking Goober's ire, I jumped to the back of the chair, trying to get a look outside. He understood what I wanted and pulled the curtain back, tucking it out of the way. There was a courtyard outside, with benches and a firepit, the edges trimmed with bright red and yellow and blue flowers.

I've been out there. All the cats were allowed out there.

I pressed my face against the glass and looked up; mesh covered the square opening between the walls. Birds could not get in; cats could not get out. There was a tiny fragment of memory, of darting out the window and down a covered ramp, a chorus of tiny meows greeting me.

I had litter mates.

"Good boy!"

I know you did, too. But you remember yours. You remember your parents. If you wanted to badly enough, Will could arrange for you to see them.

Goober snorted. "If I didn't know better, I'd swear you were talking to each other."

You don't know better, then.

"I don't suppose you know when Hyrum is coming back?" He held the tablet up. "I owe him an apology. He was right. I'm the one who fucked up the data."

You owe him one for more than that.

"I still don't get it. Him, I mean. Is he some sort of untapped genius or just a guy who got lucky with an idea...?"

Yes.

"I was such a fucking asshole to him. I keep trying to tell myself that if someone had warned me that he was developmentally delayed I wouldn't have literally taken away his crayons, but... Yeah, shouldn't have mattered. And yet, I do stupid shit like that all the time."

Oh, I get it. I'm the priest and this is your confession.

Make amends, Goober.

"Good boy!"

Goober bent forward in his chair, reaching out to ruffle Thor's fur. "You have the softest bark of any dog I've ever seen."

He learned to use an inside voice. You're welcome.

After a few minutes of pets, which became tummy rubs when Thor rolled over, Goober sat back and began poring over his work. It seemed like a good chance for a nice nap, so when Thor began breathing softly, I closed my eyes, trying to remember more about the courtyard and the other cats that lounged out there with me.

I woke an hour later, when a soft knock on the door jamb pulled me out of a dream. Drew was there, leaning against the jamb, arms folded, amused.

"There you two are. I thought you'd found a way to make a break for it."

Do not say the w-word, Drew. Thor will go nuts.

"Good boy!"

"Are they always so chatty?" Goober asked. "I felt like I was carrying on a conversation for a while."

"Wick has always been mouthy." Drew came in and sat on the sofa, rubbing Thor's head, right between his ears where he liked it best. "Thor imitates, I think. They weren't bothering you, were they?"

We were not, Goober insisted. He found the lull of Thor's breathing to be soothing, and my tail occasionally flicking against his neck reminded him of the cat he'd grown up with. "He was a birthday present, I think I was five. He was an amazing silver tabby called Jane, followed me around like a puppy and stretched out on the back of my chair while I studied. Flicked my ear the same way Wick is."

"He," Drew repeated.

"He didn't seem offended by the feminine name and he just seemed like a Jane."

What's Goober's real name?

"Any pets now, Christopher?"

"Topher, please. And no. Once I'm settled here, though? Definitely, there will be cats."

And now the awkward pause. You weren't really looking for us, were you?

"Your gel run two weeks ago," Drew started.

Goober—he was still Goober to me, mostly because I enjoyed the name and Will was firm about not calling him Nancy—held his tablet up. "Data is fixed and retests are complete. The last run showed insignificant—"

"I'm not here about the errors or the numbers."

Goober set the tablet aside with a sigh.

"Hyrum covered your ass, you know. Until I viewed the security recording—"

That made Goober sit up straight.

"—I had no idea what you'd done to make him trash the Emperor's office. You took his things, you called him names, and made him feel like complete shit."

"I know. I'm a raging asshole sometimes."

He's already working on his apology.

"That won't fly here, Topher. I don't care how brilliant you are or how hard you were recruited to come here. Treat anyone like that again and you're gone."

He's trying to understand Hyrum. And he actually feels guilty.

He's also kinda young, Drew. His brain isn't done cooking.

"Not gonna lie, I am not always a nice person. But I am trying."

Drew gave him a short nod. "Hyrum will be back on Thursday. If you want his forgiveness, two donuts with chocolate frosting and some ice-cold chocolate milk will go a long way toward that."

"Only two?"

"If you give him more, he'll eat them all at once, and there will be regrets. Probably tears, too, because once his stomach hurts, he'll decide it's punishment for being greedy, and he sees that as a sin."

"Just so you know, had I understood that Hyrum is developmentally delayed—"

"Not how we'd describe him."

"—it wouldn't have made a difference. I'd have still been an asshole. Whatever his issues are, they weren't the reason. Though I wouldn't have inferred stupidity. Even I have limits. I'd kick the shit out of anyone who said that to my little brother."

Drew gave careful consideration before he spoke. "Understand. As far as our family is concerned, there's nothing wrong with Hyrum. We don't view him as disabled or delayed, or any other label you might stick him with. He's just Hyrum, and he has his strengths and weaknesses, the same as everyone else. He deals with his through play, and we strongly encourage that."

Tell him about the volleyball games.

He sucked in a deep breath, as if he were thinking deep thoughts, even though I knew better. "He's not alone in that, you know. Even notice how your colleagues seem to vanish at the same time? You look up from your desk, and they're just gone?"

"At random times. I've noticed."

"Most of the time you'll find them on the grassy strip between the street and the beach. Usually they knock out a game or two of volleyball, but sometimes they just toss a disc around, or even just take their lunch out there. Play is a stress release, and everyone is welcome to take the breaks they need. It's good for your mental health."

He probably hasn't been invited.

"Don't wait for an invitation," Drew went on. "Just go. You don't have to play with them but showing interest...you might find that assholish edge softening."

"Good boy!"

Drew patted Thor's head. "In a minute, big guy."

"I'm getting along with everyone for the most part," Goober said.

"Good to know." Drew started to get up, but Goober wasn't done.

"I am curious about Hyrum, though. The Emperor tells me the reserve air pack was his idea and design. He knew at a glance my data was wrong, even if he didn't know why. How?"

"He's not weighed down by the things that should or shouldn't work and since he knows we won't make fun of him and will listen to his ideas, he thinks out loud. It takes him time to give his ideas structure, but he's open to suggestions—as long as he's taken seriously. That air reserve was scoffed at by more than one engineer here. On paper it shouldn't have worked. But the seed of his idea and how hard he fought for it?"

"It germinated."

"He doesn't know how it works, exactly, but he understood how he intended it to function. With your data? He's seen the worksheets and he's used the software enough to hear warning bells go off when something doesn't seem right. But he isn't always sure what the problem is."

"So, like anyone else."

"Like anyone else." Pushing up off his legs, Drew got up. "Come on, furballs. Let's go for a—"

Don't say it!

"—walk."

Thor sprang up and began hopping on his back legs, pawing at Drew with his front, barking louder than he had when he was trying to join the conversation. Drew knew better; you never say the word, you spell it. We all knew that.

Goober apparently knew that, too, and he laughed as we headed out.

~

Thursday morning there was a little brown bag on Hyrum's desk, and along with it a bowl filled with ice, holding two cartons of chocolate milk. In big black block letters was a message on the bag: HYRUM, I AM SO SORRY FOR HOW I TREATED YOU, TOPHER.

Hyrum tilted his head as he read it, his eyebrows knotting together.

"Who's Topher?"

Goober.

The guy who was mean to you in Will's office.

This is his peace offering.

He peeked into the bag, eyebrows relaxing as he broke into a big grin. "Donuts! And they're the good kind!"

Chocolate milk, too.

Hyrum snatched up the bag and the milk. "I gotta say thank you. Where is he?"

Room seven, probably. He likes to sit there while he goes through his notes.

He didn't even make it inside the room before he squealed, "Topher, thank you! These are my favorites!"

Goober was in the chair by the window. He'd been staring at his tablet, but set it on his lap, and this time he greeted Hyrum with a smile. "I had inside information. But I'm glad it made you happy. And I mean it, I am sorry."

"Sorry makes it better. You want one? I'll share."

Goober did not want a donut. He claimed to have eaten a shamefully large breakfast that would take most of the day to digest and wanted Hyrum to have both.

"Okay. Thank you." He bounced once on his toes. "Oh. I should take these to Will's office. I'm not supposed to eat at my desk on account of one time I spilled root beer on it and the computer made all kinds of noises. And then I got a new one. A computer, I mean, not a desk. I cleaned the desk really good."

"We've all been there." Goober gestured to the sofa. "Food is allowed in here."

"Food is allowed everywhere but the red door rooms," Hyrum said as he sat. "The no eating at the desk is just for me. But it's not a rule or anything. Drew just said it was a good idea to not eat there on account of computers aren't supposed to burp."

"No one should eat at their desks," Goober said, picking up the tablet. "Everyone thinks they're careful enough, but we've all spilled at one time or another."

"Even you?"

He nodded. "My first real job out of college, I spilled a cup of water onto a system terminal and shorted out some terrifyingly expensive equipment. I was panicked, thinking that I'd lose the job over it, but my supervisor shrugged it off and said he'd turned over a mug of coffee onto a schematic illustration that took weeks to draw by hand. It happens."

"It happens to me a lot," Hyrum chuckled.

Goober tapped the screen on his tablet. "I have fifteen data runs to process. If you have time today, would you show me how to use the propriety software? It's vastly different than what I'm used to."

"Is that why the numbers were out of place?" Hyrum asked as he bit into a donut.

"Most likely."

"That's okay. When Drew and Will were teaching me how to use it I made lots of mistakes. But they showed me how to fix them. They didn't even just fix it themselves. They let me do it."

"You do a lot around here, don't you?"

"Kinda. At first, I washed a lot of jars. Drew is *really* picky about how clean his jars are."

"What happens if they're not clean enough?"

Hyrum gave a light shrug. "He just says 'Dude, you gotta clean them again. I see smudges.' So then I clean them again, on account of that's what I said I'd do."

"He's very patient with you, isn't he?"

"Uh huh. So's Will and Jax and Aubrey and Oz and everyone at home."

"Must have been nice to grow up that way."

He shrugged again. "I dunno. I didn't move here until I was forty-two. My daddy was really mean. And my mom, I dunno. I never got to have any fun and Daddy took my toys away when I was twenty-two, I think."

"I promise, I will never do that again. I thought you were just goofing off, but that isn't a good reason."

"You said sorry. Do I got any chocolate on my face? I get it on me sometimes."

There were smears of frosting on his chin and cheeks, but all he managed to do with a napkin was push it around a bit. Goober took a clean one and dabbed water on it, then told Hyrum to tilt his head back a little. He would help.

Goober, to my surprise, was gentle and tender, and seemingly quite practiced in helping another adult wipe food off his face without making it seem weird.

He's done this before.

Ask him if he ever helps anyone else.

"Do you know someone like me?" Hyrum asked.

Goober weighed his answer. He sat back down, using the pretense of picking his tablet up again to give him another moment to think. "You remind me of my little brother," he finally said. "I think you're more mature and more capable of taking care of things by yourself, but yes. A bit like him."

The idea excited Hyrum. "Can I meet him? What's his name?"

"His name is Riley. Right now, he lives in Montana with our parents, but when he visits, I'd be happy to introduce you."

"Does he visit a lot?"

"Not yet. I've only been here a few weeks myself. To be honest, since my thoughtless action the other day, I've been thinking about him a lot. Maybe trying to get him to move here to live with me."

Hyrum had no idea what to say about that.

Do the parents not want him?

"Won't that make your mom mad?" Hyrum asked.

It probably would, but Goober thought it might be worth the fight. "Our parents have never allowed him any kind of freedom. He's never had a job—working here makes you happy, doesn't it?"

"I like working here. I also work on Alcatraz with Zed sometimes. And I get to ride my bike that Santa gave me wherever I want!"

Riley couldn't ride a bike; he'd never been given the chance. He had a tricycle when he was small, but it wasn't replaced when he outgrew it. He'd gone to school until he was twelve, but there was never an academic element to his education. School was merely a place to send him for a few hours a day, mostly to give their parents a break.

"But I bet he liked it," Hyrum ventured. "I went to school when I got here and I had fun even though I didn't learn a lot on account of I knew that stuff already."

"He loved it. I wish they hadn't stopped sending him. The thing is, I think if someone took the time to teach him, he'd be every bit as capable as you."

"Maybe your mom and daddy would let him come so they can have time alone," Hyrum mused. "My mom didn't think I would want to live here forever but she saw how much better I like it here and she stopped fighting my sister about me. Now she's even happy that Eli adopted me."

"King Eli?"

"Uh huh. He's my daddy now and he loves me."

"Doesn't that make your sister your sister-in-law, too?"

Hyrum giggled. "She's lots of things. She's my teacher when I want to learn about new things. But she stopped teaching me fractions on account of I hate them."

"Well, who wouldn't?"

"They're minuses," Hyrum sighed. "I can already do minuses."

"How do you feel about decimals?"

"I don't know what that is but if it's like fractions, I'm not gonna do them."

"I'll remember that."

Hyrum wadded up the now-empty donut bag and dropped it into a nearby trashcan and got up. "I gotta get back to work. But when you want me to show you that program, I will."

"Couple hours," Goober said, picking the tablet up again.

Hyrum hesitated at the door. "I like that you don't pretend about me. Lots of people here do, on account of they don't want to hurt my feelings. But I know I don't know a lot and it's okay. I hope you get your brother, because I needed my sister and I didn't even know that."

I lingered for a minute.

"Wick, if I ever...feel free to growl at me."

I'm sure I will.

I'm a biter, too, just so you know.

He went back to work, and I headed out to help Hyrum. I don't think I ever had to growl at Goober again.

But then I met his parents.

~

Kyle and Julie Gifford arrived at Ozoo's main door two weeks later with a quiet and anxious Riley. They waited in the lobby for Goober to join them, and I watched from a ledge near Hyrum's AFMB display. Kyle Gifford was short and stocky, his dark hair long enough to tuck behind his ears, and he dressed in faded, worn jeans and beat up work boots, his too-large black t-shirt tucked in neatly. Julie Gifford was taller though not by much; she was dressed similarly to her husband, but instead of well-worn woot boots she wore bright red tennis shoes and clutched a red cross-body purse to her side.

No one was grabbing that purse, not if she had anything to do with it.

Riley was a thinner version on Goober; his hair was neatly trimmed and carefully combed; his jeans were not faded but nearly new with a carefully pressed crease down each leg. His hands were jammed into his pockets and stayed there even as he bounded his way to the display case.

He examined every inch of that chest plate as he could without taking his hands out of his pockets and his breath fogged the thick acrylic surrounding it. I watched him, noting how his eyes clicked back and forth, eyebrows knotted and then unfurled, and braced myself when he sucked in a heavy breath, because years with toddlers taught me that the next thing to happen would be loud.

"Dad come look and see what Topher talked about!" His voice boomed in the lobby, loud enough to make the security guard twitch. "It got shiny on it!"

Dad did not come over to see the chest plate. "Inside voice, cowboy," he said, glancing over. His focus was mainly fixated on the archway that led into the lab's office, where he'd been told Goober would come from.

Be as excited as you want. It's okay.

Riley heard me and broke into a wide grin. "A kitty! Hi, kitty!"

Still, his hands stayed in his pockets.

Let me guess. You were told to keep your hands in your pockets and not touch anything. You can touch the case. It won't break.

Riley looked over his shoulder. "Mom, look, there's a kitty and he's talking to me!"

Will heard Riley from his office and ventured down the hall to see if there was a problem. No one was manhandling me and I was calm, so he quickly decided all was well.

"His name is Wick," Will told Riley. "He's quite friendly and enjoys being petted as long as your touch is soft."

He did not take his hands out. "Hi, Wick," he said, this time quietly. "I'm Rocko."

I thought your name was Riley.

Will picked me up. "Wick is happy to meet you, Rocko."

I'm sure Will had more to say, but Goober came out of the office and we suddenly did not exist. Rocko's hands finally came out of his pockets and he launched at his brother, grabbing him in a Hyrum-worthy hug that involved arms and legs and quite a bit of hopping.

While Goober's family hugged, Will returned me to the ledge and was about to head back to his office, but the parents were looking at him expectantly, so Goober made the introduction.

"Emperor, these are my parents, Kyle and Julie. Mom—"

Julie dropped into a hard curtsy and Kyle was about to bow, but Goober caught his arm.

"Thank you, but that's not necessary," Will said, amused. "'Emperor' is merely a nickname in my case, not a title."

Well, you technically are the King's brother, so…

Neither one had a clue how to address him.

So, what. They call you 'Prince William' or what?

"Please, just address me as—"

"Emperor," Goober cut in. "It might not be a title, but it is the name you've known him by for the last thirty-five years."

"Well. Now I feel old," Will said. "Enjoy your day, Mr. Gifford. Wick, you can follow me."

I *could* follow him into the main office, where Hyrum was reading numbers on his computer screen, but I remained on the little ledge where I could snoopervise Goober and his parents. Once Will was out of sight, the level of anxiety ratcheted up several notches, and Rocko's hands went right back into his pockets.

"Cut to it." Kyle's voice was calm yet hard, and he was not happy to see his older son. "This is it, isn't it? We've expected it since you took this job. Now that you have money—you brought us here to take your brother from us."

"Dad."

"We knew it wasn't just an invitation to see San Francisco. I told your mother, I told her. Once you left for that job in North Dakota, I told her, 'Julie, that kid is coming for Riley sooner or later. He never did care for the way we raised them.'"

"That's not true," Goober said. "And this is not the place."

"It will *never* be the place," Julie hissed.

Goober's hands went to his hips and he sighed, watching Rocko sway slightly from the balls of his feet to his heels as he gathered his thoughts. "I'm not trying to take him from you. I want to help make his life better."

That was not what Kyle wanted to hear. "Nothing wrong with his life. Nothing. We do the best we can for him."

"I know. I agree."

"Then what's your problem, Toph?"

"Your lives, all of yours, could be better. Move here, and Riley can go back to school. Work. He'd—"

"I'm Rocko!"

"Sorry, kiddo. Rocko."

Julie seemed to soften a tiny bit, but Kyle looked like he was just getting started. "School and work? You know better. That boy will never be any better than he is, and you know it. He's as mature as he's ever going to get. He'll never be smart enough and he sure as *shit* will never live on his own. That boy is *broken*. What do you expect—"

The thing about the way sound carried in the lobby is that is also carried into the offices. I heard the footsteps before Goober did and expected Will to stomp out, angry and filled with a million things he wanted to say about broken people, but the steps were softer and hesitated at the entryway.

"Hi," Hyrum said, almost shyly. "Is everything okay? I'm Hyrum. I work with Topher. He's really nice, he brought me donuts and chocolate milk, and yesterday we had brownies together. Drew says he's trying to fatten me up, even though I already eat a lot and never get bigger."

Goober's parents had no idea what to say.

"You work with Topher," Julie said after a few beats.

Defiance dripped from Goober's voice. "Technically, he's my superior."

"And he's..."

"He reminds me very much of my brother." Goober turned to Hyrum. "This is Riley, my little brother. He likes to be called Rocko."

"Oh! I been wanting to meet you!" Hyrum gushed.

Rocko pulled his hands out of his pockets and I assumed he was going to shake Hyrum's hands, but he went right for the hug and Hyrum gave it as good as he got.

When they parted, Goober pointed to the chest plate. "Rocko, this is the piece of Prince Andrew's space suit I told you about. Hyrum designed it."

"I had lots of help," Hyrum said.

"It has air!" Rocko shouted. "Lots and lots of air!"

"It also has tiny computer thingies. Do you want to see where I work? And I can show you where your brother does lots of work, too."

Julie looked to Goober, the unasked question, *Is this safe?*

"Just the office, okay?" he said to Hyrum.

"Okay. There's lots to see through the windows!" He reached for Rocko's hand. "Let's hold hands so you don't get lost, okay?"

Kyle didn't take his eyes off Rocko until he was through the entry to the office.

"He never holds hands," Julie murmured.

"He's excited," Goober pointed out.

Kyle wanted to know about Hyrum. How could he be Goober's superior when he was more interested in donuts and brownies. Someone's boss, when meeting parents, would point out the work they were doing, not...snacks.

Snacks were how Goober was bonding with not only Hyrum, but others in the office. He did as Drew suggested; he began reaching out instead of waiting, and he asked them to call him on his bullshit. In two weeks, he'd brought baked goods five times, enough for everyone. He was beginning to follow others outside, even if he only sat on the sidelines to watch and enjoy the fresh air.

He was still an asshole at least twice a day. He caught himself more often than that and stepped away from his own attitude. But the effort was noticeable, and much of it was directed at being kinder to Hyrum.

Goober gestured to the display. "He's earned his place here. I haven't, not yet. And before you ask, yes. He's exactly how you presume."

"Like Riley," Julie said.

"He's what Riley could be, if you just give him a freaking chance."

He did not say freaking.

~

Goober Gifford's dad is about to have a stroke right out there in the lobby.

"I hear them," Will said. "It's none of our business."

They're kinda making it our business. Maybe you should offer them a room to talk, or something.

"Or I can sit here at Hyrum's desk and keep an eye on him and Rocko."

They were standing in front of the window that led into the gel formulation room. Hyrum bounced on his toes, giggling, while Rocko had one hand plastered against the glass. He yelled "Hello!" to the engineer currently manning a batch of thick, red goo, and when the engineer grinned through his plastic face guard and waved back, they both erupted in loud, squealing laughter.

Hyrum won't let him open a red door.

"Not intentionally, no. We don't know Rocko, however, nor how strong he might be. Hyrum might not be able to stop him."

Rocko was about as big around as Hyrum but lacked the lean muscle that years of bicycling and toddler slinging had given Hyrum. I wasn't worried that he could force Hyrum to do anything; what he could easily do was make Hyrum cry, and I suspected that was why Will watched them closely.

Goober wants Rocko to live with him.

"His name is Christopher. And I am aware."

His name is Goober until I'm convinced that he's not one.

"You still haven't forgiven him for the incident with Hyrum."

I haven't forgotten, let's just leave it at that. And I'm not convinced he wants what's best for Rocko.

"Why not?"

Rocko isn't Hyrum. It might be like expecting Hyrum to be like you. He wants his little brother to be high functioning, and that might not be fair.

"Or he simply wants better options than his brother has in Montana. He clearly offered his parents a place here, as well."

His left ear twitched; he heard Goober's footsteps at the same time I did. I looked up; Will looked at the computer screen, Hyrum's work still on display. The parents followed and while Goober headed across the room to get his brother, they waited a few feet behind us, whispering to each other.

"Give them a night together," Julie suggested. "He'll see. It's not as easy as he thinks."

"A night? Give him a weekend. By the second night he'll beg us to take Riley home."

So which is it? Riley or Rocko? He likes Rocko, you know.

Will reached up and scratched the top of my head. To the Giffords, it looked affectionate. I knew better. He wanted me to shut up.

Will didn't always get what he wanted.

"Maybe the Emperor can convince him to give up the idea. He's got to know what it's like."

Without looking up, Will said, "I understand what life with Hyrum is like. I cannot use that information to determine how life with your son is."

"But he's your brother, right?" she asked. "King Eli adopted you both."

At this, Will turned and then got up to face them. "As adults, yes. But I don't live with Hyrum. He lives with his sister. Even so, Hyrum and Rocko aren't the same person. I can't compare them any more than I can compare Christopher to Prince Andrew."

Kyle picked up where Julie left off. "It's hard, though, isn't it? The constant supervision. The yelling and crying. Never a moment of peace."

Will's sigh said more than his words. He really didn't want to get into it. It wasn't his business, and they weren't listening; Hyrum and Rocko were different people. Since they weren't letting it go, though, he decided to humor them.

"Life with Hyrum isn't like that. He's self-sufficient and if he chose to, he could live on his own. However, that would break the Queen's heart and there isn't a member of the family who would be happy to see him leave."

You would if it were the best thing for him.

"He works here so you can keep an eye on him, right?" Julie asked.

"He works here because he's needed here. Andrew and I value his insight."

At that, Kyle snorted. "Even Topher admits Hyrum used the word 'thingy' a dozen times to explain his air tank. So, what, he makes things up and you just, what, create something to make him think he did it?"

Will folded his arms.

Damn, dude, you pissed him off.

"As with anyone in this facility, we listen to Hyrum's ideas, give him time to flesh them out, and create concepts from those ideas. We do not engage in intellectual subterfuge."

Kyle did not believe him and was probably about to say just that, but Rocko was sprinting across the room squealing "Kitttttty!" while looking right at me.

Goober was hot on his tail, trying to stop him.

"I wanna hold the kitty!" Rocko shouted. He had one arm out, trying to reach me, but Goober grabbed him from behind and the parents barked, "Stop him!" at the same time.

"Kitty cat!"

I took a step back, just in case, but was limited by the surface area of Hyrum's desk.

"Leave the cat alone," Kyle said.

"Kitty!" His voice exploded. "Kitty, kitty, kitty! C'mere, kitty!"

The hairs on my ears twitched. Rocko was as focused as a toddler near a birthday cake and I didn't want to be the frosting he made a grab for. I searched quickly for an escape route; forward put me within his grasp, and there were too many barriers in my way. Backward requiring darting between people, which might give me a second to get ahead.

I stood on all fours, just in case.

"Wick isn't a toy," Goober said to Rocko, trying to tug him back a step or two. "He's tiny. You could hurt him."

"I wanna pet him."

"Not right now."

"He said." Rocko jabbed a finger toward Will. "Said kitty liked it."

"Topher said not right now," Julie said, gently. "Maybe later."

"Nope. Now."

I took that as my cue and bolted from the desk, squeezing between the Giffords on my way to the floor. I needed someplace safe, someplace I could get up too high for anyone to reach me, and the only place I knew for sure was Will's office.

Rocko's footsteps thundered behind me, with Goober and parents right behind, yelling at him to stop. I knew better; he wasn't stopping until he had the kitty in hand, and my gut said it would not be any definition of careful or gentle. I scrambled on the tile floor, trying to get traction, but the slick surface made getting speed difficult, and Rocko was too close for comfort.

Once I hit the doorway, I turned right, into the large workspace where Hyrum enjoyed stretching out to draw. I leaped onto the sofa, then to a bookcase, and finally onto the shelves where the still-broken frame lay.

"Come on, kitty!" Rocko yelled as he jumped to reach me. "Pets!"

Goober had his arms around Rocko from behind, tugging him back. Their parents were still yelling at him to leave me alone, yet neither came close enough to help Goober pull him back.

Where the hell are you, Will?

Calmly, with Hyrum a step behind, Will entered his office, and just as calmly went to Rocko and stood as a blockade to keep him from me.

"I want the kitty!" Rocko insisted again. "He's not Jane. His head don't flop over."

While Julie and Kyle told him, again, "maybe later," Will firmly and simply said, "No."

"But I want—"

"No."

"You said pets!"

"No."

Hyrum moved to Will's side with his back to Rocko, looking up at me. "Are you okay, Wick? You look scared."

I've been better.

I don't think I want him to hold me, dude.

"He's got a thing about cats," Kyle explained. "He doesn't know how to hold them and tries, well..." He set his hand on his throat. "Yeah."

What the hell happened to Jane?

Will ignored him.

"Let me pet the kitty," Rocko demanded.

Again, "No."

"Why not?"

"I said no. I don't need a reason."

Rocko huffed out an exasperated breath but relaxed enough that Goober let go. "Okay."

"Now do you get it?" Kyle grabbed Goober's shoulder and spun him around. "It's this, all day, every day. He can't bathe himself. He barely has control over his bladder and bowels. He can't shave. He can't tie his own shoes. And his temper... You really want to deal with this?"

Goober held fast. "Yeah. I do."

~

He sent his parents and brother to his apartment with the promise that he would be there in half an hour. Will wanted to speak to him, and I saw the trepidation in Goober's eyes and heard what he didn't say out loud: *I just got my ass fired, didn't I?*

Once Rocko was safely out of sight, I jumped down onto the sofa and allowed Hyrum to scoop me up and kiss the top of my head. He knew I was scared, but it didn't escape me that he hadn't been. Either he was confident that Rocko couldn't catch me, or certain that Will wouldn't let anything happen, but he hadn't run after the Giffords and he hadn't yelled for Rocko to be nice.

Will sat on the sofa, arms folded. "Your brother is not

Hyrum. It would be both unfair and a mistake to assume they share the same capabilities."

"I don't—"

Will held a hand up to stop him. "That being said, I appreciate what you'd like to do for him. And I suspect he is not as delayed as your parents presume."

"He's a handful, I know that. But they're holding him back, I know that as well."

"At what age would you place his behaviors?"

Goober gave a half shrug. "Last time he was evaluated? They said three to four."

"My experience," Will said, "is that a toddler's response to being denied something they want is 'why.' Yet Rocko asked 'why not?'"

"And you think that means something."

"It was an age appropriate response. There may be nothing more to it than that."

Does anyone ever tell him 'no?' I only heard 'no' from you.

"There was no tantrum, no crying when I told him 'no,'" Will went on. "Simple acceptance once he understood I was serious."

Goober admitted, it was not something his brother often heard. "They're doing the best they can, Emperor. Too much of it is, well, ineffectual. And frankly, wrong. Until the incident with Hyrum..."

"You dealt with Hyrum the same way you've been taught to deal with your brother," Will guessed.

Goober's sigh was tangled with regret. "No requests, just orders. If there's a distraction, remove it. If he gets off track, yank his ass back to it, and get him going again. Don't be nice about it, because if you're nice, he'll think you're kidding. Yet never tell him no, because we can't hurt his feelings."

"I don't get it," Hyrum said.

"Good for that," Goober said. "Remember how I said I was an asshole? That's part of how I learned to be one. Someone doesn't do what you want? Bully them into it. I honestly don't think that was my parents' intention, but it's the result."

Taking him away from them isn't going to suddenly make everything better.

Will repeated my musing, with his own history-teacher spin on it.

"That's not my expectation," Goober said. "I just think he'd do so much better here. There are schools—"

"There are schools in Montana. Schools from which they chose to remove him."

"There are better schools here," Goober insisted. "And he would be less isolated. My parents live out in the middle of nowhere. My guess is that's half the reason they stopped sending him to school. Between his lack of progress and shuffling him around, it probably got to be too much. Getting him to school in winter? Forget it."

"Lack of transportation?"

"That and lack of funds. My dad is a machinist, doesn't earn a lot." Goober closed his eyes, bracing for the realization that had just hit him. "They used what money they had to send me to university. Goddamn."

In that, Will didn't hear a reason to remove Rocko from their care.

"He needs more, Emperor. They need a break."

"They might not want a break."

"But they'll never know how badly they need one until they take it."

"Maybe they just need a babysitter," Hyrum said. "When Will and Aisha need a break I watch the babies so they can go out and have dinner and drinks."

"An evening out isn't enough, Hyrum. They haven't had a break since he was born."

"And they're not going to hand over their son," Will said. "I certainly would not hand over mine."

"Maybe they would," Hyrum offered. "My mom did."

Not exactly willingly, dude.

"Spend the weekend with your parents," Will suggested. "If by the end of it you still believe remaining here is in your brother's best interests, figure out what it would take to get your parents to relocate. Breaking them apart should not be your first action. Become a family again first."

He was dismissed.

And by the look on his face, not really looking forward to the weekend.

~

"A job," Kyle said, arms crossed. "It would have to wait about six months. I'm in the middle of something."

"Middle of what?" Goober pressed.

We were on the playground across the street from Ozoo, which had been built onto the grass that stretched between the street and Crissy Field Beach not long after the complex opened. Hyrum and Rocko were the only ones playing; Will was not ready to allow his children an introduction to the younger Gifford, not until he was certain Rocko's impulses were better controlled.

"I'm contracted to build framework for a project out of Chicago and San Francisco," Kyle answered. "Some crackpot thinks he's building a transporter. He sent the specs, and what the hell, it's a damned decent payday."

Crackpot.

I wish I could laugh out loud.

"The crackpot wouldn't happen to be Finnegan Blackshear, would it?" Will asked.

"Know him? He's got to be bat crap bonkers. Not that I care, he's offering twice the market rate for the work. Julie did the math. If I deliver on time, our bills are paid for a year."

The earth could not open up and swallow Goober fast enough.

"Relocate to San Francisco and work with the crackpot right here," Will said. "Both crackpots, actually. I imagine Richard Van Hoff is the Chicago arm of the venture."

Goober cleared his throat. "Dad, Finnegan Blackshear is the Emperor's father."

Kyle snorted, amused. "And he thinks he can create a transporter?"

"He's certain of it," Will said. "For that matter, so am I. He and Richard have managed small scale transport, inanimate matter. The next step is living tissue."

Kyle leaned back, trying to decide how serious Will was. "The contract is just for multiple copies of the frame and housing for control units. How much more will he need?"

"Parts that currently do not exist, I imagine," Will answered, despite knowing exactly what Finn needed. "Your experience lends itself to the creation of tool and die patterns, correct? He'll need materials beyond the scope of your contract."

Living in San Francisco suddenly made sense. "And if I were here, I'd be that much closer and more likely to be of use to him. It'd be a hell of a leap of faith. If I move my family here and his project tanks or he goes in another direction?"

"The job offer with Ozoo stands. Phase three of our expansion begins next year. We will require the manufacture of equipment fitting exact specifications on a large scale. Currently, there is no one within the city who can meet our demands."

Ice cream bike coming at us from the left. Hyrum will hear it in about two seconds.

I was off by a second. Before Kyle had a chance to say anything about the offer that had just been extended to him, Hyrum leaped from the swing set and ran to Will, Rocko right behind him.

"Ice cream man, Will! Is it okay? Will Aubrey be mad if I get ice cream this close to dinner?"

"Eat three bites of everything, she won't even notice," Will said.

Kyle tapped Goober's arm. "Give your brother some money. I didn't bring any cash."

"I got money!" Hyrum declared, turning to catch the bike before it got too far. "Come on, Rocko!"

You wouldn't make that offer to Goober's father without a reason.

You already know. He helped Finn build it in the last timeline.

"You'd have a job here, Dad," Goober ventured. "A great job. Mom wouldn't have to work unless she wanted. The city is ripe with programs for Rocko."

"Expensive shit," Kyle grumbled.

"And I'd pay for it."

"Not expensive," Will said. "There is no cost for needs-based adult education. Rocko has the right to utilize Pacifica's schools. You could remain in Montana and shuttle him here every morning if you chose to."

"We're not a charity case," Kyle grumbled.

"It's not charity. Were you charged for his schooling in Montana? You should not have been."

Rocko's education was free. But it was the transportation costs that ate away at his paycheck and adding to the burden were restitution fees for damages Rocko incurred. The bigger he got, the bigger the damages. They reached a point where there was no money left, not if Goober was going to finish his education.

When Goober opened his mouth to apologize—stiffing Rocko out of an education was never what he wanted, he could have found a way—his father stopped him.

"We made the hard decision. Riley had grown and learned as much as he was ever going to. School was nothing but day care at that point and we chose to spend the money on the son we knew would make the most of it."

"But—"

"We knew you'd take care of your brother when the time came. We also knew that if we'd asked, you'd have paid his transportation fees to go back to school. But he's a tornado, Toph. Even if we'd asked you, he—"

Rocko threw his head back, screaming "Sprinkles!" so loud that Hyrum had to take a step back.

Kyle grunted. "So maybe we could afford to pay for everything he breaks, but the costs of getting him to school? I couldn't ask that."

"This city is imminently walkable," Will pointed out.

"Weather's amazing, too," Goober added.

Kyle grunted. "If you like fog."

"Beats the hell out of ten feet of snow overnight. Take this job and you'll have the money, Dad. I have the money. Even if it just means getting someone to be his, I don't know, handler so Mom can catch a break now and then. Or keep an eye on him in school. But you know I'm right, living here would be best for him and damned good for you."

Hyrum and Rocko each had an ice cream cone in hand, walking carefully to make sure nothing was dropped. Ten feet away, however, Rocko spit out a bite of ice cream and tossed the cone aside, yelling, "Yuck! Gross. Yuck, yuck, yuck!" His hands went to the sides of his head and he let out a frustrated scream. "I hate that! Yuck!"

Hyrum stopped, unsure what he should do. Kyle was already on his feet, headed for them, wanting to stop Rocko from escalating, but he was half a beat too late. In one motion Rocko let go of his head and then slapped Hyrum's cone out of his hand, hard enough that it sounded like he'd slapped him across the face.

Will stiffened, but he didn't get up.

I'll go bite the little bastard.

Do something.

I waited for the tears, for Hyrum to run to Will crying that it wasn't fair, just because Rocko didn't like it that didn't mean he should throw his to the ground, too. Instead, he let out a long breath while Rocko stomped on his cone, sending bits of ice cream flying, and watched as Kyle ran to his son.

He yanked Rocko away, snapping about manners and not being mean.

"I'm sorry," Goober said to Will. "I think he's had enough for the day. But oddly, that's progress. Last time I saw him, he would have thrown himself on the ground, too, and ripped out a chunk of hair."

"Take them home," Will said. "And stress to your father, whether his work continues with mine or not, the job offer is genuine and includes moving expenses. We'll need his skills."

Hyrum picked the cones off the grass because he refused to leave garbage on the ground, and he was certain they had too much sugar to leave for birds or squirrels to eat.

After he tossed them into the trash can, he wiped his hands on his pants.

"Is it okay if I don't want to be friends with him?" he asked

Will. "He's not nice. I think I should be friends with him on account of he needs friends but my tummy says no."

"You don't have to be friends simply because you feel sorry for him."

Hyrum scrunched up his nose. "I don't feel sorry for him. I know how he feels and he probably wants friends but I dunno, Will."

"That's fine. But I don't think he's being mean intentionally."

"I think he is." He sat on the bench next to Will and snuggled close. "When we were on the swings he called his daddy a dumbass and a bunch of other things. And he wants to swing Wick around by his tail on account of he thinks it would be funny. He doesn't know a lot of words, but he knows how to be mean."

"It still might not be intentional. Rocko doesn't have impulse control and that's not his fault. But I won't ask you to play with him again." Will pressed a kiss to his temple and then got up. "Come on. It's a short enough walk to Ghirardelli. The ice cream there is far better, I believe."

He jumped up. "Can I get a sundae? With lots of chocolate sauce?"

Will reached for his hand. "Hyrum, I think today, even I'll get one with lots of chocolate sauce. Don't tell Rhys or the twins, all right?"

That made Hyrum snicker. "Okay. I don't want their feelings hurt on account of we went without them anyway. Do you think Rocko's mom and dad will move here?"

Will nodded. "The job we offered is too lucrative for Kyle to pass up. But you won't have to see Rocko."

"Topher thinks Rocko and me are the same."

"You are absolutely not the same, Hyrum. No more alike than, say, Jay and Zed. Both have their strengths, and both have their faults. Comparing them isn't fair."

"Sometimes people aren't fair."

"I'll give you that point," Will said.

"Is Finn really making a transporter?"

He already did.

"Really?"

"It's taken him some time to admit that he created the transporter when he created the portals."

And time to figure out why he kept turning bowling balls inside out.

"Why'd they go inside out?"

"When you remove matter from one place, without replacing that matter, you create a bit of a black hole. He understood this, but he wasn't replacing the matter quickly enough. Once he did—"

Once Aisha fixed his math.

"—he was able to rectify the problems."

"I don't know what that means."

It's like making cookies. Finn took away some flour for one thing without replacing it with something else. Without the flour, the cookies kind of don't work.

"They're not cookies then."

"Exactly. They're nothing like what you intended. Finn just needed to find a way to transport objects without creating nothing."

A whole lot of nothing.

A massive sucking hole of nothing.

"He coulda used oatmeal," Hyrum reasoned. "Sometimes I take away a little flour and use some oatmeal so the cookies are healthy and then we can have some for breakfast."

"In a way, he used a bit of scientific oatmeal to fix the problem," Will mused.

"Does that mean that you're gonna let people know about your bracelet?"

"No. Not for an exceedingly long time. Let's allow Finn to commercialize his transporters first, all right?"

"Okay. That's nice to do since he's so old."

"You've met Liam Finnegan, Hyrum. He's an older version of Finn. Age is not a reason to be nice to my father."

I'm telling him you said that.

"He knows Liam, Wick. He'd agree."

"If I meet him again I'll be nice anyway."

Because you're a good person. I might bite him.

"Wick," Hyrum giggled. "No you won't."

I'm a biter, dude. He knows that.

We crested the short hill that led to the aquatic park, where the beach was dotted with swimmers and sun bathers, and where Hyrum's friend, Ash, was picking up small rocks. Hyrum waved and Ash yelled out, "Hi, Hy!" but we didn't stop to talk to him, and he went right back to gathering stones.

"How come you like holding hands with me?" Hyrum asked Will suddenly. "I never see other boys holding hands unless they're boyfriends."

"I love you, and you're my brother."

"You did it before Eli adopted me, too."

"Do you want me to stop?"

"Nuh. You never hold Jax's hand."

"Jax has cooties," Will said.

Will still isn't all that comfortable touching people except for you and Aisha and his kids.

"Really?"

Will nodded. "I may never be entirely comfortable, Hyrum. But I will always make the effort for the people I love."

We headed up the hill to Ghirardelli, Hyrum tugging Will along.

"I'm telling Jax you want to hold his hand now. And kiss him. On account of you *love* him."

"I do love, Jax, Hyrum. But—"

"Jax and Will, sitting in a tree. K-i-ss-i-n-g." He let go of Will's hand and raced forward, laughter trailing behind.

I hope he never changes.

"Everyone changes, Wick."

Give me this one, Will. Since I'll probably still be here thirty years from now, I want to believe that Hyrum will still giggle his way through kissing things and stupid jokes, that he'll still sleep with Chuckles clutched tight, and that he loves life as much as he does now.

"Chuckles, sadly, might not survive as long."

He made it through your childhood, Will. He'll make it as long as we need him to.

"Never tell him that, Wick."

I know.

Chuckles will remain a mystery.

He's magic and magnificent.

"Chuckles or Hyrum?"

Yes.

NO MATTER THE WHEN

"How long before the Florida masses begin clamoring for David Munson's release?" Drew asked.

Jax glanced at his watch. "How long ago did the interview end? Thirty seconds after that, I imagine."

Red and Jax were still dressed for the second co-interview they'd given, which they had once again co-opted and turned into a moderately staged conversation with a reporter who was aware that she'd lost control of the topic, but did not care. This was the King, bantering with his brother-in-law, casually informing the world that the former First Minister of Florida was so much worse than anyone had ever supposed, and because of that, how Pacifica wanted the country to change.

Red continued to press for David's release; Jax deflected the notion. David had, after all, been instrumental in the destruction of a shuttle in flight, an attempt on his own brother's life. If he wasn't directly responsible, he was an accessory. And there was the matter of a dead Second Minister, though David insisted his hands were clean on that one. David Munson was in a Pacifican jail in San Francisco, held in solitary, and he oddly didn't seem to mind.

David also didn't agree with Red, something left out of the interview. They'd met with him together, to discuss the enormity of Levi's crimes, and wanted his input. He'd seen their first interview, when Red asked Jax to let his brother go.

David Munson declined. "Release me, and I'm a dead man. There are too many left from Dad's Quorum who wouldn't blink at the suggestion I be killed for the things I know. I'm not innocent, but neither are they and they're all corrupt enough that resorting to murder to cover up their crimes is nothing."

He had kids; remaining in Pacifica's custody might protect them from fallout over the things he'd done. "I hate what the son of a bitch did to our sisters and to Hyrum, but I don't want to die, Red. And I refuse to risk turning my kids into targets. We're all safer if I stay here."

"If I could assure your safety?" Jax pressed.

"You can't." He looked to Red, who was about to argue on his behalf. "I've done more than you realize, Red. I belong here more for those things than for anything else. You know what happened to Dad, right?"

"Russia—"

"Russia didn't kill him. It was me."

Red blurted out, "What?" while Jax calmly asked, "How?"

David Munson didn't sneak into a federal prison, string his naked father up by his ankles, and then gut him like a deer. But he knew who to bribe, who was most capable of getting to Levi without being noticed, who could bypass some of the strongest security in the world. "I acted out of anger, but I have no regrets. When I realized the enormity of it all? That he probably hadn't stopped with his own family. I just...reacted. That trial. Hearing what he'd done to Aubrey, and seeing what he'd done to Oz. I'd never met her, knew nothing about her, but when the Emperor picked her up and carried her out of the courtroom...I understood then what it meant for someone's blood to boil. He tortured her, Red. We all know he did. God knows what else he did to her."

Jax was dubious. "You knew how to find a hit man."

"I'm a lawyer, Jax. One who protected the interests of the Church of Florida. Of course I knew how to find a hit man. *Dad* knew how to find a hit man. For a while, I thrived on imagining the look on his face when the man he'd used more than once popped into his cell and ended him without a word."

He begged them to stop looking for a way to release him. What they wanted was petty revenge, and it would change nothing. Letting him go, putting him front and center in a vendetta against a dead man would only turn him and his family into targets. He was content to remain in the hands of Pacifica's Royal Guard, where he had a room instead of a cell, knowing that his wife and children were taken care of. It was what he felt he deserved, and the only thing he had left to give them.

So Jax and Red went into an interview during which they had intended to announce David Munson's forthcoming release, and instead poked at the tainted legacy of Levi Munson one last time, with the promise to his family that after this, they would let it go.

The talking head interrupted their banter long enough to ask the question that had begun to resonate online: why was David Munson being held in Pacifica for a crime committed against Florida's First Minister?

"Because," Jax reminded her, "Pacifica does not have a death penalty, whereas had he been tried and convicted in Florida, he would have been executed. Despite his crimes, the simple truth is that his brother, the man against whom the worst of those things occurred, did not wish to lose him. My wife, your Queen, did not wish to lose him. And it was within my power to grant that."

Fresh from the news studio, they headed for the balcony with Drew, Will, and Hyrum, with bottles of good scotch and cinnamon whiskey. Hyrum carefully set the bottles on the end tables, while ice clinked against glass as Will got ready to pour.

The surprise was Red, who had never allowed a drop of alcohol past his lips, when he accepted the glass Hyrum held out to him. It was filled with ice and Drew's favorite cinnamon beverage; no one expected Red to drink it and assumed that he took it out of politeness toward his little brother, and that he would simply hold it.

He watched as Hyrum sipped at his drink, gave a half shrug, and imitated his younger brother. He winced when it bit back, but as the flavor settled with him, he told Hyrum it was good— why hadn't he introduced it to him sooner?

"On account of you're the First Minister and no one is allowed to drink in Florida. But I figure you're not in Florida right now and since you're stirring the shit, you might want to drink."

Drew choked on his drink mid-sip. "Stirring the shit, Hy?"

"That's what Eli said. Not your baby. My daddy. He said that right after he said, 'Son, what the hell are you wearing? You look like a lipstick tube exploded.' But he wasn't mean, he likes my pink jeans and shoes. Then we talked about Florida and Red, and he said, 'Well, Red is stirring the shit, that's for sure.'"

Red held his glass up as if he were inspecting it. "We're about to relax the rules regarding alcohol," he said. "The Prime Minister feels it's time to allow it into the country based on Pacifican law, and I'm apt to agree."

He no longer had control over what became legal in Florida, but the PM consulted him, given that 99.9% of the population belonged to the church.

"That's going to get complicated," Drew mused. "What's the legal age, then? Follow Pacifica, or follow Midlam? I could have started drinking beer at sixteen if it had appealed to me. Yet here, Oz had to wait until she was twenty-one."

"Like she waited," Jax sighed.

"I asked Aubrey for permission," Will said.

Red reminded them that it was not up to him. "Though if asked my opinion, I would choose to follow Pacifica in this. I'd like there to be a modicum of maturity in those who will choose to indulge."

The door squeaked open, and Eli stepped out, sniffing. "I smell cheap booze. Give it to me."

Hyrum giggled and poured another for Eli.

"What's the topic tonight?" Eli asked as he pulled up another chair. "World peace? Economic recovery in China? Girls?"

"The potential legal drinking age in Florida," Red said.

"They wanna be like Pacifica," Hyrum offered. "Twenty-one."

"It was almost twenty-five here," Eli offered. "If my wife had her way, it would have been."

"Seriously?" Jax asked.

"She filed a formal petition with the council, even," Eli said. "Granted, her position was owed to having a thirteen-year-old son who had discovered beer, belching, and malt-fueled farting. She hoped that by lowering the hammer she could gain more control over you."

"Yeah, that wouldn't have worked."

"She knew that. She was grasping at straws. She also found the idea of telling you a change in the law was your fault appealing, and if you didn't like it, stop being such a little bastard and perhaps we could revisit the matter."

"The absence of alcohol would not have resulted in his not being a little bastard," Will snorted.

"I needed Aubrey for that," Jax said.

Eli didn't want to contemplate the kind of man Jax would have become without her. "I imagine I don't want to know the kind of man I would have become without your mother, either."

"What kind of man would you be if she was still alive?" Hyrum asked.

"A happier one," Eli answered, though not as sadly as one might have expected. He leaned over and kissed Hyrum's temple and added, "Having you in my life makes me very happy, son. The babies make me happy. But I would be happier if she were here."

"I'm glad you're my daddy now." Hyrum slugged back the rest of his drink, which was his third by my count. "I would have been happier when I was little if you'd been my daddy then."

"So would we all," Red murmured.

"You were a good big brother," Hyrum said. "You made David stop picking on me when you caught him, and you read me bedtime stories. Daddy never did that. I asked him once and he said, 'Hyrum, do I *look* like I have time to read to you?' He looked like he had lots of time on account of he was sitting there watching the news, but I didn't ask again. But then you came in and said you had a new story to read for me and we went upstairs, and I got to sleep in your room with you."

"I remember that," Red said. "I overheard you ask him. That was before Aubrey left. She held you in her lap while I read to you."

"She was making sure my feelings weren't hurt," Hyrum said.

"Your father never once read to you?" Eli asked. When Hyrum shook his head, Eli put his glass on the closest table, declared it bedtime, and told Hyrum they should go read together. "It's been too long since I read bedtime stories to my son. I would like to, if you don't mind."

Hyrum popped up and wobbled a bit. "Yay! Drew, is it okay if we watch movies tomorrow instead? The old ones that Mom would spank me for?"

"She wouldn't spank you. But sure, tomorrow."

"She would spank me twice!" he giggled as he headed for the door.

Red watched them go. "Never in a million years would I have thought I would see him drunk."

Drew chuckled. "Yeah, well, we could say the same about you. When you get up, stand carefully. The first drinks really nail you."

He heeded Drew's advice and got up carefully. "You're not kidding. My legs feel like I ran halfway across the city."

That made Will laugh. "No, they don't. I've run across the city—"

"You're in shape," Red argued. "I am not. And before I'm tempted to take a third drink, I'm going inside to spend some time with my sister before I fall asleep, which I believe will be quite easy tonight."

He's tipsy. Even Hyrum didn't get that tipsy at first.

"Shame he didn't stay out here to help finish the bottle," Jax mused. "What would Red Munson look like with his guard down so far it was nonexistent?"

"Like Hyrum after three shots with music blasting," Drew said. "Dude dances like a madman, even if there's not a dance floor."

"With anyone?" Jax asked.

"Nah. He just cuts loose and lets himself have a great time. He'll get Oz and me to dance, and anyone else who looks interested, but he doesn't dance *with* anyone, really."

"Dancing leads to kissing things," Will chuckled.

"My mother would have loved Hyrum," Jax sighed. "And she would be a little jealous of his ability to just...play. She would mother him half to death, all the while trying to figure out how to let her own guard down."

Will thought that if Hyrum had been in her life, the Queen's stoic side would have crumbled. It wasn't possible to stay at arm's length in public with him. If he wasn't jumping at Eli—carefully, he had learned—or at Jax, he'd grab her hand to pull her along, excitedly showing her all the things he loved along the way.

"As reserved as she was, she would never allow him a moment of doubt where her feelings for him were concerned. And he would love her every bit as much as he does Eli. And Aubrey, too."

They mused about what kind of men they have become without the women in their lives. I wondered what would have become of Hyrum if he'd had Donna in his.

Imagine if Hyrum had come here when she was alive. When Jax and Aubrey married.

"Imagine how broken he'd have been when she died," Will countered.

Just assume she hadn't.

Jax let that settle. "We'd all be happier. I imagine she'd be the happiest of all."

~

I waited at the foot of the stairs leading up to Will's apartment, listening for the night music. Soft sighs, a baby gurgling, gentle snoring. Jax and Aubrey had been asleep for hours; baby Eli was awake, cooing to the toys that dangled over his crib. Hyrum's bare feet slid across the wall; when he woke in the morning there was a good chance his feet would be on his pillow and his head hanging over the edge of the mattress.

I heard Will's steps above as he crept quietly around the apartment, listening as he put his shoes back on, and then as he gently closed the door behind him.

"I had a feeling you'd be waiting," he whispered when he was halfway down the stairs. "You're coming with me?"

I am if you're going to see old Drew.

"I am."

I was just there. He clipped a note to my collar with a time to meet him.

He unfolded the note. "You went to see him."

I went to see Lux and Seven. But I found a way to talk to Drew, well enough that he's expecting you.

Old Drew couldn't understand me, but he'd figured out that I could type with my nose. He set a computer tablet on his table and waited patiently while I tapped my nose on it, until I'd managed a complete, typo-riddled paragraph.

He didn't mock me for how badly I butchered my spelling and grammar; he was impressed and only complained a little about the smear of feline snot on the screen.

"I appreciate this." Will tucked the note into his back pocket and then picked me up and set me on his shoulder. "I was prepared to call him from the lab and wait until he had time. And this might take some time."

Not as much time. He's already thinking.

By the time we got there, future Drew would have been thinking for nearly a week.

~

Old Drew's private workspace in the Ozoo complex made Will's former playground under Union Square seem claustrophobic. With the lights on and display grid off, it seemed to stretch from the borders of Fort Point to the far side of Marina Green, which I knew was impossible, but there we were.

Still, it was immense, and was wholly underground. My first thought as we exited the elevator was that one good earthquake would destroy this place, until I remembered that this version of Drew had designed Ozoo's newest testing facilities, and he employed the same engineers and architects responsible for creating new structures that could, theoretically, withstand the worst earthquake the world had ever known.

San Francisco had nearly crumbled under the last one; if

this technology held as well as its testing suggested, it would survive one significantly worse. And because of the way it had been built, with thick walls containing thousands of miles of electrical wiring and tiny projectors, Will chose to not jump directly to the workspace; we went to Drew's office instead and rode his private elevator down.

He was reasonably certain he could jump through those walls, but not willing to risk his life on it.

How secret is this? Like, do Oz and the kids know about it?

"I would be surprised if Oz didn't," Will said. "I can't say the same about their children."

Which one of the kids followed in Drew's footsteps? Liam or Ben? I can't remember.

"Ben, I believe, though Liam's work isn't far off."

Was Liam named after you?

"I have no idea."

Too many Williams and Liams running around. Even your grandmother calls you Liam. Why not 'Billy?' You'd have been a stellar Billy.

He hated that as a nickname for himself. He loved that Aisha often called him 'Bilbo' but Billy irritated him into cantankerous silence. The door slid open before he could remind me of that with colorful words and gestures; bitching at me once we were in Drew's playground would have been rude.

Old Drew waited not far from the elevator door. He stood at a desk that looked an awful lot like a podium, with a glass-like cover and controls that glowed. It was a replica of the keyboard our Drew had seen for the first time while we were stuck in Saint Francis. His exposure to it was accidental; when Will used it late one night, believing everyone else to be asleep, Drew slipped out of the office he and Oz used as a bedroom, and it—along with the hovering projection—had enthralled him.

For this Drew, the simulator was in the future, yet everything about his workshop suggested it functioned the same way. The grid-patterned walls were covered in the same projectors and nanobot-filled tiles as the simulator of Finn's creation. The lighting was comparable. The floor floated, and I knew if Will set me down, I would be able to run at high speed, yet move only a few feet. Before I reached the farthest wall, the floor would gently turn and nudge me in another direction, and I wouldn't feel any of it.

This Drew created the system that inspired our Drew to explore nanotechnology. I wondered who had inspired him.

With no projectors running and the dampening tiles turned off, sound here carried well; if I meowed now, anyone in the furthest corner would be able to hear clearly. Without intending to, people who visited this room probably spoke softly, without understanding that there was more bouncing around than their voices. Every exhaled breath, every swallow, every heartbeat—I could hear it all, including the evidence that Drew hadn't eaten in a while and his stomach was protesting the oversight.

"Emperor. Wick." He gave a short nod when Will stepped into the room, and he seemed pleased to see us. "No Jax?"

Will felt it prudent to keep Jax out of this until he knew for sure what he was going to do. When he explained beyond the things I'd been able to relate, Drew sighed and then nodded; there was no reason to get Jax's hopes up, no reason to tell him anything at all if it seemed as if nothing was going to be done.

Without any small talk, Drew set about booting up the system. There was, Will later told me, enough computing power in one of Drew's fist-sized systems to send a thousand people to Mars and back, and a thousand times over. Will mused that three centuries earlier it would have taken all of Texas to house the computing power this version of Drew utilized at a whim. Texas, and perhaps part of Midlam.

It may have been a hyperbolic musing on his part, but I understood what he meant. Drew was good at taking large things and making them tiny.

Section by section, the lights dimmed. Drew waited until there was only the essence of twilight, and then he flicked a switch, activating the projectors. Suspended in the air—essentially the prototype for Finn's simulator—a long, slow-churning ball of loosely packed filaments appeared. Line after line was painted in shades of glowing blue, the color owed to the track lighting. In that light, Will's pink self was a curious shade of purple, and old Drew's hair glittered pink.

But the display, with its fine blue lines, caught my attention. *It really is spaghetti.*

This was Drew's tactile illustration of time. It was a three-dimensional model and hung above and before us, extending as far as we could see. Will slowly moved under the display to get a better look, hands clasped behind his back until Drew told him it was safe to touch. The display was meant to be manipulated by hand. Old Hyrum had been right; it resembled a blob of spaghetti hanging in the air, noodle upon noodle, twisting, touching, with tiny pockets in between.

Spaghetti without the sauce, he'd told Will. I thought the sauce would fit neatly in the spaces and wondered what they were really for.

"Null space," Drew said. "Each line—or noodle, as Hyrum says—represents a specific line of time. The spaces between, those pockets, are null space. Void of relative time, yet at the same time totally encompassing of it."

Oh. I don't want to go back there.

"The portals made the ships obsolete," Will said. "There's no longer a need to utilize null space in the same way."

Drew considered it. "For you. The question remains, will it be necessary for Finn to again find a way to move through time, or will the portals—having not existed until he reaches his thirties—remain? And if they remain, will he fully understand them, having not created them?"

That depended on when you talked to Finn. He'd led Will to believe that stepping into a portal and heading for any part of the future, save the one he grew up in, might mean walking into nothingness. Yet Will also believed that if someone could use a portal to get from this When to his birth When, they could also get to all the points in between.

He hadn't tested his theory, because why would he? Aisha would kill him if he disappeared into nothingness.

"Look at the Old Mint," he argued. "From the moment the lock was initiated and isolated from time, we've been able to access it, place new data in it, and access information across all timelines."

"Yet nothing new went in from Finn's final 'well, this didn't work' entries following his determination that what he'd attempted hadn't worked, until the next cycle began. The Old Mint was probably always accessible, yet between those loops, no one utilized it because there was nothing in it that they needed."

So it was there even before it was built? Like, the Vikings could have found it if they'd landed in San Francisco?

"The space it occupies was likely guarded by the lock, but without the building," Drew mused. "No building, no data storage."

Will didn't think so. He felt certain Finn would always need to return to the date the lock was originally placed and do it again. He could access it until the end of time, but only from the original date it went live. Prior to its activation, the building had housed many different things, and no one was affected by the lock. It had been a site for the printing and storage of currency; clearly things were removeable. For a short time, it had been a gym. People moved the equipment in, and they were able to take it all out, and it was probably not the same people.

The time lock may have existed, but it was not active.

Whether Finn left it alone after each failure, save for the amount of time spent recording those failures, was due to apathy or loss of access, neither of them knew. Finn made his final entries, and never went back.

What if he really screwed up by not going back?

"What do you mean, Wick?"

What if he went back, say, a year later, only to find out that the world was still there after he and Jo left? And people were waiting there to tell him? I mean, he sent me into the portal and I didn't come back, but that doesn't mean I died.

"Explain," Will said, though he paled a little and I understood why.

What if I went into the portal and just couldn't get back? Not because the world ended, but because of something else? You went into it instead of me the last time, and you got stuck. I got stuck with you when I followed. What if I was just stuck?

"Wick—"

Think about it. Zed sniffed your fear. I don't think he smells what I feel. All those timelines where I went in, if I were stuck, he wouldn't have smelled it. So they guessed I was dead. But for all we know, I was stuck, and the world went on just fine. Or maybe I went all the way through, and someone was there and went, 'Ooh look at the kitty, I'm taking the kitty home,' and I just couldn't escape to return home? Lots of things might have happened, but that doesn't mean I was dead.

Will's purple-tinted pink face drained to a lovely shade of lavender.

Drew pointed to the giant spaghetti blob. "This is just a pinpoint-piece of the overall puzzle," he said, running his finger along the length of one thin line. "In every timeline ever created, surely there are millions in which he's right. Equally, there are millions in which the world ended. Millions where none of us existed. Millions where we did but were fundamentally different people."

He flicked his fingers, splaying his hand open. The display flattened and the blob expanded, until the lines looked less like spaghetti and more like broken glass, fractures spreading out like an ambitious spider web that ran from floor to ceiling. As the image settled, I saw what Lux did: snowflakes on frosted, fractured glass. Thin cracks, cracks extruding from cracks, overlaid with thousands of delicate flakes, each with equally delicate fingers.

"You've changed time before," Drew went on, not expecting Will to answer. "Sometimes it sticks to your life, sometimes it doesn't."

"I presumed owing to proximity," Will said.

He'd changed time for Oz, saving her life after having witnessed her lifeless body dragged from the water. He'd changed time for Drew, twice. Those instances, he lived close enough in time that the memories of what had gone wrong stayed with him, but no one else around him seemed to know.

That was why we were here.

Could he change something decades after the fact and return to his own life?

Drew pointed to a line that had several offshoots, and by pinching his fingers together, then splaying them apart, magnified it. "Presume this is your prime timeline. And here—" he touched a juncture "—is where you changed something that stuck with you. Note the hair-like lines that connect them. This is why you remember what you fixed, and why no one else does. You stepped back into your own life, having literally changed time."

He pushed that one aside and plucked out another line. "Now presume this one is your prime line. But its offshoot doesn't have anything connecting it. This is a line in which you changed something, but when you went back to your own time, the change didn't, for lack of a better term, hold." He tapped his finger on the spot where the line diverged. "This moment is the creation of a new timeline. And this is why you can jump to this When and spend time with us. Our Emperor didn't suddenly appear as if we'd never lost him. We remember his death. We remember our grief."

"Because I lived too far away from when I died," Will said.

Drew nodded. "The only way to change that would be if one of us had stepped back and fixed it close to the event, and we're too far from it now to do anything that would bring him back to us. The farther from it you are, the less likely the changes will hold."

How long?

"A day, at best a week, I would think," Drew answered. "Any longer and that new line has gone too far to bend at all, or the thin threads that connect the lines break. But you can clearly jump from one line to another. Any changes you make will only affect the timeline in which they occur."

Or they create a new line.

"Or that," he agreed.

So if we try to save Donna, we're saving her for someone else. We can't ever have her back.

"Even if you went back and told yourself what to do, she would exist only for them," Drew said. "Every scenario I plot, that's the outcome. And really, it might be for the best."

Not for Eli.

"You don't know what else you'd be changing," Drew said. "Suppose you managed to figure out a way that she lives, and lives for you. Then what else doesn't happen? Oz and I don't marry? We wouldn't have our children, and they're making significant contributions to the world. Zed never gets close to Sophia? His heart shattered when she died, but he would never trade those few years he had with her, nor the children they had together. There might be a hundred things you'll remember, things you treasure, that never occur."

"And then what might happen," Will sighed. "If she'd ever known what Aubrey had gone through..."

Levi Munson would have died twenty years earlier.

"Or war," Will said. "Bloodier and costlier than the war we did have."

Risk assessment.

"Hyrum," Will murmured. "If war had broken out before it did?"

Get him out first.

"Risk assessment," he repeated. "I had questions, now I have answers. Saving Donna wouldn't be at all like my father finding my mother again. And I understand, the Jo he lost and the Jo he currently loves are fundamentally not the same. But I had hopes of finding a way..."

"Donna died young, Emperor. To replicate what Finn managed would mean pairing Eli in his late seventies with his fifty-something wife. He'll have lived years that she'll feel were owed to her. That might break his heart even more. She might not have the same feelings toward the elder Eli."

So create a new timeline. Not for us. For her.

Will's fear was that this was complicated in ways it hadn't been when he'd previously changed things. When he saved Oz's and Drew's lives, it was because those were things that weren't supposed to have happened. He corrected and prevented mistakes. He'd helped fudge a future timeline; one version of Jo changing her When to be with old Finn hadn't happened yet, and his being there placed it within his timeline.

"Donna was always supposed to die," he said. "In every document regarding her life stored in the Old Mint, her death is recorded. To change that would disrupt time, and the effects of that concern me."

"How so?" Drew asked.

Will wasn't certain he would return to his own timeline if he interfered on so large a scale. Having thwarted time's intentions, negating Donna's death, he wondered if he would wind up back home, with Aisha and their children, or if he would skip ahead from the moment he changed Donna's existence and then remain in that new line. "Regardless of what it means for Eli, I would not choose to live out my life without Aisha and our children."

Drew shifted the flattened display, zooming in on one timeline and one juncture. There were spidery fragments hanging from both, places that connected timelines in tiny segments. "This is, as near as I can tell, where you saved Oz's life. It's less of an intersection and more like a detour." He traced his finger over the finer line, highlighting it in red. "It starts here, forms a tiny bump, and goes right back to its own prime line."

It was a correction and not a change.

He moved further down the line to another bump. "This might be where you saved my life when I was twelve. The same thing, though more prominent. I'm not sure why."

Will assumed it was, again, proximity. He'd only gone back a few hours to save Oz and fewer hours still to save teenaged Jax; he went back nearly a decade to save Drew. "I returned to the expected When then, but again, it was a correction and not the creation of an aberration. There were also several versions of me involved. Tying our timelines together, so to speak."

Where does the timeline go when Will lived?

Drew plucked the line from the rest to isolate it, to a place where one line completely diverged from the other. There was the When in which he died, but that was a short line. There was also the line in which he lived, and it continued on.

Your death timeline just sort of ends. What happened to it?

"This is an approximation," Drew said. "The computer extrapolated the data, and this is the visual representation. The lines may be so close together that we simply can't differentiate them."

So you're jumping from one line to another when you come here to visit.

"If that's true," Drew mused, "then you should be able to go back, save her, create a new line, and still get home. You can't stay there to see what happens. Save her and get out."

But you're just guessing, really.

Finn could be right, and this When erases as our When moves along.

That was Will's predicament. Who was right? Finn and his erasure theory, or Drew and his notion that there were completely new timelines created with each change?

He wasn't sure he wanted to prove either theory.

And in that moment, neither was I.

The elevator did not ping before the doors opened. There was simply the soft sigh of the car inside coming to a stop, and then a louder sigh as the doors opened. I heard it before it settled but Will twitched when the doors slid open; Drew merely turned to see who it was.

"Grandpa," Will said lightly. "Nice to see you. How are my grandmother and father doing?"

Eli was equally amused. "She's wonderful. Your father, on the other hand, just shit up one wall and across the floor. Someone should have warned us about loose diapers and baby swings."

"Someone warned me. The warning doesn't help. It still happens."

Drew wanted to know what brought Eli to this When and the workshop. "Not that I'm not happy to see you, but there's typically a purpose to your visits here."

"Not really. We brought Finn to visit with his grandparents and Mom said you were here with the Emperor. I thought I'd take the chance to see him now, since we've only met the one time."

Twice.

"Twice for me, Wick," Will corrected.

Ask him about his eyes.

"Why would I ask Eli about his eyes?"

The color.

"I can see the color of his eyes. They're green."

"No, they're not," Drew grunted. "I presume your Eli flummoxed you with his inexplicably deep blue eyes?"

Will nodded.

Eli gestured for Drew to touch the keyboard, and when he did the lights dimmed further. He pulled a small case from his pocket and then pressed fingers to his eyes, pulling every bit of green from them and dropping it into the little case.

"Contacts. I opted for green because half the family has green eyes."

Will peered at him closely. This Eli's eyes were the same near violet as baby Eli's were, and even with the light low they were bright and piercing. "Fascinating. Why lenses? Why not have your vision corrected?"

There was nothing wrong with his vision, and as Drew increased the lighting in the room, Eli began to squint, and Will thought he understood.

"Light sensitivity?"

It was more than that. Eli was extremely sensitive to light and spent most of his childhood in sunglasses, but there were things that the sunglasses couldn't dull.

"Oz has synesthesia," old Drew reminded Will. "Eli? His is amplified beyond my comprehension. He was, what, eight or nine before we realized that he doesn't see life the way the rest of us do."

"I see an expanded spectrum," Eli said. "Colors that don't exist for other people. A wider range of the UV scale. Your hair, for example. With the contacts in, it's just black with a slight blue tint depending on how the light hits it. Without...your hair is comprised of a range of greens, blues, and magentas."

You're a bird, dude.

"Combine that with a cacophony of sound that never ends, and my life was complicated. Every breath you take makes a sound. Mom sees bodily sounds as somewhat of an aura. I see them as an onslaught. I've adapted now, but it was miserable when I was younger. Dad created lenses that block higher UV light, mostly because he was afraid that I'd begin shooting lasers from my eyes."

He stopped squinting, having adjusted to the light. "I am highly disappointed that didn't happen. Uncle Hyrum got all the fun stuff."

"I never knew this about you," Will said. "I don't believe I ever saw you without green eyes when I was a boy."

He still looks a lot like you.

You know who you both remind me of?

"Jax?" Will ventured.

Donna.

Can we look at the spaghetti again? I think Lux is right, it looks like snowflakes on fractured glass, but there's more to it, and we need to know.

~

Old Jax was old. The years had wrapped around him with quiet dignity, but he felt the weight of them pressing on his bones and he was certain that the days ahead of him were few. Will could not, would not, visit this When without seeing him; he had become comfortable with the idea of plucking a day off the end of his own life and inserting it here, where his presence was wanted and he wasn't alone.

His gut told him he would outlive Aisha by many years, and if he could spread them out over time, all the better. If he spent some here, he was with loved ones. In his mind, that meant he would not suffer as long with the grief of her passing, and if he timed it right, he might not suffer at all.

So we stayed longer than we'd intended, though not just because Will had literal time to spare. We stayed because Jax didn't feel well. He wasn't ill, exactly; nothing felt right to him and hadn't for several weeks. He moved slowly, as if every muscle and tendon in his body ached, and his appetite was off. He was hungry, he welcomed food, but when it was placed in front of him the best he could manage was half, and that bothered him.

Will watched him pick at his lunch but didn't say anything. Jax managed to eat but it was less than he needed, and the question of whether this was a habit or just a bad day was answered when Aubrey sighed as she took his plate away and remarked that he needed to eat more.

"I ate," he grumbled. "It was good. I'm watching my weight."

"Watching it do what, sweetheart? Vanish?"

Scotch has calories.

Will agreed, scotch had calories, and they were more effective when consumed on the balcony while enjoying the cool air.

"I am glad," Jax said as he carefully lowered himself into the chair, "that you visit us. I hope you keep coming when I'm gone. Aubrey will need you. She'll need Aisha."

"Stop," Will sighed. "You're not dying."

"Feels like it."

He poured out a short shot and handed it to Jax. "You forget, I haven't been born yet. You are entire chapters in my history books. I know when you die, and it's not for many more years."

Jax answered with a grunt.

"See a doctor. He'll slap a patch on the back of your neck, and you'll feel better within a day."

"Like you know what my problem is. I'm old, Emperor. That's all."

Will tilted his head as he looked at his elderly friend. "You're shitting your brains out, Jax. You have an irritable bowel. Get it addressed and you'll feel better."

"Fuck you. And is that really in history books? 'King Jackson suffered a months-long case of the trots?' Fuck me, too."

"History books are incredibly comprehensive in the future."

For a flicker of a moment, he believed Will, then sighed and told him to do nasty things to himself again.

It really is in the books. There are volumes on the royal family's medical history. Oh! Tell him about his upcoming infected nose hair. Something he can look forward to.

"What's that, Wick?" Jax asked.

"He simply wants you to get better. No one is ready to let go of you."

Liar. But that's fine.

"You have your King, Emperor. I don't think you'll grieve much when I'm gone. I've lived well and long enough, and you know it. And you'll be here to see it happen all over again."

"Presuming I outlive you."

"You're bastard enough, aren't you?" he snorted.

"Given the choice, I would not outlive everyone I love. Not you, not my wife, not Wick."

"Yet, you will."

"Perhaps." He sipped at his scotch, then sighed. "I've been curious. You were incredibly accepting when I first showed up here. As if you weren't the least bit surprised, despite declaring that you were mad at me."

"I wasn't."

"How?"

Slowly, Jax leaned to one side, pulling out his wallet and then fishing in for a well-worn slip of paper. As he unfolded it, he said, "After you died, when I was finally able to face your belongings—which took more than a year, mind you—I found a very old and very worn book on your nightstand. And I read it."

He'd only intended to flip through it, but the pages were soft and he understood as he touched fingers to it that this book held meaning for his Emperor. Hours later he realized he had stretched out on the bed that Will had not slept in for half a year, surrounded by things that Will hadn't set eyes on in the last few months of his life. In one terrible moment, he felt as far from his Emperor as he thought he ever would, yet also closer than they ever had been.

"There was a line that stuck with me," Jax said. "Long after I set the book down, it rolled around inside my head. I felt as if you were whispering it to me, and I took it to heart. It took more time, still, but I knew that you wouldn't let me pass on without seeing you again. You'd died in my life, but that didn't mean you would die in the next."

What'd it say? Tell me.

"'Tuesdays With Morrie,' a book by a man named Mitch Albom," Jax said as he handed the fragile paper to Will. "'Death ends a life, not a relationship.' The book kept falling open to that page. I knew you were trying to tell me something."

After looking at Jax's tight, faded-ink scrawl, Will nodded. "Indeed. I read that book many times in the year before I thought I would die. And I hoped you would find it, and that you would keep it."

"I treasure it. Oz has sworn to keep it. Sam as well. As long as that book exists, I believe you'll keep coming back. You'll live, one way or the other. So will I."

"In a roundabout way, that's why I'm here."

Jax raised an eyebrow. "If you tell me you're dying, I'm chucking you over the balcony. I'm still strong enough for that."

"As far as I know, I am not." He explained what he'd spoken about with old Drew, the timelines and how they splintered one from another. What he had known he could not do but considered anyway, and what he wanted to do despite Drew's warnings of everything that could go wrong. "I am aware that it will set in motion a timeline that will no longer resemble your own. My own. Relationships might change. Children might not be born. I don't know."

"But you wouldn't do this until after I marry Aubrey."

"And not until after Oz and Zed are born. I would do it in the last week, in the moments I am certain she would agree."

"You telling me? Or my father?"

Will nodded. "I will involve Jax, if he chooses to participate. I am far less certain about Eli. I would like your input, regardless."

Jax inhaled deeply. "Ah. There should be one timeline where my father's heart isn't broken. Drew is positive it won't change anything for us?"

"He is. As it is, I have changed things considerably. I'm alive for one. I've married and had children. None of that carried to now."

"You're still gone. Living there didn't change that here." He slugged back the rest of his drink and stood. "Do it. Don't ask Dad. Just do it. And when you do, give her a message from her very old son."

"She knew, Jax."

"I know. But what I wouldn't give to tell her that one more time."

~

I went into Oz's old room to sit on the wide bench window seat with Lux and Seven while Will headed for the lab. He wanted to see Finn and was reasonably sure he would be there. If not, he would call Finn, because even as late as it was, his parents would be awake.

After drinks on the balcony with Jax, he accepted Aubrey's invitation to dinner; it was less an offer and more of an order—you will have dinner with us—and while they ate, Seven jumped onto a vacant chair and as I had on so many nights, he stood on his back legs so he could stare at them, willing someone to give him food.

When that didn't work, just before Oz cleared the table, Seven ran into Hyrum's room and quickly returned with his piece of foil. He dropped it at Will's feet, pawed at his leg, and asked, *'Cheese?'*

"He offers that foil to someone every day," Oz mused. "Hyrum says he's asking for cheese, but apparently any food will do."

It was currency. Seven decided that the foil meant food, and whichever human he offered it to was obliged to get him something whether it was time to eat or not. Will humored him and offered several bites of chicken and a few slivers of cheese. Now he was curled up on the window seat, too full and sleepy to do anything else.

"Does it get easier?" Lux asked as we watched Will enter the elevator on Union Square. *"Keeping them all straight in different Whens?"*

It's like knowing more than one person with the same name. The hard part is remembering which one said what and when. Especially the Finns. There are so many of them.

Lux was only familiar with two, and he rarely saw the Finn from my When, which made things easier for him. He was amused that his Eli was an adult and mine was an infant; when he visited, the first person he looked for was baby Eli, hoping to cement those new-person giggles in his mind.

Your Eli lives in the future. How often do you see him?

"More often these days," Lux replied. "He comes because of family. I sense that he wishes he could stay, but his work keeps him away. And there's his wife and child."

Yet another Finn.

"Drew thinks there are more out there somewhere, older Finns that skipped to other Whens before the end of their worlds. He wonders how close they are, and if they keep tabs on the family."

Could be hundreds. It depends on how many stayed and faced the meteor.

"They would be alive now though, wouldn't they? It only took one Finn to succeed. Once he did, the rest lived."

And others didn't. I'm not sure I want Will to carry through with what he wants.

"He's creating a new destiny for others. It doesn't have to match his own."

I know. But there's no way to know how things will change if Donna lives.

"Things might be better."

Drew pointed out that people might not be born. He might not marry Oz. Without that, there's no Eli. No Finn.

"But the knowledge of how to save the world will be passed down in their family, regardless."

No Finn, no Jo. No me.

"But you wouldn't feel that, Wick."

Still. No Jo, no you. Not like this, anyway. I'm not sure I like this, Lux. I loved Donna and want Eli to have her back, any Eli, but I can't imagine not existing.

"It didn't bother you to not exist before you were born."

You're not allowed to make valid points when I'm contemplating life.

Seven rolled onto his back and stretched, reaching for my tail with his front paws. He let loose a tiny meow as he yawned. *'I'm here.'*

I flicked my tail at his face. *I can see that.*

Tiny claws swiped and missed.

My tail is not a toy.

'Yes it is.'

I allowed its capture and tolerated the touch of a tiny tongue to its tip. *'I'm here,'* he repeated. *'Not there.'*

Not where?

'There. Not stars. Not loud. Not fire.'

He released my tail but remained on his back, gazing at me upside down. Seven didn't yet have the words to express the concept skipping through his mind, but I understood. He'd been listening. He had a grasp on my concern. He understood who he was.

You're here and not there. I did exactly what Will wants to do.

"In a way," Lex allowed. *"You remained within your own timeline, affecting yourself. The Emperor proposes altering the line of someone else."*

I know. But I wanted to bring Seven here knowing it meant his absence in the lives of others. I was fine with that.

"Will is not bringing Queen Donna home with him."

It's still a big change, and years after the fact.

Seven flipped over onto his belly.

'No more sad. Play now.'

"Thundering Herd of Elephants?" Lux suggested. *"We rarely get to play, and with a third cat, it should annoy the people even more."*

Seven got to his feet, tail twitching. He wasn't sure what the game entailed, but it meant playtime and he was all for that.

I hadn't played at all when I was him.

Life was survival and nothing more.

I popped Seven on his head with my paw. *Run, little dude. Run fast and run hard, and we'll be right behind you.*

~

We headed for Will's birth When the next morning. We jumped from old Jax and Aubrey's living room to the one in which Will had grown up, where Finn waited with glasses of iced tea for Will and himself, and food for me in case I hadn't eaten. It took a moment for me to be sure which Finn this was—the Finn of our When or the Finn Will had seen a few hours earlier—because he never seemed any older or younger, and it was hard to tell sometimes.

They looked alike and smelled the same. I often needed to hear him speak to be sure. Older Finn had a deeper tone to his voice. It was the gravel that came with age; King Eli was beginning to speak with it as well. Old Hyrum didn't have it and I wasn't sure why.

"I asked them to meet us at a coffee shop near the Embarcadero," Finn told Will as I ate. "It's usually quiet this time of day. We can talk without people staring, wondering who the triplets are."

This was old Finn. Pop-Pop.

"Liam will be there, then," Will guessed. "I doubted his interest."

"He's a grumpy bastard, but you're still his son as far as he's concerned. He at least wants to hear what you have to say."

It was a consortium of Finns.

Two of them were waiting at an outside table when we arrived. Liam Finnegan and Finn-from-our-When were arguing, hand gestures flying as each tried to press home his point, and neither noticed we were there until I jumped from Will's shoulder to the table.

"Do we need to separate you two?" Will asked as he sat. "I'd rather not have to sit between you, but I will if necessary."

The befuddlement on their faces was identical.

"We're not fighting," Finn said.

"You were yelling," Will pointed out.

Liam shrugged. "Only because he's stubborn and refuses to admit that Jo thinks I'm adorable."

Is he drunk?

Old Finn—Pop-Pop because Rhys decided he needed his own special moniker—sat next to Will and sighed. "Now ask them which Jo. Go on. It'll be fun."

"Mine," Finn said, a bit too enthusiastically.

She's Finn's wife, dude. Like, actual wife. Not displaced like JoJo. What the fork?

"I am aware of her opinion regarding each of you," Will said dryly. "And not why we're here."

Pop-Pop Finn already knew what Will wanted and had given the others a brief rundown on his intention and concerns. Finn—Will's Finn—thought he needed to take more time to consider it and study all the possible variables, while Pop-Pop thought he should take a leap of faith. He believed Drew was onto something with his theories, but he also thought the Finns were right: the timeline would erase as Will's new one pushed forward.

"How can you both be right?" Will asked.

Pop-Pop cupped his hands together. "Drew envisions time as spherical, with lines that overlap, often touching. With each change, a new line begins. That doesn't mean, for example, that your timelines, the one in which you died and the one in which you live, aren't the same line. They're connected, and one is erasing the other as you move along."

"And we each have our own basic timelines," Finn added. "It might not be so much that the lines are straight, nor that the new ones created are equally straight. I think our basic lines spiral. And touch. There's more truth in each theory than there is supposition."

Snowflakes on broken glass, spiraling and maybe connected. Hm. DNA strands?

Will looked to Liam, who seemed less sure. "Give me time to think about it. I have hundreds of years of data from traveling in time that these two don't, but the information is recessed deeply enough in my brain that I should review it first."

"I thought you gave up physics," Pop-Pop said.

"Eh. Well."

Liam gradually left physics as he turned to writing and then genetics, but he'd continued with theory long after he lost his Jo, and long after he'd thought himself to be utterly alone. "You realize, there are several lines of Finn between him and me," he said, gesturing to Pop-Pop. "I've had more time than you know. More time than even I'm certain of."

Will leaned back and considered it. "How old are you, really?"

"Damned if I know. I've made time my playground, William. I've left here for other Whens more times than I can remember. I live the years and wind up back here. This is the first time I've chosen to stay for the end of the world, though. Imagine my disappointment when it didn't."

Didn't he want your DNA before the world survived?

"I did," he answered. "It's not my first rodeo, though. I've looked for ways to find him in every When without dropping into his life. This was the first time I actively sent anyone after him."

"And how is Dallas Engle doing?" Will asked, a bit snippy. "The child she carried is doing quite well. He's bright, funny, articulate. My son's best friend."

He had no clue. "Her grandmother and I have a quiet agreement to not speak about her. She's been well taken care of, though, if it matters to you."

Will had made sure George had a forkton of money on hand for any custody battle, but he was unaware that Liam had equally banked Dallas.

Liam waved the notion off with a flick of his hand. "She didn't see any of it until the boy was in his father's care. Did that bastard pay you back? He didn't have to fight her. She didn't want the boy."

George had tried to give the money back. Will consented to repayment of the original amount he had deposited in our When, but the accumulated interest and residuals he deemed unnecessary and believed that all of it should be set aside in trust for Isaac. That was even before Will and Aisha had fallen in love with the little boy.

Isaac had been born because Liam wanted another Will; Will felt somewhat responsible for his existence.

While Liam had offered apologies in the past, he hadn't really meant them. He wanted his son's clone and had done whatever he could to accomplish it and felt no sorrow over loving and missing Will that much. Now he huffed in amusement as he looked over the rim of his coffee cup and asked, "Did you really admit to your late-life virginity in open court?"

"Jesus, Liam," Pop-Pop sighed.

Finn poked his pointy finger in Liam's direction. "Hey. He admitted Aisha has been the only woman in his life. For all anyone knows, they humped like rabbits in their teens."

"What others think doesn't matter," Will said.

"Find me another adult male who would admit that," Liam challenged.

Finn might have been about to admit that he'd been in his later twenties, but JoJo—Pop-Pop's Jo—arrived and the discussion died. She gave each other them a kiss on the cheek, except for Pop-Pop, who got one on the lips.

Does it bother you when she kisses them? I asked him.

"Wick, it's not as if she walked up and sucked their tonsils out. No, it doesn't bother me."

Are you still thinking about having that old fart's baby? I asked her.

The translation changed as the question came out of Will's mouth, and she knew it. "Come on." She patted Will's arm. "What did he really say?"

"That. But he called Liam an old fart."

Liam's laughter exploded, causing heads to turn to see what we were doing.

"I am not having his baby," she said, and not for the first or even last time. "He can have my DNA when he's ready."

What about your Jo? I asked Finn.

"Same. Though she's said if she has another, it will be mine." He looked at Will. "I'm never sure if she's serious or not. We're kind of...old."

"Not too old," JoJo said. "When I was her age, several of my friends had their first babies. She's got a good ten or fifteen years yet."

Will chuckled. "Go for it, Dad. I wouldn't mind a little brother or sister."

Uncomfortable, Finn sighed. "Let's just get your current issue settled. If you don't come back, maybe then we can start on your replacement."

Liam leaned forward. "I've seen how that ends, Finnegan. It ends in you going half out of your mind, forming a semi-cult in a misguided attempt to clone him. And I'm telling you now, it won't work, no matter how many other children you sire. You'll spend centuries running through portals, trying to outrun the inevitable, and you'll never get him back."

Finn had been kidding, and Liam was half-kidding, but I felt the same spasm as Will did: what if time tried to correct itself, sending him off into another timeline, leaving Finn and Jo without their son?

~

After Liam left to dive into his old research notes and Finn headed for home and his Jo, we went into the lab with old Finn. In two hundred years it hadn't changed much; it had been retrofitted with new safety equipment and the simulator was behind the back wall, but the Finns had taken care to leave it close to how it looked right after Will handed over his playground to be remodeled into a multi-level lab.

I doubted it was from some sentimental need to keep is as a touchstone to the past. They were just lazy.

"No question, I would give Liam a chance to research," Finn said as the lights flicked on. "Out of all of us, he's time traveled the most and knows where and in which When he's been. He may have hopped a timeline or two, and if he has, he knows how to get back."

"I hear a 'but' in there."

Finn reached under the island in the center of the room and

turned the computer display on. The sides slid out, projectors lifted, and a keyboard appeared. "But. I suspect his answer will be the same as mine. You've already created new timelines and you manage to come back."

"The differences being the enormity of the change I propose making and my proximity to the events I've changed before."

Dude, we both lived. That's pretty huge.

Finn's fingers glided over the keyboard, and a minute later a miniature version of Drew's floating wad of spaghetti-time appeared. "This is a small section of his predicted paths of time. You've seen it?"

Will nodded. "I spent several hours with him, discussing and essentially dissecting it. How did you get this? He guards it carefully."

"Will." Finn chuckled. "He's my grandfather. He's why I became a physicist. My theories and many of my practical applications were built on the foundation of his research. He also wasn't a physicist. He was a computer specialist, an engineer, and a mathematician. He had brilliant ideas—" Finn gestured to the display "—but he understood that his varied interests hadn't given him a full understanding of some of his own theories."

He invented the time lock, didn't he?

"An engineering marvel," Finn said almost reverently. "He invented a lot of things, Wick. He was the first to pinpoint null space and the first to theorize it could be utilized to get from one When to another."

He kind of had a head start on that. The idea, anyway. He'd been using portals for years.

"Yes, but he also understood there was a possibility that at some point the portals would be gone, because I hadn't yet invented them. He worked on much of that in his later years, knowing he would pass his work on to me."

That breaks my brain a little bit. I know you used portals after he was born.

"They were able to use portals until the actual date of his birth," Will said. "Until we loop around to that point again, we won't know what happened to them."

"Paradoxically, they might not vanish because I no longer need to invent them. As long as the Old Mint stands, so will the solutions we were looking for."

Every loop of time provided more information, more data to store in the time-locked Old Mint. At the heart of it was Drew's work, and that's what Finn had built upon to create his time machine, and then later, the portals. "Without everything he did, we wouldn't have been able to work as quickly as we did. He created such a finely layered foundation that what would have ordinarily taken fifteen years to build, we were able to do it in less than two. All of those things he's playing with right now in your When? The nanobots and the gel and the finely-honed computer systems? All of those made it possible."

Finn thought Drew was slightly off the mark with the display we were examining. "He was more right than wrong. At the time, most many-worlds theorists were looking at time as a flat object, with billions of timelines spreading from one."

That was what Drew had shown us when he flattened his display. The fractured glass, lines shooting from other lines.

"He also believes that all of time is happening at once, that there's nothing linear about it. Hence, the spherical nature of his model."

He found places of time with lines that touched and then whispered to people, at least that's what Hyrum thought.

"Something like that," Finn said. "I admit, I don't fully understand it. I've gone back to study notes in the Old Mint, and it seems to be the first time he's done that. And I'm not sure he's done it *yet*, so..."

He flattened the display. "I think he's on the mark about the tiny filaments that extrude from timelines when you change something. They function as bridges."

"And proximity to event?" Will asked.

Finn nodded. "The further you get from the point of change, the less likely it is that you can go home. But." Like Drew had, he traced a finger over the center line. "Even if you make such a major change, that filament, the splice that connects slivers of one line to another, will still be there for a while."

Like string cheese. Pull a piece apart and there are the little cheesy strings that connect them. Keep pulling and they break.

"The string cheese theory," Finn chuckled. "Just don't hang around after you save her, Dash. Bring her here, and the moment she's cured, take her home and then get out."

"How much time do you think one has in order for the change to stick to one's own When?"

"I wouldn't risk more than an hour with this. Less if possible."

"Drew theorized I might have as long as a week."

Finn shook his head. "Not a risk I would take."

"Presume there was something else I wanted to change. If I needed to go back several months, would that change be there when I returned?"

Finn didn't think so.

"Pity," Will sighed. "I've had notions of keeping Drew from being harmed on his Elysium trip."

"Why? That was a major factor in much of his early work. It gave him focus, making sure something like it never happened again."

That gave Will pause. He'd thought that this was the first time Drew had been injured, that this Drew hadn't gone to Elysium until he was older.

"He was older than your Drew. Lost a leg and a foot. Keeping that quiet was work, from what I understand. He stayed out of the public eye for a good six months while his new appendages were cloned. I'd leave that one alone, Will."

Did he have Shivan stuffed into a drone to help him?

"He had a gutsy general, Wick. They both nearly died."

"Anthony Myers," Will said. "He's refusing a medal of commendation for his actions and is threatening to retire to live on Elysium."

He's still there, isn't he?

"Indeed. He is currently functioning as interim commander."

So just make him the regular commander.

"That would essentially be a demotion."

"Listen to the cat," Finn said as he turned the computer off. "Some things are meant to be."

~

Old Jax waited for Will just outside the elevator door on Union Square. There was still an air of royal elegance about him, his straight back, hands clasped behind it, feet a bit less than shoulder width apart. He waited for Will the same way he had waited for so many other people that the world had declared to be important, though this time there was a softness in his eyes, want and sorrow mixing with newly etched grief across his brow.

Will hadn't expected to see him. He picked me up from the lab's table with the intention of heading through the portal, until Finn glanced at the message that had pinged on his phone. "My grandfather," he said, somewhat amused, "would like a word with you."

The doors hadn't slid closed before Jax said, "It occurred to me, this might be the last time I saw you."

"I'm coming back," Will said.

"You might intend to. But to which future would you wind up visiting? This one, where there are people who love you and have already grieved your loss once before, or the one you're about to create, where you'll continue to exist. Where my mother will continue to exist."

"I'm coming back," Will repeated.

Jax wasn't having it. "You don't know what will happen. Once you change my mother's life, your timeline might be tethered to that one. Presuming you can get home? The next time you go forward, it might be to there."

We've been here so many times we're probably tied to this one.

Will, he's old. Take him to the bakery so he can sit down.

Jax was certainly old but he didn't need to sit. Still, guiding him in that direction gave Will a moment to gather his thoughts. They took a table away from the door, and Will set me where I could get to Jax if he needed someone to purr for him.

"If I find my way home," Will said as he sat down, "I have no doubt that I'll return here rather than there. This is the line in which I will be born. If I create a new timeline, there's no guarantee that I will be. If your mother survives, the resulting changes might not include me."

"Don't—" Jax's voice caught. "I'm not asking you to not do this. I absolutely hope you will. Yet the idea that I might never see you again? I feel as if I just got you back."

A promise wasn't possible.

"And the rub," Jax went on, "is that I'll never know. If I never see you again, I won't know if it's because you couldn't escape that When, or if you were able to get home but not here. So. I came to see you, just in case this is the last time. Humor me, Emperor. Will."

Will got up and skirted around the table, bending over to kiss Jax's head. "I'm getting you coffee and a scone—"

"Coffee makes me shit my brains out these days."

"All right. Tea and a scone. By the time you finish it, I'll come back. Wick and I will go do what we need to, and we'll return before your tea gets cold."

What he placed on the table in front of Jax was the biggest cup of tea they had, causing Jax to mumble about having to get up to pee, and then what the hell was he supposed to do if Will didn't come back by then? How long would he wait?

"If I don't return within an hour, go home. Go home, get Drew, go through the portal upstairs. Pick a date before I've left and warn me."

"But *you'll* be lost to me. That will be some other Emperor."

"It will be me," Will promised him. "Just me before I came here this time."

Jax grunted and then stood up. "Give me this. Have the guts to say goodbye to me."

Will cupped his old friend's face between his hands. "Jax. I love you. I will do everything I can to come back, but if I don't... I've treasured my visits here, and I will miss you. Not the younger Jax. You. And I will mourn not seeing you again."

With a sigh, Jax reached down and ruffled my fur. "That's as good as I'll get from him, isn't it?"

Probably.

"I'll wait a while, Emperor." He sat down again, reaching for his tea. "Good luck."

Will scooped me up. "Goodbye, Jax."

~

You can't do any of it without asking Aisha first. Don't even bring it up with Jax until you do.

Aside from Aisha, he wasn't sure he would discuss it with anyone other than Finn and Jo. There was no hurry; whether he went back now or a year from now, he would end up at the same time and place. He could wait another fifty years, if he knew for sure he would live that long, but there was something about the idea of living all those years knowing he could do something for Donna, and the notion of waiting made him uncomfortable.

But if you waited, and wound up stuck there, at least you'd have lived out your life with Aisha.

"The thought has occurred to me."

Why does it matter so much to you? It doesn't bring her back here, and she was kind of afraid of you.

She hadn't been, in the end. And he knew more now; the things about him that bothered her were hidden in the shadows of how much she cared for him. Given the chance to live, she would be able to show her Emperor how much she cared, and he wouldn't have to live with the feeling that he'd somehow wronged her.

In the next timeline, he hoped that he would live again. He was sure of it.

We arrived home several hours after we left, whether by his intention or inattention, I wasn't sure. We'd used the upstairs portal which defaulted to his thoughts over mine, so it wasn't my fault. If he'd wanted to get home right after leaving instead of lunchtime, that was all on him.

He bypassed his apartment and kept going down the stairs, so it was intentional. I expected the sounds of little kids playing and laughing, but from halfway down the stairs the only things I heard were the low rumble of Hyrum's voice and Rhys's high-pitched giggle.

Rhys was at the table with a bowl in front of him, and he held a spoon that was too big for his hand; he was up on his knees, bent forward, trying to not spill, and when he spotted Will he stayed where he was but squealed, "Daddy!"

"What," Will asked as he bent over to kiss his son, "are we having for lunch?"

"Chocolate soup!"

Hyrum was in front of the stove. His breath hitched as he clutched at his shirt, and he began bouncing on his toes. "I just wanted to—"

Will held up a hand to stop him. "It's fine. I was simply unaware that chocolate could be made into soup."

"And there's toast, too!" Rhys said. "With lotsa butter."

Opening the refrigerator door under the pretense of looking for a drink, he used it as a barrier and gave Hyrum the chance to explain without Rhys watching.

"We were at the playground and a bigger kid was teasing him and I don't know but I told him he was mean and it was too bad for him because I was gonna make chocolate soup for Rhys and all he was probably gonna get was a sandwich, and then I *had* to make it. But it's just hot chocolate, I promise. I'm sorry."

"It's fine. Just don't make this a habit, all right? And perhaps never offer this to Alex and Charlie. They'll demand it daily."

Relieved, Hyrum nodded.

"Where are your brother and sister?" Will asked Rhys as he closed the door. "As well as your mother and aunt."

"Shopping. Hyrum and me didn't wanna go, so Aunt Aubrey said we could go play and then come home for lunch. But she said we couldn't go get pizza again, even though we wanted to."

"Again?"

Rhys dunked the toast into the bowl. "We had pizza yesterday."

"Oh!" Hyrum looked deflated. "We shoulda gotten cheeseburgers. She didn't say no cheeseburgers."

Take a deep breath. Inhale, hold it, exhale. It's better food than if Aisha cooked for them.

"Why?" Hyrum asked me, while looking at Will. "Are you okay? Are you hungry? I can make you a sandwich. I was gonna make me a ham one. With pickles. And mayo. And maybe cheese. Cheese might be too much, though."

"I'm fine, Hyrum. Wick is just being…Wick."

But he wants a sandwich. He hasn't eaten since lunch yesterday. Or maybe dinner. But he's hungry.

There was no point in refuting me. Hyrum had already put several pickle slices on a paper towel to soak up the juice, and he began scooping mayo out of the jar. Before he sat down to eat, he opened a can for me, reasoning that if Will hadn't eaten, then neither had I.

"How come you didn't eat breakfast?" Hyrum asked Will.

"I had errands to run early this morning."

"Daddy went to see Pop-Pop," Rhys said. "Mommy said they might have coffee or maybe even bananas."

"Bananas," Will repeated.

"Because you don't like tasty breakfasts and Pop-Pop would probably have a bagel or muffin. You like fruit."

"There was coffee," Will said.

There were also three Finns. I think they're starting a club or something. Finnegan again and again and again.

"There's three?" Rhys's voice cracked higher. "I know two."

"There's a third, but he goes by the name Liam Finnegan now. We met for coffee to discuss some theories about time travel."

Hyrum brightened. "Was Drew there? Was I? Did you see Jax and Aubrey?"

"You were not there, sadly," Will said.

Hyrum sighed, disappointed.

You were visiting Elysium. Old Hyrum goes there with Zed sometimes.

"Really? Does that mean someday I'll get to go there, too?"

Will nodded. "I assume that both you and Rhys will go there one day."

Rhys pushed his mostly empty bowl away. "How come you never see me when you go there? I'd be a grown up. Do I live somewhere else?"

"I don't see you, nor Charlie and Alex, for the same reason.

In that When, I never had the birthday party that brought your mother back into my life, so you weren't born. That's why everyone there is always so excited to see you. It makes them happy that we had you here."

You're an original, kiddo.

Hyrum opened his mouth to say something but thought better of it. Will had taken him through enough portals that he grasped the concept of time travel, but that he should also not consider the people he met along the way to be the same people in his life. He knew the Emperor had died in other Whens.

Rhys did not. "Do you ever see you?"

"I have met with myself in several Whens," Will said. "I have not seen myself in that one, however."

Before Rhys could ask why not, Hyrum said, "Your Daddy is super busy in all his times and I bet he just works a lot there since he doesn't have you at home to go play with."

That didn't satisfy Rhys. "Doesn't anyone have kids you can play with?"

"They did," Will answered carefully, "but those children have grown and are now adults. I don't imagine they're interested in playing with me."

"I would!" Hyrum blurted.

"Indeed. But you're a very busy man, too."

You go to space a lot. I bet that sometimes you play with the kids who live there.

"I wanna go to school there," Rhys said. "Uncle Drew said there would be a school soon."

What about school here? You get to play with Isaac. And when Blackshear Academy is open, you both get to go there.

"I forgot about that."

"In a castle!" Hyrum squealed.

"I hope there's a moat. We could swim in it."

"Or fill it with fish! Like those giant goldfish with the big eyes!"

"Or a mermaid. Lots of mermaids."

Hyrum took a huge bite of his sandwich, looking quite thoughtful as he chewed. "They're not real yet, but I bet Drew has scientists at Ozoo who could make some. He'd just have to find some ladies who don't mind having fish babies."

"Hm. How would the boy fishes have sex with the ladies? Fish wieners probably aren't big enough."

Charlie spared Will the contemplation of interspecies copulation when he ran into the apartment. He yelled "Daddy!" in one long, all-the-way-across-the-room breath and jumped into his lap. Before Will had the chance to acknowledge his daughter, much less Aisha and Aubrey, Charlie blurted, "Daddy, Mommy made me try on clothes and I didn't want to and they itch and she got mad at me 'cause I didn't want pants I just wanted shorts—"

Will set a finger over Charlie's mouth. "Take a breath."

"Yes, I am the world's worst mother," Aisha said as she bent over to kiss Will. "I refused to allow our son to run around the department store in his underwear. Or less."

"Horrible woman," Will chuckled.

"I got a new dress," Alex announced, climbing onto the chair next to Rhys. "It's black and it has shinies on it."

"Sequins," Aisha said. "And just a few around the hem."

"It's not fair. How come Rhys didn't have to go shopping?" Charlie whined.

"'Cause my suit fits," Rhys answered.

Aisha sighed. "Next time, we take him to see the Kovlovs. Surely he can stand still long enough to be measured."

"Don't count on it," Aubrey said, amused. She dropped a kiss onto Hyrum's head. "What was lunch today?"

Sheepishly, "Soup. Do I need to get a new suit? My old one still fits. It's blue. Is blue the right color for the party?"

There's a party? Why wasn't I invited?

"Any color you choose is fine," Will told Hyrum. "And it's not a party. It's a dinner reception for Robert Lopez. Your attendance is not required."

Maybe not required but I'm going.

"Can you behave?"

Of course I can behave.

And I will.

Unless there's a fly.

~

After multiple terms as the governor of Texas, Robert Lopez was, not so quietly, retiring from politics. At the head of his final month in office, Jax wanted to give the governor something he truly loved: attention. This was an official—but not formal—reception, attended by the most influential people in the perceived free world, heads of state who wanted to offer their well wishes.

Well wishes were accompanied by the dangling of post-political carrots in front of him. He'd publicly stated that he was open to new ventures, and while he felt tied by loyalty to Texas, he wouldn't pass up something incredible even if it meant relocating. Jax thought it was a message to his home country—make me an offer I can't refuse, keep me here—but the governor was not one to retire into a private life of leisure, nor did he wish to be propped up in the corner only to be used on occasion for publicity. Robert Lopez wanted to stand in front of the world, partly because of his ego, but largely because he wanted to make a difference.

Pacifica offered him a platform from which he could jump in any direction. The dinner was held in the massive Westin ballroom where Oz and Drew had their wedding reception; it was one of the few places large enough to hold everyone who wanted to attend, allowing space enough for manipulative mingling followed by dinner and dessert.

The royal family dressed in funeral finery. Black suits, shirts, ties, shoes. Hyrum gave up the powder blue suit with the neon pink shirt he'd wanted to wear when Drew and Oz brought up the idea of digging out the black suits they'd worn for Aubrey's 50th birthday; Sophia and Navi wore flowing black dresses, Aisha a black pantsuit, and Aubrey had Jax nearly drooling with her shiny, very form fitting black dress.

Will dressed as he had on all the evenings when he'd stood guard over the kids at state dinners; with his neatly trimmed beard and clipped hair, his carefully tailored suit was a worthy substitute for the intimidation tux. Instead of standing watch, keeping a careful eye on things, on this night he would be seated at the King's table while Vicat and a dozen other guards monitored the royal tiny tots.

Guests were already milling about the room by the time we arrived, and to Rhys's and Marco's relief, nearly a dozen of them were children. There was an appropriately sized series of tables and chairs near the King's, spaced close enough that the kids would be able to talk and yell at each other without upsetting other guests; just past those tables was a large, thick rug surrounded by toys and books, guards standing close by.

Hyrum circled each low table, reading place cards out loud, becoming increasingly frustrated when he couldn't find his name.

"You're at the King's table," Drew told him. "Why would you sit here with your knees jammed into your chest?"

Hyrum shrugged. "At church stuff I was always at the kids' table. Daddy said I would have more fun on account of the grownup tables were boring. And he wasn't lying, the grownups were super boring. But mostly I think he wanted me to keep an eye on Joe and Spencer. I didn't mind."

"We're not boring," Drew said. "And you're not a child."

"But someone has to sit with them. They're just babies."

Drew tilted his head in Vicat's direction. She hovered close by, surveying the room, appearing every bit as threatening as Will. "She'll keep an eye on them. Besides, this is the kids' chance to have some fun without adults hovering and telling them to behave. They need to get to know each other, because they'll be dealing with each other for the rest of their lives."

"'Til they're old?"

"Pretty much." Drew pointed to a young woman approaching the bar. "I've known her since I was Rhys's age. Her name is Yuki, and Sophia's brother is half in love with her."

"Does she love him back?"

"I'm not sure. They've had an on-again, off-again sort of relationship for years." He pointed to someone else. "That's Gerard Ming. I've known him since I was eight or nine. We met at one of these dinners and became pretty good friends. He was even at our wedding."

"Okay. But I'm still gonna try to keep an eye on the babies."

"Keep an eye on Eli," Drew said. "Your dad, not my son. Things like this are hard on him."

"How come?"

Drew led him over to the King's table. "Something you'll notice at every official event he attends. Eli always has an empty seat to his left. That's where his Queen would sit, if she were still alive. He wants everyone to remember her and how much he misses her. I think it hurts him a little bit."

"Then he shouldn't do it."

"He does it because she was important, and he never wants anyone forget she *should* be here. I think a part of him believes that she's there, right next to him, keeping him calm."

"Okay."

"Is it going to bother you to sit next to her seat?"

"Nuh. I can still talk to him and see the babies from there. Where's Wick gonna be?"

On a hover cart. I'll check on the kids and get you if I think they need you. That way you can talk to everyone else and not worry about them.

"Okay. Is there a place for you to sit so you can have dinner?"

People will feed me while I'm on the cart. Most of them like to sneak bites to me and the kids are really generous.

I had to promise that if no one offered me things to nom upon that I would tell him, and also that I would help keep an eye on Eli before Hyrum felt comfortable with the seating arrangements. Even so, he mumbled his feeling that someone needed sit with the kids, but neither of us wanted to tell him the kids probably wanted an adult-free dinner so they could complain about the clothes and the food and how stupid everyone and everything was.

Alex and Charlie were the youngest ones at the kid's table and while no one expected them to sit still, Vicat was on hand and in charge of their security. She was the first guard expected to act if there was an issue, the first to step forward if an adult approached or spoke to them. Every child, Drew explained, was hands-off unless with a parent. No touching, no shaking of hands, no guardian-free introductions.

"I can't talk to the new kids?" Hyrum asked.

"You can but keep some distance between you. Their guards might step forward, but only so they can hear what you're saying."

Everyone knows who Hyrum is. No one's going to freak if he sets a hand on some kid's shoulder.

Before Hyrum's anxiety over doing or saying the wrong thing to a child he'd never met escalated, Drew promised that if the reception ended early enough, they would watch a movie before bed. He'd discovered an archive of late twentieth century movies, and they watched them together after baby Eli was asleep.

"I promise," Drew said for the tenth or fifteenth or one hundredth time, "these aren't movies that would get you in trouble. They're just super old, that's all. And don't tell your mom about them if you really think she'd mind."

"They're really funny," Hyrum snickered. "Oh. Oh. Oh. Don't tell her I know what a doobie is."

"Hyrum...*she* won't know what that is. I'm not sure anyone in this room other than you and I know what that is."

Well, I do.

Toke a doobie, bro. Or a big fatty. A blunt.

"Wick."

Hey, I'm watching them, too.

Find me a Felicia. I want to tell her 'bye.'

King Eli mingled, winding his way through clusters of guests, looking very much in his element. His laughter boomed, and as he made his way from group to group, there was a lot of shoulder clapping and women wagging their pointy fingers at him. It took him an hour to make his way around, and he looked a tiny bit relieved when he finally stopped where Jax and Aubrey were in conversation with Robert Lopez.

"Where's Maria?" Eli asked Robert. "Did she find an excuse to not be here?"

Robert pointed to the far side of the ballroom, where his wife had baby Jonathan in her arms and was gently bouncing him. "The grandkids are more interesting than the rest of us.

Better conversation, too, I imagine. What about you? Where's your newest son? Sophia tells me he's the light of your life."

"Sophia is not wrong." He waved Hyrum over. "He might be the most interesting of my boys."

"Yeah, thanks, Dad," Jax grumbled, though he wasn't really upset.

Hyrum strolled up, nearly swaggering, with Drew right behind him, and when he was close, he blurted out, "What up, bitches?"

Immediately, he clamped his hands over his mouth and *Oh, no* slipped out in muffled surprise.

"Sorry, my fault." Unapologetic, Drew was trying not to laugh. "We've been watching movies from the late twentieth century and repeating lines to each other. He's memorized a lot of them."

"Hyrum!" Aubrey's glare would have, were Hyrum paying attention, melted him into a puddle of embarrassed goo on the floor. "What *else* do you have to say?"

Hyrum's fingers parted a bit so he could be heard but his hands stayed where they were. "Homeboy don't play that?"

"Hyrum!"

"Homegirl?" He turned to Drew. "I don't remember what they called girls in that movie. Hoes?"

"My day is now made," Robert chuckled. "Don't ever change, Hyrum."

Aubrey was grinding her teeth together to keep from saying anything more and it didn't help that Jax laughed right along with the governor. Hyrum was spared from her probable, inevitable lecture on appropriate language by the flickering of overhead lights, indicating that it was time for people to seat themselves, as dinner was about to be served.

Hyrum paused at the table, unsure. Donna's place card had been switched with his and as he reached out to move them back, Eli put his hand on Hyrum's.

"Leave it. I moved them."

"But she should be next to you! If she's here and I sit there I might squish her on account of she wants to be next to you!"

Everyone stood beside their chairs, waiting for the King to sit, and the King was waiting for Eli to be ready. He leaned closer to Hyrum, making sure he was listening. "Son, whether I leave a seat for her here or not, she's with me. She doesn't care where she sits. And there's that still, small voice in my head telling me that this is what she wants. I can feel it as certain as I can breathe."

"Like a burning in your belly? Red says that means you found a truth."

"Exactly like that."

"But you miss her."

"I miss her every moment of every day, son. I also feel her here, and she is genuinely happy that you're with me. She knows how much I love you."

Dinner waited another minute while Hyrum hugged Eli as hard as he could. When they parted, Jax nodded and pulled Aubrey's chair out for her. Hyrum stepped behind it because Jax was still the one who was supposed to sit first, even though he wanted to hold her chair for her.

They'd learned to time it; Jax's butt hit the chair a fraction of a second before hers. It was noticeable enough to suit protocol but close enough that it felt like they'd sat at the same time.

"One day," he told her, a long time ago, "we're going to rewrite the protocols and I will damn well seat you like a gentleman."

She didn't mind, so she didn't push it.

Or she didn't push it when it came to whose asterisk hit the chair first. She did push the boundaries where public displays of affection were concerned. If she felt like kissing him, she did. If she wanted to hold his hand, well, no one could stop her. A reporter once asked Jax why they seemed to chafe against tradition; the King of England had never been seen smooching his wife, nor with his arm around her. They certainly didn't hold hands in public.

"Pacifica is not England," he replied dryly. "There will be no 'eyes left' order when I choose to show my Queen affection. I'm sure the world can stand to see the occasional kiss or two."

Zed was fourteen, right at the age where any proof of adult affection was gross. He sighed and said, "Yeah, but the rest of us would like it if the groping stopped. Holy hell."

No one asked King Eli what he thought; he and Queen Donna had held to old protocols, but I knew he wished they'd done exactly as Jax and Aubrey chose, and had been open in public.

Twenty years earlier, that hug, his enthusiastic embrace of his son at a public event, never would have happened.

Dinner was thick slices of roast covered in gravy, with potatoes and vegetables and bread with an aroma that had even my carnivorous mouth watering. "Comfort food," Eli said happily. "Beats the hell out of the highbrow questionable taste-fest usually served at these things. I am relieved I don't have to choke down escargot again."

"But the babies won't like this," Hyrum said sadly, looking to the table where the royal tiny tots were seated. "There's no one there to cut their meat and to remind them that if they eat three bites of everything, they get dessert."

Their meat will come pre-cut. And I'll remind Rhys and he'll remind them about three bites.

As I neared Rhys, he leaned forward and told Charlie to sit still. This was grown up stuff and they had to be good because if they weren't, Daddy would be upset, and he didn't want that.

Daddy won't spank anyone if that's what you're worried about.

"I know but it's still not good when he's mad. It makes my tummy hurt."

"But I'm *hot*," Charlie whined.

I edged closer to the table. Instead of roast, there were pizzas and chicken fingers, and the server who placed drink cups in front of each of them said that if they preferred the adult menu, she would get plates.

No one wanted the adult food.

Charlie wasn't done whining. "I just wanna take off my jacket. It's hot in here."

"I'm not hot," Alex boasted as if it were an accomplishment. "I'm cold."

If Marco had an opinion on the temperature, he was too busy shoving food into his mouth to share it. I turned around and headed back to let Hyrum know they were fine with the food they'd been given, and then made the rounds to all the tables. Surely people wanted a chance to say hello and offer me bites from their plates.

I was not wrong. After a lap around the room, I'd eaten enough that I was a whisker and a half away from needing a nap. I decided to sweep around the kids' table again; only Marco was still eating, and Charlie was squirming and had tears in his eyes.

Meltdown in a few seconds, I told Will as I approached. *Someone is not happy—*

"This is bullshit!" Charlie's high-pitched little boy voice exploded throughout the ballroom. He'd gotten to his feet and was tugging on his suit coat, trying to get it off. Rhys scrambled to stop him, but it was the sight of Will quietly standing and skirting the table that made both boys stop talking.

I made a beeline behind him.

"Explain," he said evenly, looking down at his sons.

Rhys launched into an apology, swearing he had tried to stop Charlie, but Will held his hand up.

"I want to hear from your brother. Charlie?"

The suit coat was on the floor and he was tugging at his collar, trying to unbutton it. "Daddy, I'm hot. I'm really, really hot." He looked up; his eyes were rimmed with red and tears spilled over, but this wasn't temper and he wasn't afraid of his father's anger.

Will placed his hand on Charlie's forehead. "You don't have a fever."

"But I'm *hot*!"

"I believe you," he said as he crouched down to Charlie's level. He ran fingers through Charlie's hair, and settled a hand on his back. "You're sweating a bit."

"He's sweating a lot," Alex offered. "Can I have his coat? I'm cold."

Rhys picked it up and handed it to her.

"Daddy, please," Charlie cried. "Can I take my shirt off? I'll leave my pants on. I promise."

"I'll take his pants if he gets to take them off," Alex said. "My legs are cold, too."

Will. His fingertips.

He held onto Charlie's hands, closing his fingers over them to keep anyone else from noticing that they were turning red.

"Please?" Charlie sobbed.

Will undid the top buttons on Charlie's shirt and made sure he had on a t-shirt, but before he gave Charlie permission to remove it, Vicat stepped forward, two backpacks dangling from each hand.

"Complete changes of clothes for each of them," she said. "Shorts and t-shirts, as well as jeans and sweatshirts." As Will stood, clearly surprised, she added, "This was Hyrum's idea. Kids have accidents and he wanted to be prepared. I can take them home, but if you'd prefer that they stayed…" She held the backpacks out to him.

As Will took them he whispered to Charlie, "Stick your hands in your pockets, cowboy. All right, who wants to change into play clothes?"

Around a wad of pizza Marco asked, "Will the food still be here when we get back?"

As Will herded them into the nearest restroom, I reported to Drew and Hyrum, and Aisha followed Will. Eli watched them leave and then snorted, "Tonight, I sincerely wish Donna had been here to see this. Between Hyrum's bitches and Charlie's bullshit, she would have been amused."

"She would have been horrified," Jax said.

"If it were you, she'd have been publicly upset, and then laughed about it privately. But these kids? I'm not sure she could have stopped herself from laughing when Charlie erupted."

"I wish I met her," Hyrum said. "You don't talk about her a lot but you did a little tonight. I liked that."

Eli nodded. "Today is her birthday, Hyrum. She's been on my mind all day. And I believe I'll be telling you more about her. I want you to know her."

"Hell, I want to hear the stories, too," Oz said. "My memories mostly center around the fudge she made for holidays and sitting on her bed reading to her. I don't think she even cared what we read. She just didn't want to be alone."

"She wanted to hear your voices," Eli said. "She had a notion that if you read to her, she could focus on that and cement the sounds of you into her heart, and then she'd be able to hear you through eternity." He looked at Zed. "You realized before your sister did that she was going to die. But instead of crying about it, you made her tell you all about her favorite books, and which story she would want to hear last and forever. Later you asked her what she wanted you to remember, and very quietly she said she only wanted her truths to be told."

"Speak to the truths of their lives," Zed said, softly. "Send them off with their favorite things, speak their truths, and then mourn. No matter who. How could I have forgotten that she's the one who taught me that?"

"Because most of that came from you. Those were your ideas, Zed. She simply laid out a foundation for you to build upon."

"Did you do her funeral?" Hyrum asked Zed.

"I was just a little kid then," Zed answered. "That was a long time before I started working at Alcatraz."

"Too bad. I bet you would have done a really nice one for her. Did she get a nice one?"

Donna was given a funeral worthy of her royal status, attended by people from around the world. There were heads of state, Olympians—many of the people she'd defeated on the track—and as many Pacificans as could fit safely into the venue. It was beautiful and stately, but Eli shook his head and said, "It should have been better. It should have been more private. She would have preferred private."

"We could do one for her. I went to one once that was years later. I think Daddy said it was a remembrance ceremony. It was pretty, and no one cried on account of they only wanted to say happy things."

Eli didn't think a ceremony was necessary but speaking about her was. "We'll do that," he said. "We will speak her truths, and I'll tell you stories about her life. Did you know she was an Olympian? Such a fast runner. She won gold medals, even."

Hyrum sucked in a sharp breath and bounced in his seat. "Was she on TV?"

Eli nodded. "She was. The entire world saw her win her first gold medal. But even better...I was there when she won. That was the day I met the woman who would be the love of my life."

Hyrum snatched the nametag off her empty plate. "And her name was Donna and she was beautiful!"

"Donna Domenico, the most beautiful woman I will ever lay eyes on."

I made a mental note to repeat the conversation to Will.

It might matter.

~

Later that night, after everyone else had gone to bed, Will explained to Jax what he'd been considering. I'd related the conversation with Eli that occurred while he was busy helping the kids change into play clothes; after they returned in shorts and t-shirts—the boys, not Will—with Alex in jeans and a sweatshirt, everyone in the room under thirty began removing their suit coats, and nearly every tie was loosened, including Jax's. If the King relaxed, so could the masses.

That was the dinner Robert Lopez wanted: informal, friendly, with him at center stage. He happily allowed himself to be entertained with notions of ambassadorships and prominent cabinet positions, but by the end of the night, the one that appealed to him the most was the one Eli offered him.

Come to San Francisco, serve as a Consortium liaison, and spend most of your time with your daughter and grandchildren. We'll grab Finn, get Will's grandfather, and become drinking buddies. Oh, and there's already a substantial bank account set aside for bail money. Will made sure of that.

Robert wouldn't commit to anything, but Maria was certain of it. There might be regrets over anything else he might choose, but there would never be any if they spent the rest of their days doting over their grandkids.

After the dinner, out on the balcony, after musing over the success of the dinner and then what gift Charlie was growing into—those glowing red fingers were nothing like Hyrum's or Rhys's—Will told Jax he was seriously considering jumping back and taking Donna to his birth When to be cured.

"It would mean nothing for us, really, but everything for the people in that When," he said when he was finished. "Saving her creates a new timeline, one which I believe we would no longer be able to access. But we would know. Somewhere in time is a When in which she lives."

"There already may be timelines where she doesn't die," Jax mused. "This one isn't necessarily on infinite repetition."

"But this one, we would be sure of."

Tell him all of it. If you don't, I'll tell Drew so he can rat you out. It's important.

"The caveat," Will went on, "is that by creating an entirely new line, there's a slim chance I won't be able to return to this one."

Jax turned toward Will with a start. "Then you're not doing it. You have a family here and you're not abandoning them to save the life of a woman who would hate you for that."

He had no intention of abandoning his wife and children. There was still the research Liam Finnegan was engaged in, a careful examination of the travels he'd taken through time, the lives he led while hoping to bury the pain of his losses. If he decided the risk was too high, Will planned on letting it go.

"I keep coming back to the idea that my living changes this When so fundamentally that it is likely an entirely new timeline, yet I can still jump forward to visit you in your elder years."

"But *you* didn't die here. Some other Emperor died. If you had, and we'd gone back to change that, you might not be able to move forward. Or laterally. Whichever."

"Possibly."

You changed things. Even things that happened a long time ago. You saved Drew.

"That was still something that happened within a short amount of time, Wick. I changed that within a day."

But we were there, we heard you talking to yourself. And then you were there waiting for us when we went through the portal. That was years in between.

"I was there because I remembered, that's all. On that day you encountered three versions of me. The me of that When, who had changed Drew's death within hours, a me who went back to make sure it happened, and...me. And yes, I remember it all."

"The inside of your brain must be like the inside of a blender," Jax said. "But don't do anything until you talk to Liam. And I'd like to be there."

"To make sure I don't go to her if he says it's a bad idea?"

"To go with you if he says it's possible. I want to see my mother again, Will. I want to be there."

"It will be beyond painful—"

"I know that. But come on, do you regret being there with another Emperor's mother when she died, and do you regret plucking another Jo from another When to save her life? Holding her while she died had to be the worst thing you've ever been through. Would you give that up?"

Can you still get to the When where she died? After getting her to leave another When to go with Finn?

Will shook his head. "I cannot."

And you brought her into your timeline, so you can't even tell from that.

"Then let's go see that cranky old bastard and hear what he has to say. And whatever we do, we don't mention this to my dad, at least not yet. Let's not get his hopes up."

I don't think Will wanted to tell him, ever. Nothing he did would bring Donna back to Eli, and it might hurt too much to know that it had been a possibility.

~

Liam Finnegan's Maiden Lane office was impeccably tidy, though it smelled like old men and talcum powder. Jax hesitated once inside, pausing to take in the sight of this twentieth century office that had been recreated six hundred years later. The rich, deep-colored wood was authentic and highly polished, which made him wish that fabricated woods were less common in our own When. It was gorgeous, and he admitted to a stab of envy.

"Redo my office like this," he told Will as they made their way toward Liam's desk. "What kind of wood is that? Is it antique?"

Will ran a finger over the edge of the massive desk. "Mahogany. Rare and expensive, but contemporary, relatively speaking. Older than my father, perhaps."

"So. An antique."

Liam's voice boomed from behind a partly opened door on the far side of the room. "Your father is nearly five hundred years old. The desk, no."

"I meant his natural years," Will chuckled.

Arms loaded with notebooks, Liam came out of the storage room and dumped them on his desk. "The King is correct, either way. He's an antique." He squinted as he looked at Jax. "Have we met? I mean, clearly, we did in another life. You kept me somewhat sane after Dash died, as I recall."

Jax held his hand out. "We have not."

"Well, good to meet you again. Please don't take offense if I don't recall the details. I remember knowing you, fondly, but I can't honestly say those years aren't covered by an inch of cerebral dust."

"He's your great grandfather," Will reminded him.

"Eh. So he is."

You remembered Will.

He gestured for Will and Jax to sit in the large comfy chairs on the other side of his desk. "You never forget your biggest regret. Not that I regret *you*. I regret not protecting you."

"I understand."

You tried to have him cloned.

He waved his hand. "I lost my damned mind for a century or two. But I did that *because* I remembered him. I don't remember all of them."

Will leaned forward, resting his elbows on his knees. "All of whom? People in general, or your other children?"

"Damn, Will," Jax snorted.

"He has intimated that there were women other than my mother. Why not children?"

"You didn't expect me to live alone all those centuries, did you?" Liam asked. "Of course, there were other women. None knew how old I truly was but...I lived. As fully as I could once the grief had let go of me."

"And is time littered with my half-siblings?" Will pressed. "Understand, I'm merely curious. I'm not judging, and I feel a bit hopeful."

Liam studied Will's expression, looking for truth. When he was sure his long-removed son was curious and not critical, he nodded. "A few. Dozen. Or so. But no, don't ask me who they all were, I don't remember most of them other than they existed. The last one was born, eh, a hundred years ago. Maybe more. One fifty?"

"Just how old are you, really?"

"Haven't a clue. I've jumped through portals at the last minute, lived through the years that bring me to the end again, and escaped more times than I can count. I've ventured back as far as nineteen-thirty, lived through it all, and then jumped back to other Whens. I've lived through racial strife, political upheaval, the demise of the United States, earthquakes, floods, and I damn near ended in Florida when King Jackson burned it off the face of the earth. I've done Florida more than once." His fingers drummed against the desktop as he considered it all. "If you'd asked me before, I'd have said seven, eight hundred years. Did you ask? You might have. But my reality is closer to two thousand. Maybe three. Possibly four. Slim chance of five. Some of that was spent stuck in null space, hm, a few extra times. Not all lessons are well learned. Remind me to tell your father to remove that broken transponder. Every now and then it spits itself back to life."

He'd built new time machines, hoping to circumvent some of the events of his life. "For a while I had the notion that I could bounce off null space and wind up in my own life, old body, and fix everything. The only thing that happened was that I wound up where I'd been, following a younger me as he went about making my mistakes."

Why didn't you tell him? You couldn't have jumped into his body, but you could have told him what to do.

"I didn't know what he should do. Everything I knew about the end of the world was already available to him in the Old Mint."

But you could have told him to not make Will keep so many secrets.

"Those secrets resulted in the life I have now, Wick," Will said. "We've discussed—"

"I wanted to," Liam interrupted. "I weighed the notions of telling him against not, and decided it was a matter of dealing with certainties over wishes. The world was more important than one person."

"That person was your son," Jax said coldly.

"The world," Liam leaned forward just a touch, matching Jax's tone, "is more than even my son. But if I'd known I would go on? I never would have—"

Will sighed. "Stop. I'm here now. You're here. I admit to curiosity. What about my half siblings? Their mothers. The other lives you led."

Every time Liam escaped the end of the world, picking random eras to live out what he hoped was the rest of his life, he moved beyond San Francisco. There were years alone at first, but eventually the loneliness caught up and he sought out friendships. He fell in love dozens of times, married, had families. "I've had a hundred different names, William. A few wives. I loved them all, even if I don't remember them well. You are, truthfully, the child I carried with me always. The one I never forgot."

"And my mother?" he pressed.

"How badly will it break your heart? I won't lie to you."

Will already had a sense that Jo was a whisper in Liam's memories. "It won't."

"She was my first love. She bore my first child. She was always there in me, somewhere, but I often had to think hard to even remember her name. Her face faded from my mind a long time ago. Until you showed up with Wick and a wife of your own, I can't honestly say I'd thought about her in fifty years, at least not in ways that had little to do with my writing."

His stories of the Emperor, the volumes Finn read to him as a small child, rarely mentioned the Emperor's mother. The notion that Liam barely remembered her didn't surprise Will.

"You mentioned getting out of Florida before it burned," Jax said. "You were a Floridian?"

"Once or twice. Maybe three times, for a bit. I was curious. Here was this exodus of pious people, clamoring to live in a post-United States theocracy, weaving their government around a church that was questionable in terms of the Christian state they claimed to want. I'm an atheist, but I allowed for the possibility that their lifestyle would bring me a taste of serenity, so I decided to give it a try. Maybe the religious life was the one I sought."

It was not. He found himself living on the very edges of Florida's social norms, inserting himself into the church for the sake of survival, while trying to remain as anonymous as possible. The life of a single man was not possible, especially in the earliest days of Florida as a country; there was constant pressure to marry, whether a relationship existed or not.

He lived as Doyle Keats, a quiet, seemingly introspective middle-aged man whose wife had passed away. When that wasn't enough to keep curious eyes off him—widowers tended to remarry within a year, rarely went longer than two—he began seeking companionship of the women in his local congregation, hoping that they would either tire of his keeping them at arm's length, or that he would find someone he genuinely wanted to live with.

After three unsatisfactory, frustratingly chaste relationships, he met Andrea Benson. She was in her mid-twenties—an old maid by Floridian standards—and he realized quickly that she was a simmering embodiment of untapped genius. Her formal education ended at age fourteen, but books had never been withheld from her and her father actively sought out texts she would find interesting. Liam believed she had given herself an education that outpaced one she would have received in a Floridian university, and it was untarnished by the religious trappings that covered up the glaring omissions intentionally inserted into the formal curriculum.

She was curious about everything, wanted to learn whatever the world had to offer, and he had as much to teach.

"I fell for that woman. She was interesting and engaging. She also wanted children, something I had no reason to deny her. I knew she would raise them to think for themselves, and if there were girls, well, our daughters would get an education even if I had to provide it myself."

"Were there?" Will asked. "Daughters?"

He had to think. "She bore seven children, I think. Two were girls. Brilliant, the lot of them. A few of them were frighteningly bright. Two were quite a bit like you, precocious and…gifted."

Will twitched. "How so?"

"With a touch, they could hear what others were thinking. The one boy, though, he could sit completely still, then reach over and touch you, and shock the hell out of you. As they aged, they discovered a myriad of abilities."

"Before or after your stints in null space?" Will pressed.

"After the third, I believe. Maybe the fourth. Why?"

"Just curious."

"The youngest boy? He was unique." Liam sounded as if he were moving far away from us, losing himself to a memory he was finally able to touch after years of reaching. "What was his name? That boy could hear a whisper across a crowded room. He could burn things to a crisp or freeze them solid, just with a touch. It took everything to keep him safe, away from the gossips and witch hunters. His brothers stood like a wall, making sure no one noticed. I don't think he developed control until he was a teenager.

"There were so many times that I wished he had known my Dash. My oldest boy, he was the reason I knew that he could be taught to control it, yet I was still so angry…" Liam looked up, sadness pulling at him. "Your mother knew, Will. She knew you could control yourself. And she never—" his voice cracked "—I could never find it in me to forgive her for it."

"I know. But I've forgiven her. So has Finn."

"Spencer," Liam said as the name came to him. "His name was Spencer. I wasn't especially fond of it, but it was a family name. Andrea said it went back to one of the early prophets."

"It's a common Floridian name," Will said.

"And not why you're here." Liam reached forward and grabbed a notebook off the top of the stack. "I've pored over centuries of notes."

"That took time, I imagine."

"Hm. Ten years?"

Jax twitched. "Ten years? He asked you to look, what, two weeks ago at best?"

"Well, this wasn't going to be a quick thing. I went back a bit to give myself enough time to research. I have looped back more times than I care to remember, but I can't find an instance where I thought I'd jumped a timeline. I also can't find a reason why you can't make a change and then get home. You're tied to your own When, Dash. Time is going to flick you off the wrong one and slap you back where you need to be."

"You've seen Andrew's model of time?" Will asked him.

"I built my theories from it. You knew that, right?"

Will nodded.

"The thing is, he's not wrong. He's also not right." Abruptly, Liam stood up and went to the other side of the room where there was a coffee pot and assorted condiments. He grabbed a saltshaker and came back, shoving aside his notebooks. "This is time," he said as he poured out a long, thin line over the top of the desk. "Prime line."

He poured out a second line next to it, making sure the starting points touched. "This is the next When, these touching points are where something new occurs. And as it progresses, it melds with the prime." He slowly ran his finger over the desk, pushing the second line into the first. "The changes you've made, they're just grains of time heaped one upon another."

"But to make such a fundamental change?"

Liam shook out a few more grains and nudged them away from the prime line. "It will offshoot. I have no doubt. But you'll make the change so close to your own When that there's nowhere else for you to go but home. This is the dog, and you're the flea. Or, if you prefer, these are the grains of time, and until they're out of your reach, you can hop from one to the other."

Maybe that's how you saved Oz. You frog leaped on the grains of salt and then jumped back.

"Proximity to the event," Will said, mostly to himself.

Or maybe it's all wrong. What if all those noodly lines aren't just one prime line? What if everyone has their own timeline, like Finn said when you were all together, all wound around each other, and the places where they touch are events where people change things with and for each other? Drew's model might be of individual's lines, not a bunch of different timelines.

"I'm not sure that would change anything, Wick," Liam said.

But it would mean that we all travel along our own timeline, back and forth, and because it's a singular line, they can get back to their own When because there really isn't any other When for them. Just...their own line.

Will didn't see a way that so many timelines could veer away and merge, remaining cohesive enough to allow people to continue to interact with one another. Unless, he mused while tapping a finger on the salt spread out over Liam's desk, they were all so intertwined that the filaments Drew envisioned kept them all connected.

Time is like a tapestry and the lines are the threads that make it whole. And the salt is there, too. Places to leapfrog along on your way there and back.

Liam didn't dismiss the notion. "The cat might be as right as any of us. Just don't stay there for long."

What about anchors? That's what keeps him home.

"Most need an anchor, but not all. I still don't know why, even after all this time. I don't."

Salt deficiencies?

He chuckled. "Many deficiencies, Wick."

"Then we do it," Jax said, a tinge of hesitation catching in his voice.

"Indeed." Will got up and Jax followed. "One more question, Liam. Are you still planning on having a child using my mother's DNA?"

"Seems selfish of me now, doesn't it? After proclaiming I needed to clone my son."

"Not so much selfish as inexplicable. You've raised children. The implication was that you had not."

"But I didn't protect the one I should have. I wanted to get it right with him. But no, I have somehow lost that zeal."

"Why the hell didn't you just go through a portal and *ask* him for his DNA," Jax challenged. "It would have been that simple. Just ask."

"Because seeing him, speaking to him, knowing he was going to die again, would have destroyed me. Consider that, King Jackson. You won't walk away with your mother. You'll see her, love her, breathe in every mote of her, and she'll be as lost to you as she ever was."

~

"He remembers." Jax glanced over his shoulder at the entry to Maiden Lane. "All the talk of losing the details of his life? Bullshit."

"I believe he has difficulty recalling without an impetus. You clearly don't like him. Perhaps that's why you think he's lying?"

"I *should* like him. I like Finn. He's just not…Finn. He doesn't feel like Finn. He looks like him, sounds like him, but he's got an underlying edge of total bastard and no, I don't like him."

"You're angry that he let me die."

"Of course I'm angry about that!" Jax stopped, hands balled into fists. "He knew you would die. And he could have stopped it. The son of a bitch has been living for at least two millennia and never tried to stop it."

"And I understand why."

"How? How in the hell can you justify that?"

Will nudged him to keep moving. "Because no matter how he comes off to us now, he's still Finn. He's still the man who gave up having the life he truly wanted because *someone* had to do the work to save the world. My father has always been a bit scattered and has always lost details while trying to see the bigger picture. His heart is good. I don't imagine Liam is all that different now."

He formed a cult, Jax argued. In his many lives, he likely lit the fuse for all of them, including the ones who believed the Emperor was immortal and combed through the days of his birth When for proof. Liam was the reason Will had been dragged into court over support for a child that was not his and carried none of his DNA. He was intrusive, and not especially sorry about it.

"Consider what his admittedly wayward efforts brought into our lives," Will said. "Isaac is a wonderful little boy. His existence has given George a path toward redemption. As intrusive as all of that was, I am grateful for having Isaac in my life, and for being able to know George as someone other than the brute he was as a child."

It was a damned good thing, Jax mused, that Will was not in line to be King. "You're too forgiving."

"Says the man who did not have George executed."

"I did that for Jay," Jax grumbled.

"I have other examples."

"Oh, shut up."

"Regardless. If you feel affection for Finn, then reasonably one might argue that you've forgiven him for the same decisions you hold against Liam. They chose the same thing, Jax. Liam has simply had to live with it longer."

He never forgot and he still feels guilty. There was no winning.

"Indeed. There are a hundred other things he could have and perhaps should have done, but he didn't see those things in front of him."

"You think he's right about this?"

Will paused at the portal entry. "I think he believes he's right. I still think it's a risk."

But a risk you want to take.

"A risk I choose to take," Will agreed.

Are you telling Aisha and Aubrey?

They hesitated. Neither wanted to. Neither wanted to give them a chance to demand they not go. But before he stepped into the portal Will nodded. Not telling them was unfair and cruel. What he was less certain about was telling Eli.

"No matter the outcome, his heart breaks," Will said. "Do we want to do that?"

Jax didn't answer.

He didn't have one to give.

~

"Every time we go through a portal, we're taking a chance," Aisha said, breaking a long silence. They sat at the dining room table with coffee and scones that went untouched; she and Aubrey listened to Will, from his explanation of old Drew's time theories to Finn and older Finn's work based on those theories, and then Liam's notion that it didn't really matter. They understood that Liam spent years combing through his notes; he hadn't reached his conclusion lightly. "I accepted a long time ago that you often jump around in time without my knowing, and yet you always come home."

Aubrey's voice was soft. "But this is an unknown."

"He and I have been dozens of places through the years," Jax reminded her. "He's changed more things than he's admitted to me. He's a complete change to a timeline as it is, yet he can go forward and still come home."

"Have you gone back, William? Gone back and reached the timeline where you died? That moment?"

He'd gone back; he'd waited to see what would happen.

He entered the portal instead of sending me, I followed, Oz yanked us out, and Drew coughed up the idea that Finn used to save the world.

There was no reaching the moment he'd died in all those other Whens; he never saw Finn send me through the portal instead.

"This isn't the same," he said. "That ties directly into my own life. This does not."

Where Jax melted under the weight of her stare, Will did not. He continued to meet her gaze, even as she leaned forward, eyes locked on his. "You're not telling us to get our approval. You're telling us because you've decided. How cruel would I be to say I don't want him to go? To save his own mother's life? You understand that I can't say no, and I can't ask him to not go with you?"

"Whether he goes with me or stays, it changes nothing for *his* mother. She's gone, Aubrey. There's nothing that can be done for her. This is to save the mother of the Jax in the timeline coming up behind us. You can most certainly say no, and I won't take him with me."

"Hey," Jax grumbled. "I'm right here."

You don't really get a vote, bro.

Will snorted. "Bro?"

It's the new 'dude.'

"He gets a vote," Aubrey sighed. "Of course, he gets a vote. But we're all going to agree, aren't we? If you can create even a single When out of a million where Donna lives, we owe her that. But don't ask me to not worry. I'm already terrified. And don't you dare do this without telling Eli. It will matter to him, more than it matters to you."

"That may not be the best idea," Jax said. "To know that some other him gets a lifetime with her, while he still carries his grief?"

"Jackson, you will tell your father, or I will."

"Tell me what?" Eli's voice cracked from the stairs. "What did the little shits do now?"

"This is less about what we've done and more about what we want to do," Will answered. "You may have an opinion."

He came over to the table and plucked a scone from the plate. "If it's about pastries, I certainly do. Who made the scones? I love scones."

"I did," Aisha said, waiting for him to set it down.

He bit into it anyway. "Liar," he said around the bite tucked into his cheek. "Now tell me, what is it I need to offer an opinion on?"

Jax shrunk back in his chair and stared at the cup in front of him. Will set his arms on the table and leaned against them, and without hesitating said, "While it would mean no changes in our own lives, your life, we want to go back in time and prevent Queen Donna from dying."

He took another bite. "You can do that?"

"With risk, but risks we feel are acceptable."

"So why didn't you do that before?" Eli swallowed, then sipped at the coffee Aubrey poured for him. "When you were younger."

Donna Blackshear was supposed to die. It was written in every historical document regarding her life he'd seen in the Old Mint. In every known When, she died from the same disease on the same day, and Will hadn't considered the possibility of changing anything then.

"Cogency of the timeline, protecting it to get my father home after he was lost here, was the only thing I concentrated on. I believe you were, too, to a point. When you knew he was here, lost, you didn't come home. You stayed in Scotland, playing with my grandfather."

"I had orders, too," he sighed.

"Truthfully, I don't think it occurred to me then."

Eli wondered if changing Donna's life would do harm to Finn's success in preventing the end of the world. "She would hate it if she lived and then life for everyone ended, even two centuries later."

There was the Old Mint. He was certain the information would be available because it was there now. Regardless, he only needed a few minutes with himself to pass along everything he needed to know. "If I'm going to change the timeline, I might as well go all the way."

"Then do it."

He was not upset at all, something that surprised Jax. "I thought your heart would break. We can't bring her back to you."

"If you can help her, no matter when she is, then you damn well do it. I survived before, and I'll survive again."

"Eli," Aubrey sighed.

"I'm fine. How will you do it?" he asked Will.

"We'll jump her forward to my birth When. Mass will do the rest."

Eli reached for another scone. "Well, get to it. Time it right, and there might even be some of these left for you."

They both twitched as if they were going to get up and run for a portal. Aisha reached for Will's hand, pulling it closer to her. "I have one request. Really, a demand. Find yourself and tell that son of a bitch that once Donna is all right, he needs to get his ass to Las Vegas, because there's a woman who has a little boy, and they both need him. She'll believe him when he explains why he walked away from her. Let him see the life you have now, and why he doesn't want to wait for it. Because he's going to live, Will. Tell that Emperor he's going to live, and there's no point in waiting."

~

"I chose this time and location because we were in the living room and your mother was the only other person in the apartment." Will sat at the edge of his sofa, tapping coordinates into two jump bracelets. "And I am choosing to jump to where we already are because I feel an explanation is in order. It's also the easiest way to ensure that we'll be able to see Donna without interference."

"You don't think they'll interfere."

The young Emperor would not be surprised to see himself suddenly appear, and it would only take Prince Jackson a moment to adjust to the idea that he was looking at himself. He'd time traveled; he'd gone into his own past to snoop on his parents. That these versions of themselves were poking around time would practically be expected. Will assumed that their arrival without use of a portal would be chalked up to technological progress. And they would help, he was sure of it.

"Once the Prince understands we're there to save his mother," Will ventured, "I expect zero interference."

He's not going to interfere no matter what. He's you. He'll be curious.

"Indeed. Yet I hope they shove curiosities aside well enough to stand guard."

Someone needed to make sure that neither Oz nor Zed entered the apartment while we were in Donna's bedroom. Aubrey would understand if suddenly confronted with older Jax and Will, but the children would not, and it was better that no one had to explain our presence to any of the guards.

Will chose the day that he had given his memories to his Queen. Her knowledge of who he truly was would be necessary to avoid terrifying her; she'd had moments where clarity slipped from her mind, and she was aware of that. If presented with these older versions of her son and his best friend without having glimpsed Will's memories, her anxiety might be overwhelming.

As expected, Jax was on the sofa, lesson plans scattered across the coffee table. The Emperor was halfway across the living room with beer bottles in hand, and when we appeared in the middle of the room, he raised an eyebrow as he handed a bottle to young Jax, who slammed it down and sprang to his feet.

"So, that wasn't a dream," the Emperor said. "You truly can move without a portal."

That gave Will pause. "You remember?"

"I sincerely appreciated the assistance in getting a decent night's sleep, but I also do not now regret informing you that you were unable to suppress my memory. I am biding my time, Emperor. I haven't forgotten her."

"How?" Will sputtered.

You done didn't finish the job, genius.

"Wick."

"I had a notion of what you wanted to do," the Emperor said. "It was there in your mind when you touched me—close the window, close off my thoughts. If you were capable of that, surely I was capable of ferreting out the information you were tucking away in my subconscious."

You should just tell him now. And then maybe let the Prince know that you can talk to me because his mouth is hanging open and flies are gonna wind up in there.

Oh. Hey. Where am I, anyway?

The Emperor reached up and tickled my chin. "You're downstairs with Aubrey. She's preparing dinner for the Queen, and you're...helping."

Ah. Snoopervising.

"I didn't realize I looked like that when I'm confused," Jax said. "I'm you. You know that, right?"

The Prince nodded. "No, I...the cat."

"I'll explain later," the Emperor said.

Dude, just tell him. Wick is over four hundred years old, closer to five, and I totally have long conversations with him while walking barefoot on the beach with my sandals dangling from my fingertips.

He pulled his hand back. "How old?"

Will held his hand out, inviting the Emperor to touch him. "It will be easier and much quicker this way. And I have a message to deliver while I'm at it."

"What?" the Prince blurted. "He never touches—"

"He does now," Jax said. "Besides, I'm pretty sure he touches the hell out of himself all the time."

"Really, Jax," Will sighed.

"I'm not wrong."

"This will be somewhat of an info-dump," Will told the Emperor. "You'll need time to process it, but the most pressing will be on the surface."

After a long minute, the Emperor took a step back, his eyes darting back and forth as he absorbed everything Will passed along. The idea that I was so old was tucked into the back of his brain while he parsed the two main things: we were here to take Donna to someone who could cure her, and Aisha was—whether she realized it or not—waiting for him in Las Vegas.

"You could wait until your forty-third birthday," Will said softly, "but why? What we're about to do will send your timeline on a new trajectory, so you might as well bare your truths, and then get the girl."

"She may have forgotten about me. I was just a crush."

"Emperor. I have met her eighty-year-old self, one who watched from a distance as her Emperor died. She never forgot, but part of her did resent his absence."

Oh, tell him about the kiss. She's smokin' hot even when she's old, and she kissed him and made his toes tingle.

"Indeed," Will said. "When we're done here, if you're half as intelligent as I hope I am, you'll get on the first shuttle to Vegas."

The Emperor turned toward the Prince, his face flush with hope. "They're here for your mother, Jax. They want to take her to my birth When, where she can be cured."

"Forward? You can't go forward. Dad—"

"He lied to you," Jax said. "Granted, it was to protect the work Will's father is doing and to protect Will against the promises his father exacted from him before he came here, but you can go forward. Hell, your father has gone forward. He met Will when he was a little boy."

"Who?"

He doesn't know your name, dude.

Will gestured to the Emperor. "His name is William. He'll explain as much as he can while we're with your mother. I assume you have no objection."

"For saving her life? Why the hell would I?" He turned to the Emperor. "*You* could have?"

The Emperor shook his head. "I never believed that I could."

"And he's not lying," Will said. "It's complicated, and he doesn't have all the facts. Only rules imposed upon him when he was a teenager. As far as he knows, the Queen's death is a fixed point and should not be changed."

"Then why?" the Prince asked, his voice cracking.

"Because I now know better," Will said. "If she lives, it will merely create a new timeline. The future remains unaffected because it will be a different future."

"You know all the questions that spin in your head that you've never dared ask him?" Jax asked the Prince. "Go ahead. He's now free to answer. But don't forget the bigger thing—he's here as part of an effort to save the world, so if your shorts get in a knot, get over it."

The Prince folded his arms, a spark of defiance in his eyes. "So sayeth the Crown Prince of Pacifica?"

"No. So sayeth the King of Pacifica, Midlam...and Florida."

The pinkness faded from the prince's cheeks.

"No, my father isn't dead. He just got tired of the job." Jax exhaled hard. "His heart was broken. He walked away from the throne because he was shattered and didn't know how to function without her. So please, listen to the Emperor, just accept what he says, and let us help her."

They agreed to keep watch, and we quietly made our way down the wide hall. Jax hesitated at the door; he wanted to be there, but the reality of what waited inside that bedroom finally hit him. This was his mother in her final days of life; this was how she had been when he'd last told her that he loved her: thin, weak, and so very tired. Through the years he'd intentionally focused on her life before being told she was going to die; he'd wanted to remember his mother as happy and healthy, and he was about to paint over that image with the truth.

Will whispered to allow him to enter first. She now knew that he could travel in time; it might be less jarring if she saw him before Jax.

Donna was on her back with the comforter pulled up to her chest. Her eyes were closed though she was awake, and I knew she had heard us enter but was too stubborn to look. Eli often stood in the doorway just to watch her breathe, comforted by the slow rise and fall of her chest, and she'd found her own comfort in knowing he was there. She'd lie there, listening for the soft sigh that often escaped him, or the impatient shuffling of tiny feet—Oz or Zed coming in to read to her. If we left her alone, she would grumble, without opening her eyes, that whoever was standing there had better have chocolate, even though she was past wanting to eat any.

If it was Oz or Zed, she'd peek at them and smile, then claim that a kiss was just as good.

If it was Eli, well, sometimes she cried, because the end was near and she could feel it and there was nothing she could do to make it easier for him.

I had no idea what she did when she thought it was the Emperor.

I did what I could to speed things along; I jumped off Will's shoulder onto the bed, and my tiny thud caused her to smile and then open her eyes.

Visitors. Hello. I've missed you.

Will clasped his hands behind his back and lowered his head, an appropriate bow for a familiar royal, and said, "Your Majesty."

"Emperor," she breathed. "You were just here. Did I fall asleep?" She sat up, exhaling sharply. "How long was I asleep? I promised Eli—"

"Ma'am, please, look up at me. Really see."

She squinted. "Wick, what's he going on about?" Then as it hit her, she grinned. "Oh! You're him, but older. Your beard! How wonderful! I never hoped that you would come see me. Well, granted, it's been all of, what, an hour or two? That was such a gift, Emperor. I am grateful I had the chance to finally know you. Oh! Tell me, how are they? My son and husband? Did they come to grips? Did they—"

"Ma'am," Will chuckled. "Would you like to see your son? A much older though perhaps not wiser Jax?"

Her hand went to her mouth. "Could I?"

She's taking this way too well. How many drugs is she on?

Still uncertain, hesitant, Jax stepped into the room. He was not the King, not the imposing figure who could stare down any other head of state and make him wither. He was a little boy again, terrified, wanting to run to her and be enveloped in her arms while also wanting to run away in case she was upset. He opened his mouth to speak, hesitated, and when he managed, his voice caught and broke. "I don't know what to call you."

Donna scooted until she was sitting upright, and then tossed the comforter aside, patting the mattress in an invitation to sit. She was dressed as she often did when home alone, in running shorts and an old race shirt, and across the room left heaped on the corner chair were her well-worn running shoes.

They had probably been sitting there for a year. Eli left them there when she died, and no one touched them until he surrendered the apartment to Jax and Aubrey. The last I'd seen of her gold and black shoes was on the day Aubrey carefully wiped off the dust, wrapped them in tissue paper, and then placed them in wooden box with other trinkets she wanted to keep close.

She'd thought that when Eli was ready, she could create a shadowbox with the shoes and Donna's medals, but it hadn't happened yet, and I wasn't sure it ever would.

The running attire hung loosely on her. Her once muscular legs and arms were thin, skin clinging to bone; it had happened so quickly, mere months had robbed her of her strength, and in a day, perhaps a day and a half, she would slide quickly from brightness into confusion, her breathing would become labored, and she would fade as her family said their goodbyes.

This was, I realized, the last day that saving her—with consent—would be possible.

"I don't care how old you are or where you're from," she whispered as she embraced him. "I'm your mother."

As was habit when he was younger, Will averted his eyes. Displays of affection were rare, but when they happened, he did as he'd learned was an unspoken rule: give them privacy no matter how many people were in the room. On the other hand, I didn't care. I climbed onto Jax's shoulder so that I could touch my tongue to the tip of her nose while he held her.

"Tell me everything," she said when they finally parted. "Aubrey, the kids, all of it. And you, Emperor." She looked up. "I want to know about you as well. Please tell me you found a way around your issues."

Spoilers.

"Oh," she whispered. "And Wick. Tell me he lives at least a few years longer than I. This adorable little man deserves more time."

Jax's hands were still on her arms. "This isn't your Wick. It's Wick, but...we brought him with us. He's still alive."

Damn straight, and I want another kiss.

I stood on my back legs and patted at her.

"Jax, pick him up. He wishes to kiss his Queen again."

He did as he was told, and then set me next to her. "We can't tell you anything about the future, Mom," he said. "Granted, our lives here may take other turns, but Will informs me it would be wrong to set expectations, and then have them not happen."

"But I won't be here to expect anything. I know that. I've found some peace with that. I only want to know that you're all right."

"You'll be here, if we have anything to do with it."

She didn't understand but didn't want to waste any time demanding they clarify things for her. "Just tell me you're happy, and that my grandchildren are well."

Didn't you tell her all this? So she would know what they would be up to?

Will pretended he hadn't heard me.

"So very happy." He spoke softly, so soft that I wasn't sure Will could hear him. "Aubrey and I celebrated our thirtieth a few months ago and she's every bit as wonderful as she was the day I met her. I adore her."

"My grandchildren?"

"Oz and Zed are both married and are very happy. You'd be proud of them. They've become incredible people and are creating their own paths. Every bit as stubborn as Dad, but warm and kind."

I hear big footsteps. Too big to be either of you.

"And Eli?" she ventured.

His voice boomed from the hall. "What about me?"

Some guards you have there. I cocked my head to listen. *Oh, they're arguing.*

"You've aged well," he said to Jax as he entered the room. To Will, "You, on the other hand, don't seem to have aged at all."

"I've been informed that I am a freak of nature."

"Eli, you know?" Donna gasped.

"I do, and apparently you do as well." He turned to Will. "Popping in here now could have gone badly. You could have frightened her—"

"She knew who I was," Will said. "Your Emperor told her this morning."

"And so much more!" she gushed. "He placed his hand on my head and let me see. He's from the future Eli. *Two* centuries."

"How much did he tell her?" Eli asked Will.

"Why I'm here, when and where I'm from, why I didn't seem to age along with Jax. As much as she needed to know to be certain that I would be here for him, and to find peace."

"And your lineage?" he demanded.

"Wait," Jax said. "*You* know?"

"I've known him since he was a little boy, Jackson, though I doubt he remembers me." He took a deep breath. "This is not the time. I saw the two of you on the bridge, you know. The day the Emperor kept Jax from falling. From time to time I've wondered if you would come back. Never would have thought it would be now."

You're wasting time, dudes. Just tell him why you're here and let's get on with it.

"Still mouthy, I see," Eli said.

Donna rubbed her hand on Jax's leg. "You didn't answer me. How is he?"

"Even now, his heart hurts. He abdicated not long after and then ran away to play with the Emperor's grandfather in Scotland. He's only returned in the last couple of years. Being home is hard for him, because he feels you everywhere and I think he feels like he hasn't lived up to your expectations."

"Eli." Her gaze shifted to meet his. "Oh. I am so sorry. I wouldn't do this to you for the world."

Eli popped Jax on the back of the head. "That's mean, Jackson. I don't care how old you are now. I never thought you would be cruel."

Jax stood to face him. "But it's the truth. You're just now starting to come out of the fog, but you still *ache* for her. You're staring down two decades of misery, and you need to know that."

"I do not."

"Listen to him," Donna urged. "If you listen, perhaps you'll be able to pull yourself out of it sooner."

"If you listen," Jax went on, "you won't wallow in it at all. We're not here because I wanted to break my own heart by seeing her again so close to her death. We're here to prevent it." He looked down at her. "You don't need to die, Mom. We're here to take you where you can be cured."

"There is no cure."

"Not here. Not now."

Knees weak, Eli took Jax's spot on the bed. "You mean to take her into the future."

"To my birth When," Will said. "The King's personal physician is waiting, and he has everything set up for her treatment."

Eli stared at the floor, refusing to look up. "I could have taken her there," he murmured. "I could have spoken to Finn. Why didn't I? Why didn't he tell me? He surely knew."

"What my father knew was that Donna Blackshear died too young from a disease that was difficult to cure. He had no information to suggest that she should be saved from history. And given the work he was doing, he avoided making any major changes, in case it derailed forward progress."

He relied on the failures of every When behind him, Jax explained. Altering anything major unrelated to his work might have meant changing details that could lead to success. But he'd figured it out, and the data was secure; it would travel in every When from now on.

"Because of that," Will said, "we feel confident that nothing will prevent him from making the same discoveries this time around. The Emperor has my knowledge on the matter now, so. Here we are."

"You can save me," Donna whispered. "Should you? I've accepted my fate. What if—"

"Do it," Eli ordered. "Whatever it takes. Whatever it costs."

"Eli, not if my living means destroying their futures. They're happy. The grandkids are happy. I won't risk that."

"It will have no effect on our lives," Will said. "Once we bring you home and return to ours, our lives continue on as they were."

He explained as much as he could about Andrew and Finn's theories of time, and how this would create a new timeline. She listened carefully, though Eli was restless and only allowed Will to go on because she wanted to hear it.

It was Jax she focused on. "Does this mean you'll go home, and not have your mother? Why are you bothering?"

He nodded. "I understood what I would be left with when Will proposed all of this. All I need is to know that *you're* alive, and the Jax who sits in the living room with the Emperor will have his mother, and his children will grow up with their grandmother. And his father's heart won't be shattered."

"This seems so unfair."

"No, what was unfair was that no one recognized your symptoms when it was early enough to help you. But now we can, and we will."

"It will also help Jax," Will said. "He'll face the same fate in his mid-forties. Your presence and your experience will help him understand what's happening to him. And your Emperor will be able to take him forward."

She burst into tears. "Not you."

Jax allowed a tiny smile. "I'm fine, I promise. And having survived it, I can tell you that the treatment is painless. You'll sleep through it, and when you wake up…you'll have a headache and forever to look forward to. Then you'll have most of time as a playground. Dad can take you places you've only read about."

"Tell us what to do," Eli said.

Will gestured for him to get up. "Ma'am, are you well enough to stand? If not, Jax will carry you."

She reached out for Jax's arm and pulled herself up. "Just give me a few minutes to change and make myself presentable. The Queen does not appear looking like this."

"No need. Where we're going, you aren't the Queen." Since Jax had a grip on her, Will reached over and tapped his jump bracelet, then grabbed me, took Eli by the arm, and a blink later we were standing in the hospital corridor, where Mass and Finn waited.

~

Donna, vigilantly reserved Ice Queen of Pacifica, bounced on her toes and clapped her hands, then spun around as she absorbed every detail of the corridor with bluish metal walls and track lighting that ran along the floor and ceiling. Her excitement could not be contained; she darted to the wall and ran her fingers over the coarse surface, then touched the chairs that lined the hall near Mass's office and leaned in close to examine fluid artwork on the wall.

These pictures moved; they were video clips programmed to look like textured moving paint, and it took every reserve she had to not touch them as well.

Eli waited quietly as she bounded from one thing to another, an amused smile tugging at his lips. When she'd looked at everything in the hall from the corner to Mass's office door, she ran to Eli and threw her arms around him, squealing "this is the most wonderful thing I've seen in such a long time!"

Will turned to give them privacy in their embrace, but he was the only one. Mass simply waited, and when she let go of Eli, Finn gave a courteous bow of his head and said, "Ma'am."

Her eyes flew open wider. "I know you! Finny!" She launched at him as well. "Call me Donna. You're Eli's friend, not a royal subject."

"All right," he chuckled. "Donna."

"Oh, how I hate that term. 'Royal subjects.'" She turned to Eli. "We're doing away with the formalities, Nicky-bit. If I'm to live, then I want to live like a normal human being. Once we're home, we're walking across the Square together, and we're holding hands. I miss that. Just holding your hand."

She's giddy. This isn't like her at all. She should be too weak to stand.

"Indeed," Will whispered.

She finally took note of Mass, who stood near Finn, waiting patiently. "I don't know you." She held her hand out to him. "I'm Donna. Your patient, I presume?"

"Brian Massimo." If he understood the royal protocol that had been in place prior to Jax's reign, he chose to ignore it. "I am the King's—" he nodded to Jax "—physician. I'm familiar with your disease, but I would like to run a complete scan before we begin treatment. Make sure there are no surprises."

She reached over and plucked me off Will's shoulder, snickering. "Wave Wick over me. Cat scan."

"I know Wick a little too well," Mass said, gesturing to the door just down the hall. "His fees are exorbitant and he gets his fur on everything. We're better off sticking to the certified medical equipment that I have free access to."

She latched onto his hand and tugged him toward the exam room.

"This is uncharacteristic," Eli said softly. "Jax? Emperor? Am I wrong?"

"Her defenses were lowered in her last few days," Will explained. "Fuel that with adrenaline and a new well of hope, and you have this. Uncharacteristic, yet something we could have expected."

"How close to the end is she?"

Finn clapped Eli on the shoulder to get him to move. "Not at all, not now."

"But had the boys not come for her?"

"Three days." Finn spoke as if it were a simple fact and not the dusty reality of her life.

Donna's joy curbed as she entered the exam room and immersed in the cacophony of sounds and enormity of the diagnostic equipment. This was the same room in which Jax had been diagnosed, where we stood and watched as the evidence of his disease appeared on the monitors over the examination table.

Mass explained what he was about to do; it would take only a few minutes, and when the scan was complete, he would have a three-dimensional view of everything inside her body. While he spoke, he set about turning the monitors on, flipping switches, and he reached for one on the underside of the table.

"Heat," he grunted as he bent over. "The table is cold."

"Hey, I never got that," Jax grumbled.

"Well, I like her," Mass countered.

It was warm when I got on it.

Donna ran her fingers over the edge of the table. "How many more years will it be before this is invented?"

"Similar scanners are already in use in your When," Mass said. "The technology we'll employ today is significantly refined, and the research into that will begin in approximately twenty years." He glanced at Will. "How old is Andrew, in her When?"

"Andrew Van Hoff?" she asked. "He's just a little boy."

"He's a bright boy with an incredible future ahead of him," Eli said. "Come on, let's get to it. Hop up on the table for the good doctor."

She reached over and tugged on Mass's shirt. "Are you? Good?"

Jax was horrified, but Eli laughed. "He wouldn't be Jackson's physician if he weren't."

"That's not what I meant," she giggled, sitting on the exam table.

"I know. But that's the answer you're getting. Come on, lay back so he can get to work."

Donna wiggled her eyebrows and settled back, arms at her sides. Her eyes followed the track of the scanner, but her head did not move, and she barely drew a breath until Mass told her she could sit up.

The images from Jax's scan lit up parts of his head where tendrils of the cancer had wound its way through his brain. Donna's lit up most of her body; it had metastasized everywhere, into her liver, intestines, choking off her reproductive system, and there were strands winding around her heart.

"Odd. Only the lungs seem unaffected," Mass mused. "Frankly, I'm surprised you're coherent. You should be in agony—"

"I am," she said, calmly.

"Yet you're not medicated out of your mind. You should be."

The drugs made her sleepy, sleepier than she cared to be. If life was winding down, she didn't want to miss any more of it than she had to, even if it meant living in her bed, moving as little as possible, waiting for the people she loved to come see her. "They've been very good about that, even the Emperor. But I am looking forward to being outside, seeing people, and playing with the grandchildren again."

"We'll take them to the beach," Eli said, reaching for her. "But first, let's get this done. What's the protocol, Doctor? How difficult will it be, and how uncomfortable—"

"Not at all."

He led them out the door and down the hall to the first door on the left. It was the same surgical suite where George had spent months recovering from brutal injuries that should have killed him. Jax had been saved here. The tank had been replaced after Jax's surgery; the new one was twice the size, long and wide but not as deep, and the gel sparkled under the bright OR lights.

Donna's excitement faded quickly, and her steps faltered. It was almost too much to take in, and if not for Eli's arm around her, she would have sunk to the floor.

We need Aubrey. Aubrey could make her feel better.

"I'm all right," she said after a moment, patting Eli's hand. She asked questions about every piece of equipment. What was is this for? What does it do? When she settled on the tank, stepping over the forbidden blue line to rest her hands against the side, Mass didn't order her away. He went to her side and reached over, sticking his finger in the gel so that she could see it was harmless.

"You'll float in this. The tiny metallic flakes are nanobots, and they're the powerhouse behind the procedure. They make everything we'll do here possible. In the simplest of terms, they'll eat every cancerous cell in your body without damaging the rest."

"I'll float," she whispered. "Won't I? My body will float on the surface?"

Show her the pictures. You took pictures when Jax was in there.

Will fished his phone from his pocket and picked through a seemingly endless photo stream of his kids, scrolling with his finger until he found the set taken during Jax's surgery.

"Perhaps a visual might help," he said, handing her the phone. "This is literally all you'll do. You'll be suspended in the gel's center while the nanobots remove all signs of cancer from your body, and while they repair any damage."

Dude, tell me you didn't take a picture when he had the raging boner. No mom wants to see that.

"Emperor, for God's sake, he's nude," she sighed, trying to hand it back to him.

"Go ahead," Jax said. "I'm not that modest and you've seen it all before."

With another sigh, she took the phone back. "I am never looking at my son the same way again. This doesn't look awful. You were just suspended there in the center of it all? And felt nothing?"

"I had a bit of a headache after. Mass slapped a pain patch on me, and an hour later I was fine."

"What's this?" she pointed at the respirator, and then looked over at the table where hers waited.

"It keeps you breathing and prevents any of the surgical gel from getting into your nose and mouth. You'll be asleep before it goes in and won't wake until after it comes out."

As he did with Jay and then Jax, Mass explained each step, minus the method used to expel the nanobots when the surgery was done. She hung on every word, stepping from point to point as he told her what each piece of equipment was for and what information he gleaned from them. Eli listened, but instead of moving with them he rooted in place, watching, soaking up every curve of her.

Jax was also focused on her; he had limited time with her and wanted to sear her in his memory. Eli watched with gratitude and joy he could not quantify.

"Will I sleep?" she asked when he patted the exam table, indicating for her to hop up. "I mean true sleep, not that unconsciousness one usually associates with surgery."

"Both. There will be times when the computer senses that you need restorative sleep and will adjust the anesthesia to allow for it while still keeping you under. When we wake you up, you'll have the sensation of having slept and the restfulness that comes with it, although you'll also wish you'd gotten a few more minutes."

She hopped up onto the table. "So, typical."

"Personal question," he said, ignoring the bare whoosh of the door as the technicians entered. "How much weight have you lost, and when?"

She didn't know. The scale had been removed from the apartment to prevent her from obsessing over it, and she avoided mirrors because she was afraid of what she would see. Mass wanted a rough idea, and turned to Eli, who held his phone out to the doctor.

"This picture was taken three months ago. The one before it, six months. That might be more telling."

He'd snapped a picture of her as she passed by him in the living room, wearing a tight cotton shirt and running shorts that fit well. Her legs were still lean and muscular, and through the shirt it was easy to see that she had the washboard abs Jax wanted, though not badly enough to work for.

Mass flipped back and forth between them. "It looks like you've dropped around sixty pounds, if we account for the loss in lean muscle. You weigh—" he glanced up at the monitor over her head "—just under fifty kilograms right now. How tall are you?"

"Five-eight."

He didn't want to alter her appearance too much, but he wanted to give her extra time in the tank to allow for some lean muscle growth. "The nutrients we feed you will be calorically dense enough to put roughly five pounds of body fat on you as well. You'll look like someone on the mend, but not someone miraculously better overnight."

"Doctor Massimo, I don't care if I look like death warmed over when this is done, as long as I'll live to see my grandchildren grow up."

"Barring an accident occurring elsewhere, I can promise you that."

"Unless I drown in there," she kidded.

"No one has ever died in the tank. It's not possible."

"Still." She beckoned Eli over. "I'm not saying goodbye, but I insist on telling you how much I love you. And propriety be damned, you're kissing me."

When Will turned his head, Jax jammed his elbow into his ribs. "Stop it. You're not a servant. No one will explode if you see them mash lips together. Though I might drop if there's tongue involved."

Donna snickered and leaned to the side to see past Eli. "Boys. You, too."

It was Will's hand she reached for first. "I know, I know. I won't touch you without invitation after this. But I need to thank you, properly. I will never be able to repay this wonderful gift."

He bent and kissed her fingers. "Ma'am. Gifts are not to be repaid." When she didn't let go of his hand, instead pulling him closer, he also placed a kiss on her forehead.

"I believe I do, too, and I'll tell him so," she whispered when he stepped away.

Eli and Will stepped back, closer to the door so that she could speak to Jax privately. They were quiet, though, and the techs were respectful enough to not interrupt, so I listened carefully, because I am not always as polite as I could be and I'm not sure why anyone would expect me to be.

"When you get home, you tell those beautiful children how much I love them, and I miss them. It doesn't matter if I still get to see them grow. I miss *your* children, Jackson. I already feel that deeply. And Aubrey—she must know how much I treasure her, despite our beginning."

"She knows. She loves you just as much."

"I'm proud of you. Please tell me you know that. The Emperor—" she glanced at him "—has told me perhaps more than he should have. More than I can sort through so quickly. But if you're half the man he's shown you to be, the world is so very lucky to have you."

"This world will be luckier still. It needs you."

"I will miss you, King Jackson. Baby bear."

"I love you," he said, his voice riding on breath. "I never really had the chance—"

"I heard what you didn't say," she murmured. She kissed his cheek, then his forehead. "Keep Eli company. He won't do well, waiting for me."

I wanted to tell her things, too, but Mass pushed us out the door.

She knows I love her, too, right?

"Wick, out of everyone, your feelings were always the least in doubt."

In the hallway, Eli focused on the OR door, willing it to open, wanting an invitation back inside. At some point he would be allowed in; the old, not-so-comfortable comfy chairs were will in the corner and only needed to be pulled to the blue line. I expected Will to tell him that, yet he didn't.

Mass came out a few minutes later, and he didn't tell Eli, either.

"She's sedated and being placed in the tank now." He didn't take it personally when it seemed as if Eli was ignoring him. "I expect this to take four and a half to five days—"

That made Eli turn. "Days?"

"—and I am not fudging the expected duration this time. This cancer has spread to nearly every nook and cranny in her body, and we'll need extra time to make sure the nanobots get it all."

"Were we unclear on the amount of time needed?" Will asked Eli. "I apologize. It often seems unnecessarily lengthy, but the alternative is the barbaric surgical techniques of the twentieth to twenty second centuries."

"Hey, we still need that from time to time," Mass said. "It wouldn't be an option in this case."

Eli spoke softly. "Then I just go home and wait? How? I can't be in another century while she—"

"We'll stay at my parents' apartment," Will said. "You can spend as much time with her here as you like."

Until the OR was ready for a visitor, Mass suggested we wait in the cafeteria. He intended for Eli to be wowed and amazed by the things he could see from there, without knowing that Eli had spent significant time in this When and kids flying around in jetpacks was nothing new. It would not be the welcome distraction it had been to Aisha, and later to Jay, Drew, and Oz.

"I heard the sound of a portal up there," he said as Will pulled up the menu to order coffee. "How?"

Will didn't look up. "Because there's a portal. Finn placed it there a few years ago, when my oldest son needed surgery."

"Son. You have children. I am surprised, Emperor."

"Perhaps not as surprised as I on most days."

"Couldn't just use the portal on Union Square and then walk through the front door?"

"The circumstances of his surgery benefitted from secrecy."

"Bio-dad didn't know about Will being from the future," Jax snorted.

"Jay is Aisha's son," Will explained. "I claimed him as my own, with his father's permission."

There was Eli's distraction. He wanted to see photos and didn't care if they would spoil some future event that might not even happen. While Will searched for the file that had photos of all the kids, from Jay down to Zed's newborn, Jax pulled up the video compiled from news footage of Will and Aisha's wedding.

"Listen to the crowd cheering for you," he said as he handed his phone over. "You'd been in Scotland so long, and they were thrilled to see you."

Eli's eyes flicked toward Jax. "You're wearing your uniform. You married them by King's decree?"

"There was no way in hell we were letting him scare her off again. I stapled those two together for eternity."

"I know her, don't I? She used to team up with this one to lie for you, as if I didn't know where you really were."

Eli was treated to the story of Will's wayward love life, peppered with Jax's opinions, which were easily summed up with a simple, "He was an idiot." Will repeated the same assurances he always offered Aisha: he would not change anything, because it brought Jay into his life, and even if they'd never reconnected, the world needed Jay.

"And yet you just told yourself to go find her," Jax said.

"Well, I'm an idiot but I'm not stupid. She has Jay now. The Emperor can save that boy years of grief."

What about his surgery? He got a better deal by coming here. Can this Emperor still do that?

There didn't seem to be a reason why he couldn't. Even if the timeline split, the same people would be there. Mass would be there; he would recognize the Emperor and there would be little to prevent them from jumping forward to get it done.

"That might not be a choice they'll make, regardless," Will said. "He'll be young enough that the process will be far less complicated."

Until someone reminds Aisha that he can't have kids of his own. If he comes here, he can.

"If he finds her and marries her," Eli said, "I will remind him of the possibilities. May I ask what his issue is?"

His issue is a giant asterisk of a stepfather.

Will gave Eli the short version; George Denton would not be allowed to impose his will; he was certain of that. Between the Emperor's standing and the notion that Pacifica's King would take a vested interest in the young child who would be renamed Jimmy and then Jay, there was little chance that George would be able to twist things this time around.

"This really will be a whole new When." Jax touched the picture on Will's phone; it was Hyrum holding Rhys, and they were giggling wildly. "Why don't we just pick up the snow globe and shake the shit out if it?"

"Indeed."

Eli's eyebrows knotted. "Explain."

"Hyrum Blackshear, formerly Munson," Jax said. "Save him and then end Levi Munson before he has a chance to destroy Midlam."

~

Quiet tension blanketed the room as Eli absorbed archived news broadcasts of the first war between Pacifica and Florida. Will connected his phone to the living room video monitor and selected a series of reports he'd stored, reports that condensed the information without sacrificing the important details. Eli watched as Midlam fell amid an onslaught of centuries' old technology, and the fighting that occurred while Will hid the royal offspring in a Denver safehouse, and then while he marched across Colorado with Drew and Zed in search of the kidnapped Oz.

He pressed his hands to his mouth to keep from crying out as he watched Levi Munson's final Thanksgiving broadcast with Oz chained to an electric chair, wires puncturing her skin, the evidence of his brutality painted across her flesh in black and purple, with flecks of blood everywhere. He saw in front of him Oz at eighteen, but his mind's eye imposed over that image the little girl who had, just a day before, announced that she was going to be a "begetarium, but the kind that eats hot dogs" because the meatloaf placed in front of her was "grosser than boogers."

Eli remained tightly wound through coverage of Munson's trial and only softened when Aubrey took the stand. He allowed himself a few tears when Oz testified, and I heard him swallow against them as Will plucked her from her seat and carried her from the trial chamber. When he could speak, his voice was soft.

"Oz has grown into a formidable woman, hasn't she?"

"I can't begin to tell you the half of it," Jax agreed.

"She's such a stubborn little imp."

"That won't change. None of this broke her, Dad. She bent, but…no, she didn't break."

Using the remote he picked up from the coffee table, Eli backed up to Levi's Thanksgiving broadcast and paused it just as Oz had her arm cocked back to punch Munson in the throat. "Tell me how to prevent this. No, tell me I can rid the world of that despot now. I've wanted to since—"

"You know he's Aubrey's father," Jax prompted. "She thought she'd hid it well, but…we're pretty sure Mom knew, too."

Eli gave a slight nod. "My gut rolls every time I see that man. There's something about him…he wants the world and I have no doubt he'll align with the devil to get it."

"Russia," Will said.

"Same thing." Eli sighed and leaned back, pressing fingers to the bridge of his nose. "How did he carry out an attack over Chicago? They don't have the technology."

"Airplanes," Jax said. "They few six bombers out of Canada."

"*Canada* allies with them?" Eli blurted.

"Not in the least," Will replied. "They were able to get the aircraft into the country by deception."

He took the remote and pulled up images we had seen years ago in Jax's office of Florida's boneyard, a storage area for broken relics. We watched as the wall came down and Floridians marched out of the country under the guise of escape, and Eli noted the same thing I had: the boys who were told they were men, who would fight and die for Levi Munson's megalomaniacal ego.

"I'd kill the bastard tomorrow if I could," Eli said. "His Second Minister is young and not ready to assume the throne, so to speak."

Jax nodded in agreement. "He's close, but he hasn't been anointed yet and without that he doesn't automatically become First Minister. But there's someone you need to focus on first, before you find a way to unseat Levi."

Will sorted through files until he found the video he was certain Jax wanted to lead with.

"Hyrum," Jax said. "Aubrey's little brother. Save him first. Get him the hell out of Florida and under your protection, nail down his custody so he can live with your son and daughter-in-law, and then do whatever the hell you want to Levi."

We watched Hyrum on his first Christmas with us, as he stopped at the head of the hallway, his excitement bubbling at the sight of the bicycles Santa had brought. Will and Jax both laughed softly when he squealed, and we kept watching until Hyrum dumped out his stocking and found Lazybones' whiskers.

Eli leaned forward as he watched, his head cocked to the side just a hair. "What's wrong with him?"

"Wrong? Nothing," Jax answered. "At this point, this Christmas, his mental age was roughly six or seven years old, with brilliant spikes of wisdom that seem to transcend age. He's made significant leaps since he came to live with us, but he will always exist somewhere within a childhood that never ends, and he will become the light of your life."

~

There was little information available about the Munson

children in Eli's When. He knew about Redmond because of his position as Second Minister, and he had guessed that Aubrey was the oldest daughter based on her name and reticence to discuss her childhood. Names of the sons were public knowledge; there were no circulated photos and the media was generally respectful of privacy where the minor offspring of public officials was concerned.

Until Jax listed the names of all of Levi's children, Eli wasn't sure if there were daughters other than Aubrey or not. But what stood out to him was the absence of Hyrum's name on the known lists of Munson male children.

Hyrum would not, Eli vowed, make his trek across Midlam. The war would be thwarted and he would make sure that Hyrum was living with Jax and Aubrey long before then.

But that walk was important to him. He didn't understand that he was a man until then.

"There are other ways to raise up a man," Eli said. "Wouldn't it be better for him to come to that realization through love and knowing that he's treasured?" He gestured to a photo of his our-When counterpart laughing with Hyrum. "You do treasure him. I can see that. I can't imagine that he would be less so with us."

Jax sighed. "He might even be a bit happier. Oz and Zed are still young, and he had no playmates in his twenties. His toys were taken away, he was stripped of his ability to find joy in play. Bring him home soon, and they'll all benefit by his presence."

What about Bree? He won't be there when she's born.

"Remove Levi from the equation, and he'll still have a close relationship with her. Red would permit nothing less," Will said.

When they weren't at the hospital waiting for updates on Donna, they were in front of the computer, formulating strategies to bring Munson to his knees before he had the chance to align with Russia. Will knew where the functioning airplanes had been stored, where they obtained fuel and parts, and how Florida had gained admission to the Winnipeg airshow that gave them access to Chicago.

We sat in the cafeteria late on the 4th day, crafting plans while we waited for news.

It was a war that could be won without a shot being fired; Eli was certain that Pacifica could take Florida without destroying it, and the wall would come down well over a decade sooner than it had.

"Midlam might never become part of Pacifica if this happens," Will mused. "Not unless you foster the childhood dreams of the crown heirs and encourage their hope to unite once they both ascend the throne."

Jax didn't think it mattered. "The only thing those two need to do is fall in love, get married, and have little Eli. And then shove him into the future to make sure Finn is born."

Eli huffed, a bit amused. "The future gets complicated. Send them back to visit us when the kids are teenagers, let them see what they have to look forward to."

The awkward pause that formed was impossible to ignore.

"What?" Eli asked.

Will was the one who answered. "Once we leave, your timeline will undoubtedly diverge from ours. There's little chance we'll be able to return, not past the moment we brought Donna here. I've made fundamental changes to my own history before, but not one of this magnitude, and I truly do not know what that will do."

Old Oz and Drew have come back to visit themselves, and you lived in our When but not theirs.

"We travel along a fusing timeline, Wick," Will answered. "This may take such a sharp turn that no merge occurs."

"How sharp a turn?" Eli asked.

"Uncertain."

"You can get home? If you've made this big of a change, can you get home?"

Jax looked down, unwilling to meet Eli's gaze. Will took a beat before replying, "I am reasonably certain that if we deposit you back into your bedroom in your own When and immediately jump, that we can return to our own."

That was not the answer Eli wanted. He got to his feet, fists clenched. "How could you, then? If you can't get home—Donna will never forgive herself. How could you do that to her? Or your children? Your wives?"

"How could I pass up a chance to let my mother live?" Jax countered. "The risk seemed—"

"You have *him*," Eli shouted. "In any When, you have the Emperor. All you needed to do was *tell* him. You could have just told the Emperor, my Emperor, what needed to be done and then gone home. For God's sake, you could have come *here* afterward and waited if seeing her meant that much to you, but you should have told him, Jackson. Everything this Emperor can do, so can he. You should have told him."

Every nervous moment of the last four days poured out of him. Tears he had managed to hold back poured over his cheeks and his breath came in tortured, heaving sobs. "You're my son, even..."

Well, now you might have two of them.

"Wick, hush," Will whispered as Jax pulled Eli into a tight hug.

"Tell me why," Eli whispered.

Will gave a light shrug. "Truthfully? We didn't think of it."

"You didn't think of it." Eli pulled back from Jax and dropped into his chair. "The boy genius, the adult idiot."

"I was the boy genius," Will said to Jax. "You're the adult idiot."

"Kiss my ass. And now you can never make fun of Finn for all the things he didn't think of. We now have proof. It's genetic. We're all so focused on what we want to get done that we're stupid in how we do it."

I could have told you that.

Will tapped the top of my head with his pointy finger. "Really, Wick? Then why didn't you suggest it?"

You didn't ask my opinion.

"When has that ever stopped you from giving it?"

I would have answered, but the cafeteria door popped open and one of Mass's techs was there, informing us that they were ready to pull her from the tank. In another hour, we could see her.

~

King Eli paced the corridor, pausing at the OR door every time he neared it. He refused to sit, refused to wait in Mass's office, and refused to engage in conversation. He wanted to prowl, and I felt sorry for whomever opened that door because he was ready to pounce.

"She's out of surgery," he grumbled. "Why won't they let me in?"

Because she has a vacuum cleaner wedged up her asterisk and no one wants to see that.

I was on Will's lap and felt him move with the chuckle he managed to contain.

"They need to clean her up and then wake her," Jax said. "I've been assured that the bathing is thorough and upsetting to view. You're better off out here."

"I watched that woman push you out along with a disturbing amount of blood and feces. I hardly think—"

"But you didn't watch as someone rolled her unconscious self over, hiked her hips up, spread her cheeks, and scrubbed."

Eli stopped in front of Jax.

"The cleansing is somewhat internal as well as external," Will said. "No, you do not wish to observe that happening."

Jax snorted. "He would know. He watched his wife come out of the tank. Mass only allowed it because nothing seems to faze this bastard."

Will gave a light shrug. "Matters of biology aren't worthy of upset."

"My kids shit all over him when they were babies and toddlers. He never blinked."

They almost got a smile out of Eli. "The Emperor nanny. Oz calls you Empy sometimes. Does she still?"

Dude, I'd forgotten that. We totally need to bring back the Empy.

"She does not," he answered Eli while ignoring me. "They call me by name now."

"But they think of him as their uncle," Jax added. "You formally adopted him when he was forty-two."

"Did I now?" He resumed pacing. "I wanted to grab him

when he was a boy, you know. Grab him and bring him here, prevent all the misery I suspected he was facing. But to do that, I would have had to tell Finn who his son would become. He didn't know, not then."

"You did?" Jax asked.

Eli had access to the Old Mint, and he wasn't shy about using it. Will's identity was not difficult to ascertain; Eli had read as much as he could find about his descendants but was limited in viewing information that occurred past his own lifetime. "The system refused to give me access to my own future, and that of my son. But all of Finn's and William's was there, and I managed to fit the puzzle pieces together. And this one—" he paused to pet my head "—I never did come to understand why Finn brought him to us so early. He could have brought him through on that last day."

I needed to be in Jax's backpack on the bridge when he was six. Otherwise he might have climbed higher because the weight of me didn't make it snag on the metal. And if he had climbed higher, if he fell, well, there would be a tiny Jax-splat on the road.

Finn had no way to know that sending me ahead was crucial to Will becoming the Emperor. He simply followed his gut.

The OR door popped open when he was on the other end of the hallway. Mass stuck his head out and waved him in, and he nearly broke into a run getting there.

"It's a shame he doesn't like her," Jax chuckled.

"Are you prepared to say goodbye?" Will asked. "She'll be ready to go home within the hour. We shouldn't take the time for extended conversation once we leave here. We need to jump them back to their bedroom and leave immediately. If you have anything left to say, you should do it now."

Jax wasn't ready. He stood on shaky legs—leaving her behind was becoming too real—but he made his way to the OR door and knocked on it, waiting for permission to enter, lest she still be in a state of undress.

What about you? Do you want to say goodbye?

"I shared my feelings with her when I gave her my memories, Wick. I won't rob Jax of even a moment of this time. But if you need to give her a kiss, I can let you into the OR."

She knows I love her, right? She won't forget.

"Indeed. Next to Eli, you're her favorite Blackshear. She'll never forget."

I thought she might put Jax a little higher on the list, and she would especially put Aubrey and the kids ahead, but we discussed it anyway, waiting as Jax said the things he wished he had told his mother before she died. He was in the room for half an hour, and as the door started to open Will reminded me that Jax was probably upset, and this was one time I was not allowed to mock him for it.

His eyes were red, but he was more at ease than he had been when he entered the room. Eli came out right behind him, his face flush with wonder and joy, and his grin was flush with amazement.

"Not a sign of it," he marveled. "And she looks younger! Still too thin, but…"

"By design," Will reminded him.

"Mass says she'll be ready to go in about five minutes," Jax said. "If you want—"

"Let's just get them home," Will said gently.

Eli's voice came at us from the rear, even though he was standing in front of us. "Wait. Just…wait."

Our Eli had come through the portal, with Liam Finnegan right behind him.

"Dad." Jax went to him, reaching for his arm, rubbing it gently. "I'm not sure you should be here."

"I know my heart will break, Jackson."

Other Eli, the King, cocked his head a touch. "I'll go in and warn her that he's here. She'll want to see him. What he needs to tell her…I imagine he has regrets. I would have."

"Dad," Jax breathed again.

Eli watched his younger self go into the OR. "I wasn't there when she died, Jax. I never…" he swallowed against the lump in his throat. "I understand she's not my Donna. Yet, she is. This *is* the woman I loved and lost so long ago. There is a direct tether between us. And I am aware this will be the last I see of her."

Will stood and put me on his shoulder. "The order of

words," he said gently. "Therein lies your regret. Say what you need to, but remember, your regret was centered around the last words she heard from you."

He didn't need to be reminded what they were. When Other Eli beckoned him in, he took a deep breath, squared his shoulders, and went inside.

Should I go with him? To purr for him?

"Not this time, Wick."

Are we ignoring Liam?

They'd forgotten he was there, waiting quietly. Other Eli looked at him, inclined his head, and said, "Finn. I'd say it's been a while, but I could look at my watch and count back that far."

"Oh, it's been longer than you can imagine."

"Play nice," Will warned. "Eli, this is Liam Finnegan. He's a far-past Finn who makes this When his home."

Eli stuck his hand out. "Nice to meet you, then. How far past?"

"Can't honestly say," Liam said. "Could be the one before the Finn you know. Possibly two. Or three. More likely fifty or sixty."

"And you brought your Eli here."

Liam shook his head. "He came on his own. I just tagged along."

Will's eyes narrowed. "You're not the tagging-along sort. What are you up to?"

"I took another look at my data. Poked around a bit. I'm less certain now than I was before regarding what might happen to you. There are simply too many what-ifs."

As Jax blurted, "What?" Will calmly asked, "How long did you poke around?"

"A couple of years. I still think my theory of merging timelines is correct, more so than Andrew's theories built upon the many-worlds idea. But there's a kernel of uncertainty and it's not a risk worth taking."

"A risk we have already assumed."

"Not entirely." He exhaled, long and slow. "You're not taking them home, Dash. When Eli is done in there, you're going home with him. Since you're here, where you have been a hundred other times, your odds of portaling to your exact When are significant. And you need to use the portal. This one, no other."

Other Eli nodded in agreement. "I can get us home. If you have the means to assure that you land where you came from, then do it."

Will wasn't convinced. "My concern is that if you go through the portal and don't end up seconds after you left, you'll be displaced."

"Nonsense," Liam uttered. "This is still their future, until it isn't. They'll travel in their own timeline, the same as you will. The timeline won't diverge until the moment she's home. But I'll go with them, to control the portal."

Eli bristled. "I am capable—"

"I know you are," Liam said. "But I am exponentially more experienced, and I can take you to the blinking moment after you left." He looked to Will. "There's a portal in the multi-purpose room now, correct? We'll use that one."

"How did you know?" Will asked.

"It's always been there," Liam chuckled. "You just didn't know it until Finn opened it."

Finn was aware of Liam's intentions and would arrive soon to see him off. But as an assurance, Liam handed Will a mosquito drone, and asked him to send it through the hospital portal when they were on the other side. "If you get to the When you belong in, send it."

"How will we know?" Jax asked. "The corridor might look the same, but we could be in his—" he nodded at Other Eli "—When."

Aubrey was home, waiting for his call. "Just ask her for the word Finn gave before he left. If she knows the answer, you're home."

"Presuming—"

"Don't overthink it, Dash," Liam said. "Just ask the word. If she answers 'mousebreath,' you're where you need to be."

"That's two words," Jax argued.

"One. It was an online magazine in the twenty first century

and I quite enjoyed it. Everything was written from a cat's point of view. Look up the archives, you'll be amused."

"You might get stuck," Will reminded Liam.

He shrugged. "If I get stuck, I get stuck. There's nothing holding me here, and what's a new timeline over this one? Hell, I'd get to experience an entirely new When. The Queen lives, the King doesn't abdicate. Everything going forward will be a surprise. It should be interesting."

"If you get stuck," Eli said, "you can help me remove Levi Munson from the face of the earth."

Liam grinned. "Fun. See, not only will it be interesting, I'll be useful again. I can't remember the last time I was truly useful."

The grating grain of sand that had been between Liam and Will dropped, and Will reached for him. "You're useful. Thank you."

"You're him, no difference in my heart." Liam said, not wanting to let Will go.

"I know." He pulled back and placed a kiss on Liam's forehead. "For the record, I hope you're able to return."

"Maybe not right away," Liam said. "Oh, I'll make sure I can, but after that? I might want to play for a while. Don't look for me for a week or so."

Look for me if you need a friend there. Just give me cheese and I'll like you forever.

Liam's eyes widened as the memory of finding me flooded his brain. "You ate the meat out of my sandwich," he murmured. "You were so small. Your voice was tiny. How could I—"

That Wick hasn't forgotten. And that Emperor's opinion about you hasn't been tainted by the whole cloning business. You'll be okay there. Probably even happy.

"That would be the first time in centuries," he said.

You fart dust, don't you?

~

Twenty minutes later, after nearly—unintentionally—convincing Liam that his life would be far better there than home, our Eli left the OR. His eyes were bloodshot and puffy, his nose gurgling, and he walked up to Other Eli and said, "Treasure her, or I swear I will find a way—"

"She's my soul, every bit as much as she's yours. I would give her the world if it were enough."

Eli's breath hiccupped. "After she died, I found her journal. She'd never tell you. But the one thing that pained her about this life was losing the freedom to travel, and she was sad that she would never see the major wonders of the world without the world coming with her. Find a way, Eli. Find a way to take her to every place she dreams about, without the guards and reporters and paparazzi following. Use the damned portals if you have to but take her to see the world. You have time."

Other Eli nodded soberly. "World enough, and time."

Eli leaned closer to his younger self. "Read her that poem now and then. It's among her favorites. She loves how it sounds coming from you. And goddammit, don't let her stand aside in public anymore. Take a page from your son's book and love her openly. She deserves and wants that as much as she fears it."

Shy, reserved Donna Domenico Blackshear was about to be pulled out of royal tradition and into the normal life she craved, ready or not.

"You were in there for nearly an hour," Jax said. "What did you talk about for so long?"

Jaw set, Eli said sternly, "I will give you my soul, Jackson, but I won't give you that."

"Fair enough."

"Did you give Will the drone?" Eli asked Liam.

Liam fished it out of his pocket and handed it over. "It's programmed to activate with the portal. Just turn it on, it will come to me on its own. I'll send it back as confirmation of reception."

"Are you sure about this?" Will asked him. "The King can escort his Queen."

"The risk is mine to take, Dash. Their odds of getting home are better with me controlling the portal."

Will gave him another hug and kiss, and then without looking back, we entered the portal.

~

No one said a word as Will tapped the tiny drone to activate it and as he sent it in the direction of the portal. It vanished in a wink and he stepped back, shoving the tips of his fingers into his jeans pockets while he waited, surprised when it popped back trailing a slip of paper with Liam's inky scrawl.

'Did you call home? Reply.'

Jax fished his phone from his pocket and tapped on Aubrey's name; when she answered I could hear her frustrated voice sigh, "Oh, Lord, don't make me say it."

"I don't make the rules, angel. What's the word?"

There was another sigh. "Mousebreath. Really now. Mousebreath. Oh, just get home."

"Turn around, we'll be there."

After Will sent the drone back, Jax reached for Eli's arm, they both tapped their jump bracelets, and we were home, in the living room. Aubrey came out of her little kitchen office and after seeing Eli she started for him, but he held a hand up to stop her.

"I need to feel this, Aubrey. Don't take it from me."

He would still feel the pain, but she could take the worst of the stinging out of it. Still, she nodded as if she understood and didn't move again until Hyrum's door popped open and he started down the hall.

He was pumping his fists in the air and shouted Eli's name in one long breath as he bounded down the hallway. There was no stopping him, though when he saw Eli's face he skittered to a stop, considered the sadness wrapped around his chosen father, and without another word put his arms around Eli.

"Are you okay?" he asked in a whisper. "I'll make you some cookies. That will help, all right?"

Eli held him tightly. "I'll be fine. I had a hard day, that's all. Jax also had a hard day, so make some cookies for him, too, all right?"

Hyrum reached for Eli's face to squish his cheeks between his hands. "Okay. Do you want chocolate chip or wiener cookies?"

"How about both?" Aubrey pried Hyrum away from Eli, turning him toward the kitchen. "There's already dough for both, and we can make enough to go around. You get started and I'll be in to help in a bit."

"I got it! You make Jax feel better!"

Eli left to shower and said he would be back later, though no one honestly expected to see him for a while. Unlike his father, Jax wanted Aubrey to take the edge off the pain and held his arms out to her with a promise to explain everything in a few minutes.

Are we just going to stand here and gawk?

"Do you have anything better to do?" Will answered.

Food would be nice. I didn't get breakfast.

None of us ate before leaving Finn's apartment for the hospital. As soon as Aubrey heard that, she shoved Jax toward the table and told Will he needed to sit down, too, and there would be sandwiches in a few minutes.

I got to eat first.

I rank higher with her.

"How come Eli is sad?" Hyrum asked as he shoved trays loaded with little balls of sugary goodness into the oven. "You look sad, too, Jax."

They explained over lunch and dessert—Hyrum set aside a plate of cookies specifically for Eli—trying to keep the conversation where Hyrum had hope of understanding. He listened quietly, eating a few more cookies than he knew Aubrey liked, but when Jax finished explaining, Hyrum set his cookie down and smiled.

"I'm glad you got to see your mom and tell her you love her. Did she say it back? It's always nice when they say it back."

"I did, and she did. But it was hard to leave her there, and we're going to miss her all over again."

"But you can go see her again. If she's not gonna die, you can see her the way Will goes to see his other parents."

"Maybe not," Jax sighed. "It's complicated."

Will held his hands up, palms together. "In this case time may have done this—" he held one hand still while arcing the other away "—and there's probably no way to bridge that gap."

Hyrum nodded as if he understood. "Okay. It might be hard to see her, anyway. She has her Jax and Eli. It's hard to feel like you're in the way even if she doesn't want you to feel like that."

Eli would need time to mourn all over again. Jax thought he had a handle on his feelings but allowed for the idea that he needed to do what he failed to when his mother died in this When: grieve. He'd set his own feelings aside to allow room for the enormity of Eli's, but this time he needed to embrace it.

Without saying anything, Hyrum got up and ran to his room. He came back clutching Chuckles, his stuffed rabbit, and he solemnly held it out to Jax. "If you lay down on your bed and hold him tight with his head on your face, you can cry and he makes you feel better. You can even tell him secrets and he doesn't tell anyone. He just listens and lets you cry until you don't need to anymore. You can borrow him."

Aubrey opened her mouth to tell him no, he might need Chuckles, but Jax took the rabbit in hand very gently.

"Thank you, Hyrum."

Hyrum bent over and whispered, "Just don't rub snot on him, Okay? He doesn't like that."

Jax clutched Chuckles to his chest and promised Hyrum he wouldn't, and with a grin tugging at his lips, he added, "I can just use Aubrey's sleeve when she rolls over."

Did we break them? I asked Will when we were alone. *Will they really be okay?*

"They'll be all right, Wick. It was difficult to leave her behind, but they were able to say the things they wished they had, and this time left her with peace and hope."

They might not be the same after this.

"No," he agreed, "they might not."

~

Charlie held his hands out to show Will the reddened tips of his fingers. Alex sat on the floor in front of the sofa, arranging Hyrum's borrowed and coveted wood blocks into a neat pile; she was dressed in jeans and a sweatshirt, slipper socks on her feet, while Charlie stood in front of Will wearing only thin shorts.

Sweat plastered hair to his forehead but he promised he wasn't too hot and that his fingers didn't hurt. "Is Aunt Sophia gonna make me put pants on?" he asked as Will touched one of his fingertips. "I'll be hot then."

Will assured him she would not. The reasons for Charlie's aversion to clothing had been explained to every family member; no one had a problem with a pantsless three-year-old running around, though lately Charlie had chosen to wear shorts, without explanation.

Alex carefully set a large block on top of a stack of smaller ones. "How come she's coming to watch us? Why can't we go with you?"

Because your daddy doesn't want her to go outside today.

"She's coming because Aunt Aubrey is going to lunch with Hyrum today, and I have errands to run. My errands will be boring, and you'll have far more fun if you stay here with her."

Also, he needs to keep Sophia home.

"What's Wick saying?" Charlie asked.

Will kissed the tips of Charlie's fingers, even though they didn't hurt. And then he outright lied to him. "He wants me to remind you that there are fresh cookies for your afternoon snack. Aunt Aubrey made them last night."

"I hope my fingers turn back before then," Charlie said as he looked at them, though he didn't say why, and Will was interrupted from asking by a knock on the frame of the open door.

"Red fingers. Ah, he's coming into a skill, I see."

"Liam." Will stood, ruffling Charlie's hair. "I honestly didn't expect to see you again. You've been gone a while."

It had been several months since he'd taken Other Eli and Donna home; when he hadn't returned after a week, Will assumed he was unable to find a way back.

"I considered hopping back a few weeks to time it right, but—" he shrugged "—eh."

Will gestured for him to come inside and sit. "You look a bit tired."

"Not tired," Liam grunted as he dropped onto the sofa. "Just older."

There were a few more lines around his eyes and he was a touch grayer at his temples, but it would still be difficult for someone unfamiliar with the Finns to tell him apart from the others. Will sat on the other end of the sofa and turned toward him, asking how much older.

"Hm. Well, I stayed until what should have been the end of the world. Good job on the information you planted in the Emperor's head. Armageddon averted; it was the least stressful crisis management I could imagine. After that, I hopped back to a few places, made sure I could get home, then wandered off to visit a few people. Spent time searching for things. Met a woman, stayed with her for a while. Met another, stayed longer. The usual."

"The usual," Will chuckled. "All right, how many more half siblings do I have scattered throughout time?"

"Ah. Two that I know of. Not to worry, they haven't been born yet."

"What's a sibling?" Alex asked as her tower of blocks tumbled down.

"A brother or sister," Will answered.

"I hab one, two, three siblings," Charlie announced, holding up the appropriate number of fingers.

"You also have an inordinately high metabolism, I'm guessing." Liam reached for Charlie's hand. "Are your fingers only red now, or have things been happening with them?"

"Just red. They don't hurt."

"Brace yourself," Liam said to Will. "He's about to turn into a human food machine. And once he's got enough fuel on board, he'll be able to scorch things with a touch."

"Me?" Charlie asked.

Will wanted more information. "You've seen this before."

"Pick a unique skill, I've probably seen it. This one, in twins. Well, except for the one boy who had both in him." He tilted his head toward Alex. "She's cold all the time, isn't she?"

"I like cold! I can make milk into ice cubes!" Alex boasted. "I thinked it would be like ice cream but it wasn't."

"She made fog into slushies!" Charlie giggled. "But just on the roof. Daddy said not to do it anywhere else."

Will...ask him about Valerie Munson.

"Doyle Keats," Will murmured. "How far apart are you and Valerie Munson? How many generations?"

He had no idea. Liam sat back and pondered his lineage, but he wasn't sure where Valerie came in his line of descendants. He thought she might be his great, great, great granddaughter, but allowed for one more generation.

We have an 'I'm my own grandpa' situation here.

Will's eyebrows knotted. "Perhaps not. Question, Liam. You mentioned being stuck in null space more than once. How many times did it happen before you settled in Florida?"

"Three, I think. Maybe four. Possibility of five. Why?"

The version of Jo Will had watched die thought she had created his gifts by exposing him to null space in utero. Now he thought she was closer to the truth than he'd previously presumed. "You may be patient zero, so to speak. If you fathered those children after that much exposure—"

"Sorry?"

"No," Will said, amused. "It's a curiosity, nothing more."

Does Valerie have a twin?

"Wick?"

He said the cold comes with a twin. Charlie's heat to Alex's cold. If Alex has Valerie's gift, she might have a twin out there.

He reached for his tablet to search for the children of Jacob Keats; there were ten, and Valerie was one of the youngest—and she had a twin brother named Callum, who currently occupied a seat on the Church of Florida's Quorum. He was relatively new to the position, appointed by Red following the fall of Florida.

It was something Will wanted to discuss with Liam—how many gifted people might be wandering around Florida—but his phone pinged and when he read the message, he began sputtering expletives that caused Alex and Charlie to giggle.

"Problem?" Liam asked.

"Sophia. She's running late and sending Zed to watch the kids."

No, Will, she has to come home. She has to.

He lunged for Liam's arm, grabbing him by the wrist. "I need you to stay with them, please."

Liam heard in his head what Will didn't dare say out loud. "Go."

I jumped to his shoulder as he slapped his bracelet, and we went.

~

He'd meant to jump to a spot several feet ahead of where Sophia was walking, but instead wound up three blocks behind. Still, he wasted no time contemplating the error and began moving. I found my center and balanced but had to dig in hard to keep from falling.

We were near the corner, and I felt him twitch, ready to gear into an all-out sprint, when Rhys's voice cut through the air, yelling out, "Daddy!"

Will skittered, slowing, but he didn't stop. He reached up to grab me, thrust me toward Aisha while telling her to stay put, don't move, don't follow, and he raced down the street. Sophia was two blocks ahead, looking down at her phone, and the increased noise coming from leaving the vehicle-restricted zone into the traffic-permitted area kept her from hearing Will call out.

Stop, stop, stop, stop, stop. Sophia, stop. Please.

"Where's Daddy going?"

Please stop. Hear Will.

"Oh my god," Aisha breathed. "Not today. I didn't realize it was today."

We focused on Will's back, willing him to speed up, for Sophia to hear him calling her name. The delivery truck barreled down the center of the street, its magnets clacking as they tried to realign, the air jets whining and brakes screaming as the driver tried to stop, to bring his vehicle back onto the magnetic track. It was then Sophia looked up; the truck was five feet away and Will was ten.

He had no hope of reaching her.

He had no hope of getting out of harm's way.

Aisha sucked in a sharp breath and called out his name, choking on anguish. She pressed me to her face, not wanting to see, but unable to stop herself, muttering, "No, no, no. Rhys, turn away, don't watch."

She reached for his head, trying to turn him to her, but he shrugged away.

Then the world stopped.

The truck hung in the air just a foot from Sophia, who screamed. Will used momentum to scoop her up and turn but didn't stop to question the silence that exploded around him, the bird that hung in the air just a foot overhead. He grabbed her and ran back to Aisha and Rhys, who stood with his arms spread, his palms facing up and middle fingers pointing toward the sky.

"Move," Will ordered when he was close. He ducked around the corner of the Museum of Modern Art, and only when we were out of sightline of the truck did he set Sophia down.

She babbled, "What the hell? What the hell?" until Will set her on her feet, and then locked eyes with Rhys. Understanding flooded her, and she softened. "You did this, didn't you, handsome?"

"You were gonna get squished. Daddy, should I let time come out to play again?"

Breathing heavily, Will nodded. He set his hands against the building, trying to control the nausea that had suddenly welled up, and we heard as the truck landed with a thud.

What we didn't hear was disastrous impact, the truck plowing into the other side of the museum.

"I made the air put the truck down, Daddy," Rhys said when Will's head jerked up. "So no one would get crashed with it."

Will went to his knees, reaching for his son. "How did you know?"

Rhys shrugged. "If I didn't, you and Sophia were gonna get squished. Is it okay?"

"Oh, cowboy, it's more than okay," Aisha said.

Truck driver's going to survive then, too. I don't think he did last time.

"You did exactly what needed to be done," Will assured Rhys. "Thank you."

"Sophia's still scared, though."

She pressed her back against the wall, holding onto herself, and she was trembling. Aisha handed me to Rhys and went to her, wrapping her in a tight embrace, whispering to her that it was all right. She was safe.

"What's wrong?" Rhys asked.

"She's in shock," Will answered, getting up. "We need to get her home. Everyone grab on and I'll jump—"

Sophia pulled away from Aisha, shaking her head. "No, I need to walk. I need to breathe."

"Are you sure?" he asked.

Aisha kept her arm around Sophia's shoulders. "We'll call a cab if we have to. Where are her guards? Where the hell?"

They were in the shadows where they belonged, probably trying to regroup after Sophia's disappearance from their watch. Frozen along with time, for them she was there one moment and gone the next.

Will. Across the street. At the edge of the Gardens.

He turned, placing me on his shoulder, balancing me as an excuse to look where I'd directed.

"I have something to attend to," he told Aisha. "Signal a guard if you think for even a second that she needs a ride."

Her gaze followed and she nodded, understanding. Rhys latched onto Will's hand and said he wanted to go with him; a siren blared in the distance, getting louder as it approached, and Will wanted him to go home, but there was no reason to make him leave. There was no accident to shield him from and keeping him with us gave Sophia respite from the questions Rhys would surely fire off in rapid succession without understanding that she needed quiet.

He skipped next to Will as we crossed the street, smiling, not caring that he'd again stopped time and saved another life. Two lives, maybe three. Once across, he leaped into the air and landed hard on both feet, then looked up and asked, "How come you look sad, Z-man? Are you crying?"

Silver splashed Zed's temples, his face lined with subtle folds near his eyes and lips, and he leaned against the garden wall as he tried to compose himself. He ruffled Rhys's hair and admitted to feeling a little bit sad, but it was all right. To Will he said, "I don't know how you did it, but I was there, on the other side of the street, trying to get to her, too. I blinked and she was gone. You were gone. The truck dropped and barely grazed the side of the building."

"Rhys can stop time," Will said, as if it were a perfectly ordinary thing his son could do. "He controls who retains awareness. If he'd known you were there, I'm sure he would have made sure you were able to move."

Old Zed nodded. "Thank you, Rhys."

"I never seen you here before. We always go see you instead."

"I had a notion that if your daddy didn't remember what today was, that I could get here in time to save Sophia." He blinked and a tear crept onto his eyelashes. "My timing was off."

"I was prepared to jump back if I needed to."

Were you late intentionally? I asked Zed.

"Why would he be intentionally be late?" Will asked me.

Because if he couldn't save her, then he could go with her.

"Go where?" Rhys asked.

"Wherever she wanted," Will replied, speaking softly, understanding that was exactly what old Zed had intended. He would have saved her if he could, but barring that, it was how he wanted to die. He wanted his days to end with Sophia's. "You were never intended to end that way."

"And she was. But neither of us—" He stopped suddenly, standing straighter, looking past Will.

Sophia stepped up beside Will. "I had a feeling. I don't know why. Something told me to turn around and I'd find you here."

Zed's mouth was open, and he had no idea what to say. Here was the woman he'd lost when he was very young; her heart still beat, her breath brushed across his face. She reached up and grazed fingers over the gray hair at his temple, then ran a finger down his jawline.

"Oh, you just get better with age, don't you? You're gorgeous."

He couldn't speak.

Aisha tugged Rhys away to give them space. Will followed them but stayed close, just in case, and also because he was as nosy as I and wanted to be where he could hear.

Sophia didn't make it easy, dropping to a near whisper.

"I was supposed to die today, wasn't I? That's why you're here."

He managed a slight nod, and the tears poured down his face.

"Oh, sweetheart," she breathed. "How long...how old are you now? Fifty? Fifty-five?"

"Sixty," he managed to say.

Her hands went to his; he was still wearing his wedding ring, the one she'd had made specifically for him, with thin lines running along the edges and *S y Z* engraved on the front. "Please tell me you haven't been alone all this time."

She was the love of his life; he'd once explained his choice to remain alone to Will, then without tears. He missed her every day but hadn't felt the crushing loneliness he expected, not after the first few, horrible years. He was a lot like Eli in that; he never wanted anyone else and felt that anyone he chose would spend their life feeling as if they would never measure up to his memories. And it would be true, because no one else could. His heart wouldn't allow it.

Her hand went to his chest. "I would never want that for you. She never wanted that for you. Zed. My god. Do you know how much she loved you? Even when she was harping at you to just stay off her for five minutes, she loved you so much. Deep down, it thrilled her to know that even after three kids back to back to back and how saggy it made everything on her and all the stretch marks, you still wanted her more than anything."

He wanted to touch her. His hand moved toward her face, but he stopped himself, unsure, despite how much she was touching him. She grabbed his hand and held it over her heart, willing him to feel it beat. "No regrets. She never once doubted you and felt every wonderful moment of your love."

"I still miss her. Every day. And the parts of me that left with her, I…" His breath hitched. "Tell your Zed he's a lucky man. And that now his wish will come true."

"Wish?"

His hand moved to her cheek. "He already knows, Sof. He's waiting for the lecture, for you to ask him what the hell is so wrong with him that he can't remember to get his damned implant refilled. Yet he did, he always did, but those boys—" He finally allowed himself to smile "—they were meant to be. He'll treasure this one. More than you know." A soft slip of a laugh. "He wants just one more. I wanted just one more. But if I could have had you instead…"

Sophia threw her arms around him while he cried, her own tears wetting his shoulder, and they stood holding on until Rhys squealed, "Uncle Jax!" and the largest of the official royal cars pulled up beside them. A guard popped out from the passenger side to open the back door and Jax stepped out, beckoning Will closer.

"Son, trust me, the longer you take, the harder it will be," Jax said to old Zed as Will ushered Aisha and Rhys into the car. He took Sophia by the arm and kissed her forehead, told her to take just another minute, but then she needed to go.

He gave them privacy as they said goodbye, his jaw tightening when she told Zed they would see each other again. He closed the door behind her after she climbed into the car, but it stayed put and he stepped close to Zed, his arms clasped behind his back. He tried to separate himself from the pain, but he knew this Zed; they'd met, and he couldn't keep himself from feeling pricks of anguish.

"Seeing her," Jax said, weighing what he wanted to say even as the words tumbled out. "You'll mourn all over again. The pain will amplify, and it will feel as if you've just lost her. If I'd known you were planning this—"

"Did you know she was going to die?"

Jax shot a look at Will. "No, I didn't."

"Then how?" Will asked.

"Liam."

"I had to come," Zed said. "There was a chance and I had to take it."

"I know." Jax pulled him into an embrace. "I would have taken it, too."

The guards surrounded them, facing outward, a wall of red and blue uniforms daring people to stare. When it seemed as if Zed was going to break down, Will yanked the car door open and guided him into it.

"What the—"

Will gestured to his bracelet. "Aisha has one. They jumped home."

When we were settled into the seats, Jax tapped the intercom on the panel that separated the driver from the passengers and told him to head for Union Square. He was to let us out on the far side, away from the royal home entrance; we made our way down to the lab, where Finn waited with coffee, scotch, and Liam Finnegan.

"Prince Zealand is with your children," Liam explained before Will could protest his presence.

"Jesus, how many of you are there?" Zed asked, voice still thin.

"One too many, if they answer honestly," he answered.

They plied him with booze at Finn's well-worn table, hoping to peel back a layer or two of the sorrow he would hold onto for months to come. Jax explained what they'd done for Donna, and the pain that came with it.

"We should have left it to her Emperor," Jax said. "He could have done everything we did, without adding so much onto our grief. You knew this one would save Sophia, didn't you?"

He gave a slight nod. "Still..."

Jax stared at him, weighing the guilt on his face against the sorrow in his eyes, and the understanding slapped at him, hard.

"Zed, no," he cried.

"Tell me you wouldn't do the same thing, if it were Mom. Oh, fuck. Your wife."

Jax reach over and grabbed him by the chin, forcing Zed to look at him. "I'll tell you the same thing I was recently told.

No matter how old you are, no matter the When, you're my son. She's your mother. And yes, in your shoes, after having raised the kids and seeing them off into their adult lives, I probably would have."

"I've had a good life," Zed explained. "A wonderful life. But it's missing her. It's always missing her. With the boys all grown and out on their own—I've handed my work over to others. The academy functions without me. I just feel...done. And I wanted to save her, I really did, but if I'd failed? Fine. I'd have gone out with her."

"You don't want to die," Liam said with a heavy sigh. "This one has a kid about to melt down everything he touches. The other will freeze everything. You don't want to miss that."

"And Rhys can shoot electricity from his fingers," Finn added. "He can stop time, read your mind... We're just about to get interesting and if you live, you'll get to see it. We'll bring the kids to visit and let them destroy your things instead of ours."

"If he can get home," Jax said.

"I made it," Liam pointed out. "It's simple merging of timelines, that's all, and Will has tied his to Zed's with all his visits as it is. He'll go home and this line will erase his as you progress here. From now on he'll only be able to come back to this point, not the one where the girl dies."

"Can we go rub Andrew's nose in it?" Finn wondered out loud. "We were right, he was less so."

"I'm not sure we're as right as we think we are," Liam said. "And I took no chances getting back. I made sure I went back to a point before the Queen's life was spared, and then came here. I don't know if it was necessary, but...we still might be wrong. Andrew might be wrong."

"Eh, we invented the time machine. So there."

Zed ignored them. "I can never see her again, can I? Or I can, but it would be a bad idea."

"I see your father every now and then," Jax reminded him. "Your mother as well. Granted, I'm attracted to her, but she's not my wife. She doesn't feel like my wife. I imagine Sophia would begin to feel the same to you."

"With all due respect...you haven't lost her. She's right there with you. I lost my wife before I was twenty-five years old. You've aged along with yours. My mind's eye still sees...her."

"The choice is yours," Will said. "And hers."

You can show him pictures, right? He'll want to see pictures of the baby.

"If he wishes to see photos of the next child, I will honor that."

"It's a girl," Zed murmured. "When I realized she was—well, I wanted a little girl so badly. It broke me, knowing what we'd lost."

Will offered to withhold all images if he thought it would hurt.

"Oh, it'll hurt. But you're damn well showing them to me. I'll take all the pain in the world to see that little girl live." He turned to Jax. "Granddad would take it all to see his queen live, even with another man, wouldn't he? All we want is their happiness. I'll survive. He'll survive. As long as they're happy."

"But will *you* be?" Jax asked.

He was happy before; he thought he could be happy again. Something would come along, or he would carve a new niche for himself. "Sometimes you think the brownies are done, but you check and realize you have to shove them back in the oven."

"That's an unfortunate image," Finn mused.

"You're the brownies," Liam said to Zed. "You took the dish out when it was still mostly batter and there it sits, edible enough for those who enjoy the soft innards, but you never let anyone get a taste."

Zed scrunched his nose. "Ew."

Liam tapped the table to get Zed to look at him. "You've done her memory a disservice, Zealand. You've closed yourself off to possibility because of some noble notion that you don't deserve to be happy without her, and I know that girl quite well now. She would hate what you've chosen for yourself."

"But I didn't choose—"

"You did, and you know it. And I understand. You lose the other half of your soul and feel as if moving on, even a bit, is betrayal. And then there's that voice in your head that warns if you do, if you allow yourself the comfort of companionship, you'll begin to forget her. And that is unacceptable."

"There's no one who could take her place."

"No, there's not," Liam agreed. "But listen to me, Uncle." Zed twitched, which made Liam chuckle. "Your sister is my grandmother. And don't distract me. Zed, I have lived more lifetimes than I can remember. I truly don't know how old I am. But I can promise you this—no matter what you might tell yourself and everyone else, you will never, *never*, forget your greatest love. Nor the life and the children you created together. Allowing yourself to love someone else doesn't take anything away from her and doesn't mean you value that commitment any less. You're allowed to love again. You won't forget her. And if there's a life after this one, she'll be there and she'll be glad that you made room for someone else."

"I can't," Zed murmured.

"You can. You choose not to. You're clinging to grief and this notion of a soul mate as an excuse. You don't have the years I did to get it right, Zed. It took me hundreds of years to open myself to relationships. Children. And yes, sometimes I have difficulty recalling their names, but I loved them all and mourned them all."

You remembered Will.

"I remembered Will," he agreed, not acknowledging when Will twitched because he hadn't translated. "I remembered Jo. I've loved them through every day I've lived. No one can take your greatest love from you, and those worthy of you will never try. They'll honor those memories and help you carry them. And your sons...your happiness will be a gift to them."

"Yeah, well. I'm a little rusty. I don't see myself jumping into the dating pool. With my luck I'd go headfirst into the shallow end." Annoyed, he set his hands on the table, pressing down. "I don't think I expected to go home. I've let go of everything there. Before I consider moving on, I need to carve out something new for myself. I think I'm done speaking for the dead."

Liam reached across the table with the bottle of scotch and poured Zed another drink. "Here's a niche for you. Your academy.

Half of it is a program for those who wish to learn to speak for the dead, so to...speak. Correct?"

Zed nodded.

"The other half, the quiet half, is a school for the unusually gifted. Rarely more than ten students at a time. Correct?"

"What's your point?"

"My point," Liam said, inhaling the aroma of Finn's expensive scotch, "is that there are likely hundreds, maybe thousands of children spread through time who need a place like Blackshear Academy. And who better than you to be there when I begin sending them your way?"

He'd stayed in the other When until what should have been the end of time, and then hopped around for a century more, amusing himself. Now that he was back, paying closer attention to the effects of his abuse of time, he thought that he should put his longevity to use. There were surely more descendants of his out there, people with gifts that had been left unchecked, and he felt a renewed responsibility toward them.

"I find them, bring them forward or back to you, you educate them. Or bring them here, to this Zed," he said, looking at Will. "You'll need students other than your own children, won't you? They'll still be family, even if quite removed from you. You can't enroll locals because they'll talk. But displaced students with gifts they're trying to hide at home? The academy will be a refuge."

"He'll need adult instructors," Will said.

Liam nodded. "I'm sure some of my spawn grew up just fine."

Finn frowned. "Are you saying that if Jo were not here, I would wind up essentially screwing my way through time?"

Liam grinned proudly. "And what a fine way to spend the millennia it's been." He set his glass down and got up. "Go home, old man Zed. Mourn your wife for a while, then get ready to expand. I'm going on a hunt, the kind where no blood gets shed and everyone wins."

~

"Liam left this with Dad," Will said as he handed the computer tablet to Jax. "This compilation is why he chose to remain there after taking Eli and Donna home. He wanted me to vet it before showing it to you, and he wanted you to decide if Eli sees it. It's mostly news and journal entries, but there are some photos and a considerable number of video."

Jax was in his comfy chair, feet up. He was still in his suit after a day of doing kingly type things but had kicked off his shoes and wanted to enjoy the quiet that hugged the apartment. In another hour, Aubrey would be home with Will's kids, Oz would be home with baby Eli, Sophia and Zed would come downstairs with their brood, and the sounds that swirled around him would be a different kind of music.

"So, what, does Will have three daddies now?" Jax snorted.

"I admit, I am spending more time with him. Though he's still Liam, not Dad."

Liam's layers of anger dissolved under Will's attention. He spoke honestly about his pain in losing Will and then Jo, and the years it took before he was willing to admit someone else into his life. But even then, there was guilt. He married several times, raised several families, saw them all grow old and die, and then he mourned—yet wrapped around his heart was the son he felt he had let down, and the agony of knowing he could have done so much more if he had only known that Will could be taught to control his gift.

The guilt ate at him. When he decided he was done roaming time, he settled close to his own When, and began fermenting plans to clone Will and do everything right. "I was not entirely sane by then, Dash. Worse, I knew it and didn't care. But when you walked into my office..."

"I left there under the impression that you were hovering around seven hundred years old and had never remarried. Nor had children."

Liam shrugged. "I lied. I'm not like your father, I stopped being him centuries ago. I've lost that insane curiosity and scattered approach to everything."

He thought himself to be more focused than ever, and wanted to roam time, searching for his grandchildren and their children, carrying off the ones who needed help. They were his past, true, but they were also the future. They needed Blackshear Academy every bit as much as did Rhys, Charlie, and Alex.

That prompted Will to lift Liam's hand, studying his fingertips. "You heard Wick the other day. What else can you do?"

In reply, Liam cut loose a single spark, shocking Will.

"The gifts are there inside you, William. Some more prominent than others, but if you dig you might find them. Maybe you need the academy, too."

Liam was not Will's father; he didn't think of him that way, but he allowed for the possibility that one day he would, and because of that he would allow his children to draw closer to him as well. His curiosity regarding the half siblings scattered throughout time had piqued; those children were a significant reason Liam believed he would be able to return to this When.

"I had new families in several Whens," he reminded Will. "I changed things in those timelines as much as you have in this one."

He wasn't willing to risk losing Will to a new line but was certain his living through so many loops of time had tethered him.

For now, Will detoured into the kitchen to give Jax a chance to decide if he wanted to look at the things Liam had collected, or if he wanted to hand the tablet back.

Once Liam had deposited Donna and Eli back to their apartment—Other Jax and the younger Emperor were still arguing in the living room, with no idea they'd left to begin with—he decided to do what he'd suggested: stay and play, poke around their When, meet a few people and have some fun. He saw Donna melt against Eli and felt a stab of regret; if he went home then, his family, his great grandparents and his even greater grandfather would never see this. They would know that in another timeline their beloved Queen Donna lived, but the proof would be little more than wishes that felt unfulfilled.

He had time; he could give them this much.

Liam Finnegan decided to stay in their timeline and to chronicle, as much as they would allow, the lives of the royal family.

He interfered where he never had before. He aided the Emperor's effort in getting his father home when the time came, and he made sure that Finn sought out the information he needed in the Old Mint. He drew close to the Emperor and prodded him toward Las Vegas when it seemed as if fear had rooted him to San Francisco, and he later stood with family when the Emperor married Aisha years ahead of when he'd been able to in this When.

He stayed for two hundred years, give or take a decade, leaving when he'd seen proof that the world would go on.

Liam returned armed with several tablets filled with information and left it up to Will to decide how much, if anything, he looked at, but he wanted to share the stories about Eli and Donna, and then let Will decide if Jax should be given a choice.

Jax sat with the tablet on his lap but didn't turn it on. "You've looked at all of this?" he asked as Will fished bottles of beer from the refrigerator.

"I did." Will came back with the beer and handed one to Jax. "Their lives followed new trajectories. The Emperor married Aisha Okuda when her son was still small, before George Denton had the opportunity to inflict his baggage upon the boy. He grew up with little memory of his birth gender and became Zed's best friend several years before they even met in this When. And he was a stellar older brother to Rhys and the twins."

"They were born," Jax breathed.

Will nodded. "Had Aisha and I married at the same age, Rhys would be a teenager now."

"And you're okay with knowing that."

"I am. I don't feel loss, if that's what you mean. They are, truly, different people in my mind. I am grateful the Emperor found his way back to her long before I did. I consider it happiness extended and afford it the same joy I feel knowing that Zed, your Zed, will have a lifetime with Sophia now."

It had been two weeks; she was still somewhat shaken up, but Jax worried that old Zed was broken beyond repair. Will offered to check on him but hadn't yet made the trip because Jax wasn't ready to know and going made no difference to Zed's grief.

With a sigh, Jax turned the tablet on and began reading. Will sat back, silent, and began flipping through photos on his phone. I jumped onto the sofa next to him to see, thinking he was looking at the teenager Rhys was in another When, or wedding photos of the 30-year-old Emperor and his Aisha.

Instead, he was looking at pictures of his own children. He'd taken dozens at the playground earlier in the day, before Aubrey arrived to take them for lunch with Aisha at the university cafeteria. Isaac was with them, and I thought Will felt a little wistful, seeing him crouched in the sandbox, helping Alex build a castle while Rhys helped Charlie dig a moat.

As far as he knew, Isaac was missing from the next When.

"Talk to the cat," Jax said after a while. "It's too quiet and I don't enjoy feeling like I'm being watched."

Usually he thinks I'm too mouthy.

"You are too mouthy," Will said without looking up. "You're a master of unsolicited advice and unrequested observation, yet I suspect that since your cooperation is needed, you're going to clam up."

I could go check on old Zed if you want me to. Then you could sit here and talk to yourself.

"Only go if you wish to visit Lux and Seven."

I saw Lux yesterday. He came to see baby Eli. Seven was afraid to come through the portal with him. I think he's afraid he won't be able to get back and he's practically imprinted on Hyrum.

"You're allowed to see your friends more often, Wick. And these days I imagine Lux prefers that you go there. I don't think he's entirely comfortable with Thor."

Only because Thor licked his entire face in one massive tongue swipe. He's a juicy kind of dog.

Oh. Did Aubrey tell you that Charlie left burn marks on the table? Right next to the ones Hyrum made.

He set the phone aside and got up to look. Next to Hyrum's scorched handprints were two tiny ones, placed intentionally, for no reason other than he thought he could.

She wasn't mad. They had a talk about asking permission first, and about the odds of setting things on fire.

"He did this on purpose?" Will asked. "He was able to control it?"

"Sure," Jax said, "let's ignore the scarring of a very old, probably expensive table left to me by my mother."

"Added value." Will ran a finger over Charlie's handprints. "I am favorably concerned that he controlled this rather than doing this without meaning to. I'll replace the table if it bothers you."

Jax grunted. "If it bothered me, I would have replaced it years ago. Zed carved up the underside when he was six. I still don't know where he got the knife."

Screwdriver.

You wanted a new table last year. You really need one now.

"Beside the point." Jax pointed to the tablet. "This article. King Eli advocating for a doubling of the basic income entitlement. Fifteen years from now. Does that Jax ever become King?"

"Concentrate on the parallels, not the future," Will said. "But at this point in your life? No, Jax was not King. He taught high school history in the morning and political science at the university in the afternoon. But back up a few years. There are news clips regarding Florida that you'll find more interesting."

Jax sank further into the chair, his beer going warm as he perused the detailed information Liam provided on the end of Levi Munson's reign over Florida and Red's ascension to the First Minister's seat. Eli did what Jax had avoided: he bullied his way onto Florida soil, made sure his meeting with Levi was televised, and hurled every accusation at the First Minister that he knew to be true. He publicly accused him of pedophilia, incest, verbal and physical abuse of his children and his wife, and slathered onto that cake of truths was a frosting made from Levi's own journals, in which he chronicled his rise to the head of the Church of Florida, his glee in discovering the blatant lies upon which it had been founded, and—something Jax did not know but was not surprised to learn—that he'd ended his own father's life to take the seat.

Aubrey offered public confirmation of the things she knew her father had done, and quietly wrestled Hyrum from his mother's clutches, promising to keep secret the things she now knew about her mother while also assuring her that his gifts would be cared for and controlled. She stood by Valerie when she issued her own public statement, verifying everything and offering up whatever proof she could.

When asked how King Eli came to possess Levi's personal journals, Valerie arched an eyebrow and said, sincerely, "The Lord works in mysterious ways."

Levi Munson died at the hands of his own church, executed for heresy, and Red became the youngest prophet the church had ever followed, including the years before the United States dissolved and Florida became a theocracy.

There was no war. The Emperor never fled with the royal offspring and Oz never faced the evils of her grandfather. Zed was still somehow shocked into discovering his ability to hear the newly dead, but it didn't happen because the shuttle was struck by lightning.

They led quiet—though not simple—lives until Drew and Will formed Ozoo and Oz launched the Wastelands project.

"Giving Eli that information saved thousands of lives," Will told Jax. "Chicago stands. Shazia remained Queen until Andrew was in his thirties, and rather than force him to the throne, she offered Midlam to Eli, supported by a national referendum of the people."

When presented the option—become a part of Pacifica now or wait for King Andrew to merge with them later, when Oz took the throne—the nation shrugged and asked, "Why wait?"

"Do I want to know when and why Jackson took the throne?"

"King Eli opted to retire in his late eighties."

"Huh. He would still be King."

"And you would still teach history." Will took the tablet and pulled up a photo. "The last official portrait of King Eli the

Second and Queen Donna of Pacifica. They enjoyed long lives, and Liam believes they were every bit as much in love at the end as they were in the beginning."

"How old?" Jax barely managed a whisper. "And yes, I want to know."

"She lived to one hundred nineteen and died peacefully, at home. Eli lived only a few hours longer. Oz told Liam that he seemed determined to go with her and passed away while napping on the sofa, waiting for the coroner to arrive."

"Then we did it. They got their happily ever after." He swallowed his tears, swiping to another file. His eyes narrowed and he held the tablet a little closer. "Who's this?"

"Me," Will chuckled. "Liam wanted to be sure I knew that regardless of the changes, the baby Emperor was born, right on time."

What about me? Do you know?

Will took the tablet and went to another photo. It was five-year-old Will with a tiny cat perched on his shoulder, and he clutched a stuffed blue rabbit to his chest.

"Suffice to say, you were brought into my life, though I suspect under different circumstances."

I wonder if I ever had to be Seven, and then Merlin.

"What about Hyrum?" Jax asked.

There were more photos, and Will searched for the right one. It was of Hyrum running across Union Square, his arms thrown open, mouth wide with joy as he aimed himself at Prince Jackson. "He became Hyrum Blackshear almost from day one," Will said. "Liam feels that our Hyrum has grown more than this Hyrum did, but he was happy, and his happiness was infectious. He was surrounded by love and always had playmates. I suspect that will matter most to Aubrey."

There were only two things Aubrey was concerned about. Hyrum was one; she hoped the Hyrum of the next When would be spared his march across Midlam. The other was that Donna lived, and that Eli understood how fortunate he was, given the risks Jax and Will had taken.

Everything else belonged to someone else's lives; they

were us, yet they were not us. We threaded our lives around our pain, embraced our joy, and celebrated the wonder of it all.

The elevator dinged and Jax turned the tablet off, handing it to Will with the request that no one else see it, not yet. Hyrum's voice echoed up the stairs as he shouted "Eli!" which was followed by his feet slapping against the stairs, sprinting up to reach his daddy.

The noise of Hyrum was followed by children laughing and shouting to be heard over each other, and a minute later they poured into the living room together. They spread out through the living room, spilling into the kitchen, and after a few minutes of chaos, Eli snatched a bottle out of Jax's liquor cabinet and nodded toward the balcony.

"I love the little bastards," he said as he dropped into a chair near the railing, "but good god they're loud."

Jax took the bottle from him and began pouring scotch into glasses. "Is that why you only had me? You enjoyed the quiet that much?"

"You were a noisy little shit, too." He took the glass Jax held out and sniffed at the contents. "Ah, I grabbed the right one. We were never fortunate enough to have another, not for lack of trying. But don't feel bad for it. We were content with you."

"You seem to be in a better mood."

"My heart hurts less," he admitted. "This morning I woke, and my first thought was that she's out there, somewhere, somewhen, and today she woke up, too. She rolled over, told her Eli that if he snores one more night, she's going to smother him with his pillow, and then went about her day as if she had never been so close to dying. Right now, she has everything she dreamed of, and they're all just as loud as the ones we're out here to get away from. She's happy, I know she is. And that's all I ever wanted."

"And having been able to say those things you wished you had?" Will asked.

"Be careful what you wish for, Emperor. But yes, I'm grateful I was able to say them, even if to another Eli's Donna."

They turned when the door squeaked open and Zed came out.

"You." Eli pointed at Zed and his finger followed him until he sat. "Leave nothing unsaid to that girl of yours. Say it now, mean it deeply, and say it always."

He had no idea what they'd been talking about, but he nodded anyway. "We've been saying a lot of everything the last couple of weeks. All of this is why you never let me meet my other self, isn't it? Because of Sophia."

Will nodded. "He would not have been able to keep his loss to himself."

"How broken was he?" Eli asked. "Merely sad about his own loss yet grateful our Sophia lives, or did seeing her again put him into a tailspin?"

Jax thought he was all right; he would mourn, but it would settle with him. "It's settling with you. With me. I just hope his family is able to help him deal with it again. I'm not sure they can understand, not entirely."

With that, Eli stood. "Well, I understand. And he's still my grandson, right?"

Jax nodded.

"Then I'm going to see him." He bent to kiss Zed's forehead. "Seeing you with Sophia gives me clarity, Zed. Let's see if I can impart some of it to another you."

Will offered to take him, to make sure that he could contact Zed. It wasn't as simple as picking up his phone and calling. The number was the same, but the technology a little bit different, and if he used the portal upstairs there were any number of people he might startle.

"They expect Wick. They expect me. You, not so much."

He already had plans to meet Finn for a drink. "No reason we can't pop forward and take Zed for a glass or two. Hopefully I have things to say that will help ease his pain a bit. If not, at least I'll finally get to meet the old grandson I probably won't live to see."

"Damn, Grandpa," Zed groaned. "You'll still be here when I'm your age."

"Don't ask Finn about that," Will said. "And don't presume. But also don't worry. You're too stubborn to die before your grandchildren grow old."

Jax watched him go back inside, and as he hugged and kissed Hyrum before getting into the elevator. "Do we let him see Liam's chronicles?"

"Eventually."

The door popped open and Hyrum skipped out, blurting, "Eli said I could have a drink with you! But I have to promise to not say yuck because it's not cinnamon and it might burn."

Will poured him a glass and then set the bottle down when Zed waved him off. "Sip this. It's not the kind you drink just to feel a bit drunk."

He nodded enthusiastically, then drained the glass in one long, slurping sip, giggling after he swallowed. "You know what? Mom says sometime when I visit I should bring her some cinnamon whiskey because she's old and it's time to take up drinking. Red said it's okay, too! He's making it so the church doesn't get mad about it anymore. Did you know that Daddy had booze in a special closet in his office? Even though it's a sin?"

No one was surprised.

"One more, that's it," Jax said when Will poured another drink for him. "Aubrey—"

"She'll have words," Hyrum snickered.

"Quite a few, I imagine."

Zed wanted Hyrum to remain sober. There were things he wanted to discuss, and they involved his uncle and his job. "I'm stepping back from Alcatraz," he said, watching for Hyrum's reaction. "The castle will be complete in about a year, and the school should be ready to open not long after. With the search for students and teachers underway, I think I need to focus on one thing, and the academy is it."

"Who's gonna speak truth for dead people?" Hyrum asked.

"I'll still do that, but not as the director. And I'd like you to move over to the school, too. You relate to kids better than anyone else and they respond to you—they'll all be scared at first and I think having you there will help calm them. I'd like you to be a recreational director."

"What's that?"

"You would lead play time. Just like you do when you take the kids to the park. Make up games, get them running and burning off some energy, and keep an eye on them so they can have fun without worrying about teachers sucking the fun out of things."

"I can do that." He slugged back the rest of the drink and got up. "We're going to have story time now. They want to hear about Noah and the flood, but I bet Rhys has things to say about that."

Give it ten minutes. He'll be pleasantly buzzed and arguing with a four-year-old about the animals eating each other on the ark.

"That went better than I expected," Zed mused. "I thought he would be upset about leaving the mortuary. Remind me to make sure he understands he's not obligated to the school. He might prefer to go full time at Ozoo." He sighed and reached for the bottle, ignoring Jax's surprise. "Marco has a gift. I think. I'm not sure if he realizes it or not, or if he's been using it and we haven't noticed, but I'll be damned if he doesn't."

While Zed held his infant son, trying to coax a burp out of him, his two older boys sat on the living room floor, playing with toy cars. Jonathan spotted a sippy cup on the table and told Zed he wanted it, but Marco—who was on his belly, stretched out on the floor—said he would get it.

"I looked down for maybe three seconds to wipe drool off the baby's face, and Marco had the cup in hand. He never moved. He was still on his stomach, right where he'd been, yet he was handing it to Jonathan."

"Telekinesis," Will mused. "Interesting."

It was more worrisome than interesting to Zed. Marco was nearly five; if he could call everything he wanted to him, life could become far more complicated than it already was. He hoped he was wrong, and that somehow Marco got up, went to the table, and was back on the floor that quickly.

"You know he didn't," Jax said. "It also explains how the kids wound up with cookies the other day, when they hadn't left the living room. There was a plate on the counter, Aubrey said they could each have a cookie, but before she got from her office to the kitchen, they each had one."

"They snuck one before she said—"

"I don't think so, son."

"It could be worse," Will said. "Charlie appears to be on the precipice of melting everything he touches. Alex, freezing things. And Rhys..."

Liam said you could probably do all those things. You just never realized it. Zed will grow into Aubrey's empathy soon.

He was already showing signs of it. Aubrey thought his touch was why Sophia hadn't panicked more after Will and Rhys saved her life. If Zed could grow into gifts, why not everyone else?

I bet Oz has something tucked away that she doesn't know about. If Liam was his own great, great, bazillion removed great grandpa, even Jax and Eli might have untapped gifts.

"They aren't related by blood," Will said. "Not until his birth."

Liam humped his way through history. They might be. Besides, loops and spaghetti noodles and snowflakes on glass. Who really knows?

"Incest. Wonderful," Jax sighed, though he didn't sound like he thought it really was.

The door opened again and Aubrey came out, nudging Jax to move over so she could sit with him. "I need five minutes," she sighed.

"Mayhem?" Jax chuckled.

"They're setting the table for dinner. Rhys pushed the highchairs over, Charlie is yelling that he doesn't need one, Jonathan is yelling that he does, and at least three of them have already declared the menu 'yucky.' I tagged Aisha, so she's it right now."

"Hyrum went in for story time," Jax said.

"That ended when Jonathan sneezed on the book. It was a productive sneeze," she sighed.

"Question," Will started. "Does the name Doyle Keats sound familiar?"

"My great, great, great, grandfather. Why?"

Jax snorted a laugh into his glass.

"He's also Liam Finnegan," Will told her.

Will had a theory, one that meant Jo had not been far off in her assumption that she had caused Will's ability to hear thoughts because she'd exposed him to null space when she was newly pregnant with him. Liam had spent, he guessed, over a thousand years in null space, given the number of times he'd been stuck there. The cumulative effects were likely why the things they considered to be gifts were passed down through Valerie Munson's lineage.

Liam was her great, great grandfather.

"That means my nieces and nephews also might—" She sucked in a deep breath. "Good lord. The secrets that family has kept."

While Liam flitted through time looking for his gifted descendants, Will decided he would take Hyrum to see his mother and while there, press Red for more information. The academy would be available for them, as well, and it was only a year from opening.

"We're really doing this, then," Jax said. "Blackshear Academy. We have to protect the hell out of it, Will. Protect the kids who study there. If the general population were to find out—"

"Protecting the children is a large part of why you decided holding onto the throne was important," Will reminded him. "And my father—both lines of him—have been working on a version of the simulator, in which visitors can be misdirected, should the need arise."

What about Isaac? He doesn't have a gift. Will he still be able to go to school with Rhys?

Will nodded. "He's from the future, Wick. And his father is contracted to work for the school. Regardless, Isaac always has a place with us."

Until those kids burn the place down.

"Wick," Will sighed.

They fell silent, watching people on Union Square as the sound of the kids—laughing and squealing and at least one argument—crept up from the other side, and they sipped Jax's

Very Expensive Scotch until Aisha was heard telling everyone to pick up their toys, it was time for dinner.

Instead of getting up and heading for the table, Jax put the cap on the scotch, sat back, and asked, "Have we done the right thing, Will? Not just saving my mother and Sophia, but everyone else we've mucked around with. Is time going to bite us in the ass for it? Some demand of a sacrifice to make things balanced again?"

Our lives were on repeat, Will pointed out. One line after another, time's gift to make sure it kept going along with us.

Maybe we're just doing it over and over until we get it right. Not just us. Everyone. Time will keep looping until the world is filled with more good than bad. Infinite second chances. And when time decides everything balances in favor of good, it can rest.

"Perhaps," Will said, allowing for the possibility, "time can rest a bit now. Perhaps we've finally gotten it right, and it will quit flicking at displaced people like they were fleas. Or maybe we'll never get it right, and time will loop around us as long as it exists."

"You're a little buzzed, aren't you?"

"No, but I am tired of worrying about keeping the timelines as pure as possible, and tired of trying to juggle what happened before with what will happen next. We do what's moral and ethical, as much as we can, no matter the When we're in. If it bites us in the ass, it bites us in the ass. But we'll do it, because that's who we are."

Dude.

Speaking of biting in the ass. We totally forgot someone. Like, weeks ago. He's still waiting.

He had to think about it, but when he remembered, his eyes went wide. He reached for me, told Jax he would be in for dinner in a minute or two, and started to reach for his jump bracelet.

"When to?" Jax asked.

"I left you sitting at the bakery, waiting to find out if I succeeded in getting to your mother and then home again."

He hasn't shown up to tell you to not go, you know.

"Still," Will sighed.

Jax was going with us. No argument. He grabbed onto Will's arm, said dinner could wait, and a blink later we were standing on Union Square looking at old Jax. He was picking his scone apart, flicking pieces of it onto a napkin, determined to not finish it or his tea.

If he didn't finish, he didn't need to find out whether we were stuck somewhen else.

"Hello, me," Jax said, amused.

Tension drained from old Jax's face and he smiled when he looked up.

"As promised," Will said. "We did not find ourselves stranded in a new timeline."

"And my mother?" old Jax asked.

They sat across the table from him, and I leaned against his arms to purr while Will explained everything. The scone and tea were forgotten; dusk fell as they spoke, the temperature dropped, and when the streetlights clicked on, old Jax's phone pinged. Aubrey wanted to know where he was and if he was all right, and then asked them to come upstairs for dinner.

"If we're not hungry enough to eat when we get back, my Aubrey will have words to say," Jax said.

"Hyrum," old Jax chuckled. "He still threatens to have lots of words to say about things. Yet, he rarely does." He began to push up from the table, trying to stand. When Will popped up to help, he waved the Emperor off, grunting that he still had it in him to get off his own asterisk.

"She knew what I wanted her to, didn't she?" he asked as Will cleaned up the bits of scone.

"I told her I loved her," Jax said. "She was certain, no matter the when, no matter what happens, we will always love her. There was no doubt. Mom...well, she wanted us to understand that we were what she lived for. And she wanted Aubrey to know, too, despite the distance she felt she'd put between them in the beginning. Oh my God, she loves Aubrey."

"Loves," old Jax sighed.

"Loves. She's out there, Jackson. In another When, she's alive and happy, and she will be for many more years."

He gave a slight nod. "As long as she's happy."

"Are you all right?" Will asked.

"I am. I'm content, Emperor. And wondering now how much I should tell my father. If at all."

"Consult Aubrey," Jax suggested. "If you tell him, tell him together, and make sure she has a hand on him."

Will picked me up. "One other thing. If you tell him, also tell him that his regrets over the order of the last words he said to her didn't matter. The only thing she gave weight to in those last days were of how much she was loved. She knew what he intended and felt it deeply."

You don't really know that, I said to Will when we were back on our balcony.

It didn't matter. He wanted old Jax's father to understand that his Donna heard what he'd meant. The order of words was less important than the way he'd said them.

Jax pulled the door open, and they paused. The noise had leveled out, the kids were all at the table, waiting to be fed, and Hyrum moved from highchair to highchair to make sure each of the smaller ones was secure. Somewhere, in another When, Jax's mother also flitted around a dinner table, and in yet another When his father was consoling his heartbroken grandson. It all made sense to him, and it all felt right.

"We got it right. All of it. Didn't we?"

Will chuckled and nudged him inside.

"Little bit, yeah."

Also by Max Thompson

The Emperor of San Francisco: The Wick Chronicles, Book One
Ozoo: The Wick Chronicles, Book Two
Forked: The Wick Chronicles, Book Three

The Space Between Whens: Wick After Dark, Book One
The Blessings of Saint Wick: Wick After Dark, Book Two

The Whens of Wick: Return of the Wick Chronicles, Book One
The Book of Hyrum:Retrun of the Wick Chronicles, Book Two
JUMP: Return of the Wick Chronicles Book Three
The King of Saint Francis: Return of the Wick Chronicles Book Four

Waiting to Inhale: Wick Shorts Book One

The Psychokitty Speaks Out: Diary of a Mad Housecat
The Psychokitty Speaks Out: Something of Yours Will Meet A Toothy Death
The Rules: A Guide For People Owned By Cats
Bite Me: A Memoir (Of Sorts)
Epistle: A Love Letter
There Once Was a Cat From Nantucket

Visit Max online at his blog, The Psychokitty Speaks Out
http://psychokitty.blogspot.com
or on Facebook
http://facebook.com/thepsychokittyspeaksout

Books one of his people (K.A. Thompson) wrote

The Charybdis Novels:
Charybdis
As Simple As That
Finding Father Rabbit
The King and Queen of Perfect Normal
The Flipside of Here

It's Not About the Cookies
Rock the Pink

Visit K.A. Thompson online at her blog,
Thumper Thinks Out Loud
http://kathompson.blogspot.com